MAJOR ERIC "⟨" W9-CFX-690

Top of his class at the Air Force Academy, the icy paragon picked by computer to fly the super-secret Nightwing Eagle to the limits of the earth's atmosphere, he carries a dread secret that could destroy him...

CANDY JAMES

Topper's beautiful, desperate wife, embroiled in an illicit love affair that cures her loneliness but may destroy her marriage...

CAPTAIN SIMON "MOONBIRD" McALLISTER

The "space freak" from MIT whose contempt for the military is matched by his talent for trouble and his desire to work in the top-secret "Hot Victor" spaceship program...

NANCY GLASS

The jaunty daughter of the powerful Chairman of the Senate Armed Services Committee becomes the pawn in "Moonbird's" quest to get the assignment he wants...

SENATOR MORTIMER GLASS

Unscrupulous promoter of the sale of the F-15 Eagles to the Air Force—despite doubts as to their safety...

EAGLES

A novel that soars with all the drama, excitement, intrigue, and secrecy of the great fighter planes it so beautifully describes.

EAGLES

M. H. Davis

FAWCETT CREST • NEW YORK

A Fawcett Crest Book
Published by Ballantine Books
Copyright © 1980 by Maggie Davis

Library of Congress Catalog Card Number: 80-14471

ISBN 0-449-24557-8

This edition published by arrangement with William Morrow and Company, Inc.

Manufactured in the United States of America

First Ballantine Books Edition: September 1982

For *Jumbo* and *Beeper*
and *Charge* and *Grovel* and *Duck* and *RV*
and *Bronc* and *Redneck* and "*WL*" and *Puppet*
and *Sammy Durden*
without whose help this book could not have been written

And thanks to *Nancy, Barbara, Karen, Tana* and *Jeanne*
for their particular support

Part 1

```
/*   1500 HOURS   */
```

1

The passengers from the National Aeronautics and Space Administration Visitors Center stepped out of the green bus at the end of the runway and began to file into the splintery wooden seats of the reviewing stand. The north side of Langley Air Force Base was a dusty, treeless field that offered no shelter from the steaming July sun, but the fifty-odd, mostly middle-aged sightseers in Bermuda shorts and barebacked sundresses were still good-naturedly entertained, still obviously enjoying their free, hour-long NASA tour.

"Ladies and gentlemen," a voice said from the overhead loudspeakers, "on your right you will see the F-15 Eagle, the Air Force's new supersonic air superiority fighter, taxiing to the runway for takeoff. In a few minutes, the F-15 will perform a thrilling flight demonstration to illustrate to all of us here today this remarkable aircraft's capabilities."

There was a sudden ripple of distraction in the reviewing stand, and heads turned. Another NASA bus drew up in the area and discharged a smaller, rather noisier group with several children in it. As the latecomers made their way into the seats, a few of the tourists sitting there bent forward and frowned, cupping their hands to their ears.

"The F-15 Eagle," the voice of the Air Force Public Affairs Office announcer went on, "is a truly unique development in advanced military jet fighters. It has, among other totally new features, a central computer which not only monitors the Eagle's systems, but also plans flight maneuvers and advises the pilot of vital target information. During training and combat, the pilot will wear the helmet containing the HUD, or Head-Up Display, which, when connected to the central cockpit computer, projects a lighted display on the visor of the pilot's helmet, superimposing this running account on his field of vision. The HUD computer display gives the pilot necessary data on the position of other aircraft in the vicinity, his air speed and altitude, and a general picture of location and target sighting."

The heads in the reviewing stand turned expectantly to the right. Conversation had died; all attention was focused on the silvery shape approaching the runway, its engines emitting a distant, ululating shriek.

"The F-15 we will see today is part of the First Tactical Fighter Wing stationed at Tactical Air Command Headquarters here at historic Langley Air Force Base, Virginia. The pilot of today's Eagle, Major Eric James, is the regular demonstration pilot for the F-15 and a veteran of advanced fighter operations."

There was a sudden, earsplitting roar on the right as the pilot advanced the throttles of each twenty-five-thousand-pound jet engine. The Eagle made a slow turn onto the runway and could now be seen as a strange, alien shape, squatting powerfully against the concrete, its outlines shimmering in heat waves.

"Our pilot has a total of two thousand forty hours' fighter time in the F-15 Eagle. Major James is a flight leader in the 17th Tactical Fighter Squadron here at Langley and is currently Top Ace of the Month in the First Tactical Fighter Wing. Incidentally"—here the loudspeaker voice broke from its official tone to impart some information of friendly interest— "Major James was top of his graduating class at the Air Force Academy some years back and made one of the highest averages ever recorded in flight training. With a record like that, we can see why he earned the tactical call sign of Topper. So from now on, we'll be referring to him as that—Topper."

The crowd smiled appreciatively. Several hands lifted to point out the faraway white and silver dot of Major James's helmet, visible through the acrylic plastic canopy of the F-15.

Almost directly across the runway of the airfield, in the tower of Langley Air Traffic Control, Tech Sergeant Regina

Murphy lifted her binoculars and trained them on the reviewing stand. As she always did, Sergeant Murphy counted the crowd—which she correctly estimated as numbering about sixty—and searched for the presence of any VIPs, such as visiting NASA officials, who might be in it. God, she thought, it looked hot as hell out there! She could see that several of the men had spread white pocket handkerchiefs over their heads to cover vulnerable bald spots. Behind the stands, a line of women and children had already formed at the door of the metal Porta-Johnny by the parked NASA buses.

A bare ten minutes before, Sergeant Murphy's binoculars had followed the tall figure of Major Topper James in his anti-G suit as he made his way down the flight line and climbed the yellow ladder to the cockpit of his Eagle. Major James was one of Sergeant Murphy's favorites; although she had never come any closer to him than her position in the Langley traffic control tower, she could see, even at that distance, that Major James, swaggering along in the peculiarly encumbered gait of fighter pilots, was one of the men in the squadrons—if not, in fact, the entire Langley base. And nice on the radio, too; Major James had a deep, sexy, friendly voice that one recognized right away, and it always stood right out from the rest of air traffic. He was, in Sergeant Murphy's estimation, really a doll.

As soon as the acrylic plastic canopy of the F-15 had closed over Major James's silvery blond head, Sergeant Murphy had given orders to Ground Control to hold the traffic pattern, delaying, among other things, an incoming cell of two KC-135 tanker planes and the takeoff of a small C-7. During the quarter of an hour it would take Major James to go through the demonstration flight, Langley Air Force Base was, in effect, all but closed to anything except top priority flights and emergencies. The orders came down direct from the office of the commander of TAC, General Algernon Couch. The General regarded the F-15 Eagle demonstration flights as his own personal public relations project; every Friday the year round, an F-15 with Major James at the controls took to the air over Langley to illustrate to the world—and particularly the taxpayers on the NASA Visitors Center tours—that no matter what they might have heard, the F-15s were not only miracles of design and advanced technology, but also trouble-free and totally depend-

able and worth every penny of their cost. Which was some
fifteen million dollars per jet fighter.

As a consequence, General Couch took a strong interest in
each demonstration flight. His offices at Tactical Air Command
Headquarters overlooked the Langley runway, and he could
nearly always be seen standing at the windows at the appointed
hour on Fridays, monitoring the proceedings through his field
glasses. If the General left the base early for a round of golf,
as he sometimes did in the summer, he drove his car to the
edge of the flight line to sit and watch the air show before
leaving the area.

Sergeant Murphy lowered her binoculars. It was curious
after so long a time, but she always felt very uneasy just before
every demonstration flight. She always said that if something
was going to go wrong on the damned demo show, she would
just as soon it happened on somebody else's Friday tour of
duty. Not that anything ever had—Major James was, by almost
universal agreement, just about the best pilot in the whole
United States Air Force. He and the test pilot from the aircraft
manufacturer had worked out the very first demonstration flight
pattern during the first definitive production of the F-15s, and
Major James had been flying it ever since. A copy of the ribbon
flight diagram was scotch-taped to the tower windows for the
traffic controller on duty in Local Position to follow during
every Friday show.

But just knowing the diagram was there, and that Major
James was going to take the F-15 Eagle through all those
dangerous dives and rolls and climbs, was enough to make
Sergeant Murphy uneasy. As many times as she had looked
at the flight pattern, and as many times as she had seen Topper
James take the F-15 through it and had been assured that it
would work over and over again without anything going wrong,
Sergeant Murphy still watched the demo flight with a distinct
lack of pleasure.

At the top of the eight-thousand-foot loop and as the demonstration flight was drawing to a close, two members of Major
James's own Topper flight—usually Captain Moonbird
McAllister and Captain Beeper Farris—would appear from the
northwest to sweep in and make a low pass at the runway,
hurtling, it seemed, right over the heads of the spectators. As
the two F-15s throttled up to full power in a thundering roar

that shook the sky, they climbed from the airstrip to join Major James for the final "vertical departure"—a maneuver made possible by the F-15s revolutionary new-design engines. At the top of the climb, the two wingmen peeled off from Major James's center Eagle like the unfolding petals of an aerial fleur-de-lis. It was a great moment—the finale always brought the tourists to their feet with yells of delight.

It had already been announced at 1st Wing Headquarters that Major James would step down at the end of the summer, returning to his regular duty on Friday. His two wingmen, McAllister and Farris, were in hot competition to replace him as demo pilot. Sergeant Murphy often thought that few people could tell how intense that competition was, unless, like herself, they were in a place like the control tower to observe it. The barreling entry of the two F-15s was often a wild chase in the style of the Thunderbirds, the Air Force precision flying team, as the two tried to show how close they could fly off each other's wing. Thirty-six inches was the legal minimum, but Sergeant Murphy could swear she had seen them closer than that.

The loudspeaker narration down at the reviewing stand murmured in Sergeant Murphy's headset. She was patched into the voice of the demonstration announcer down at the stands as well as Langley air traffic, and today she was also keeping an eye on her new air traffic controller-trainee, Airman Ronny Masarek, who was working Local Position for the first time.

Sergeant Murphy covered the button of the microphone in front of her mouth, considering whether to speak to Airman Masarek and check out what he was doing. He certainly seemed to be applying himself; he was bent over the radar bright screen with an air of almost paralyzed concentration that, since he was so new and eager to please, Sergeant Murphy found rather endearing. She had forgotten to tell him that the Local Position Controller didn't use the bright screen all that much; it certainly wasn't necessary to keep your head stuck right in it. But she decided not to say anything. Air traffic control was tough duty, and it was a good sign when a trainee took everything very seriously.

Airman Masarek was young, maybe twenty-two or twenty-three, Sergeant Murphy judged, and certainly very good-looking. Not as handsome as Major James—nobody was—but still pretty cute. Standing over him, Sergeant Regina Murphy could look down at the top of his head and see that Airman Masarek had been so recently close-cropped by an Air Force barber that only a few dark, turfy ringlets showed across his skull. Airman Masarek was tall and had to slump rather awkwardly in his chair to bend over the radar screen. He kept his thumb pressed against his left earpiece to shut out the ceaseless sounds of radio static and the voices of military flights in the Norfolk area which flowed through the Air Traffic Control tower speakers.

Sergeant Murphy put her hand on her trainee's shoulder, feeling the warm skin and tense muscles through the light summer-uniform shirt. Airman Masarek started violently at the touch and whirled around to face her. Sergeant Murphy only smiled reassuringly. She bent down to tell him he was doing just fine. The green light of the radar scope reflected in her pretty freckled face, casting a purplish hue on her short red hair.

A few feet from Local Position, the Traffic Control Supervisor, Master Sergeant Tom Bullock, leaned his elbows on his console and advised a C-130 transport of a thunderstorm moving eastward in the Williamsburg area. On the other side of the glassed-in, air-conditioned cylinder of the air traffic control tower, Airman Rosalie Tenchman, slender and neat in a short-sleeved light blue shirt and dark blue uniform skirt, stood at her position and sipped a cup of coffee, monitoring the VHF frequency of civilian aviation through her headset. The SOF, the Supervising Officer of Flying, Major Mattingly, whose duty was rotated with other tactical fighter wing officers, had gone below, taking an informal break and a smoke while things were quiet.

"It's not too long," Sergeant Murphy assured Airman Masarek; "the demo flight only takes fifteen minutes." As she spoke, the firm, sexy, friendly voice of Major James sounded in her ears. "Langley," it said, "this is Topper demo Eagle taxiing for takeoff."

"Roger, cleared for takeoff," Sergeant Murphy told him. She lifted her binoculars. Another voice in her headset, this time the announcer on the field below, said, "Now, ladies and gentlemen, the pilot of our F-15 Eagle, Major Topper James, will take off."

The silver dartlike body of the fighter jet at the end of the runway began to move. As it picked up speed and rushed toward the reviewing stand, the faces and bodies of the spectators there seemed to shrink before the impact and speed.

"The large Trueham engines," the voice went on, "with their revolutionary thrust-exceeding-weight ratio, enable the F-15 for the first time in aviation history to accelerate and sustain a completely vertical climb."

The gleaming body rose abruptly like a projectile rocketed skyward. The faces in the reviewing stand turned up, mouths slightly ajar.

"Now the pilot is demonstrating his ability to climb vertically by rotating his Eagle to ninety degrees. Once in a climb, the pilot will roll the F-15 Eagle to position for a split S maneuver. Following this, he's going over the top of his climb upside down and will then come down from this altitude to make a pass at the field at only three hundred feet, going four hundred and fifty miles an hour in the opposite direction from takeoff."

Out of the corner of her eye, Sergeant Murphy detected a possible spot of trouble and quickly covered her mike. "Catch the whirlybird," she told Airman Masarek.

A large Sikorsky helicopter with Marine Corps markings was moving down at the west end of the runway, and the voice of the pilot asked the tower for clearance for takeoff.

"Sheesh, where's *he* been?" Sergeant Murphy said under her breath. Air traffic was on hold, now; only top priority flights were allowed once the demo flight was in progress. And noisy, ugly distractions such as helicopters and conventional prop aircraft—which General Couch found aesthetically unacceptable—were to be kept out of sight.

"Langley, I've got an ETA at Quantico in ninety minutes," the Marine complained.

Oh, shut *up*, Sergeant Murphy told him silently. She didn't know what a Marine whirlybird was doing out there, anyway. Probably, she thought, some transient put into Langley for minor repairs. As if in answer to her thoughts, the Marine voice informed her quite crossly that he was carrying two colonels back to Quantico from a Langley meeting and wanted to get the hell out of there, air show or no air show.

Sergeant Murphy looked at Airman Masarek and shook her head.

"Up above us now, Topper will roll the F-15 Eagle one and one quarter times and perform a left-hand three-hundred-sixty-degree turn. This is done while Topper is sustaining seven 'Gs'—or seven times the force of gravity—while traveling at four hundred and twenty miles an hour. The capability to pull high G forces and sustain airspeed makes the F-15 outperform any known threat in the world."

At that moment, Sergeant Murphy knew, the straining body of Major James would be hitting seven times normal gravity, which would drag the flesh of his face down painfully and inflate his anti-G suit to clamp his thighs and abdomen tightly, thus keeping his blood in his upper body. His vision would already be narrowing in a closing tunnel of blackness that fighter pilots called the *Star Wars* effect. The demo flights were punishing work. After the show when Major James climbed down from the Eagle, his anti-G suit would be mottled with sweat, his blond hair wet and plastered to his head.

"Emergency—we have an emergency; Topper Three has hydraulic failure."

There was a sudden, urgent mix of voices in the tower room, that of the Traffic Control Supervisor, Master Sergeant Bullock, and other new ones, high pitched and loud, standing out from regular air traffic noise.

"Roger, Langley," one of the new voices blared, "this is Topper Three and Topper Four, two F-15s, twelve miles west of Langley, full stop. Topper Four is chase."

Lights began to flash on the Local Position console in front of Airman Masarek. Sergeant Murphy quickly reached over his shoulder to punch the channel selector. Hydraulic systems failure could be anything—and from what Sergeant Murphy was hearing, the F-15 in trouble was one of the two scheduled to join Topper James in the final moments of the demo flight. Master Sergeant Bullock was standing up now, looking toward the northwest, his hand cupping the mike button at his mouth.

The voice down at the reviewing stand said, "The superb cockpit visibility enables the pilot of the F-15 to search the skies better than any other fighter. The advanced radar designed by Hughes Aircraft serves as the eyes of the Eagle and extends far beyond the pilot's vision. It enables the F-15 to detect intruders from treetop level to maximum altitude."

Down below on the airfield, emergency procedures were already in progress. The flashing red lights of fire control trucks had begun to appear at the end of runway zero-seven. The fire equipment was closely followed by the squad cars of the Langley Air Force Base security police, who took up positions on the perimeter roads to keep ground traffic clear of the landing strip. The runway and the area around it blossomed with twirling, flashing emergency beacons. The crowd in the reviewing stand turned away from the demonstration flight taking place above them and regarded the commotion at ground level with interest. A white-painted van raced up the runway, and two figures in yellow asbestos suits, hooded and ominous, jumped out. The fire control crews continued ahead, trying to anticipate the spot for touchdown.

At Local Position, Airman Masarek sat alert, his hand hovering over the buttons of the console, although Master Sergeant Bullock was now personally directing the emergency. Sergeant Regina Murphy stood behind her trainee, trying to keep her attention focused on the demonstration flight. There was nothing she needed to say to Airman Masarek at this point, anyway; it was a waste of time to try to speculate on the degree of emergency involved. Every emergency was critical until the aircraft was safely on the ground.

The voice of the announcer down at the reviewing stand continued to read the script, mingling with the amplified sounds of Major James's thunderous gasps as he thrust his F-15 into the five-thousand-foot climb indicated on the ribbon flight diagram.

Sergeant Bullock asked Topper Three for another landing gear check. Captain Beeper Farris answered that his landing gear was down and added that he hoped it would hold.

Sergeant Murphy shut her eyes for a brief moment. It was going to be bad enough. Because somewhere General Algernon Couch, Commander of TAC in all the continental United States, was surely watching this entire performance. Major James's Eagle had just gone into a breathtaking dive, but hardly anyone noticed. Attention was focused on an ambulance roaring past.

And when the two F-15s came in on emergency mode, Sergeant Murphy knew, it would be even worse. Captain

Moonbird McAllister would be flying "chase" on the wing of
Captain Farris's disabled Eagle; by longstanding military tradition, no fighter jet was abandoned in flight or left to land
alone. A wingman always flew "chase" right up to touchdown,
when the escorting fighter accelerated and climbed away.

"Down the back side of the circular loop," the voice reminded Sergeant Murphy, "Topper James will now accelerate
for a square loop."

At this point, the F-15s were normally cued to join Major
James for the final figure. There was no way for him to know
what was taking place, Sergeant Murphy was sure. He was
probably oblivious to everything except what he was doing.

"Note the square corner as Topper pulls the Eagle into a
vertical climb. He will maintain airspeed and pull the F-15 over
on its back."

"Yeah, yeah," the irritated voice of Captain Farris was saying on the tower speakers, "I have three gears and they're down
and locked." Another voice broke in, that of Topper Four,
Captain McAllister. It said something unintelligible.

Suddenly the voice of Captain Farris burst out: "You asshole—when we get down I'm going to kill you!"

Airman Rosalie Tenchman looked up, eyes widening. Sergeant Bullock made no move to show that he had heard. He
continued to stare through the tower windows toward the northwest.

"Up yours!" the other voice responded promptly.

Sergeant Murphy looked around. They were on the open
Langley frequency and could be heard all over the area. For
a moment she wished the SOF, Major Mattingly, were up there
right now so he could hear this.

At that second, the two Eagles became visible over the west
end of runway zero-seven, so close that their wings seemed to
be supporting each other. The jets dispensed with the "break,"
the 360-degree turn that would align them with the runway for
landing, and instead thundered straight on. The heads in the
reviewing stand swiveled quickly. Major James, all unseen,
sent his Eagle into a magnificent dive. A line of automobiles,
stopped by the security police, backed up along the perimeter
roads. Drivers stood outside their cars, hands shading their
eyes, watching the Eagles come in for emergency landing.

The two F-15s roared in, astonishingly coupled, sweeping

down for the runway. The NASA tourists were on their feet, but uncertainly. Was this all part of the show, or wasn't it?

The first Eagle touched the runway, and its landing gear, seen only as a blur at that speed, appeared to hold. Its engines went to full idle with a sudden termination of the thundering bellow, and it slowed. The second Eagle swooped away. For a second, there had been the illusion that the second Eagle had been so low that its belly scraped the surface of the runway. A voice in the control tower murmured, "Jesus." The second Eagle did not stop. It raced straight ahead, gaining altitude, its nose thrusting up and aimed for Major James's F-15, which was mounting in the final climb of the demonstration flight.

Langley Air Traffic Control had fallen suddenly silent. The voices of other flights in the area came through the speakers, but no one moved. The controllers stared as Captain Moonbird McAllister's F-15 rose to position itself on the wing of Major James, to join in the final vertical departure. What had been done had been done so quickly and smoothly that it had seemed all of a piece: the jet coming down the runway on Captain Farris's wing and so low it appeared to be only a few inches off the concrete; then going to a blast of afterburners to climb into the midst of the demonstration flight. The maneuver had been beautifully executed, exciting to watch, and wholly unnecessary.

In that minute, Sergeant Murphy breathed a silent prayer for a miracle, for General Couch to be engaged on the telephone, or in the men's room—somewhere, anywhere, so long as he couldn't see what was happening.

Captain Beeper Farris's F-15 rolled to a stop at the end of runway zero-seven, fire trucks racing after it. High above Langley Air Force Base, Captain McAllister had joined Major James at the top of the vertical climb and was in the process of peeling off to make one-half of a lopsided aerial fleur-de-lis.

"Now Topper has been joined by—" There was a pause as the loudspeaker voice seemed to be checking the script against what was actually going on. "Now he pulls the fighter down the back side of the loop, ladies and gentlemen. In the dive, he will—both Eagles will—roll and position themselves for landing." The voice, having apparently skipped several paragraphs, said, "The F-15 fighter represents the Air Force's dedication to insuring that we have the resources to meet our adversaries anywhere in the world with a force unequaled in aviation history."

Captain Farris's F-15, surrounded by fire trucks and emergency vehicles, cut its engines. A small puff of gray smoke issued from somewhere under the fuselage in the vicinity of the landing gear and drifted lazily away. The asbestos-suited figures approached, carrying their canisters of fire-fighting foam. The acrylic canopy opened and Captain Farris appeared, shaking his head. Sergeant Murphy's binoculars followed Captain Farris as he stamped off angrily to a waiting van.

"The combination of the F-15s powerful engine, good pilot visibility, excellent maneuverability and dependability, as well as lethal armament makes it a formidable addition to freedom's arsenal. And thank you, ladies and gentlemen," the voice down on the field said with heavy finality.

The crowd in the reviewing stand was on its feet. It waited, hesitated, and then a flutter of handclapping began. No one moved to go back to the buses. Men, women, and children clapped enthusiastically as Captain Beeper Farris climbed into the van and disappeared. The clapping mounted as Major James and Captain McAllister, side by side, turned their F-15s into a 360-degree turn and swiftly roared in for landing.

The demonstration flight was over. The two Eagles immediately taxied off the active runway for the flight line. The fire control trucks and crews still clustered around Captain Farris's F-15, but the asbestos-suited figures had already lumbered back to their vehicle. Traffic was moving on the perimeter roads. One by one, the flashing red lights went out.

The handclapping in the reviewing stand sputtered away. The crowd turned now, gathered up belongings, and began to file out of the seats. The green NASA buses started their motors. Behind, in the area surrounding the reviewing stand, the litter of half a hundred blue programs covered the dusty grass.

Sergeant Murphy unplugged her headset and moved over to the Local Position console. Her trainee, she saw, was still on his feet, still staring beyond the tower windows to where a Coleman tug was now hooking onto the nose of Captain Farris's F-15 to tow it away. The voices of local traffic, neglected for a quarter of an hour, buzzed into her headset, the voice of the Marine helicopter the most insistent.

"Roger, Marine Zero Four Six," Sergeant Murphy told him,

"you are cleared for takeoff on runway zero-seven. There is emergency equipment in the area, so exercise all necessary caution."

Sergeant Regina Murphy discovered that in the past few hectic minutes she had snagged her middle fingernail on something. It was split painfully down to the quick. Dammit, a good long nail, too, she thought, examining it. She stuck her finger in her mouth impatiently and gnawed at the broken edge.

"Roger, honey," the Marine voice said, "cleared for takeoff it is."

2

Candy James, in shorts and halter and licking one of her daughter's lollipops, made her way across the heat-softened surface of the shopping center parking lot, two-year-old Emma following some yards behind in a yellow terrycloth sunsuit, the dirty pants bottom wagging over her fat legs. The bag boy with the shopping cart full of groceries brought up the rear, slouched over the handlebar, guiding it listlessly with his elbows. The time and temperature indicator on the Tidewater Bank opposite them blinked lighted figures: 4:01, then 94°. A hot and comfortless wind blew across Mercury Boulevard, carrying the grit of the highway with it, raising a small cyclone of paper and trash in front of the A&P.

Candy lifted her heavy brown hair from the back of her sweating neck and felt the lollipop snag and pull. Carefully she reached back and disentangled it and put it back in her mouth. She was going to have to wash her hair again, anyway; when it was this hot, it was best to wash your hair twice a day, or the acid in perspiration attacked the hair shafts and robbed them of their basic protein. She had been told this by a hairdresser several years ago, and she had found it to be true. Fortunately, she had good, strong hair, bouncy, with a natural curl, and it hadn't succumbed so far to acid or anything else really worrisome.

Candy turned around slowly to look at her daughter. She thought about putting Emma into the shower with her, too, when they got home and wondered if the time saved would be

16

worth listening to Emma's screams. Emma could be a beast when she wanted to, and she hated showers; all she ever wanted to do was sit in the bathtub with a thousand plastic toys around her and make a mess.

The bathroom, Candy remembered as she watched the time on the bank clock slide to two minutes past the hour, was a mess, too. And she didn't know when she was going to get around to cleaning it up. *And* the kitchen, *and* the family room—Topper had had pizza and beer in the family room watching the "Late Show," and paper plates and things were still all over the place.

She was not—and she admitted it—very well organized. Topper was patient and good about it and hardly ever complained, but she knew sometimes it bothered him. Topper was very well organized himself. He was always making helpful suggestions. Clean shirts, he kept saying. And, honey, why don't you put yourself on a schedule, start at the bottom of the house and work your way up?

Candy sighed. That was easy to say, but actually that would take weeks, months—she didn't even want to think about it. She supposed she had to do something; even her mother said that. And she had more or less learned by now that if you waited to shop for groceries until you were down to the last can of soup, then it *always* interfered with something you really wanted to do. Like a tennis game arranged on the spur of the moment when somebody called you up to see if you were available for doubles. Or, as for instance—Her mind struggled with the thought. Well, when—and if—*Rick*. She drew the lollipop out of her mouth and stared at it pensively. Not "making love," she told herself. You couldn't use that term with somebody who was only seventeen years old and with whom you played tennis. It was just sex.

The bag boy was asking her if she remembered where she had put her car. Candy stared at him. The bag boy had been watching her, especially her bare legs and bra. You could tell what he'd been thinking.

Not that it bothered her particularly, she thought, feeling kindly toward the bag boy; it was just one of those things. It always happened. She eyed herself with practiced objectivity in the windows of the parked cars and saw a tall girl, notably naked in sun halter and tennis shorts, hair drawn back in a pony tail like her daughter's, face partly hidden by giant, stylish sunglasses. She was reminded that she had a pair of matching terrycloth shorts like Emma's, but the shorts had disappeared mysteriously somewhere in the laundry. The tennis shorts, she saw, fit her better, anyway. The figure of Candy in the reflecting glass walked with a charmingly unselfconscious motion that centered in knees and pelvis and displayed, with suitable detachment, the best of a magnificently endowed, very healthy body. The bag boy, still watching, tripped on the wheel of the grocery cart and caught himself.

Candy smiled. The bag boy, she guessed, was about sixteen, probably a high school football player. He wore a faded black T-shirt with the words *Darth Vader Lives* across the front. In the side window of a Ford Torino, Candy saw his eyes move from her legs to the middle of her bare back with a heavy, speculative look.

Candy reached out a hand to her daughter, and Emma ran to catch up. It was all right if the bag boy kept staring, as long as that was all it was. At home her trophies as Miss Nebraska State Fair, Miss Fidelity Insurance and First Runner-up, Queen's Court, Ak-Sar-Ben Grand Ball, stood beside Topper's gold statuettes of football and track awards and his Air Force models of the F-4 Phantom and the F-15 Eagle. She was used to it.

The old Dodge station wagon stood down at the end of the line of cars parked in front of the bowling alley looking, in the glaring sunlight, even more in need of a paint job than it usually did. The original color, she remembered, had been so pretty. In spite of Topper's making fun of it by calling it *Pepto-Bismol* pink. Candy opened the tailgate for the bag boy and then took Emma around to the front and opened the door and put her inside. She had left the windows rolled down, but it was still blisteringly hot inside. The plastic seat covers burned to the touch.

"Be careful, hon," she told her daughter.

A few months back, Emma had released the brakes on the station wagon when it was parked in the driveway, and Emma and the Dodge had rolled into the street and halfway to the corner of Pinecrest Drive before Topper, racing after it, had managed to catch up with them. Now Topper was violent on the subject of not leaving Emma alone in the car. Candy warned her daughter not to touch anything, then went back to the bag boy. She saw he had moved the picnic chest and beach toys to one side and was putting the groceries in very neatly. Candy leaned against the burning metal of the tailgate and watched him.

The bag boy wore extremely tight blue jeans which revealed, quite clearly, the enormous bulge in his crotch. She couldn't help staring at it curiously, because she was sure he knew how it looked. It was really very sexual. She had read in a magazine somewhere that at age sixteen or seventeen most boys were at the height of their sexual powers. If true, it certainly did account for a lot of things. Although she was sure, at that age, that boys didn't really have an opportunity to use those powers, heightened or not. From what her brothers told her, teenage girls weren't actually all that available. It was no wonder high school boys were always so incredibly horny.

Candy took the empty lollipop stick out of her mouth, studied it for a moment, and then threw it away. Six months ago, she told herself, she wouldn't have been caught dead thinking about such things.

She heard a noise from her daughter and looked back and saw Emma standing up in the front seat of the Dodge, twisting the steering wheel with fierce energy. It was so hot, and Emma never seemed to slow down. She wished the bag boy would hurry up. All the frozen food would melt. Everybody agreed Langley was one of the worst places to be stationed, especially in summer. Air Force families hated it almost as much as they hated bases away out in the middle of Texas.

But you had to go where they sent you, she told herself. And at least the Texas desert was dry. At Langley, from the beginning of June until the end of September, life could be an endless round of searching for someplace bearably cool. Like the Officers' Club and the swimming pool. Or the houses of friends who were lucky enough to have central air conditioning and who could afford to keep it turned on. Or even indoor shopping malls—there were some lovely ones in Norfolk with fountains and indoor gardens and terrace restaurants where, she also reminded herself, you could spend a fortune if you weren't careful. And cool, dim cocktail lounges—if you wanted to meet someone and not be seen. Except that Rick always got carded if he ordered anything stronger than beer.

Candy wondered suddenly if she had remembered to turn off the window air conditioner in the bedroom or straighten up the bed. She wondered if Topper would notice. He certainly noticed the electric bill. He reminded her week after week to keep the bedroom air conditioner turned off during the day and the door closed, so as to hold down the terrible utility bills. She told herself that the first things she had to do when she got home were to rush in and make up the bed, turn off the air conditioner, and look around for any small things that might have been left behind. Such as a comb. Or one of Rick's tennis socks.

Emma suddenly squealed. Candy turned and saw her daughter hanging out the front window on her belly, both hands lifted to the sky. She couldn't help being struck at that moment by how much Emma looked like her father; people always commented on it—Topper's determined chin, the same pale cornflower eyes, the yellow sunstreaked hair.

A flight of B-15 fighter jets hung sidewise in the air above Langley Air Force Base, aligned like a shining school of angelfish, the sun brilliant on their metal sides. There was no noise; they were too far away for the scream of the jets to be heard. The Eagles turned, standing on edge, needle-nosed, flanged as arrows. The four silver bits banked in unison and came silently roaring back.

The bag boy stopped what he was doing and stood with his face turned up, hands at his sides, entranced. Candy looked at her wristwatch. It wasn't Topper—she didn't think he had an afternoon flight. Or maybe that was yesterday. She frowned. She did try to keep track of these things so she'd have something to talk to him about.

The leading Eagle climbed straight up, breathtakingly vertical, heading into the sun like a pointing finger. As though dragged behind it in some invisible force field, the three others rose after it. Candy watched the bag boy. It was some mysterious male thing, this fascination; no woman could really understand it. Every boy in Hampton—in the world, probably—wanted to be an Eagle fighter pilot.

Candy rubbed her fingers over her sticky mouth. And not only the boys, but the men, too. And the pilots themselves; don't forget that, she told herself.

At home Topper had a collection of cockpit tapes that he

o
St
be
fill
jet t
gasp
to gr
workii
o'clock
faster,
And at t

On Su
making lo
something

Emma w
started towa

Daddy, C   Friday!
They were su   ...fficers' Club. She
still had to unl   ...en they got home. She still
had to straight   ...e bedroom. She hadn't even called a
baby-sitter. And all the damned girls were dated up on Fridays.
The bag boy came down the side of the car toward her. There
was the distant sound of jets overhead as the flight of Eagles
circled in their approach to Langley, flashing over, rolling in
unison, cleared to come in, now that the demonstration flight
was over. Candy didn't look up. She fished in her handbag and
gave the bag boy two quarters.

"Daddy!" Emma screamed.

"Oh, honey, please." Candy was in a big hurry. She pushed
Emma over in the seat and took her place behind the wheel.
She patted her hand across the hot plastic seats, then bent
forward to search the floorboard. She groped under the pedals.
She picked up an empty animal cracker box.

"Oh, sweetness," Candy moaned. "What in the hell did you
do with Mommy's car keys?"

aptain Simon McAllister came out of the rear door of Maintenance Debriefing and into the corridor which led to the squadron equipment room and saw Captain Farris standing by the Coca-Cola machine. There was no one else around, so McAllister assumed Beeper was waiting for him. Captain Farris's slender, well-made body and handsome face appeared to be rigid with some strong emotion. He still had his flight maps and information pack under his arm, and he carried his HUD systems helmet in its sling bag dangling from one hand.

"You son of a bitch," Beeper said, coming toward him, "I'm going to kill you."

Simon McAllister eyed Captain Farris with considerable caution. Beeper was, in his opinion, a major irritation, another all too common Air Force Academy zoomie with a superabundance of military attitudes which, unfortunately, Beeper persisted in regarding as solid virtues, and which, Simon McAllister was convinced, contributed to his greatly limited mindset.

Still, he reminded himself, he had to be careful; he had a lot of important things going for him at the moment, and he didn't need someone like Beeper to screw them up. It was too damned bad, though, that the Air Force was filled with small-town types with Grade B minds who were never sure in situations like this what in the hell they were reacting to. At that moment, he knew, Beeper didn't have any clear analysis of what was bugging him, only that, whatever it was, Moonbird McAllister was the cause of it.

"Listen, asshole," Simon McAllister said reasonably, "why don't you knock it off."

"I'm going to do the Air Force a favor," Captain Farris said between clenched teeth, "and kill you before you kill somebody else."

He put the helmet bag down carefully on the floor, straightened up, and before McAllister could react, shoved him backward with a straight-armed blow in the middle of the chest. McAllister fell against the Coke machine. The heavy metal cabinet slammed noisily against the wall, all the soft drink cans inside crashing against each other. Beeper moved in, threw a punch at McAllister's head, and McAllister ducked.

"Christ," Beeper cried, "I'm really going to kill you! I'm so damned sick and tired of your crap I'm going to beat the shit out of you!"

McAllister sidled along the wall, away from the Coke machine.

"Ah, cut it out, will you?" he said. He was beginning to lose his temper. "Why don't you stay out of that shitpot if you can't fly it? Draw another tail number!"

Beeper Farris made a choking noise. He followed McAllister and, hampered by his anti-G suit, still managed to lay a couple of punches hard into McAllister's ribs. McAllister grunted. He backed off and hit Beeper on the side of the head. Beeper absorbed the blow heavily. Out of the corner of his eye, McAllister saw the rear door of Maintenance open and one of the airmen step out into the hall. The airman stood there, surprised and interested. Beeper caught McAllister off guard and punched him in the mouth. McAllister staggered back.

Christ, that does it, he thought. He was surprised to see red dripping down the front of his flight suit. In a minute, someone was going to get on the telephone back there in Maintenance and spread the word. He wondered how fast he could get under Beeper's guard and really cream him. It had to come to a stop somehow, and quick.

"Fuck you and fuck your theories," Beeper panted. He swung a roundhouse blow that missed. He recovered quickly, slipping a little on the flight gear that lay scattered under their feet. "I'm tired of having you screw me up, you arrogant bastard—I'm so fucking tired of hearing about your fucking MIT degree and what a hotshit you are and your goddamned—"

At that instant, McAllister fended off Beeper's wavering left and got a straight shot for his face. His fist landed squarely on Beeper's handsome nose.

Beeper went down. As he started to fall, he grabbed at the front of McAllister's flight suit with both hands. He held on, dragging McAllister down with him. They both grunted loudly as they hit the concrete.

In the equipment room, Major Eric James put his helmet on the storage stanchion in front of him and stood looking down at it, taking a moment before unbuckling his belly pads to decide how he felt. Not tired, he told himself. He turned this over in his mind to see if this was really so and decided it was—although tired was an acceptable reaction. He had heard that sometimes you were hit with a sudden, paralyzing exhaustion that could take you off your feet, no matter where you were or what you were doing. And if true, that was worrisome. He had seriously considered, at one point, canceling out the demonstration flight. Up there was no place to put the Eagle through its flight pattern and discover you were so maxed-out you couldn't lift your hands.

As it turned out, there was no real cause for worry. The demonstration flight had gone off well—if anything, just about normally.

Major James tugged thoughtfully at his ear. He was fairly certain he could eliminate the possibility of an attack of the shakes; he'd never had that sort of reaction and was not, as far as he could tell, susceptible, for which he was heartily thankful. Nor did he have any urge to go off looking for somebody who had a bottle in his desk. Although that was fairly normal, too. Instead, some twenty-four hours after nearly crashing into the Atlantic, he found he was still feeling very good. He'd been checking it out all day, waiting for something to hit him, bracing himself to deal with it, but so far—nothing. Not that he was particularly pleased with this; the fact that there was nothing made him uneasy and even faintly embarrassed. A stress reaction was more normal, to be expected, and therefore more easily accountable. Not to feel anything at all was almost pretentious; suggested a kind of grandstanding. He was a modest person. He didn't want to give the impression, even inadvertently, of anything that might add to what he considered to be his already inflated reputation and to the names that had become attached to him as a consequence: Iron Man; the Flying Dutchman; the Top. *Topper*.

Almost absently, Major James put his hand out to touch his helmet and the tactical call sign painted there, his outsized palm and fingers easily covering the word. The rounded plastic shape was still warm from the sun that beat down through the Eagle's canopy.

Not tired and jumpy, he thought. Not like the rest of Topper flight who, comparatively new to the experience of probable death passing closely and quickly, even mundanely, were still a little shaken, although trying hard not to show it. He thought: It's worse when you're around to see it and can't do a damned thing about it.

Yesterday, coming off the dive on target and just beginning to climb, there had been a sudden, simultaneous shock of noise and motion, a giant *Boom* that had blown his feet off the floor of the cockpit and jacknifed his knees to his chest. His head had jerked back violently, and he had cursed. At that moment, he knew, the blowout of both engines was throwing a ball of flame about a hundred feet long behind the Eagle. He had had just about enough breath in his lungs to yell, "Knock it off! Knock it off!" into his mask to bring Topper flight off the target exercise and into emergency mode.

And in that same second when he was reacting to the massive physical blow to his body, he had to be alert enough to make a series of decisions: to reduce power on both engines to idle, to pick the engine that had the best chance of restarting—which was number two, with the lowest temperature and highest RPM—and shut it off. And at that altitude, and considering what he was into, not without a sharp, futile pang of regret— you hated to kill an engine for any reason. And then quickly, in a sudden limbo of nothingness, to feel the Eagle responding to the prolonged drift, the wandering, aimless drag of no power. And the agony of waiting for the engine to cool down to 700 degrees centigrade so that you could put it back into idle. And hope like hell it would start.

If he'd felt anything in that moment of wavering between

sky and gray water, it had been the cold, real clutch of gravity deep in his bones.

The rest of Topper flight had seen him not rising off the target but suddenly dropping to mush along the far side of it, on a path only a bare fifty feet or so above the water, heading straight for the Maryland shore. There had been a burst of agonized yelling in his earphones: *Eject! Eject! Eject!* over and over. Below, the surface of the Atlantic was as gray and shining as the hard cold steel it would approximate if the Eagle hit it at that speed. And it was maximum risk to eject—he was close enough to the surface to get out and stand on it.

He was working like hell to keep the faltering Eagle going when his wingman, McAllister, made a split S to drop down behind him, following him closely. The first sign he'd had that Moonbird was right behind him was when the loudest voice of all cut through the squawking voices in his headset and said, "Topper—it's Moonbird, I've got a visual."

He heard it with only part of his mind. But the warm and reassuring sound of his wingman's voice did what it was supposed to do; it was nice as hell to know Moonbird was on the job.

Still, if anything stood out in his memory, it was not the frenzied voices of Topper flight yelling for him to eject, not even McAllister's lightning reaction—not even, at that moment, the recognition of how close he was to hitting the surface of the water and turning into an instant ball of fire and scrap metal. What was engraved on his mind was something else. The eerie silence. The shutdown to total stillness.

They called the F-15s "bricks with short wings." No power, and down you drop. He'd seen the temperature figures on the engines falling slowly, and he remembered watching them, mentally forcing them to cool off faster. Shutting down was hairy anytime; there was only a gut chance at an altitude of less than a hundred feet. He'd been close enough to the water to see the waves breaking, the beads of white foam sliding off their tops. Number one engine was still too hot to do anything with, but number two, when he gave it full throttle, caught with a gush of power, throwing him sharp left. McAllister, close on his wing and only a few inches above him, quickly cut on his afterburners and scampered out of the way.

The trees and houses of a Maryland shoreside village were

rushing at him fast. He eased back on his one engine to climb, buzzing the hell out of the town as he rose. As if that wasn't bad enough, as he was pulling up over a church steeple, number one engine caught with a roar. By that time, he guessed, there wasn't an unbroken window in the place. He'd limped the Eagle back to Langley. Moonbird covering him, and he had spent the rest of the day at his desk writing out a massive, detailed report on his engine failure. And waiting for the expected reaction—any sort of reaction—to hit him. He'd taken his wife and daughter out to the Pizza Hut for dinner. He'd gone home and watched "Hawaii Five-O" and the eleven o'clock news and had gone to bed and slept for eight hours. Still okay. Now he was trying not to worry about it.

Topper James unbuckled the tight girdle of his groin and belly pad. A stream of sweat, suddenly released, dripped down his thigh. He laid the pressure pad on top of the helmet and slowly unzipped the front of his flight suit. On either side of him, the rows of helmets stretched like the brightly colored skulls of some alien tribe, the computer visors lowered and dark, the snouts of the oxygen-radio masks hanging below. On his right, the helmet on the post said "Boots" for Captain Malcolm Snyder, the element leader in Bullet flight. On the left, he saw that Beeper's and Moonbird's stanchions were empty. He guessed they were still in Maintenance Debriefing. Beeper had to file on his hydraulic systems emergency, and McAllister always spent a lot of time back there, driving Maintenance personnel to the wall. And Maintenance usually retaliated by filing their own reports back to Squadron Command on the unreasonable demands and overbearing attitudes of Captain Moonbird McAllister.

The telephone rang at the far end of the equipment room, and he saw Master Sergeant Dennis Neroda, the equipment room supervisor, lean across his desk to answer it. Topper picked up the pressure pads he'd draped across his helmet. In a few minutes he was due in debriefing to go over the mysteries of the hydraulic systems failure in Beeper's tail number 74033. But that was going to be a minor project compared to the paperwork still waiting for him on his stall stagnation problems and engine failure of the day before. The realization that equipment problems were piling up filled him with the usual sense of frustration; at some point, they had all been telling themselves for months, the situation would approach critical. Was critical. Had passed critical. Wearily, he reminded himself that whatever it was, he was still going to have to turn in another hour's work on the engine failure report before he could go off duty.

He was suddenly aware that Sergeant Neroda was signaling him from the other end of the equipment room. The Sergeant held his hand up and wagged it, still talking into the receiver. The Sergeant's mouth formed words Topper could not hear at that distance. Suddenly Sergeant Neroda lifted his arm higher and jabbed his index finger in the direction of the rear door and the corridor leading to Maintenance; his mouth moved in an exaggerated pantomine of a single word: *You*.

Not knowing what it was, but alerted by the urgency of the Sergeant's stabbing finger, Major James started for the door.

At approximately ten minutes before the hour, the oncoming shift of air traffic controllers mounted the ten flights of stairs to the Langley control tower and reported in to Master Sergeant Tom Bullock, the supervisor of the outgoing shift. As the new crew milled around in the cramped space of the tower room, a small thundershower about a thousand feet across and as opaque as a granite wall dropped unexpectedly out of a low purplish cloud at the west end of the runway, temporarily obscuring a KC-135 tanker holding in position for takeoff. The shower marched down the concrete path of the runway. After a few feet, it was pierced by the nose and then the wings and fuselage of a small T-39 transport just coming in for touchdown.

"Christ, what weather."

Tech Sergeant Alois Rodriguez, the oncoming shift supervisor, made the obligatory remark of Langley tower personnel as he stood at the windows and watched the T-39 disappear into the deluge. Above the tower at five hundred feet and dropping, another T-39 asked the controller for a runway check on the moving rainsquall.

"I'm getting a helluva car wash out here," the voice of the KC-135 said on the loudspeakers.

"Roger, hold your position," Airman Ronny Masarek told him. "It should clear out in a minute." He monitored a landing roll of the last flight of Eagles being sent to Ground Control and checked out a C-130 transport as it came downwind, turning on its base leg to the runway.

The new crew going on duty moved about the tower, looking over the weather report strips on the spindle above the console, putting away two six packs of soft drinks in the small refrigerator under the tower windows. Tech Sergeant Murphy sat beside Airman Masarek, turning sidewise in her chair to watch him, her cheek propped on her hand. Without letting him know it, she had been studying his profile, the thick black lashes and the wide, determined curve of his mouth as he spoke to local air traffic. Pretty cute, she thought again. It had occurred to her that there could be plenty of difficulties involved in what she was thinking, but nothing that couldn't be worked out. As the new shift controller came up beside Airman Masarek, he started and quickly looked up at Sergeant Murphy.

"Just unplug," she told him. "This is Ed Nyers—he's relieving you."

"Langley tower," the KC-135 said on the loudspeakers, "how about it?"

Airman Masarek stood up, and Sergeant Nyers slid into his chair. The rainsquall passed over the tower, a brief spurt of raindrops dappling the glass.

Airman Masarek stood behind Sergeant Nyers, watching him, holding the cord of the disconnected headset. The new shift was in position; the takeover had gone smoothly. A flight of F-4s reported their position east of the airfield. Master Sergeant Bullock was already at the ladder of the stairwell. Airman First Class Rosalie Tenchman had disappeared below.

"Well, that's it," Sergeant Murphy said brightly. "And that wasn't too bad for a first day, was it?" She stood up, tiny and brisk beside Airman Masarek. She pulled off her headset and patted her short red curls, looking up at him with a warm, flickering glance.

On Fridays the eight-to-four shift usually went over to Pepe's Pizza, just outside the Langley West Gate, to have a beer. Sergeant Murphy considered asking Airman Masarek if he wanted to join them, but she hesitated. She thought of Tom Bullock and Rosalie Tenchman and the crowd from the Communications Building. What would they say? *My God, Murph— not another one!* Sergeant Murphy bit her lip. Monday, she thought. Airman Masarek was cute, but there was no need to rush things.

Airman Masarek hovered uncertainly, getting in her way. A faint tinge of excitement colored his cheeks. "That was some day," he finally blurted. He followed Sergeant Murphy to the stairwell.

Turning to back down the ladder steps, she looked up at him. She gave him a dimpled smile. "You're off duty now," she reminded him. "Take off your headset and hang it up on the rack."

The color in Airman Masarek's face deepened to scarlet. He pulled off the headset with a violent gesture and looked around for a place to put it. Sergeant Murphy laughed.

"Oh, you'll get used to it." Her voice floated back up the stairwell. "Today was nothing. You should see it when there's *really* something going on!"

Major Randolph Slyke, the Operations Officer of the 17th Tactical Fighter Squadron, was on the telephone to the public affairs office of Tactical Air Command Headquarters at Langley Field. He sat with his slightly balding head bent, writing at great speed on a large yellow legal pad. To anyone passing by, Major Slyke, glimpsed through the open door of his office, appeared to be terribly busy and totally absorbed in an important telephone call. In actuality, Major Slyke was on "hold" and had been for ten long and infinitely tedious minutes, and the legal pad before him was covered with nothing more profound than some estimates of how many square feet of ready-mix concrete he would need to extend the end of the driveway through his backyard and into a newly constructed family barbecue area.

Originally Major Slyke had been called by Miss Marguerite deHaviland, secretary to Colonel Jonathan Dietrich, Chief of TAC Public Affairs, with the request that he hold on for a minute, please, Colonel Dietrich would be right with him. About three minutes later, a somewhat breathless Miss deHaviland came back on the line to apologize for the delay, explaining that just after she got Major Slyke on the telephone, Colonel Dietrich and his visitor had stepped out into the hall to catch General Couch, and they were still talking out there. But Miss deHaviland assured him they would be only a second.

Colonel Dietrich said he wanted to be sure to speak with Major
Slyke before he went home.

Randy Slyke guaranteed Miss deHaviland that he would
stay on the line for Colonel Dietrich. He heard Miss deHaviland
hesitate. Then she wanted to know, uh, if Major Slyke had,
uh, any plans for the evening. Major Slyke, leaning back at
his desk, lifted a hand to rub the tired muscles at the back of
his neck and grinned. He could think of several snappy retorts,
but since he didn't know Colonel Dietrich's secretary except
for a few brief and businesslike exchanges over the telephone,
he decided to forego being funny.

Major Dolph Bauernhauser of Dolphin flight peered around
the door. Randy Slyke covered the mouthpiece of the telephone
and looked at him inquiringly.

"We scrubbed out." Major Bauernhauser had just come back
from a Sidewinder exercise on the Atlantic weapons range.
"The telemetry screwed up and scrambled the scores."

Randy Slyke lifted his eyebrows even higher.

"Bullet flight scored nine thousand hits. And no misses."

"Oh, for Christ's sake," Major Slyke murmured.

Because, uh, the breathy voice of Miss deHaviland was
going on, Colonel Dietrich was tied up himself for the evening
and had this important visitor who—At this point, Randy Slyke
heard a male voice in the distance calling Miss deHaviland
away from the telephone again. Major Slyke, who was not
about to hang up on a department chief and a bird colonel,
especially one engaged in conversation with the Commanding
General, waited.

"Talk to you later," Dolph Bauernhauser said and disappeared. But Major Slyke had spotted Topper James in the hall.

"Top!" the Ops Officer called. "I want to know what in hell
happened out there."

"I'm sorry," Miss deHaviland said again, "but it *does* look
like Colonel Dietrich's going to be tied up for a few minutes.
He wants to know, can he call you right back?"

"Sure," Randy Slyke said, "tell the Colonel no problem. I'll
be right here." He hung up and got up from his chair. He started
around the desk. At that moment, Major James appeared at the
door. "Topper," the Flight Ops Officer repeated, "what the hell
happened out there?"

Major James wore his flight suit and carried a clipboard;

he had obviously just come from a debriefing. He stood easily and gracefully for a man his size, but his figure still filled the doorway. Major Slyke, a small man, looked up and then turned and went around his desk and sat down again, putting it between them.

"Beeper had a hydraulic systems failure." Major James fixed Randy Slyke with Major James's peculiarly pale-eyed stare.

Randy Slyke picked up his pencil and made a note at the top of the concrete estimates sheet to reschedule the weapons shoot right away. During the weekend, he thought. It was going to be unpopular as hell. But the squadron's time on the missile range, Randy Slyke knew without consulting his board, was cut back for the coming week to accommodate some transient F-105s from the Virginia Air National Guard. And the range belonged to the Navy to start with. Early Sunday morning was going to make everybody unhappy.

"Your element leader's gone over to the medics with a busted nose," he said, not looking up. "The wing commander called and wanted to know what in hell happened out there."

Major James said nothing. Major Slyke continued to write. "A little misunderstanding," Major James said finally.

"A little misunderstanding, hell," Major Slyke said. "Somebody from Maintenance called in here and said there was a goddamned riot going on out there. Then they tell me somebody took a swing at somebody in Bronco flight when they came through."

There was an extended silence. Finally Major James said, "It's been a tough day."

Randy Slyke tossed down his pencil irritably. "Is he engaged to some Senator's daughter, or what?" he wanted to know. "I hear he's got connections with somebody on the Senate Armed Services Committee."

Major Slyke detested politicking. He was a dirt track man himself and believed in going up the hard way. But, as he would be the first to admit, a little Washington influence got you everywhere. It certainly didn't hurt to have a politician for a friend, or some big industry head who gave generously to one of the national political parties and who could drop a good word on your behalf. Congressional representatives rated high, depending on what House committee they served on. A Senator who was a member of the Senate Armed Services Committee carried very big weight, indeed. Especially if it looked like you were going to marry his daughter. Nobody, Randy Slyke knew, had ever been kicked out of the Air Force for that.

Major Slyke had no problem with Captain Francis Farris, a team player who knew the system and generally got along very well in it. Captain Simon McAllister was another matter. Major Slyke had a deep distrust of Eastern establishment structures like the Massachusetts Institute of Technology and any of its cum laude graduates who drove Porsches and had seemingly important Washington connections. In Major Slyke's estimation, Captain McAllister was deliberately and obnoxiously larger than life, even for a fighter squadron, and the Ops Officer was considering various means of dealing with the difficulty.

Major James regarded him somberly. "Not exactly engaged. But she's Senator Glass's daughter."

Major Slyke grimaced. Senator Mortimer Glass was indeed a member of the all-powerful Senate Armed Services Committee. He was the Chairman. Randy Slyke thought it over for a minute before he said, "What *is* not exactly engaged?"

"I don't know," Major James said honestly. "Some sort of arrangement."

Randy Slyke assumed an ironic expression. "I hear he has some sort of screwball apartment with space movies and wall-to-wall women. Is he some sort of freak? He's supposed to be trying to get into experimental test pilot school."

For some months—no, Major Slyke corrected himself, ever since he'd been in the squadron—Captain McAllister had not let them forget that he was just passing through, just making his required fifteen hundred hours in advanced aircraft before going on to the Big Time. Which, as Randy Slyke understood it, was test pilot school and then ARPA, the Advanced Research Projects Administration, the Skunkworks and the supersecret experimental fighter-craft being worked on there, and, eventually and in natural progression, the wonders of outer space. Major Slyke wished Captain McAllister well. He could barely restrain himself, but the prospect of getting Captain McAllister out of his hair—especially away from the flight operations counter where McAllister hung around hustling for high-visibility assignments such as instructor pilot, weapons and tactics instructor, and practically anything else he could think of to promote his ambitions—filled Major Slyke with limitless joy.

In the squadron, perhaps the whole First Tactical Fighter Wing, it could be said that nobody appreciated Captain Moonbird McAllister except, perhaps, and unaccountably, Major James, his flight leader. Topper wrote McAllister's evaluation reports, rated him highly, and seemed able to live with him. Which was apparently more than anyone else could do. Not that McAllister was a bad pilot; in fact, he was almost as good as he said he was. But the truth of the matter was that virtually no one in the 17th Tactical Fighter Squadron would stand in Captain McAllister's way if he truly wanted to go on to, as he saw it, Better Things.

"I hear he's even been up to Edwards, bugging them about what a good test pilot he'd make. Tell me," Major Slyke said, "is this all with the Senator's help? I just want to know what we're dealing with here."

"The apartment's a joke," Topper James said. He hesitated. "He told me they once took a Volkswagen apart at MIT and put it together again in somebody's room. They're big technological types."

The Ops Officer stared at him.

"What I'm trying to say," Major James said, "is that he's probably not your basic fighter pilot's fighter pilot. But I can't fault him as a wingman; I wouldn't want anybody else. Also, he's got an instinctive feel for the equipment. He'd make a good test pilot. Hell, I think he's bored." Major James's expression was strained. He was not given to personality analyses. "He bites his nails."

"I don't care if he shaves his balls," Major Slyke said, "I can't have this crap going on. The wing command is down on our ass about what happened out there. I'm going to give your pal two weeks' simulator time. He can work his butt off learning to fly an airplane again. Unless," Major Slyke added, looking down at his papers, "you want to argue about it."

Major James didn't answer. Randy Slyke shuffled through the legal pad sheets and then opened a desk drawer and closed it. He pulled a sheet of paper to him and started to write.

Major James let out a long breath. "I'll straighten it out," he said. "Beeper had a hot start going out, or thought he did, and while he was checking out his engines, McAllister pulled out in front of him. That's what started it. You already know about the hydraulic systems malfunction. Something's wrong with that tail number; it's giving more trouble than all the other troubles we've got put together."

"I'm going to come down hard on his ass," Major Slyke said, not looking up. At the moment, he did not want to discuss engine failures and other factors affecting their highly publicized air superiority fighters. He'd had more than his share of table pounding and the usual ultimatums: Either you get it fixed, or I'm going to quit—and I'm not going to quit so you damned well better get it fixed. To which Major Slyke gave the usual answer: People are working on it.

When all was said and done, their troubles with the Eagles were what they had to live with—and not bitch. Although he knew the futility of *that;* in the pressure-cooker environment of an Eagle fighter squadron where every member was a prima donna by definition, bitching was the name of the game.

Slyke flipped the circular file on his desk, looking for the number of the TAC PA Office. He couldn't wait forever for Miss deHaviland.

"Write me a report on it," he said.

Major James set his large jaw adamantly. "Randy, I've got enough paperwork."

Major Slyke looked up, remembering now. "Topper, how do you feel? The demo show go off all right? I can give you a couple of days free if you want."

"I feel fine," Major James said with infinite patience. "I just don't want to have to write any more reports on equipment malfunctions until I've finished the one I'm working on."

Major Slyke considered this. "Get back to me tomorrow. I mean Monday."

The telephone rang, and Major Slyke answered it.

"Oh, Major Slyke," Miss deHaviland's voice said, "I'm so sorry for all the delay! Colonel Dietrich will talk to you now."

When he looked up again, Topper James was gone.

4

It was six o'clock by the time Topper James turned in his hour's work on his engine failure report and arrived at the Langley Officers' Club. It was obviously TGIF, Thank-God-it's-Friday, and the parking lot showed it. Even the auxiliary parking lot across the road was filled. And so was the Officers' Club bar, with the usual single girls from the base offices and NASA and their male opposite numbers in the civilian strata, as well as the regular Friday night crowd of TAC fighter pilots who staked out the area around the bar itself as their traditional territory.

Party time, Topper thought. The voice level was already several tens of decibels above that of other weekday nights, compounded by the blare of recorded disco music. He stood just inside the entrance, still wearing his flight suit, looking at the press of bodies three and four deep at the bar and wondering if it was worth the trouble to try to get a beer.

The place seemed to be unusually crowded for a hot July evening, but he supposed everybody had had the same thought. A nice cold drink before going home. He looked around. The 27th Tactical Fighter Squadron was there, most of them still in flight suits from a late afternoon mission, and the 94th, the famed Rickenbacker *Hat in the Ring* squadron, projecting the subtle image of hot pilots and tough men. A group of Israeli F-15 trainees stood near the door to the television lounge. Beyond them and about midway in the crowd were ten or twelve Egyptian Air Force officers in fancy uniforms. The Saudi Arabians were down on the bar stools at the far end.

Always, Topper observed, the careful geometric separation of the allies.

Just beyond the Egyptians, Topper caught a glimpse of Major Dolph Bauernhauser with the rest of Dolphin flight standing glumly around him, drinks in hand. Dolphin flight was sore; their computer scores for the Sidewinder missile shoot had been garbled along with the rest. Major Bauernhauser talked earnestly. Topper watched Dolph's bent head, his gestures, with sympathy. Dolph was probably late for dinner at home, but there he was, trying to smooth the troubled waters of chronically failed electronics systems. Topper looked for his own flight. Everybody had problems; at least Dolph Bauernhauser didn't have a damned feud on his hands.

A stream of traffic pushed Topper ahead, and he moved with it. On Friday nights the Officers' Club offered, in that period known popularly as Happy Hour, a free hors d'oeuvres table or mini-luau, as the club bulletin referred to it—an all-you-can-eat affair with flaming hibachis and platters of braised chicken wings and miniature meatballs which, along with cherry tomatoes and chunks of pineapple, were to be put together on skewers and toasted over the hibachi fires. The mini-luau, set out only in the summer months, was intended to draw the members of the Officers' Club and their families away from the outdoor pool—where they lingered past dark and after the lifeguard had gone off duty—and into the cocktail lounge and the bar where business usually slacked off in July and August. The mini-luau was a roaring success, but it created a traffic jam at the doors of the bar that looked like the last days of Saigon. As Topper elbowed his way past the table, he grabbed a couple of tomatoes and ate them hungrily. Dinner with his wife was still more than an hour away.

He spotted the head and shoulders of Simon McAllister deep in the crowd. Beside McAllister, he could make out the face of Beeper Farris, eyes half shut in a mass of purple flesh, a large strip of beige surgical tape stretched across the distended plane of his nose. McAllister's mouth showed some damage, too; his upper lip puffed up over his teeth like a chipmunk's. He bent toward Beeper, talking fast, both hands held with thumbs together in the classic gesture of flying airplanes. Around Beeper and Moonbird were Captain Forrest Harmon, Beeper's wingman, Captain Elbert Shaun, Captain William

Cooke, and others of the 17th Squadron who went variously by the tactical call signs of Nizzard, Moose, Grits, Livid, and Churn.

Topper stopped just beyond the mini-luau table. He had told Beeper and Moonbird to have a drink and get it straightened out. Now they were at least talking to each other. McAllister was making a conversational point and, as always, pressing a little too hard for it, his vivid, sharp-featured face almost in Beeper's. Topper observed them for a moment, holding his place in the jostling crowd. McAllister was always doing some damned thing to keep the pot boiling. There was an established procedure for delays on takeoff; when you saw that the pilot ahead of you had some sort of equipment trouble—in this case with his engines—you called to ask what the delay was and if it was going to be long, then asked his permission to move out ahead of him. Anything else was grounds for murder.

Topper looked around him. He disliked crowds. A beer would taste good right then, but he didn't want to go to the bar where Beeper and Moonbird could see him. He wanted them to stay with it for a while. At some point, he was reminded, perhaps next week, he was going to have to have a talk with McAllister about calling the wing commander and inviting the Colonel and the Colonel's aide, Major Sickle, out to lunch. Apparently McAllister's idea had been to promote his application to test pilot school and the letters of recommendation that were to go with it. But Tom Sickle had called George Gazenove, the 17th's commander, wanting to know what in the hell was going on. The Colonel didn't have time to lunch with some fighter jock over in the 17th. Or did he? Even the wing command had heard peripherally that somebody somewhere in the wing was dating a Senator's daughter.

That was pretty barehanded, Topper thought. It wasn't that McAllister didn't know what subtlety was, but that rather, coming from a background of some wealth and influence and seeing the Air Force as only a stepping stone, he lacked respect for the military and the people in it and didn't bother with protocol. McAllister was certainly smart enough; his college transcripts showed his major in mathematics in undergraduate studies; he had a graduate degree in physics, as well as aerospace engineering. But he was a nut, Topper told himself. A real nut. Even if you were born with a high don't-give-a-shit factor, at least you could learn to cover it up.

Although, Topper had to admit, McAllister wasn't exactly unique. In the sixties, some of the astronaut candidates for the Apollo moonshots had passed through the squadron, all hell-bent, too, for the Big Time. According to what he had heard, they hadn't exactly made themselves well loved, either.

Topper turned and made his way out of the bar. In the hall he flagged down a waiter to see if someone could bring him a beer in the main hall of the club.

Built in the baronial style of the early twenties, the main hall was undergoing major renovations, and Topper found there was no longer any place to sit. All the leather sofas and battered coffee tables had been taken away. The evidence of new construction was everywhere. A door had been cut through to the back hall, and the framing was still unfinished. The massive hooded fireplaces were still intact, as were the great hanging Tudor-style lighting fixtures, but the casement windows that overlooked the greensward and the back of TAC headquarters had been ripped out and replaced with large sheets of modern plate glass. Gone, too, were the crowded rows of framed photographs that had covered the walls of fighter pilots of World War I, Langley Field, in their leather helmets and laced boots, standing in front of wooden hangars and ancient biplanes.

The east wall of the main room had been filled with larger, more formal photographs of World War II tactical fighter groups massed before P-40s and P-38s and some aerial color shots originally featured in the *Look* and *Life* magazines of that era. There had never been, as far as anyone knew, any permanent displays from the Korean or Vietnam wars.

Now, with renovations underway, the walls had been swept bare, the pictures apparently carted off to Air Force archives somewhere. To cover the east wall, already peeled down to the laths, a bank of portable canvas display panels had been set up, and a poster on a stand announced an exhibition of paintings from the United States Air Force Art Collection. In the middle of the main panel was the Space Shuttle, painted nose-up in a giant scaffolding that was in turn held by an outsized crane.

Topper was not much interested in art, but since he was killing time and wanted to avoid the bar, he bent down to take a look at the painting and the Space Shuttle's underbelly. The shuttle's experimental skin was composed of an epoxy matrix, laid in tiles. The Navy's F-18 Hornet was supposed to be made entirely of the stuff. Topper saw that the artist had worked the Space Shuttle's tiles into a smooth mass for a more pleasing effect.

Next to the painting of the Space Shuttle was another artist's concept of an F-15 Eagle in flight against a cloudless blue sky. Topper stepped back to take a good look at it. The card underneath said:

> The new dimension in air superiority. The F-15 Eagle will outperform and outfight any enemy supersonic fightercraft in the foreseeable future; it is a single-placed, fixed-wing Mach 2.5 class twin engine aircraft whose primary mission is air superiority. A low wing loading and superb thrust-to-weight ratio provide the F-15 with unprecedented maneuverability. Length: 63.8 feet. Height: 18.5 feet. Wing span: 42.8 feet. Weight: 40,000 lb. class. Armament: mix of air-to-air weaponry including a high firing-rate cannon, four Sidewinder and four Sparrow missiles. Air-to-surface ordnance up to 15,000 lbs. Propulsion: two Trueham turbofan engines in the 25,000-thrust class with afterburners, making the F-15 the first fightercraft with thrust-to-weight greater than one-to-one.

It was a beautiful spacebird in spite of all its problems, in spite of all the bugs still in it. The F-15 was pictured against the open sky and, as it traveled at more than twice the speed of sound, seemingly weightless, enveloped in light and motion. Topper felt his throat constrict as he looked at it. It had its problems, some of them apparently insoluble, but it was still just what the description implied: an aircraft superior to all others.

And modifications had already begun. The latest Eagles off the production line could carry 30–40 percent more fuel, decreasing the need for the fighters to depend on tanker planes for inflight refueling. The couch—and it was a couch now, not a seat—had been increased to thirty degrees from the usual thirteen degrees, to give the pilot more "G" tolerance. And the pilot's arm now rested in a support shell, his hand pressure electrically signaling actuators which provided input to the control surfaces. Gradually, Topper thought, the Air Force had caught up and passed the people who designed movie and television spaceships and kids' toys; the reality of the F-15 Eagle looked like something he'd buy in the dime store for Emma.

The next panel brought him up short. The Dumb Machine. The card under it said "Land Attack Missile," but it was still the Dumb Machine, born to render poor fighter pilots obsolete. The painting showed a cruise missile, a Tomahawk, in flight over mountainous terrain. It looked ugly as hell—long, bullet-shaped, like a marine torpedo with little stubby wings.

The guidance system for the land attack Tomahawk employs terrain correlation for navigation updating. At launch, the system's inertial guidance platform is provided with the location of the launch platform and its target. Operating autonomously, the guidance system directs the missile over a circuitous flightpath to the target. While flying over land, downlooking radar is used to construct terrain altitude profiles along preselected segments of the flightpath.

"So here's where you are," a voice said. A hand slapped him lightly on the rump.

"Quit, I'm trying to read," Topper said.

This information is compared with the computer-stored digital map data to provide correlations to the missile's flightpath. With each terrain correlation update, the accuracy of the missile's flightpath is improved.

"The Old Man is in the dining room," Randy Slyke said. "He sent me to find you. He wants you to come in for a minute."

Consequently, the missile achieves previously unattainable levels of target accuracy. The downlooking radar operates continuously to permit the missile to follow the terrain at very low altitudes to evade radar detection.

"You ought to read it," Topper said, straightening up. "It says they're going to replace Flight Ops officers with this thing."

Randy Slyke, too, was still in his flight suit. He took Topper by the arm and steered him in the direction of the club dining room.

"He's got somebody he wants you to meet."

"Whatever it is," Topper told him, "let's make it quick." He wasn't enthusiastic about joining up with the squadron commanding officer at that hour; by now, Lieutenant Colonel Roger Gazenove was well into his weekend marathon of Dewar's and water. "You get me out of it, Randy; I've got to get back to my group at the bar. And my wife's coming in for dinner."

"Right." Randy Slyke was easily agreeable. "Just don't let him know you're in a hurry, will you? I just got him smoothed down."

It was early, and the Terrace Room was almost empty. Two waitresses were setting up the salad bar. The Squadron commander of the 17th sat at a table in the back by the windows, several empty glasses in front of him. A young heavyset man with a shock of red hair, wearing a flowered aloha shirt, sat opposite. When Topper and Major Slyke came up, Lieutenant Colonel Gazenove looked at them with an expression of visible relief.

"Well, now, here's somebody you ought to meet," he said jovially to the redheaded man.

Randy Slyke made the introductions. The civilian's name was Tony Meehan. Randy Slyke sat down at the table, moved his chair back, and crossed his legs, sprawling comfortably. "Topper," he said in a smooth, overly deliberate tone of voice which made Topper look at him quickly, "the 17th's glad to be able to welcome Tony, a reporter for the *National Globe*, while he takes a look around TAC headquarters for a story he's doing on the Eagles. Jon Dietrich of our PA office showed Tony around the base today, but Jon's tied up tonight and thought Tony would like to come over and have dinner with us." Randy Slyke smiled too cordially. "Tony was forwarded to Colonel Dietrich's office from Air Force PA Headquarters, Pentagon, and he's on the first leg of a trip that's going to take him out to Nellis and the Red Flag exercises."

Colonel Gazenove said suddenly, loudly, "Topper's the man you want to talk to. Here, sit down, Top; have dinner with us."

He leaned back on two legs of his chair to flag a waiter. "Let's get some drinks."

The reporter said, "You're pretty big for a fighter pilot, aren't you, Major?" He was grinning. He looked very Irish, with his large meaty face and red hair. But the eyes were cold, observant, and glass-green.

Topper sat down next to him. It had taken him a moment to comprehend what was happening. Damn, he thought; at least Randy Slyke could have tipped him off.

Nellis Air Force Base was right next door to Las Vegas. After the joy ride in the Eagle over the desert and a look at the Red Flag war games, the information office would probably assign a couple of people to take Meehan up to Vegas for a night on the town. The whole, extended VIP treatment. It was not a matter of whether Meehan deserved it or whether his paper was that important, but that the media drought since Vietnam had been long and tough. And what there was of it, notably hostile. Topper looked at the fattish, redheaded young man with curiosity.

A few months ago, the base had been visited by a reporter from the Richmond paper, a nice type about Meehan's age, a family man with kids—Topper had seen the snapshots of his family, passed around over a couple of drinks. A genuinely likable sort of guy. The squadron members had found him a man much like themselves, his shoptalk similar to theirs: he wasn't getting paid enough for what he did considering his skills; he'd bought a house in the suburbs that he couldn't afford; he'd just made a job switch, hopefully for the better, and was new to the Richmond area—all the middle-class goals that affected them all as they moved out of their twenties and into their early thirties. The story he was working on was some feature article for the Richmond paper Sunday supplement on the presence of Tactical Air Command Headquarters in the state; he said he'd talked his editor into doing it. They had liked him so much that a couple of fliers had taken him out to dinner, gotten drunk with him, and had just managed to get him back to his car in shape for the long drive back to Richmond.

They had been stunned when the PA forwarded a copy of the story to them some weeks later. It was a hatchet job, pure and simple, all of them portrayed as near incompetents, weirdos, paranoid military types, the Air Force their only haven in a sane society. The tactical fighter squadrons in particular were pictured as supersonic flyboys hacking around in marginally operational and essentially experimental equipment that was, at the very least, an unwise investment for the laboring taxpayer. They had all read it, passing it from hand to hand. Well, what do you expect, they had told themselves. He's part of a system; he has to write what they tell him to write, doesn't he?

But Topper had never bought that explanation. It had occurred to him several times since that the Richmond reporter might have been genuinely impressed with them and with what he saw; that their similarities to him and his old stereotypes of them having produced an unworkable conflict, he found himself adrift and without a real story. And when he got back to Richmond, he had attacked them out of a sense that, in pushing the assignment, he had put himself in a position to question his own convictions. That made sense, somehow; Topper felt he could understand that.

It had certainly been a bad deal. But now, he could see, the IO was still soliciting publicity and, hopefully, a better break. The orders came down from Washington, from the Joint Chiefs of Staff.

"They shortened my legs in flight training," Topper said. It was the standard reply, but he saw, to his surprise, that Meehan laughed.

"I'm really glad to be down here with you people," the reporter said. He was making an effort to be friendly. The squadron commander was ordering drinks. Meehan said he'd have another bloody mary. Randy Slyke ordered cream sherry. Topper stared at him. Topper ordered a scotch on the rocks, and Colonel Gazenove said make it two, doubles.

"That's really exciting stuff the Air Force is doing out in Nevada," Meehan said. His voice was peculiarly soft and quite husky for a man his size. "Full war modes, no punches pulled." He drained his glass. "Hell, I wish my paper was set up to do an in-depth piece, but that's not our style. Our readership's scaled to a first person I-was-there-riding-in-the-world's-first-spacefighter sort of thing. But we give good photo coverage— about a three-quarter page on this one, and that's a lot for us.

I've got a good photographer; I'm going to pick him up out at Nellis. He's been shooting a story on UFOs in Canada."

Major Slyke looked at Topper, who said dutifully, "Red Flag is tough."

"Yeah, well, I'm going to zero in on the gee-wow material, frankly." One corner of Meehan's mouth sagged ironically. "The space helmets with the computer flight simulations on them, the Mach Two and above stuff. I hear you guys pull out all the stops going over the desert ridges out there. The fatality rates have been running pretty high, haven't they? What's it now—over ten so far this year?"

A sudden silence settled over the table. Topper looked at Randy Slyke and saw the barest movement of his head, no. Topper looked away toward the wall of windows and the summer sun beating on the surface of Chesapeake Bay. The terrace of the club and the swimming pool fence and the side of the diving tower showed in the right-hand corner of the glass. A line of skinny kids, burnt brown by the sun, raced up the steps of the diving tower and cannonballed off, arms wrapped around their knees, plummeting silently into the bright blue water below. Topper heard a ringing noise in his ears; a bubble of air seemed to close around him. The ringing grew louder. He heard the distant clatter of dishes somewhere.

He suddenly remembered that the *National Globe* was one of those weekly tabloids on sale in the supermarket checkout stands, along with *TV Guide* and *Reader's Digest*. It carried stories about miracle cures for cancer and the latest movie star divorces. Colonel Gazenove said something about advanced fightercraft in the modern Air Force. Topper looked down at his scotch.

Whatever the dangers were in having Meehan dumped on them like this, Topper thought, it wasn't Gazenove's problem anymore. The squadron commander had only a few weeks left before he transferred to desk duty in the Pentagon, and then a year or so before he retired. Topper lifted his drink and took a swallow. The whiskey went down cold and bland as water. The strange ringing sound continued in his ears. The voices at the table were far away.

The reporter was saying that he was really looking forward to wearing the Head Up helmet out at Nellis. He'd heard some fantastic things about the system. The voices drifted away. The reporter said, more distinctly, *Yeah, but you've got something big coming up now, haven't you? I've been hearing about supersecret stuff, like suborbital fighters.* The Old Man sat and stared. Randy Slyke looked out the window.

"Well, hell, what the Air Force is doing right now is science fiction all the way. We've just closed the gap—sneaked up on it, actually, in the last few years. Listen, the Eagles themselves would have been Buck Rogers concepts forty years ago. Look what we've got now—the F-15s, the Navy's F-18 Hornets, which are right out of your television space shows, and how about the SR-71s? They do better than Mach Three, from all accounts. At twenty-five hundred miles an hour, that's the speed of a bullet from a high-powered rifle. What a comparison, huh? Man, I'd really like to get a look at one!" The reporter's green eyes glowed enthusiastically. He was talking about something he liked now; the studiedly amiable manner was gone. "In a few years we're going to see fighter jets skimming in and out of the earth's atmosphere, the Space Shuttle will be up, and we'll have it building orbiting space stations. The Russians have been working on the space station idea for years; that's what the Soyuz series is all about, to see how man can live and work in space. They're going to try and jump us again, you wait and see. The Russians got a first with Sputnik, and Gagarin was the first man in orbit—they just fell behind on the moonshots because they didn't have the money to spend. But they're going to try something again; you can bet your ass on it."

"That's interesting, all right," Colonel Gazenove said. He looked with blurred eyes at Randy Slyke, who was drawing designs on the tablecloth with his fingernail.

Topper felt the eerie stillness thickening around him. The light from the window enveloped them, sun motes dancing in the quiet. Topper's vision faded, tunneled out. He felt no vibration from the airframe, nothing from the engines, only quiet, rushing motion, gravity pulling. The stainless steel surface of the water rushed at him. Waves ran by, foam breaking at their tops. No wind. No noise. Closer, downward, closer. All in silence.

"You'll be wearing the helmet with the HUD at Nellis," Randy Slyke said.

Topper's hands were wet with sweat. His bladder was suddenly full; the small muscles in his knees trembled. He was aware that Randy Slyke was watching him. Meehan talked about tennis courts on the base. He wasn't good, but he liked to sharpen his game whenever he could. Play anybody.

Meehan was still talking. Topper stood up. He needed to get up and walk around. He knew what it was now. It was a fairly long walk to the bar.

"You're clear for Sunday, aren't you?" the Old Man said, looking up. "I thought you could take our friend here around."

He had intended to get the lawnmower out, clean the spark plugs, and mow the grass in the backyard; McAllister had decided to throw some sort of party, a peacemaking effort, at his place Saturday night; and the rescheduled missile exercise was set for Sunday morning at 0700 hours. Topper said that was fine with him. He shook hands with Meehan, said he'd see him later. He nodded to Gazenove and Randy Slyke and started toward the front of the club. It was like walking in a vacuum.

He came out in the reception hall by mistake, and he saw his wife Candy and his daughter Emma in the crowd coming in. He stopped short.

Candy was wearing a floor-length dress of some filmy flowered material. It was new, he didn't recognize it; for a moment the dismal thought passed through his mind that she'd gone shopping again, and he wondered what the hell else she'd bought. She wore her long hair to her shoulders, and around her face the curls were arranged in long, dramatically dangling ringlets. She was as artfully made up as a fashion model and too impossibly beautiful for the lobby of the Langley Officers' Club. His daughter wore a dress like her mother's and dirty tennis shoes. They both had fresh flowers in their hair. Topper recognized marigolds from the front yard. Candy rushed to him, apologetic and uncertain.

"Oh, Top," she cried, "I couldn't get a baby-sitter, I just *couldn't*. Look, doesn't Emma look sweet? She'll behave, I promise. Won't you, hon?"

"Daddy!" Emma shrieked. She grabbed Topper's leg and wound her arms around it. She held on tightly. Topper stroked her head, careful of the flowers.

"It's all right," he said. He tried to pry Emma away from

his leg. "It's okay. We won't stay long, anyway." He meant dinner.

"Oh, Topper, it isn't all right, is it?" Candy's beautiful red mouth turned down unhappily. "I swear I telephoned, but all the damned girls were busy. It's Friday night."

Topper knew she had waited until the last minute to call the baby-sitters, but it didn't really matter. Candy was Candy. He kept staring at her. She was so theatrically lovely that people in the lobby turned to look at her. He felt tired. His eyelid twitched.

"Look, it's all right," he said. "Let go, honey." He bent down and worked Emma's fingers loose. "Daddy's got something to do. I'll be right back in a minute." To Candy he said, "Take her in and get a table, order a drink, something. See if we can get dinner quick and get it over with before she gets tired." Emma could be hell in the dining room. "I've got to see some people in the bar." He picked Emma up and put her into Candy's arms. "The Old Man's in there. For God's sake, get a table way the hell away from him." He left her holding Emma.

The entrance to the bar was now almost completely blocked by the crowd around the mini-luau table, and the noise was deafening. Topper pushed his way inside and bumped into Dolph Bauernhauser.

"I thought you went home," Topper said.

"I decided to stay and get drunk." But Dolph was sober; he merely looked tired and unhappy.

Topper couldn't find McAllister or Beeper anywhere in the bar. He decided to look in the television lounge. He was fairly certain they hadn't gone home. It took him several minutes to get through the Israelis still at the doorway. When he entered the lounge, he saw Nizzard sitting on the arm of the sofa drawn up before the television set, and he knew the others were somewhere around. The sound was turned up full volume to drown out the racket on the bar side. The room was full of Tactical Air Command personnel, mostly fighter pilots, many still in flight suits, all with drinks in their hands. Topper saw McAllister in the middle of the sofa, back to him, feet on the coffee table among the glasses. Beeper was sitting beside him. Topper started for them. All the faces in the lounge, expressionless and absorbed, were turned to the bright light of the screen. The voice of Captain Kirk of the Starship *Enterprise* spoke to Communications Officer Uhura about maintaining contact with an alien craft closing fast.

Damn, Topper thought, it's seven o'clock. The local Hampton television station featured reruns of "Star Trek" every weekday evening throughout the year, the same hour-long shows which had run so long on television that they had been memorized by a whole generation. And still wildly popular in military areas; half the personnel of Langley, most of NASA and the Navy in the Norfolk bases had been raised on Captain Kirk and the crew of his Starship.

"Moonbird," Topper said, bending over the back of the couch. Beeper Farris was on his right, McAllister in the middle, and Harmon and Shaun on the other side. None of them looked up. Mr. Spock, checking his computer readouts, identified the alien spacecraft as Klingons and closing fast. Topper watched Mr. Spock's green ears.

"Yeah, Top," McAllister said, without looking up.

The red alert signal had begun to shriek through the Starship bridge. Lieutenant Uhura pressed her hand to her earpiece and looked attentive. "Go get 'em, honey," a voice said in the crowd.

"Listen," Topper said. He bent and touched Moonbird's shoulder.

At that moment, the enemy spaceship advancing on the *Enterprise* fired its lasers with considerable effect. The bridge of the Starship rocked. The red alert signal rose to a whooping scream. Mr. Spock said very calmly, "The enemy is closing, Captain."

Topper should have anticipated it, but he was busy trying to make connection with Beeper and McAllister, to let them know he was there and going on to dinner. He didn't remember until the very last second. The crowd in the television lounge had been straining forward, waiting, since the red alert light had started flashing on the bridge of the *Enterprise*.

"*Klingons!*" someone yelled at the back of the room.

Moonbird and Grits threw themselves forward across the coffee table and the empty glasses there and rolled off, dropping to the floor on the far side. Beeper toppled slowly, holding his beer high in one hand. Across the lounge, there was the thud of flesh hitting the floor, grunts and whoops, bodies falling and colliding, and the sound of chairs coming over. A wave of bourbon, beer, and scotch rose in the air and fell back wetly. The 94th went down in a tangle at the entrance to the bar, yelling in unison. Bodies fell behind them, beyond the lines at the mini-luau table and on into the packed bar itself. Diners from the Terrace Room rushed out into the hall to see.

Nizzard came down on Topper, and they hit the floor at the same time. Nizzard lay there, head down, still holding his half-empty glass in his hand. The ringing in Topper's ears faded away; the bubble shattered. "God*damn*," Nizzard said in his Alabama drawl and laughed. Topper lay on his stomach, reality welling up in him again. It was so damned stupid you had to laugh. In the rush, he never knew how many civilians managed to stay on their feet. Once in a while some bystander got pulled down by mistake.

There wasn't a fighter jock upright. A few years ago it used to be *Dead Bug*, and when it was yelled out, you had to fall down and roll over on your back, holding your arms and legs up in the air. Now it was *Klingons*.

The spilled booze on the floor was seeping across his belly. Topper lay there, his chin on his arm, his eyes closed. Nizzard kept laughing. Somewhere, the *National Globe* reporter, Tony Meehan, was seeing all this and undoubtedly asking what in hell it was all about.

Part 2

/* STAGNANT OCCLUDED
WARM FRONT */

5

Near dawn on Sunday a thunderstorm came up in the southeast, in the direction of the city of Norfolk, and moved noisily across the bay toward Hampton and Newport News. It was a large storm, full of energy; the sky turned white with repeated lightning flashes while the storm was still far enough away for the thunder to be no more than a faint, ominous roll. Simon McAllister lay with one arm propped behind his head, watching the light at the window above the bedroom air conditioner. He wasn't sleepy; in fact, he was wide awake and felt good and didn't see any reason to lie there and fight it. He had to get up in a few minutes, anyway, to get ready for the rescheduled Sidewinder shoot at 0700 hours. Lying in the dark, he savored the tight, perversely vigorous feeling that always came on him when he missed a full night's sleep. His system was full of adrenalin, a natural high that he knew from past experience would go on well into the second day without fading or letting him down. But then, he was in top physical shape: he took care of his body, he ran five miles a day, maintained a good diet, and, he reminded himself, he had watched his liquor intake at the party. That helped.

He waited until he heard the first rush of storm wind in the trees outside, and then he got up, taking care not to disturb the naked girl beside him, and went into the living room to shut the windows. The rain was beating hard against the south side of the building, and the floor was wet. He moved a chair out of the way and then stood for a moment, looking down at the street. He liked the night, with everything sleeping and dark; always had, even as a kid. The rain began to come down in hard, windblown streams, lashing over the parked cars under the street light, flooding the walks and the grass in front of the apartment house. The air, suddenly trapped in the room by the closing of the windows, was fresh and wet and smelled of sea water. McAllister lifted his arms and stretched. It had been a good party, a lot of booze and food and peacemaking efforts, and everybody had shown up with wives and girl friends, except Beeper, who was taking pain pills for his nose.

Even the reporter from the scandal sheet, he was reminded, brought along by Topper. A strange mix, but everybody had enjoyed themselves. Hell, they'd stayed long enough, practically until dawn, and they all had flights at seven o'clock.

He went into the kitchen. The formica counters were covered with beer cans and dirty glasses, and somebody had neatly stacked a line of empty whiskey bottles on the floor against the wall. He found a roll of cheese spread softening on the stove and opened the refrigerator to put it away. The refrigerator was still full of beer, so he tossed the cheese into the freezer. He could see it was going to take him a couple of days to clean up, unless the girl in the bedroom got good-hearted and decided to straighten up when she woke. He opened the cabinet above the sink, looking for the can of coffee. He was glad the party was out of the way. He didn't mind making the positive social gesture, and he guessed he owed it after Friday; it was just that he had a lot of his own friends in Washington and New York he didn't see enough of, as it was.

He plugged in the percolator. The reporter had been a surprise; at first nobody had known what to do with him. Just don't talk shop, Topper had said. As far as *he* knew, nobody had. What was shop talk, anyway? If they wanted to bitch about the rotten engines in the F-15s, that was their business. It was only the Air Force's secret, anyway, not anybody else's. McAllister grabbed a handful of potato chips from the bag in the sink and went into the living room.

The sound system was still on, but the volume was turned down, the dial on the amplifier showing a green-lighted strip. The film moved against the far living room wall, a space fighter attacking the Death Star in silence. It was a little out of focus. The projector was developing some kind of trouble, and the focus wouldn't lock and hold. He was going to have to work on it again. When the sound was up and coming through the quadraphonic speakers, though, the system was perfect; the whole room jumped with noise and motion. The rear screen projector fed into the console in the bank of cabinets, which also held the master controls for the sound and the strobe lights. McAllister stood eating potato chips, watching the spacecraft move down the metal ravine toward the Death Star's heart. The film clips came mail order from a pirate film lab on the West Coast, and the system was an expansion of an earlier, similar outfit he'd put together in college. He poured the last of the potato chips into his mouth and wiped his hands on his bare stomach. It was a pretty good setup; he'd designed it himself, every wire and circuit diagram and connection—although he still wasn't satisfied with some of the film clips, especially the sound sync. Shoddy processing every time—you could tell the films were pirated. And now the Gaevaert projector, which had cost him a bundle, was probably developing some hitch in the focusing mechanism. He was going to have to put aside a weekend to tear it all down, find out what was wrong. At the climax of the scene where the Death Star finally got a bomb in its nuclear guts and exploded like a hot new nova, he had rigged up the strobe lights to cut in. The effect was like being dead in the middle of the thing as it fissioned itself right into limitless space.

Jesus, Meehan, the reporter, had said, *you people are really into all this in a big way, aren't you?*

Since the reporter had seemed so eager to believe it, they let him believe it. Nizzard had taken him aside and told him he was building a small experimental spacecraft in his garage. Not to go anywhere, naturally, just to see if it would work. Meehan obviously couldn't tell when they were putting him on. For all they knew, it would show up in the *National Globe* in a few weeks.

A little later, he had taken the reporter into the bathroom to see the system hooked up to the toilet seat that he'd finished in the early summer. He explained that he'd had to disconnect it; some of the girls wet all over the shag carpeting in there, screaming and jumping up and turning around when it opened up with strobe lights and a high-volume sound track.

McAllister drew up a sling chair and lowered himself into

it, propping his feet up on the couch. A loud rumble of thunder
sounded outside. He supposed he should turn the system off,
but he didn't want to; the fighters were passing down into the
narrow valley on the surface of the Death Star, and Luke Sky-
walker had taken over the final bombing run. Ten seconds from
ground zero.

He leaned forward, elbows on knees, and chewed at his
thumbnail. What the hell, the apartment was a send-up; they
could laugh like hell but that's what it was there for. And in
a larger sense he was proud of it, it was a good piece of work
technically, nothing there to be ashamed of at all. He had had
a couple of sound systems people in, and they had been knocked
out by it, really knocked out. But then, they took these things
seriously. It was still a hell of a place to have a party. And he
was lucky, he had the time and especially the money to play
with it, not like most of the group, a lot of whom had kids and
were struggling along, trying to make it on an Air Force
captain's pay. At least, he told himself, the space show had
kept him busy the past year when the process of trying to make
his fifteen hundred hours in advanced aircraft was driving him
nuts.

The Death Star had blown up in stillness, spewing hot fountains of flame and galactic debris into the black velvet night.
All right, he thought, you could laugh at his space movies, but
there was plenty of reality in them; the technical research was
perfect in some of them. And if he had to give a reason for
any of it, he could say that the systems he had worked up in
the apartment were, in a sense, accustoming him to the visual
orientation of space. That's what space looked like, that's what
space felt like, if you had any imagination. Actually, Air Force
training, especially in the Eagles, provided plenty of physical
forecasting, if you took time to focus your attention and make
use of it, and if you didn't have to pay too much attention to
Air Force Mickey Mouse stuff.

He reached up and punched the tape button on the console,
and the cold, silvery notes of Schönberg's *Variations for Or-
chestra, Opus 30* flowed into the room. This was the part he
liked, coming up. Just shots of space, the light-spangled scarf
of the Milky Way spliced into some old film cuts of *2001:
A Space Odyssey*, where the spaceship was approaching the
moon station. He settled back. He liked the dissonance of

Schönberg's music, icy and clear, interfaced with the moving camera sweeps of stars and darkness. The beautiful void.

Occasionally, in some few fleeting moments of solitude, he was aware that he was not like other people, not—in the main—like the people who had attended him and nurtured him day by day for most of his existence. He had found other people's goals to be relentlessly directed toward human relationships and the world of emotions—the most confusing, turbulent, and to him the most irrelevant and disorderly aspects of living. Who the hell cared, basically, about whether the United States could enforce civil rights in South America or whether somebody's wife was leaving him? Who even wanted to think about it, since it was probably insoluble? You couldn't talk to many people, even in a university, about the sensual pleasures of math equations or the perfect isolation of a problem in physics. Who saw the beauty and symmetry in zero, the eternal, constant, and challenging void? But *there* was the real fascination and passion. It gave him a fine, calm, almost sweetly desolate feeling to watch the stars spinning around noiselessly out there. Home, earth, was just a watery ball floating above you. Life was the place that began after, not before, the decimal point.

He couldn't think of anything more satisfying. Not earthbound, restless, bored ever more. His soul reached out for it. He closed his eyes and listened.

After a while he knew it was late, he was going to have to get dressed. The storm was moving off. He cut off the film system but left the Schönberg music on. The tape would run into *Transfigured Night* and then shut itself off.

He went into the bathroom. With luck, the weather would clear before flight time, CAVU—Ceiling And Visibility Unlimited—as it usually did after a thunderstorm. He moved around, collecting his clothes. The girl on the bed slept heavily, one knee pulled up and an arm flung to the far side. She'd had a lot to drink, he remembered. Jack Daniels and ginger ale. Jesus, he thought. He decided not to wake her. She could let herself out of the apartment; she'd done it often enough. She was a big girl with a mop of curly hair, flashy-looking, big breasts and muscular, slightly sagging thighs. He wondered who was minding her baby when she was out all night. It was a cute baby; he'd seen its picture.

He took some bills out of his wallet and slipped them partly under her pillow where she could find them. He knew she wouldn't like it. She was a date, invited for the party; he wasn't supposed to pay her anything, but she was a singer in a country and western band around Norfolk and always a little hard up. He knew she could use it.

He carried his flight suit into the living room, stepped into it, and zipped it up. He was still feeling good, on top of the vibrant high of sleeplessness. A core of hollowness deep down inside, he tried to ignore. He looked around the room. When he moved on to experimental test pilot school, he wasn't sure if he wanted to carry all his junk with him. He supposed he could sell most of it. He felt restless. Hell, he thought suddenly, his whole life was slipping away from him—that was the truth! I'm fucking up, he told himself, getting no place. I've got to pick up speed.

He needed to talk to somebody. It was suddenly very urgent. He went into the kitchen and picked up the receiver of the wall telephone and dialed the area code for Washington, 202. At this hour, not even five o'clock, she would be asleep upstairs in her room in the big Georgetown house. He could just picture her at that moment. Her private line would ring, and she would roll over, making funny, sleepy faces, trying to get her eyes open. But knowing who it was. There was only one person in the whole world who would call her at that hour. Once he had called the regular line at the house by mistake and had gotten the Senator, who had raised hell. He dialed the remaining digits carefully and listened to it ring.

He tried to think of something to say to Nancy. Like, he was up for an early morning flight, just getting dressed, and he missed her. He would ask her when she was coming down. Then, it occurred to him, he could bring up the subject of his application for test pilot training. He needed some help with it, the way things were going. The Senator was the head of the Senate committee on the armed forces; he knew how these things were done. You got a member of your administrative staff at the Senate office building on the Hill to call the appropriate level of Air Force command at the Pentagon. A friendly inquiry about a promising young man now in an F-15 squadron at Langley Air Force Base who has his application in for experimental test pilot school. Wants to go on to advanced research and development, eventually, and supersecret tactical fighters. Just making sure his papers get a little attention for processing.

Nancy's voice was suddenly in his ear, rusty with sleep. *"Simon?"*

He could visualize her now, sitting up in bed with the telephone held to her cheek, the round, serious face with a slight frown. Dressed in cotton pajamas. With her long brown hair pulled back, maybe knotted on top of her head with some strands hanging down. A plain girl, not pretty: gray-eyed, thoughtful, grave. But a great, intelligent, *right* sort of girl, the kind to get engaged to. The Senator was a friend of his father's; they had gone to Choate together.

At the sound of her voice, so close and familiar, something happened. He forgot everything except how he felt at that second.

"Nan, baby," he blurted, "hell, I woke you up, didn't I? Well, listen, I just wanted to talk to you, that's all."

A gust of storm wind blew in through the open end of the hangar and rushed toward the back where the F-15 Eagle rested under the glare of arc lights. On the work scaffolding, Master Sergeant Amos Schuld turned and looked over his shoulder. Beyond the cavernous mouth of the hangar building, the storm was still invisible, only blackness out there, with the blue lights of the runways showing as pinpoint brilliants against the dark. Below Sergeant Schuld, the fightercraft was bathed in a pool of light. The girl beside him, a slender figure in olive drab coveralls, stood with her head lowered thoughtfully, one arm bent, reaching down into the metal throat of the engine air-intake scoop.

"Although the hell of it is," Sergeant Schuld went on, ignoring a roll of thunder nearby, "you can look into any engine until hell freezes over, and if the trouble is some goddamned glitch in the basic design that a micro-micrometer won't measure but which is feeding your air in at some crazy angle, then you're up shit creek. The engineers will tell you that modifications will take care of it, but they're just barking up their assholes. Now there wasn't a goddamned thing wrong with the

F-111s," he said, returning to his subject. "I worked on them in Nam from tail to nose and back again, and I couldn't see what all the bitching was about. Most of that was the damned newspapers and television picking up on what they thought was a big story, about how much the F-111s cost and how they weren't winning the war for us. But the F-111s were damned good aircraft for what they was supposed to do, and don't let anybody tell you no different. They were supposed to do anything an F-105 could do, only better. Like deliver bombs deep in enemy territory by flying low and fast enough to get under enemy radar. And they did it; they could go supersonic fifty feet off the ground, and they could damned well get off an airfield half the size you need for a Thud." He turned to the girl. "Jesus knows they could beat the Thuds any way you wanted. We used to say about the Thuds when they said they was triple-threat fighter bombers: 'Bomb 'em, strafe 'em, and if that don't work, fall on 'em.' Hand me that work light, sweetie," he told her.

Too late, Sergeant Schuld realized he had used a term of endearment again to a fellow crew chief. He looked at the girl out of the corner of his eye to see if she had noticed. He was used to calling females sweetheart, honey, and dearie without thinking; it was second nature. He said the same things to his daughter in college, to his wife, and to all females generally. It was hard to remember not to. But after a dozen years as an Air Force master sergeant and chief of tactical ground crews, he could not adjust overnight to asking some pretty young thing to hand him the work light without automatically adding sweetie. He had been briefed on this; he had been told to look at the stripes of female personnel and think ratings, the modern Air Force way. He did, but sometimes he slipped up.

Now he said, "The trouble with anything in this business is *mentality*. When you come right down to it, mentality will screw things up worse than any lousy equipment; it's been proven a million times. The mentality problem was that the Air Force was told to call the F-111s fighters and to use them as fighters, when you could see right there in the operational requirements the Defense Department issued that what the F-111 was, was a strike fighter. Which is a light bomber. Now if they had called it an attack fighter or a fighter bomber from the beginning, it would have saved a hell of a lot of money and grief. When you say fighter, you don't mean anything else but air-to-air combat. But the mentality of it was that the F-111 was what they said it was. The Secretary of Defense, McNamara, was straight from the Ford Motor Company, and his idea was that he was going to save a couple of billion dollars on the F-111 program if he treated it like a new model that Ford was putting out. That was what *that* mentality was." Sergeant Schuld turned and spat down onto the hangar floor. "Christ—an all-purpose airplane! You ask anybody, and they'll tell you that for military purposes, that damned well isn't going to work. But the Department of Defense wasn't listening. Then they got into Congress with investigations and why the F-111 was so expensive. And the Navy sweated blood—they couldn't get the F-111s down to any kind of weight for carrier takeoff. The Navy lightened the F-111s until they damned near scrapped everything but the pilot. Admirals and generals couldn't get into the mentality of it; they was jumping out of the windows on the top floor of the Pentagon every morning. The Air Force made up nameplates to get everything straightened out which said: 'Captain So-and-So Jones, F-111 Fighter Pilot' and made the fighter jocks wear them. No, I swear to God," he said, seeing the look on the girl's face, "that's the absolute truth. It didn't solve a damned thing, but some brass somewhere thought about it and decided that was a step in the right direction. So after about seven years of this crapping around, trying to make the F-111 something it goddamned well wasn't, the government got smart and cut off the modification money and all the rest of it and called it quits. The Navy wet its pants, it was so happy to get off the hook. It had tried to screw up the F-111 program from the start because it wanted to develop its own fighter, naturally. So the Navy got right on the designs for the F-14 Tomcat, which was what it wanted to do all along."

Sergeant Linda Criscio had unhooked the work light from the lip of the air-intake scoop, and now she held it out to him. Sergeant Schuld took it from her and switched it off. It was getting late. Amos Schuld still had to run a paper check on the Eagles on the flight line scheduled for the morning's 0700 hours sweep.

He realized he'd gotten off the subject somewhere, but he wasn't particularly sorry. It would give her an idea, he thought, of what could happen when you were up against the bureaucrats

and the wrong kind of mentality. Sergeant Schuld's gaze went
down the lines of the fuselage of the Eagle before them, noting
the scratches around the panels which showed how many times
they had been taken off for repairs and then replaced; the tool
cabinet still sat by the landing gear assembly where work had
been done on the burned brakes. Externally, this particular F-
15 did not appear to be any different from any other in the
squadron, Sergeant Schuld thought grimly, but it was a real
monster, full of demons. He had had experience with fighter
jets like it before; occasionally one came down the production
line from the aircraft manufacturer that seemed to have not
only the series' entire catalogue of things wrong with it, but
also exotic, recurring mysterious malfunctions which, year
after year, appeared to defy all solution.

In the case of the Eagle before him, the hairline scratches
around the panels told at least a small part of the story. The
F-15's panels were infected with bad screws and bad nut plates;
once you got the screws in, you couldn't get them back out.
They would keep turning, but you couldn't get them out for
birdshit. Sergeant Schuld had seen crew chiefs, top sergeant
veterans of thirty years, reduced to jellylike masses of cursing
impotence over such panels. In the past few months, Sergeant
Linda Criscio's revolutionary supersonic wonder had had
smoke in the cockpit from an oil leak, nearly suffocating the
pilot and forcing him into an emergency return to base; a hydraulic fluid leak in the radar antenna, causing the radar screen
to go berserk and vital dogfight information to drop right off
the scope in the midst of the action. The pitot tubes had iced
up—a damned mystery in low-altitude conditions, but that was
the only diagnosis possible under the circumstances—and
chronic hydraulic systems problems like the one it had developed during the demo flight. Not to mention one of the more
spectacular malfunctions: this F-15's ability to defy its cockpit
fastenings and pop open the canopy just as the pilot was preparing for takeoff. Its tail number was 74033, but like the rest
of the Eagles, it was referred to by only the last four digits.
The fighter jocks called it that goddamned Forty Thirty-three.

"Look, honeybun," Sergeant Schuld said, "there's been talk
that we got another hard-luck generation of fuck-ups here in
the Eagles like the F-111s, but I can't buy that because the
mentality is sure as hell not the same. Every time you get a

new-design piece of equipment, you can bet your life it's got bugs in it, and some designs, the ones that were experimental to begin with, like the F-111s, have got more than others. The trouble is, the Air Force tries to put the lid on every time it's got problems, and it don't know that never works. Because I've seen stuff work out all right. Hell, when the Thuds first came out, you couldn't have paid me a million dollars to get into any one of them. But they got them flying. They're still flying. And even the F-111 is coming up, now. All the F-111 systems that was so experimental is the stuff they put in the Eagles. Now they're talking about the F-111Es going to be replacements for the B-1 bombers they didn't get. Which means, if you don't mind me saying so, that we've come a full-ass circle. I tell you, honey, you might think the engines in the Eagles is shitpots, but at least this time there's a positive mentality working for them. Because nobody in this man's Air Force is going to want to go through what they did over the F-111s. These hot new fighters are too hard to come by, what with Congress cutting back on money every year."

During his years of service at Air Force bases around the world, Amos Schuld had built a large circle of friends in the powerful noncommissioned officers' structure, most of them supply supervisors or chiefs of ground crew operations like himself. They kept in regular touch. At least once a week, Sergeant Schuld settled himself down at the Maintenance WATS line for a long chat with a friend in the NCO system somewhere in the United States, the object being a little unofficial information exchange. Very infrequently, he boarded a transport with a requisition for some part or other that regular channels couldn't provide and paid one of his cronies a visit for an hour or two. The news passed around the NCO network this way was mostly intended to move forward the general day-to-day work of the Air Force and was nearly always helpful, accurate, and often what the military regarded as top secret-classified. Or what Sergeant Schuld and his friends referred to as the Hot Poop.

Sergeant Schuld wrapped the cord of the work light around his wrist and elbow in a circling motion, watching the girl beside him. She leaned against the air-intake cowling, her fine-boned face with its usual tranquil expression thrown into high relief by the glare of the Light-Alls. The pale olive cast of her skin was almost sallow; her large, heavy-lidded eyes were the strange color of sea water. The hand resting on the intake lip was pitted with grease, the nails broken, the fingers long and bony. The hands were the best mechanic's hands Amos Schuld had ever known, amazing hands for a woman, strong, sure, and painstaking. This particular girl had an intuitive feel for the million intricate parts of the Eagles' systems that Sergeant Schuld, in his long years in the military, had come to regard as a gift, as inexplicable as a great operatic voice or a head for quantum physics and which he usually expected to find only in grizzled veterans of the flight line like himself. He was still full of wonder at her talents, totally unexpected in the body and mind of this exceptionally beautiful young woman. She didn't talk about herself at all, he knew, but when she had first entered the Air Force, she had taken the usual aptitude tests and, following the overwhelming evidence of her scores, had been assigned to aircraft maintenance school. She was one of those rarities, a natural-born mechanical genius. She had come right up the line after ground crew training, leaving a wake of astonishment behind her. When she had been transferred to Langley Field, half the First Wing flight line had turned out to see, not believing. Women in ground crews were no particular novelty. But this one was a five-day wonder. And so beautiful you didn't trust your eyes.

Eighteen years ago, when Master Sergeant Schuld had joined the Air Force, if someone had told him he'd be spending half the night in a hangar troubleshooting with a lovely young woman who was also a sergeant and a top-rated chief, he'd have laughed himself hoarse. That'd be the day.

Well, the day—or the night, to be exact—had arrived, as he was willing to admit. And he had just turned in four hours' nonduty time for the hell of it, fooling around with engine problems and enjoying every minute of it. She had an amazing head on her; she was a goddamned wonder. He was as fond of her as he was of his own daughter. Or his own son, if he'd had one.

It was just too bad, he thought, that she was stuck with this particular shitpot. He supposed he could see the reason for assigning her Forty Thirty-three—she was probably the only person besides himself who could keep it in the air. But she had probably poured too much of her heart and soul into the damned thing. It had been up to Edwards for overhaul several times, even newborn, and she had gone right up there with it. The engines had been taken out and sent to Warner Robbins engine repair down in Georgia, and when they still didn't work right, new ones had been ordered from Trueham Engines in Connecticut. And still the fighter jocks turned in reports on engine compressor stall, fuel system failures, hot brakes, hydraulic glitches, ghostly noises, and just about everything but getting Johnny Carson on their HUD displays.

Each step of the way, the girl had been right with her Eagle. She stayed with the specialist teams when they were brought in, like a hen with a sickly chick. Tail number Forty Thirty-three looked good; it taxied off the flight line well and confidently. But from then on—it had the squadron record for aborted takeoffs—only the witchcraft she worked on it kept it flying at all.

The girl had a theory they'd been kicking around for weeks—that the problem in the F-100X engines in the Eagles centered around the guide vanes, the movable parts in the engines that controlled the air flow into the jet pods. Trouble was constant in that area. In some cases, the air flow bunched up coming off the air intake and hit the compressor blades in what were being called burbles—pockets of air that sounded like pistol shots and went hard and fast enough to hit the blades and snap them off. The result was like a small explosion, often tearing hell out of the whole engine mechanism. If the pilot's reflexes were good while his Eagle was coming apart under him, he could pull the ejection handle and shoot free of it before it disintegrated.

Sergeant Schuld draped the work light over the railing of the scaffolding and stared down at the low-swept shape of the fighter jet, its beaky nose arched and pointing down slightly, the acrylic space age plastic of the canopy poised before stubby, dartlike wings, the twin tails rising above the long sections of jet engines that were about all there was of the airframe. The Eagle was little more than a flying power tube; once you were in it, you were sitting on top of two capsules of air and fuel blasting you through the sky at more than twice the speed of sound, with a load of missiles slung underneath. It was a beautiful, lethal thing; a lot of genius, Sergeant Schuld knew, had gone into the making of it. Its computerized systems had all but eliminated anything mechanical; there wasn't a rod or a lever or an old-fashioned wire-pull left in it. Instead, electronic sensors did the work: moved the controls; monitored air pressure, air temperatures, turbine inlet temperatures, pressure ratios, and other vital elements; and fed the data to the central computer to maintain what was, theoretically, ideal operating conditions. And ideal operating conditions were an incredibly fine variance of fuel and air going into the engines and operating, among other things, the guide vanes. Which, at high speeds, altered the air intake just enough to feed the engines without starving them or drowning them out.

Linda Criscio's theory was that the chronic troubles with engine stall and broken compressor blades seemed to involve a guide vane actuation at low air speeds, especially in a climb where a combat pilot needed all the power he could get. But the guiding vanes operated off computerized fuel systems, which had interesting problems of their own.

Sergeant Schuld was convinced they weren't going to get anywhere with her theory. A team of experts from industry and the Air Force labs had been working on the engine problem for months, and their latest report stated that the investigation of difficulties with the F100X engine seemed to eliminate all factors except perhaps a flaw in basic air-feed design. Or maybe improper use by the Air Force on operational missions, i.e., pushing the unique new engines beyond their limits. Whatever it was, the committee ventured cautiously, it was probably uncorrectable.

Beyond Master Sergeant Schuld, in the shadowy depths of the hangar, was the F-15 that had developed stall stagnation four days ago in a dive on the Atlantic missile range. Major James, the pilot, had been too low and too fast to use his eject system even if he'd wanted to, and he had managed to save himself and his Eagle by skill and a bit of luck. Now the F-15 waited for an Air Force team from Edwards Air Force Base to come and take it apart. Looking beyond the Light-Alls, Sergeant Schuld could see it only as a dim shape covered by a canvas shroud.

A bright flash of lightning lit up the sky beyond the open mouth of the hangar.

"Amos—" Sergeant Linda Criscio broke from her reveries.

The words fell from pale, delicate lips. "Amos, I think we'd better pack it in."

Amos Schuld nodded in agreement. "Sweetheart," he said, "I wish you could get authorization to break down those engines. I'd just love to see you have a ball with them." They both knew that the engine pods, under explicit maintenance directives, were not to be opened up for that purpose. When it went down for repair, the entire engine unit was removed and replaced with another engine by a special crew, in an operation that was a matter of no more than an hour's time. But he knew how much she wanted to do it.

"Hell, they'll get them fixed up," he assured her. "They'll keep modifying them, screwing around with them until they work all right—the Eagles are just too damned hot not to work. And by and by, something else will come along from the Skunkworks that will just knock your eyes out—and with a whole new set of goddamned number one priority troubles. Then everybody will say, when they take time to think about it, 'Yeah, the Eagles—they were good old planes.' So what we got to do right now is keep maintaining them, rolling them out on the flight line. You can't think of anything better to do, can you?"

Crew Chief Criscio wiped her hands on the knees of her coveralls and thought about it, frowning.

"No," was all she said.

SPOON-SIZED SHREDDED WHEAT offers you . . .
The Natural Goodness of Whole Wheat

Lieutenant Colonel Roger Gazenove, commander of the 17th Tactical Fighter Squadron, shoveled several teaspoons of sugar into the bowl of cereal in front of him and read on.

A Good Source of Natural Bran Fiber

The back of the cereal box showed the enlarged cross section of a wheat kernel, graphically depicting the outer or bran skin, a white membrane under what was called endosperm, and a yolky inner heart labeled "wheat germ." There were not, he saw with some satisfaction, any send-away offers of Superman School Notebooks or notices of enclosed Miniature Plastic Tops.

No Sugar Added

Lieutenant Colonel Gazenove deliberately spooned another

helping onto the crusty mound already topping his shredded wheat and mixed it all together forcefully. If Mrs. Gazenove had been in the kitchen at that moment, she would have registered loud expressions of dismay and disapproval. Lieutenant Colonel Gazenove had voluntarily agreed to limit his salt and sugar intake as a precautionary measure for a borderline hypertensive condition Nothing much to worry about, the flight surgeon had said, just something we have to watch as we get older Older Roger Gazenove thought. The flight surgeon was still in his twenties Lieutenant Colonel Gazenove was pushing forty-two

Lieutenant Colonel Gazenove rested his elbows on the table, chewing a large mouthful of natural bran goodness without enjoyment The general malaise of a low-level hangover nagged at him Suddenly, a white crash of lightning lit up the thrashing trees in the backyard and seconds later reverberated through the house The gimballed lamp over the table blinked, leaving the room in momentary darkness, and then came back on again. Lieutenant Colonel Gazenove paused, listening for sounds that the storm had wakened his wife in the bedroom above. The rain drummed heavily on the roof.

Lieutenant Colonel Gazenove resumed chewing and looked at the clock above the kitchen sink He checked it against his wrist chronometer and saw that the clock had not lost any detectable time while the current was off. He wished to hell he could go back upstairs and get into bed and sleep as soundly as his wife was sleeping at that moment. Might as well get used to it, he thought. In a few short months he would be able to indulge himself in the dubious pleasure of sleeping late mornings, reading the morning paper in its entirety, and getting up with nothing more pressing to face than a day's round of golf And, on gloriously empty and unhurried evenings, searching out old friends at the Officers' Club bar to talk old times, old wars

Retirement, Lieutenant Colonel Gazenove thought staring at the back of the cereal box with unseeing eyes

In six weeks he was scheduled for assignment to the Pentagon in something called Tactical Planning and Development. No matter what it was called, it was still the boneyard—paper shuffling, the waiting-out time until he was finally eased out of everything that mattered At best he figured that he and

Amy would spend a little under a year in the Washington area, holed up in some apartment in Alexandria or Arlington. They hadn't planned to sell the house in Hampton right away; by the end of the year they should have made up their minds where they wanted to live. Maybe Florida. That was Amy's choice. He liked the idea of Arizona better.

Lieutenant Colonel Gazenove pushed the bowl of shredded wheat away from him. Goddamned bran. There was nothing wrong with his bowels. And he was damned if he was going to end up in Florida in some old people's condominium, waiting around all day and worrying about when and if he was going to shit. He leaned his head on his hand and stared down at the gold-flecked plastic surface of the dinette table. The early morning thunderstorm was moving off; he could tell by the sound of the wind and the slackening thrum of the rain. A whole lifetime of flying had attuned him to weather and flying conditions. He had checked out the aviation weather update at Langley tower before he went to bed as he always did, whether he was scheduled for flight duty or not.

Now here he was, up at the same hour as the kids who were going out on the Atlantic range. Knee jerk reflex, he told himself. He knew to the minute how long it took to get out of bed and fix a solitary breakfast, how long to get the sleep out of his system, how long to drive to the airfield—any Air Force field—how long to get into flight gear, how long for briefing and readiness, how long to walk from the Flight Ops building down to the flight line, how many minutes to engine start.

In the early days when the kids were little, an early morning sweep was pure hell. As a junior officer, he had pulled the worst flight duty as a fact of life. He remembered getting up in the god-awful early morning with a hangover, needing a cup of coffee, trying to get a despairing Amy to fix him some eggs while the kids, ready for the school bus, thundered and fought through the house. That grubby goddamned concrete house in the middle of nowhere, ten miles from the base, the invasion of Texas cockroaches in the carport, his off-duty time spent fixing the damned wheezing old washing machine or the damned wheezing old Plymouth. He'd been an irascible, cocky son of a bitch in those days, hard to live with, bucking for a promotion and to get the hell out of Texas. Some of the best years of his life, Lieutenant Colonel Gazenove thought morosely Nothing to do but make love to your wife and drink, raise hell and fly

God, he thought, I can't retire. How did this happen?

A sudden burst of wind hit the house, and the windows rattled. CAVU by flight time, he told himself. A beautiful time to take up the Eagles, early morning. He hoped the kids flying them appreciated it, had some time to look around and be glad where they were

In the clear morning air after a thunderstorm, the whole world was a glass bowl, free crystal-pure. In Texas that year, they had been flying the F-100 Super Sabrejets. You watched the earth slide to one side and then the other against the blue, reaching dome of the sky; you could pull back on the stick, climb, and lie back on your spine, knees up, feeling the jet thrust under you, the drag of G forces. Then a heads-over roll, standing on your forehead for a blissful minute, looking up at the green world swinging above you He realized his right hand had curled, just thinking about it, as if easing back on the stick. In the old days, you worked like hell, operating all the old mechanical systems, now, all that stuff was electronic, computer-controlled, smooth as jello

Lieutenant Colonel Gazenove looked down at his hands. He supposed he could go over to the field in a little while without being too conspicuous He had some paperwork he could do, keep himself busy until the flights came back from the Atlantic range. Then he thought about the operations officer, Randy Slyke, on desk duty down the hall. Slyke, coming in to see who was in the office, knowing damned well who it was. The knowing smile. *I thought you were going to play some golf.*

Lieutenant Colonel Gazenove got up from the kitchen table and went down into the den to pour himself a drink.

Candy James reached up and turned on the light on the bedside table She saw, squinting, that the clock radio showed four-fifteen Beside her, Topper lay flat on his fack, his length and bulk taking up most of the oversized bed, one arm above his head and partly crooked around it, noisily dreaming. Thunder rolled close by and a heavy burst of rain hit the windowpanes.

It's only a thunderstorm, Candy told herself. She looked for Topper's pillow She supposed it was on the floor again. Topper was not a particularly restless sleeper, but he was big enough, when he moved, to move everything in the bed with him. Now the flowered sheet was all wound around him, and he lay with his pale chest and shoulders uncovered. He went on talking indistinctly.

Candy bent over her husband. They were Topper's words, Topper's voice, but, in some queer facsimile of dreaming, all the voices on the cockpit tapes. Sometimes in the first few seconds of waking, she was not sure someone wasn't down below in the den playing the tape machine. *Close it up. Okay, pull it in.* Candy held back her hair with one hand and bent closer. The words murmured away.

The bedroom was almost cold, and Topper had all the sheet. She wondered if she should get out of bed and turn the air conditioner down. She yawned. Topper's eyes were lightly closed, eyelids fluttering. When she moved her head to one side, she could see his small but very pronounced Adam's apple. Topper, she said silently. She tried to will him awake so that she could pull the sheet out from under him. She tried his full name, Eric Thurstan James. In the second generation, the family had changed it from something Norwegian and unpronounceable to the simpler English version. But Topper could still say the other when he'd had a few beers, and she coaxed him enough. Topper, Candy thought.

Watch it—here comes the son of a bitch! Topper's voice said. Candy propped her cheek on her hand and watched him. With her free hand and very carefully, she lifted a corner of the trapped sheet and drew it across his chest. She saw the tremor of his lips, interrupted.

If she touched him, if she woke him, she knew he would come instantly awake. What's the matter? What time is it?

Timidly, Candy considered pulling back the covering sheet suddenly, taking this moment while he was vulnerable to probe the mystery of him beside her. She had a strange, irresistible impulse to expose him to a sneaking examination, getting so close to him that she could see the very grain of his skin, the outline of his bones—completely, finally penetrating the enigma of the being, the body she was married to. Carefully, she put the tip of her finger against the flesh of Topper's side and saw it indent with her touch. When she took her finger away, the white skin sprang back, smooth, damp, faintly cool.

Topper's lips moved. He said something about *Fox One* and *Fox Two*.

Candy felt her eyes sting, fill with tears. Please wake up, she told him silently. You don't know what's happening to me; you never do. I'm getting into this thing deeper and deeper; I think about it all the time. And how to have sex when you're not here, in places where people won't find us. Emma knows about it. Emma's going to tell you one of these days. I won't be able to stop her.

Candy put her hand to her mouth. She was afraid she would burst into tears, thinking about it. It was worse than anything she could possibly tell him. A kid, urgent and hot, touching her hand. Standing close to her. A joke, just fooling around. Oh God, she thought, how could it come to this?

Her mother always said she didn't have enough to keep her busy, what with just the house to look after and Emma. And with Topper so involved in what he was doing. And, her mother reminded her, she still had a lot to offer. Her mother thought she ought to go into modeling again, where she could buy herself nice clothes at a discount, keep herself fixed up, stay busy. She had told Topper what her mother had said, and Topper had only answered, well, maybe when Emma gets a little older. Or we could have another baby. Candy didn't want another baby. In her mind's eye, she saw the little, grasping hands of another baby and Topper removed yet another step away.

Suddenly Candy bent and put her mouth against Topper's bare shoulder. She put her hand over his wrist, her fingers closing over the face of the heavy gold watch. Her mouth moved against his skin, caressing it. Topper, Candy said against his shoulder. She heard him grunt. In his sleep he rolled over, moving away from her.

She looked down at her husband's back. She took her hand from around his wrist and moved her fingers up his heavily muscled forearms, up the massive curve of his shoulder. Topper slept on. In the depths of his sleep, she knew, the touch was familiar, unalarming, could not wake him. He accepted it. Perhaps even liked it.

Candy wiped her wet cheeks with the back of her hand. She rolled over and reached up and turned off the bedside light.

* * *

The waves, whipped by a sudden wind, churned up over the end of the pier, and a spray of sea water hit the hood of Sergeant Regina Murphy's Volkswagen. In the dark, the flying spume looked closer than it really was, she thought nervously. She glanced at the dashboard clock. Almost four-thirty. It was terribly late. Airman Ronny Masarek, silent and self-conscious for most of the evening, had only relaxed and begun to talk after they'd parked on the pier. Now he sat with both hands grabbing the steering wheel, bent forward, staring fixedly at the storm. He came from a small coal-mining town in southern Illinois and said he had never seen the beach or the ocean before.

"Jeez, look at that," Ronny Masarek said admiringly as a white-crested wave rushed up in the dark and hit the end of the pier, breaking into foaming drops. A quick flash of lightning bored into the water. At Sergeant Murphy's gasp, he turned to her.

"You're not scared, are you?" His white teeth showed as he grinned.

She shook her head. She winced as another bolt of lightning crashed nearby. She wondered if Ronny Masarek knew how dangerous it was, parked in her Volks on a pier with lightning striking all around them. She remembered that cars were supposed to be safe in a storm; their rubber tires protected them from lightning bolts. She sure as hell hoped so.

"Here, hold my hand," he told her. His voice was warm, a little hoarse.

His strong fingers closed over hers. Before she was really aware of what he was doing, he had pulled her to him. He looked down at her. She saw that his shyness had dropped away with surprising suddenness. But she started as another lightning flash bathed the beach and the Volkswagen in a brilliant light.

In the sudden darkness that followed, she found Airman Masarek's warm wet mouth on hers, his tongue moving expertly, boldly into hers. He put his hand under her blouse, his fingers moving quickly inside her brassiere, stroking her breast, touching and rubbing her nipple. Regina Murphy clutched him as a roll of thunder shook the rickety pier under them. She felt his arms tighten around her convulsively. God, in the car, she thought. She hadn't had sex in a car since high school. He held her tightly. His hand, now under her hips, guided her expertly under him. She saw her bare knee raised by the steering wheel. Airman Masarek, so tall, so shy, was coming on so confidently and skillfully it left her breathless.

"You redheaded doll," he was murmuring into her ear. "You beautiful redheaded little doll. Jeez, Sergeant, I just can't believe it!"

Obviously he didn't know his own strength. She was pinned down, overwhelmed by strong, forceful excitement. With amazing speed, her trainee had unbuttoned, unbuckled, and unzipped his uniform, and now his partly naked body was pressed against hers. He took her hand and guided it to him, opened her clenched fingers and put them around warm, throbbing flesh. My God, Sergeant Murphy thought, good grief. In a flutter of surprise and confusion, she had a hurried thought that maybe it would be better if they stopped right there, started the car, and left. Went home. Or at least somewhere else. But she melted under his powerful clutch. Her hand struggled to contain the enormous pulsing thing in her grasp. She wet her lips in anticipation and closed her eyes.

Anthony Joseph Meehan put a fresh sheet of paper into the typewriter and took a sip from the glass of gin which stood on the night table beside him. He had been drinking all night, straight through the party with the Air Force fighter pilots and into the small hours of the morning. He was still cold sober. Or nearly so. When he finished what he was doing and was ready to turn in for a few hours' sleep, he would fix himself a cup of black coffee from the hot water tap in the bathroom with the jar of instant coffee he always carried with him, get undressed and into bed, knowing he would fall asleep at once. He had developed the booze-and-coffee routine—which had the reverse effect on him it was supposed to have on the human system—while working the lobster shift at the New York *Daily News* a few years ago. From midnight to eight in the morning, he'd kept a bottle of gin in the bottom drawer of his desk to brighten up the working hours. And on his way home on the upper West Side, he had always stopped at a diner to have a cup of coffee before he tried to go to sleep.

Meehan looked over his shoulder as a flash of lightning brightened the motel room for a moment, followed by a roll of thunder. The lights blinked. He lit a cigarette and studied the sheet of paper laid out on top of his suitcase on the luggage rack beside him. He doubted he'd get to use any of the stuff he'd put down, but the notes were necessary to get the whole picture in his head.

Sludge, he told himself, just shit. He could write better than this story demanded with his hands tied behind his back. Once he got into it, the stuff fell into a formula, anyway, like all the *National Globe* crap:

As I looked over *(the desert) (a chicken farm) (the great expanse of Seattle) (her beautiful breasts)*, I realized for the first time *(how dangerous it was to fly through the air) (my fly was unzipped) (how much Congress and the taxpayers were screaming)* and that I would thrill to *(supersonic boondoggling) (the sight of her pussy) (the waste of billions of dollars on a bloated defense budget)* . . .

But he was making good money, he reminded himself. Last year, middle-range five figures, which wasn't bad in this business. Better than the Newspaper Guild scale at the *News*, better than the short stint at *Tempus-Finance* five or six years ago. Shit had its rewards.

He studied the sheet of notes.

RED FLAG: they go into these war games twice a year they approach the deadly desert ridges a few feet off the ground—as the second ridge comes up they flip over and take it upside down—check this out?

HOTSHOT FLYBOYS:

personality profile: firstborn, right-handed, high energy, high achievers
tense, overbearing, high caliber, average age—twenty-five

games played: fall on floor
TV space shows
freaked-out apartments

tactical call signs: Animal (has been known to drop to knees at parties and scurry across floor in this manner to bite attractive females on the butt)

Beeper (at low speeds and high
angles of attack, the cockpit stall-
speed warning device begins *beep-
beep-beep*, getting faster as you
approach danger stall . . . when this
kid's radio was monitored in
training, that's all they could
hear . . . big-deal call sign as a result)

Moonbird (space freak from MIT
with space-freak apartment complete with movies and light
show . . . wants to fly *Star Wars*
space fighters)

Nizzard (something they call people in Alabama)

Grits (same thing)

Call signs chosen not more than two syllables, easy
to identify on radio in combat—chosen by other
fighter jocks.
ELITE STUFF: last of mankind's warrior class?

The F-15 as real spacecraft—computer helmets, cockpit
computers, supersonic, hypersonic, plug-in anti-G suits,
etc.

Tony Meehan stared at the last line. The focus of the story,
brought down to the seventh-grade level that marketing research
studies told them made up the readership of the *National Globe*,
was wide-eyed stuff. That is, the F-15s and their fighter jocks
as the new Flash Gordon and Company. Or about as close as
he could get. But that wasn't so far out of line—nothing was,
these days. The Space Shuttle had the world on its toes, waiting
for the space age to begin.

Suddenly he thought: Hell, this is too good to sit on!

It wasn't his story, but the newspaperman in him was still
alive and well after all the years of shoveling crap.

He ripped the sheet of paper from the typewriter and put
in another and a carbon. He'd spent a few minutes in the kitchen
during the party with the tall kid from Alabama who turned
out to be a nonstop talker after a few drinks. From what this
one said, none of them were too happy about engine troubles

and the crash the flight leader'd nearly had Thursday. They were still a little shaken up about it. From what he could tell, there were running problems with the F-100X engines in the Eagles, and the Air Force, true to form, was working hard to keep it quiet.

That posed some interesting questions, if true. For instance, why no recall of the engines if they were faulty? And why was the Air Force footing the bill to try to get them straightened out? And weren't engines supposed to pass some tests before the government accepted them?

Meehan started typing.

Fred Lightfoot
Finance Magazine
10 Rockefeller Plaza
New York, N.Y. 10020

Dear Fred:

I want to give you a tip on something I've turned up re the Air Force's hot new jet fighters, the F-15s. There may be a story in it for *Finance*.

6

It was a cool night for Washington in July. A summer rain dripped musically in the walled garden, and the double doors stood open to receive a wet breeze that touched the candelabra and sent out faint streamers of fire and smudge. Simon McAllister watched George, the Senator's houseman, pass around the far side of the dinner table with the dessert, bright pink watermelon sherbet in stemmed silver dishes. The dining room was pleasantly filled with the odor of wet brick and roses in bloom and the faint, waxy stench of candle smoke. McAllister felt his eyelids grow heavy. He was relaxed, well fed, and the sleepless weekend, the Saturday night party, the early morning flight, and the long drive to Washington were catching up with him. He blinked at the candlelight. It was no time to get sleepy, he reminded himself.

Across the table, Congressman Harold Dobbins of Washington State listened politely, his head inclined toward the Senator. His plump, chain-smoking wife sat next to him, her face showing that pleasantly attentive look that suggested she wasn't really listening. Opposite the Congressman's wife was Bernard Gould, Washington lawyer and lobbyist for the AAASI, a group representing the aircraft and aerospace industries.

And Nancy. Simon looked across the table to Nancy, sitting upright in her chair, turning the dessert spoon idly in her fingers, her head bent and eyes fixed on some spot on the tablecloth. He was never really sure why Nancy looked so damned unhappy when her father was talking; by now you would think she'd be used to politicking over the dinner table. After all, she'd been raised on it. But between Nancy and her father there was a war going on that he found hard to follow.

She looked damned cute, he thought, watching her. Her long, straight hair hung fine and loose to her shoulders, and she wore a cream-colored dress that clung to her little breasts and showed the points of her nipples very clearly. He'd been watching them all evening. Suddenly he hoped he hadn't come to Washington for nothing. You couldn't tell with Nancy; she turned hot or cold depending on how she was getting along with her father. He watched her watch the Senator, who now took a cigar and very deliberately cut the end of it with a silver knife. The Senator leaned back in his chair and rolled the cigar around in his mouth to wet it thoroughly. His full, fleshy lips kept their agreeable smile. The Senator's smile was famous; it was caricatured in newspaper cartoons across the nation as the symbol of the powerful personality, subtle and masterful, that had built a twenty-year career in the Senate and gained him the chairmanship of one of its most important committees without, it was noted, making him any influential enemies along the way. The Senator was one of the best-liked, most discreet, and most feared members of government.

"Harold, it's time for some plain talk," the Senator was saying in his rich, deep voice. His lips curved around the brown cylinder of the cigar. "I'm going to save us a lot of trouble and tell you right now that I know what you're going to say."

The Congressman smiled.

The Senator laughed. "Harold," he said, "I'm going to *admit* to you that the United States military is a damned unmanageable monstrosity and that it's been that way since World War II. Hell, you can't sit on the Armed Services Committee year after year and not acknowledge the obvious. And I'm going to admit that a lot of people consider the Air Force a big fat whale, a *corpus magnus* of indulgence and overexpansion that nothing, not even Congress, is ever going to contain successfully."

"I hear you, Mort," the Congressman said.

"As for the Army—the Army's a sad case, damned near indescribable." The Senator paused to lean to one side, lighting his cigar from a taper the houseman held. "The Army never gets itself together except in times of war, and then it takes it

a year or two, with luck." He leaned back, mouthing a cloud
of blue smoke. "As for the damned Navy, the Navy grabs
everything it can get on the theory that it's locked in a life and
death competition with the other services, and that sooner or
later somebody's going to find out that boats are obsolete and
take its planes away. The Navy's convinced, day by day, that
it's fighting for its life. It gets on top of every Defense Department budget like an elephant. A damned pimp elephant.
I hate admirals. They're the biggest whores in the world."

There was a ripple of laughter around the table. The lobbyist,
Gould, kept his eyes on the Representative from Seattle and
smiled. Simon McAllister concentrated on his sherbet. It was
the same talk he'd heard the last few times, including the part
about the Navy and elephants. In a way, he knew how Nancy
felt. The scenario was nearly always the same: the important
guest, usually from the opposition in the Senate or the House
of Representatives; the good dinner; plain-talk time, just as
George was serving the dessert. The Senator's dinners had
begun about three months ago when the Administration had hit
a snag in Congress with funding for the Space Shuttle, and the
space program in general, and had been going on ever since.
Simon hadn't found himself bored; on the contrary, he felt he
had a stake here, and it was interesting to get an insider's view
of the political maneuvering as the Senator worked the Congressional landscape carefully, sometimes repeating an invitation
to a marginal case, shifting his presentation from time to time
to include new material and updated arguments.

It was hard to tell, Simon thought, if the Senator was making
any progress. Probably at this hour on Sunday night in Washington, there were other members of the Senate's military support coalition who were doing the same thing—wooing the
opposton and the fence sitters at dinner or drinks somewhere,
trying to swing their backing to the Administration's Industrialization of Space program. Plain-talk time could get pretty
heavy; there was a large bloc in Congress opposed to government programs, viewing them as enormously costly and with
no hope of immediate return. During the past few weeks, the
Senator had brought every big gun in his arguments to bear on
the crash program which—with energy shortages and world
crises—was growing even more complicated and pressing.
Fortunately, Simon knew, there was a time limit. After dinner,

the Senator usually took his guests off to the theater or a concert. Tonight they were going to Kennedy Center. Simon looked across the dinner table at Nancy, trying to catch her eye. They'd have the house to themselves then.

The Senator was talking about the military status quo and saying that, in informed opinion, there was no way to go but up. No matter what the evils of a gigantic and overweaning military structure, it was plain to see that it was so embedded in the nation's economy that to dislodge it would bring about disaster. Even the closing of a few outmoded Army posts, the Senator pointed out, brought screams of protest in Congress about loss of jobs and tax revenue. And then there was that hard fact of life—the highly profitable business of selling United States military equipment to the rest of the world. Sales to allies of the F-15 Eagles and the new F-16s, along with other sophisticated weaponry, made up a large part of the American export business, and one that was increasing every year.

Senator Glass stubbed out his cigar in the ashtray George had put in front of him. "Harold, listen," the Senator said. He leaned back and pressed his hands together, touching his fingers to his mouth. "Harold, this country is riding the tiger. There's no significant way to decrease military spending at this time; I'm sure of it. Defense considerations aside, the economy's just too shaky. People tend to forget that money pumped into the military is money spent, eventually, right in their home-towns, right in their local industries. At the moment, it's no secret the country's got its back to the wall fuelwise, consumer debtwise, and productionwise, and it can't sustain many more rough blows to its financial base. There's no way to go but up, and I mean that literally. As a nation, we've got to get into space exploration and development on a profit-making scale. And that's what the Industrialization of Space program is all about."

"Listen, Mort," the Congressman began. He put down his dessert spoon.

"No—you listen. In an economic slump of the kind we're facing, what you usually look for is a nice war to set all the wheels in motion, galvanize industry, and give everybody jobs. But we're at the point now where war's a risky business. We didn't win the last war, which we bought on the idea that it was going to be a 'contained conflict,' and anything else would probably lead to nuclear aggression and total destruction. So that's no sort of answer. What we've got to do is get Congress to throw its support behind something constructive, make an investment of some considerable proportions and back the Industrialization of Space bill. At this moment, to go into space is our only salvation. I believe that as firmly as I believe I'm sitting right here tonight."

Representative Dobbins nodded. The Congressman was young—in his late thirties—tanned, relaxed, and casually dressed in a Western-style denim suit, plaid shirt, and string tie. Senator Glass had been courting the Western ecology lobby in Congress with particular thoroughness, and the Congressman from Seattle was one of the leading opponents of increased spending for space programs.

"What's the cost overrun on the Space Shuttle so far?" Dobbins asked, looking up. "Seven hundred million was the last figure I heard quoted. And still no firm launch date, so it's going to go higher. I tell you, Mort, there's a lot of feeling in my part of the country to call a complete halt to this crazy space stuff and turn to some large-scale government programs that will do something for unemployment and the fuel crunch. Hell, we're on an emergency basis right now, as far as gas is concerned. I've had a lot of people tell me they wish we'd cancel the whole Space Shuttle thing. What's it going to do for us? they ask me. And I'm damned if I know what to answer."

Simon looked down at his coffee. In the past few weeks, the dinner conversations had gotten pretty heated. He could see the sense in the arguments against the program; as much as anyone else, he had trouble getting gas for his car, dealing with inflation, and all the rest of it. But the bill the Senator was backing involved putting the Space Shuttle into a crash program to construct, among other things, a solar energy satellite. The revised Space Shuttle agenda would mean scrubbing some of the lesser missions, such as space medical experiments and astronomical observations, but the benefits would certainly outweigh the losses. If Congress passed the Industrialization of Space bill and funded it adequately, the second or third Space Shuttle flight would begin erecting a giant solar energy platform satellite which, once it became operational, would provide solar energy power worth several billions of dollars a year according to NASA estimates. The plan would call for the platform to be constructed at government expense as part of the space program, but the energy generated would be sold to private utility companies, which would then sell it to their consumers. Profit was the key to the whole idea. Getting into space and making money, not spending it, was the factor the Administration was counting on to get the initial staggering cost past Congress.

The second stage of the Industrialization of Space program would be a revival of the project originally studied under NASA contract back in 1971 by North American Rockwell—to put a construction platform in orbit around the moon. This was a manned version of the long proposed lunar polar orbiter that had appeared on NASA budgets for years but had never managed to past Congress. The lunar orbiter would be launched from the belly of the Space Shuttle, as soon as the solar energy earth-orbiting satellite was operational, and would go on to circle the moon and provide a working station for an eventual permanent moon base.

As the Senator kept repeating to his guests, the Industrialization of Space program was coming up in the nick of time: a study commmission report had just been released by NASA, showing anyone with the time to wade through the thousand-page transcript that the earth's economic development and raw materials' supplies were fast reaching foreseeable limits. The cupboard, the Senator kept saying, was nearly bare. And programs to conserve national resources and budgetary cutbacks, even long-term ones, were not solutions.

"We're not offering pie in the sky this time, Harold," Senator Glass said. "No moonshots, no skylabs, just solid planning and profit taking. Forward-looking planning and solid figures. NASA estimates we can have mining operations and solar energy complexes set up on the moon and operational by 1992 with an investment of approximately sixty billion dollars—and that's been corrected for our current rate of inflation—which is a little more than we spent on the Apollo moonshots. We already know from the samples we have in hand that there's magnesium up there and iron, aluminum, and titanium that can be mined profitably. Most interesting is that there's a supply of thorium and uranium, which we've just about used up here on earth. Not to mention the solar energy developments. Fantastic resources—you've got to remember that a day on the moon is two weeks long."

The Senator paused, and there was silence. Finally Dobbins said, "I think we've gone over all this before, Mort."

Simon watched Nancy across the table. He doubted if the Senator was getting anywhere, but there had to be some hope or the Congressman wouldn't be there. Simon knew some of the estimates the Senator was quoting; in the past two decades, NASA had gone to Congress with space programs that would take ten or fifteen years to develop, and every year NASA had come away with only the short-range items approved. Once again Congress had demonstrated that it wasn't willing to invest in anything as costly as space expansion unless there was no alternative.

But you'll see it, he told Nancy silently, and I'll see it. Hell, I'll be living and working in space; that's what I've planned my life around, that's what I'm hustling the Air Force for. And women are going to be out there, too; it's going to be a whole total environment, eventually. I'd love to make love to you on the moon, he thought, catching her eye.

Well, it wasn't impossible. There would be women technicians working in the Space Shuttle when it went up; they were in training at that very moment. And God knows, sex didn't stop while you were orbiting in space. At least he hoped to hell it didn't. He thought about it and decided the idea was very interesting, actually very serious in its implications. Everything was pressurized up there, no space suits in the Shuttle, so that was one problem you didn't have to deal with. He watched the slow rise and fall of Nancy's breasts and the little buttons of her nipples and thought: *Standing up*. It was an awkward way to do it, but there would be a lot of people around; you couldn't take time to find a bunk somewhere. He pictured a man and a woman in earth orbit in the lab in the belly of the Space Shuttle, the blackness of the star void all around them and the earth a blue-green ball below. Screwing like crazy. He felt a stirring warmth in his crotch and looked away. But up there you were going to have kitchens, beds, sit-down toilets—if you could eat, sleep, and piss, you could certainly have sex. Would have to have sex. There was no reason to leave it out.

Nancy was staring at him. He had heard the Industrialization of Space speech so many times he could practically recite it from memory. Now all he wanted to do was make love to his girl. Lately he'd been thinking about his situation and eventual commitments, and he had considered going the whole formal route: the ring, the engagement announcement and party, the big Washington wedding. He was discovering that he needed to get his personal life in hand and align it, once and for all, with his career goals. He couldn't think of anyone more suited to his plans than Nancy. She came from the same kind of background; she was used to men whose professions were demanding to the point of obsession; she understood about limited time and frenzied pressures as they related to marriage, and she could cope with them. He saw life with Nancy as damned good, busy but filled with all sorts of rewards. They would have a large, comfortable house, a good lifestyle, a circle of friends, time for the theater, skiing, a little sailing if he had time for a boat.

And Nancy herself—she was someone intelligent to talk to, independent, educated, but not into a career or anything that would really take her away from him. Someone in bed at night. A companion, a lover, a friend. Fitting neatly into that part of his life that wasn't devoted to work. His father had once pointed out that it was best to marry a girl from a professional family where roles were well defined: men as leaders, achievers; women as graceful, independent, yet supportive and understanding partners. He certainly didn't want to make a big mistake in this area and end up with somebody like Candy James, who didn't know what in hell to do with herself and who didn't understand Topper or what Topper wanted from life. And who was going to get herself in damned big trouble if she kept on doing what she was doing.

For a moment Simon was disturbed by unease, a sense of something left unplanned or unanalyzed. Sex was tricky; with Nancy, he was sure, it would fit into the rest of a successful marriage picture—after they got a few minor problems straightened out. First, Nancy had to get the hell away from her father. Every time Simon came to Washington, it was something new. The last visit, when the Senator had gone back to his office on Capitol Hill after dinner, they had gone up to Nancy's room to make love, and the first thing that had come up was the business about the joint of grass. Let's smoke a little pot, Nancy had said.

He had tried to explain to Nancy many times before that not even in her bedroom on the second floor of a Senator's house in Georgetown, not even as far as he was from Langley at that moment, was he going to take a chance on it. He knew some Air Force types who did; some of them would light up a joint at parties, but he wasn't into that kind of craziness. It was a dumb gesture, anyway. The penalties were enough to end permanently any hopes he might have for the future.

Boozing—yes, a lot of that went on. In the world of advanced tactical fightercraft, booze was an acceptable hazard. Gazenove drank. The Old Man was your Vietnam war fighter jock, hell-raiser, hard-driving professional son of a bitch, and his veins ran amber on the weekends with Dewar's and water. Randy Slyke could lose a weekend, too, once in a while, when he decided to keep up with his wife, who was an alcoholic and a virtual recluse. Topper drank. Not often—but when Topper worked himself into one of his Scandinavian binges, he did it like he did everything else, and the end result was like trying to hold down Eric the Red.

But not pot.

The whole house had filled up last time with the stink of it, and he had been nervous as hell that the houseman, George, or Eadie Mae, the cook, would come upstairs, thinking they had set fire to something.

But he had to admit that when Nancy had a few joints, she got all smoke-eyed and vibrating in every part of her silky little skin, and she was enough to drive him crazy. To look at her you wouldn't think she was that way, but that beautiful childlike body, the little breasts, the hard little round ass turned into a lashing, squirming sex machine after a little grass. Then she wanted to do it against the wall, in the shower, thrown down on the bed and from behind, any one of the thousand and one positions in the Kama Sutra—anything. When she was like that, he couldn't help but think of the guy she had lived with for two years when she was in college, the anti-everything activist, the partner in pot smoking. She didn't talk about him, but he was the one who had gotten her into the demonstration against the neutron bomb on the lawn of the White House. The Senator had had to bail her out of jail and pull plenty of strings to keep her name out of the newspapers. The daughter of the chairman of the Senate Armed Services Committee arrested in a ban-the-bomb protest. At least that had been the end of the pot-smoking lover.

"Take Captain McAllister here," the Senator said, "a superbly qualified young man with degrees in physics and aerospace engineering, who's now serving in a fighter squadron and looking forward to being a test pilot some day."

All eyes turned toward him. Simon was not sure what the subject was. He smiled.

"Now, the Captain's generation had no trouble accepting the concepts of space development—to him and his peers, the advance into outer space is as actual as computers and color television. It's been a part of their lives—the moonshots they monitored on television in grammar school, the books on space they read in the process of making career choices." The Senator looked down the table at Simon, who kept smiling. "We do these fine young people an injustice when we delay their inevitable future. Space," the Senator said, "is to the United States in this decade what the discovery of the Americas was to Western Europe in the fifteenth century—adventure, settlement, development—a world to live in, to grow rich in." He raised his eyebrows and looked to Simon for corroboration.

"I certainly wouldn't disagree with that, sir." He wasn't sure, exactly, what he was supposed to say. He was aware that the Senator wasn't too fond of him; he gathered he was only a half-step above the activist ex-lover in the Senator's books, but he was willing to give it a try. "And if you'll pardon me, sir, I'd like to say that I think the Industrialization of Space program is going to pass Congress, and I think the American public is going to support it. The only thing is, we should have started on it ten years ago. Then we'd be into the profit-making mode now, when we need it."

Congressman Dobbins turned to him with only the mildest curiosity. "What makes you think it's going to pass Congress?"

"Well, for one thing, the program has supporters like Senator Glass to articulate the reasons for it. The Senator's familiar with complex projects, and from his years on the Armed Services Committee, he knows how to get information across with maximum effectiveness. From what you seem to be saying, Congress is going to be resistant to the cost involved in any new space program or an adaptation of a prior one. But it seems to me that if we're going to spend billions of dollars on the Space Shuttle, and I don't believe for a moment we're going to back down on our commitment to it, then we should see about getting our money back on the investment. Anyway, I don't know that the country has much choice. We haven't got any real alternatives to get us off the nuclear energy hook, and the Arabs have just about rung the bell on us as far as oil supplies go. Unless we cut back on our fuel consumption and drastically lower our standard of living—which I don't think many Americans will stand for—then a good, solid, profit-making development of space and solar energy is the way we're headed."

"Really," Congressman Dobbins said. He studied Simon for a moment and then swung around in his chair. "Captain, whether you know it or not, what you're proposing is the old 'Kleenex' approach to the world's problems. That is, use up our resources; move on to something else. And that's the biggest mistake this country could make right now. Moon mining and solar energy factories might make the utilities rich, it might make a bunch of government-aligned corporations bigger and more powerful, it might reinforce the hold of the military-industrial establishment on our economy to an irretrievable degree—it might even give the peacetime Air Force something to do. But while you space people are into this, the rest of us here on earth are not going to profit a hell of a lot. You're talking about immediate expenditures of billions of dollars by an already extravagantly overspent government to get this thing operational. And a *possible* return on the money some twenty, thirty, forty years from now. And things do go wrong in the space program, Captain—you remember the Skylab fiasco. You must consider the problem of some solar energy platform going into decaying orbit and coming down to smash Chicago. I say it *is* pie in the sky, and to hell with it. I'd like to see this country spend its money on some programs to alleviate pollution, especially by nuclear wastes, to eliminate disease, to ease world hunger, to eradicate crime and all the other problems we routinely neglect. Because in all probability, Captain, *I* will not be exploring space with you; I will be right down here in our dirty, depleted, trouble-ridden environment, serving the public. And, I hope, so will my children and my children's children."

For a moment they looked at each other with guarded, mutual distaste.

"Well, sir," Simon said, "I certainly respect your feelings about public service. But I think you'd better consider supporting this country's expansion into space as part of that service. Because it will come. The current program's been assembled by some of the top scientific minds of our generation; it's not some wild idea based on romantic possibilities. It's going to come about because the opportunity is there. You remember when someone asked Sir Edmund Hillary why anybody would go to all that trouble and risk his life to climb Mount Everest, and the answer was, 'Because it's there.' I feel that's the way it's going to be. Certainly, crossing the Atlantic in the fifteenth century was a crazy idea to most people, because any right-minded person could tell you if you did, you'd drop right off the edge of the world. But that didn't stop the Vikings or Columbus, and it's going to be the same way with space. We'll be getting into it, exploring it, colonizing it, and industrializing it mainly because it's *there*."

There was a moment's silence. Then the Congressman said, "Well, that *has* been the military's philosophy. Of course, if you want to take the analogy a step further, we could say that as long as the European nations kept busy staking out their territorial interests in the New World, everything went fairly smoothly. Until boundaries reached out and interests collided over exploration and profit taking. Then we had a series of very ugly struggles that lasted for more than two centuries. If we follow the lessons of history, I'm very much afraid we'll repeat the same conflicts with any grandiose plans to exploit space resources. After we industrialize the moon and strip it of its resources, we'll go on to Mars and see what we can do there. After we've had our space war with the Russians, of course. I'm sorry, Captain—in the next century, perhaps, when we've devoted our best interests to making the earth a better place to live on, have outlawed war and dissolved the military structures, and solved some of our pressing social problems, then I think we might be ready to carry our special brand of civilization into the galaxy. But not right now."

"I think basically you're talking about revising human na-

ture," Simon said. "And, sir, I don't think you're going to be
able to do that in the next hundred years."

"You're going to miss the concert," Nancy said loudly. She
stood up.

The party left the dining room fairly quickly. As the Senator
passed Simon, he reached out and clapped him on the shoulder.
"Good job," the Senator said.

"Well, thank you, sir." He tried to look happier than he felt.
"I don't think it accomplished much."

"On the contrary, on the contrary, it was very interesting."
The Senator chuckled richly. "Harold's a hard case, but he'll
come around. He's just holding out to make sure Boeing gets
their share."

"Come into the den," Nancy told Simon McAllister, "I want
you to see something."

He tried to put his arms around her, but she ducked and
slipped away from him. He went after her, although he was
not really interested in looking at anything in the den; he wanted
to go upstairs and make love. That was why he'd come to
Washington. The concerts at the Kennedy Center were over
by eleven, eleven-thirty at the latest, and that didn't give them
much time. He had to be up and fully dressed by the time the
Senator got back. It was a pretty stupid situation. Nancy was
twenty-three, old enough to live her own life, do what she
wanted, but as long as she lived with her father she had to obey
his rules—stay out of jail, the newspapers, and the Washington
rumor mills. That meant he couldn't spend the night with her
in the Senator's house in Georgetown. That meant she couldn't
come down to Langley and Hampton unless she stayed in a
motel.

She went ahead of him into the Senator's paneled den and
turned on the lights. He followed her reluctantly.

"Sometimes you make me sick," she said, turning around.

"What's wrong now?" he said carefully.

"Oh, God!" Her voice was full of exasperation. "You're so
busy sucking up to my father and promoting yourself, you don't
really see anything, do you? Harold Dobbins is *right*. If you
weren't so full of military shit, you'd know he was right."

It occurred to him that it was eminently unfair to be accused of a military mindset twice in one evening, when it was one of the things he felt he was currently doing his best to fight.

"What they want him to go for," she said savagely, "is another giant American space rip-off. We're going to pollute everything, dump industrial wastes and beer cans and nuclear material; it'll be the same total mess all over again! You're so goddamned naive." She twisted her hands tensely. "Bernie Gould's crowd is going to get the contracts; that's why he hangs around here. The whole AAASI *is* the space industry— they bid against contracts, but they've got so much influence in government and the Defense Department it doesn't mean anything, because what one of them doesn't get, the other will. They subcontract to each other, anyway. Don't you see how it goes? We're into total societal corruption! You're so dumb. You really believe all that Industrialization of Space crap."

"I don't know what in hell you're talking about." He didn't want to argue. Arguing led to fighting, and that was what had happened last time.

"Oh, you're really so dumb," she said. She sat down in one of the chairs, and he stood over her, thinking about a way to get her back on her feet and headed upstairs. The long cream-colored silk dress drooped over her ankles gracefully. He thought about the way she looked in bed, naked.

"You're smart, Simon, but you're really dumb. You never see the important things, do you? Every time you come here and my father starts selling his space program, don't you notice Bernie Gould is always here? Don't you know that he works for the aircraft industries? Bernie *sells* all that stuff to the government. Just like my father!"

"Yeah," he said. The last time the argument, long and loud, had been over why she stayed in the Senator's house and took his money if she hated him so much. Now, he could tell, she wasn't going to get out of the chair unless he dragged her out of it.

"Well?"

"Well, what?"

"Oh, my *God*—you come *snaking* up here from Virginia to ball me and promote your goddamned military career with my father, and now you want to pretend you don't know what's going on. Oh—" She put her hand to her forehead in despair. "Oh, damn, I really hate self-seeking. Tell me, is it nice to get fucked and work on your application to test pilot school at the same time? That's so damned efficient. You're so goddamned *intelligent* and *brilliant* and *efficient*."

"Nan, I don't make love to you to get on the good side of your father. From what I can see, that's the number-one way to get my ass chewed off around here."

"Look me straight in the eyes and say that."

He looked her straight in the eyes and said it.

"Oh, shit!" she cried. "You're just like my father. 'I certainly wouldn't disagree with you, Senator. I'm so glad you said that, Senator,'" she mimicked. "I'm fucking *fed up*. Everybody in this whole damned sick world has a game to play, and it goes on and on. I had to sit through all the crap when Bernie and my father were selling the F-15s to Congress. And everybody knew they were shit. They were scared stiff."

Simon stared at her. "Wait a minute; back up. What did you say?"

"What, that the engines don't work? That's what I'm trying to tell you! Bernie and my father come in here and shut the door and talk for hours about how long they think the Air Force is going to manage to keep it quiet. My father's not supposed to have anything to do with military contracts, you know that! It's unethical. But everything in Washington is unethical; the whole damned Armed Services Committee is unethical; they're just a bunch of burned-out military groupies. My father is just chief unethical pig, that's all."

"You mean to tell me"—he grabbed her arm to make her listen—"that somebody—your father—knew about those damned engines and didn't do anything about it?"

She pulled away from him. She stubbed out her cigarette in the ashtray and lit another one. "Oh, come *on*, Simon. My father sold them in Congress just like he's selling the space stuff now. It took him a year to do it; we were always having generals to dinner, and Bernie—naturally—and the people from the aircraft manufacturer and the engine company. They guaranteed everything would be just great if Congress would just give them the money for the Eagles, that it would put us way out ahead in the arms race and all that stuff. But boy, none of them can do anything *now!*"

Simon stood there, staring, not able to say anything.

"Listen, do you know how they're going to get out of it?"

She jumped up from the chair. "I don't mean the Industrialization of Space crap; I mean the real money-making stuff. My father wasn't kidding about a nice little war."

She went around to the Senator's desk, took a key from some hidden place on top of it that Simon couldn't see, and unlocked the big center drawer. She took out a large plastic portfolio, almost as big as the drawer itself. She laid it on the desk and turned on the desk lamp.

"Come on, I want you to look at it." Her voice was strident. "You're going to love it, especially you. After all, this is your business, isn't it?"

"Look, Nan," he began.

"You don't have to be so damned scared. You can look at it—I ought to know. You're not the only one, believe me."

He sat down at the desk. When she was up in the air like this, there was no sense in arguing with her. It was hardly a matter of his being scared.

The binder was covered with every *Classified*, *Eyes-Only*, *Top-Secret* tag he had ever see, and for a moment he hesitated. If, as Nancy implied, lots of other people had read it, he supposed it was all right. The first page said: *A Report on the Air Force Space Program Support and Defense Plan (SPAD)*.

He saw with some surprise that his fingers were shaking as he turned the pages. The thing had a portentous feel about it: proceed with caution. All he could think of was, Christ, there it was!

The Hybrid Tactical Vehicle (HTV), or Hot Victor as it was named in experimental testing, is a hybrid aircraft/spacecraft intended for tactical operations in the suborbital or near-space environment. It consists of a three-engine airbreathing turbofan "booster" carrying a rocket-powered hypersonic tactical weapons platform of the type referred to as modified BFW (Blunt Flying Wedge). HTV, in its atmospheric flight regime, will cruise at a maximum altitude of 100–120,000 ft. at a speed of more than Mach 3. In this mode, the vehicle will have a range of approximately 6,000 mi. and will be able, from high atmospheric cruise, to engage low orbital targets with weapons yet to be covered. Low orbital targets are: manned spacecraft, orbiting thermonuclear weapons, reconnaissance satellites, and ICBM re-entry vehicles in the fractional orbital bombardment (FOBS) mode.

In order to engage targets in higher orbits and ballistics trajectories, HTV will separate from its booster in a zoom climb at approximately 150,000 ft., where it will use rocket power to effect space flight. HTV is essentially a two-man fighter spacecraft designed for tactical operation against enemy aircraft/interceptor-spacecraft at altitudes from 80,000 to 400,000 ft. and speeds exceeding 12,000 mph. It is configured as a modified flying-wedge, rocket-powered vehicle constructed mainly of titanium and inconel with a vitreous enamel tile skin. Atmospheric flight attitude control is accomplished by means of conventional trailing-edge spoiler-type control surfaces similar to those used on the Space Shuttle. Attitude control at extremely high altitudes (near space) will be effected by wing-, nose-, and tail-mounted retro-rockets similar to the current generation of spacecraft.

It is emphasized that Hot Victor employs no new technology; nothing need be developed. All systems and flight parameters have been tried and proven on a variety of earlier projects. Engines for the booster are GE CFM-256, or military derivative of turbofan engines used on widebody airliners. Air frame and structural designs are drawn from the SR-71 and Dyna-Soar programs. Computerized weapons control systems promise to be the simplest of all, designed to be employed in near-perfect visibility against targets capable of limited evasive maneuvers. Hot Victor promises to be more of a construction project than a development project.

Hot Victor will present even more of a problem to the pilot than the current generation of high-speed aircraft. In a manual-fly mode, control inputs will be interpreted by the central flight control computer which will then manipulate control surfaces, retro-rockets, and power to satisfy the demands of the pilot. In automatic mode, which will comprise the great proportion of extra-atmospheric flight, the pilot, by programing a cockpit control head, will command a specific task from the spacecraft, such as closure with a target, and the flight control computer will adjust attitude and rocket burn to yield a course, altitude, and velocity to accomplish the task. General Nordstrom Williams, in the preface to the preliminary report on HTV development, notes: "The first fighter spacecraft will have several things in common with the first fighter airplanes: they will be small, lightly armed, unarmored, and difficult to fly."

The folder he was examining seemed to be prepared for a high-level conference, from the code numbers on the binding. It seemed to indicate a meeting of the Secretary of Defense, the National Security Administration, and the Director of NASA. But there was no date on it. He knew he should stop, close it up, and not go any farther, but he couldn't help himself. Nancy had known that.

He scrambled through the pages, devouring everything. There were drawings, side views, top views, cutaways. He was reminded of the rocket-powered X-15 which had set altitude and speed records almost twenty years ago but which had been almost impossible to maneuver, once it broke through the earth's atmosphere. Now they had done it. What he was looking at solved nearly insurmountable problems with the dual propulsion systems. The first of the series of HTVs, the XF-19, would go up through the earth's atmosphere, jettisoning the airbreathing turbofan engines to return to base under their own power; then it would convert to main rockets, with smaller rockets for attitudinal control. He sat moving his finger over the drawing of the engines, tracing their components as if engraving them on his memory. The government had poured two billion dollars into NASA's development of the scramjets, but he had never really seen the details, nor had he been aware that they had finally worked out the system of hydrogen fuel. According to the specifications, the air temperatures inside the engines would go to 5,000 degrees Fahrenheit and above, and the structure would have to be cooled to around 1,500 degrees by using hydrogen for both coolant and fuel. The inside of the scramjet engines was made with the new *inconel* high-heat-resistant alloy of stainless steel and titanium.

Once out of the earth's atmosphere, the XF-19 would rocket into suborbital space and chase hell out of anything sent up to imperil the Space Shuttle, Space Lab, solar energy platform, or any other American structure orbiting up there. And, of course, especially surveillance satellites. He kept going through the pages. The XF-19 would be able to strike from four primary United States Air Force bases around the world, and they were listed, with Thule, Greenland, at the top.

There was too much to absorb in a hurried, furtive reading. But he couldn't stop when he came to the section of the report that defined missile development. Manned flight versus robot flight, it was bound to be in any report; the subject was still debated, still unresolved, and of burning importance.

The limited maneuverability characteristic of air-to-air missiles is exacerbated by the negligible aerodynamic pressure Q-factor of near-space regimes of flight, necessitating a computer-operated, vectored thrust-guidance system to alter the flight path in much the same manner as course adjustments are made with present-day spacecraft. Put more simply, a space-to-space missile will be either a simple, line-of-sight projectile which may be easily evaded, or a heavy, complicated, and therefore less reliable and more expensive miniature spacecraft in its own right, having a self-contained guidance system that is subject to electronic countermeasures.

For these reasons, development in the area of space armament is currently centered on a light, fast, and simple "dumb" rocket with conventional explosive warheads, although the most recent trials suggest that more damage is sustained by the target by the aerial collision of the SS missile than by the detonation of the warhead, owing to the exceptionally high velocity involved (in the neighborhood of 16,000 mph).

The other major area of development revolves around adaptation of high-powered beam-type weapons, particularly of the infrared laser systems under such extensive development by the Soviets in recent years. [See CIA Document 24-298] Out of this has come the High Energy Attack Transducer Assault (HEAT) system. HEAT is, simply put, an exceptionally powerful laser, drawing its electrical power from a small rocket-powered turbine generator, firing a two-millisecond pulse four times per second. A target vehicle, when struck by this beam impulse, experiences a violent explosion caused by the rapid expansion of any part of the skin. A beam pulse, on striking the target vehicle, vaporizes a small part of the skin of the vehicle and simultaneously heats that vapor to a temperature of between 500,000 and one million degrees. The rapid expansion of the small volume of the superheated metal vapor causes the target vehicle to experience a violent and disabling explosion on its surface.

Simon McAllister sat back and pushed the folder away from him. He was beginning to worry about whether he had compromised himself by reading all this. He was still a chickenshit captain in the Air Force, nothing more, and this portfolio was not for his level of rank to see. He struggled with that thought, weighing his confidence in his own training and talents and the strictures of the military system under which, willingly or not, he was bound. He decided not to go any farther. He closed the book and opened the desk drawer and slid it inside. His head was so full of ideas he couldn't sort them out. Dominance in space meant armaments and support systems. It was logical. They certainly weren't going to beat off the Russians with moon shovels.

For the first time, he was aware that Nancy was gone. The clock on the Senator's desk said ten-thirty. He'd been reading for over two hours, losing himself in the report, and he hadn't even missed her. He knew he was in trouble. First get into bed, he told himself, and explain later.

He turned off the desk light and hurried into the downstairs hall. There wasn't much time. The stairwell was dark, but he couldn't stop to find the light switch. He took the stairs three at a time. He didn't know whether she had let him see the folder of the top-secret SPAD program as another maneuver in the continuing war with her father, or what. There were times, he thought, when he felt pretty manipulated himself

He turned past the railing in the upstairs hall and the door to Nancy's mother's room, still kept locked and closed after three years. Sad memories, they said. But it made him uneasy. During the two fruitless campaigns the Senator had waged for his party's presidential nomination, his wife had been slowly dying of cancer in her room upstairs in the Georgetown house The Senator hadn't been home most of the time; he hadn't even been in Washington when she died. Nancy had taken care of everything. Probably all the trouble had begun then

He turned the knob on Nancy's door, but it didn't give. "Nan," he said, "open the door."

He waited, but nothing happened. He thought: she's not in there. Then he knew she was because the door was locked from inside. What the hell, he thought. He tried to remember if she had been mad enough at him for some reason or other to lock the door.

"Come on, open the fucking door," he said loudly. He was getting tired. The sleepless adrenalin high was leaking out of him, and he knew it was going to take a hell of an effort to drag himself out of bed after they made love. There was nothing but silence in there. "Listen, you've got to open the door; you've got to go back downstairs and lock up your father's desk. I don't have the fucking key."

He lifted his fist and pounded on the door, not caring how much noise it made. He guessed if he made enough noise, she'd have to open the door. But the whole thing was so goddamned silly. He decided there wasn't time to go to bed with her, anyway. Forget it, he told himself. He just wanted her to open the door and talk to him and not act like a damned idiot.

He kept slamming his fist against the door, but nothing happened. He started yelling then and really pounding on it, and as he did he seemed to lose control of the whold damned thing and he found himself really trying to break the door down. He was fed up with this on-again, off-again shit. He'd had just about enough of waiting his time through political dinner parties and Washington conniving and backbiting and people accusing each other of being crooked. Christ, what an environment to have to live in! He was glad he was just a dumbass technological type. The whole idea of anybody—*anybody*—promoting air superiority weapons like the F-15s with defective engines that were liable to kill him and cut off a promising career before it ever got started—liable to kill Topper, Nizzard, Beeper, any of them—was so damned incomprehensible that he choked up with fury. He drove his shoulder into the door. He heard the wood crack.

He backed away, breathing hard, and started to slam himself into the door full force. He yelled at the top of his lungs. He told her that she was a goddamned cockteaser, and if he ever got inside the room he was going to kill her.

Somebody came up behind him and wrapped two arms

around his body and tried to pull him away from the door. "Captain," George, the houseman, said, "you don't want to do that. Captain, you'd better stop that now, the Senator's going to come home just any minute."

He allowed George to push him back toward the stairs. He was strangled with rage; he sounded as if he was sobbing. He had really freaked out there for a minute. Exhaustion hit him suddenly, and he staggered.

"Okay, okay," he said loudly. George had put his raincoat around his shoulders. George, he knew, had gotten his raincoat out of the hall closet and had come upstairs with it. That meant he had to get the hell out of there if he had any hopes of coming back to the Georgetown house again.

"Go to hell, Nancy," he yelled back up at her door.

7

The day was so warm and the air so saturated with water vapor that even though she had just stepped from the shower and had dried herself quickly with the bath towel, she now glistened with sweat. Linda Criscio sat down in a chair in front of the full-length mirror on the back of the bedroom door and picked up the nylon panty hose, lifted her right leg slowly, and slipped the fabric over her toes. She pulled it up, smoothing her hands over the ankle, working the nylon over her calf and up to her knee, watching the naked figure in the mirror replicate each movement. The body, striped with light from the window, bent and lifted its shoulders. The thighs parted, showing wet ringlets of dark pubic hair and the opened pink slit of her flesh.

She observed this sudden, rather greedy-looking appearance of her sex curiously. For most of her life, this part of her had been forbidden, hardly looked at, mysterious. Now that she was fully a woman, twenty-nine years old, married, divorced, and certified by these experiences to be sexually mature, it still remained largely unknown, concealed, biding its time and its appetites. She knew if her mother were to come up to her room now and find her like this, there would be a flurry of outcries, the towel or the bathrobe quickly tossed into her lap. *Marron! Rosalina, che' sta fa gen?* And who ever heard of sitting like that in front of a mirror?

A nice Italian girl with a good Catholic upbringing, too.

She did not smile. The sallow oval of her face in the mirror, the steady gray eyes regarded her gravely. She supposed she was pretty; at least, that was what had always been said of her in the family. *Linda is the pretty one.* But it was an old-fashioned beauty, the face of the lithographs in the dining room downstairs—medieval women with long noses, delicate bones, their mouths curved in pious dreaminess.

She put her hands up to her breasts and held them, weighing the feel of firm, damp flesh. In a minute, she would get up and go to the closet and put on the clothes she kept there. Her uniform, the regulation brassiere and underpants, lay carefully folded on the bed. A cicada droned in the trees in the backyard. The odor of cooking drifted upstairs, bread baking, olive oil, and tomatoes. Her brother whistled shrilly in the driveway as he worked on his car.

The room she sat in was exactly as it had been when she was in high school, even, in some ways, as it had been when she was ten. All the framed pictures stood in a row on the dresser in echoes of former selves: Rosalina Mary DiCriscio, first communion; Rosalina in black gown and mortarboard delivering the salutatory address, St. Theresa's High School for Girls; Rosalina at nineteen in a mist of lace veil and satin wedding dress, the giant train swept in front and spread like a peacock's tail by the careful hands of the photographer. The other picture, with Domenic beside her, she had burned in an ashtray two years ago.

In the driveway, her brother stopped whistling and yelled up at the windows, "Hey—Linda! Come down here a minute!"

She picked up the towel and wrapped it around her. She never liked to come home. She felt very guilty about it; she had so much leave accumulated that every year papers came through the First Tactical Fighter Wing office, questioning her about it. Once, two years ago, she had taken a vacation in Hawaii, but she had returned before the tour was up. Now, dutifully, she was home for four days because her mother and father had insisted on it.

It wasn't that she didn't like New York—she did. But once there, in the old neighborhood, she was filled with a strange restlessness. She didn't know what was the matter with her.

She held the towel about her loosely and went to the window. Her brother was replacing the fuel lines in the Nova. Leaning out the window, she looked down, saw him struggling with the slippery hoses, his hands coated with grease. He was, she reminded herself, her brother Angie, kind and easygoing; he would do anything for her. The past few years and beer and his wife's pasta had given him a belly which hung over his belt, but his arms and shoulders were like her father's, broad and powerful and covered with wiry black hair. He looked up.

"Come down, Linda," he told her. "You're supposed to be good at this, right?"

She said nothing.

A hot wind blew across the neighborhood roofs; in the distance, the ribbon of the expressway which bordered that portion of the east Bronx and the towers of Co-Op City hung in a mist of heat. A few houses down, she heard the voices of her nieces and nephews shrieking as they played in their back-yard pool. The old ginkgo tree by the garage rustled with the breeze. But inside the damp towel her skin went cold, and she shivered. *Something going on, somewhere.* To hide it, she leaned her elbows on the windowsill, turning her face.

Her brother lifted the hose, a line of gasoline dripping down his forearm and from his elbow.

"C'mon, Linda," he called to her.

He would only want her to hold something, hand something to him. They had been through this before.

Her mother had heard him. Her voice came up from below. *"Rosalina, che 'sta fa gen?"* What are you doing?

She thought: there was Mass on Sunday and the big family dinner with all the cousins, aunts, uncles. Monday—nothing; everyone would be back at work.

She had to leave. She couldn't wait until Monday.

She stuck her head out the window so her mother could hear her in the kitchen down there. The feeling was stronger than ever. She needed to go back.

"I'm going to help Angelo with his car, Ma," she called.

A few miles away, Charles W. Buldrigg, executive editor of *Finance* magazine, stood in front of the wall-to-wall expanse of his advance editorial scheduling board, a shaft of sunlight pouring through the wraparound windows of his tower office that overlooked downtown Manhattan and the vista of the Empire State Building standing waist-deep in summertime smog. Charlie Buldrigg was reading the newspaper clipping his staff writer had just handed to him.

A touch of a button on his desk, when he returned to it, would send the Barzini-designed drapes electrically flowing across the windows, blotting out the errant beam of sunshine, tripping a switch which would flood the room with indirect lighting. The massive scheduling board that covered one entire wall of the office could also be concealed by the same sort of electrically controlled drapery; when both walls were hidden and fluorescent lighting bathed the room, the furniture and the outsized Louis Quinze desk made the executive quarters invitingly elegant, a drawing room for distinguished guests, rather than a work place. Charlie Buldrigg had inherited the office from his predecessor, the former executive editor of *Finance*, whose philosophy had been that the parent company, American Cardboard Container and Can Company, wouldn't know they were doing anything important in there unless he dressed it up like Caligula's bedroom.

In the two years since that gentleman had occupied the executive editor's suite, CARDCO had cut back on the magazine division and put increased pressure on the staff of *Finance* to edit and sell magazines as profitably as ice cream containers, styrofoam mattresses, or any of the other products CARDCO manufactured. Under these pressures, the Claudian splendors of the executive suite had grown quite mundane. Although, Charlie Buldrigg suspected, it still influenced the way the magazine was put together.

He held the clipping his staffer, Fred Lightfoot, had given him up to the shaft of sunlight and continued reading.

Bonn, West Germany—The U.S. Air Force European command, reacting to a string of five crashes here of the new F-15 jet fighter in the past eight months, announced Friday it was putting some high-speed restrictions on the plane while investigators try to figure out what's wrong.

General Paul Johnring, the Air Force European commander, ordered experts from headquarters to review maintenance procedures at the 26th Tactical Fighter Wing at Bitburg, West Germany, where the seventy-two-plane F-15 wing is based.

All of the five planes that have crashed, including two in the last ten days, are based at Bitburg. At the same time, the Air Force ordered a speed-up in a modification of the twin-jet fighters' fuel-starter system.

While the maintenance review is underway, the Air Force said, most F-15s will be allowed to operate only at less than the full power settings on the plane's engines. The exception will be planes on war alert. The modification to the starter system will make it easier to restart the jet engine in flight, if necessary.

The Air Force claims there "is no single cause for the accidents and no discernible trends which might have caused them."

The headline was: AIR FORCE RESTRICTS FIGHTERS IN REACTION TO CRASHES.

Charlie Buldrigg moved the chalk in his hand from the column marked "January" into "February." From the left, across the horizontal dividing line of color-coded titles denoting their stages of preparation, the editorial assignments marched through the months ahead and into next year.

Dealing with Windfall Corporate Profits (J. Garland)
The Pros and Cons of Deregulating the Oil Industry (T. Debenning)
The Teamsters—a Federal Court Challenge? (F. Steinberg)

Under "February," Charlie Buldrigg wrote: *Trueham's Problem Child—the F100X Engines in the Eagles* (F. Lightfoot).

"What in the hell's going on in Germany?" he wanted to know.

"We'll probably never find out."

The lanky young man in the chair at the far side of the room stirred and looked up at the board critically. A tentative scheduling of the Eagles article for February put him on a tight deadline.

"The Air Force sure as hell isn't saying at this point. But TAC sent out a couple of superclassified directives to the squadrons, advising them not to push those engines too hard. Considering these are our new air superiority fighters that we contend are capable of challenging anything the Soviets have, that's not too good." Lightfoot reached up and scratched his head, looking quizzical. "Jesus, I've got to have a certain sympathy for the Air Force this time. They got themselves into a slick deal in that contract, and they're being taken to the cleaners on repairs and modification costs. It was a neat piece of work by somebody."

"Who?"

Lightfoot shrugged. "Business is business," he said, but not too loudly. "From what I know of it, once the F100X engines were accepted by the Air Force brass, they were bound by the terms of the contract to foot the bill for all future repairs and modifications. That's all right if you're thinking in terms of a normal breaking-in process—anything as advanced in design and computerized systems as the F-15 is bound to have some bugs. Unfortunately, the bugs turned out to be major and critical: engine stall at sensitive speeds, fuel system malfunctions, hydraulic systems failures. And all, apparently, hard as hell to pin down and correct. From what I hear, the Air Force has already called in a special panel of experts, and nobody can tell exactly why the engines don't work right. Trueham, of course, is in the clear. They've got their profits, and the contract is closed out. Meanwhile, in an excess of zeal, the Air Force threw the F-15 Eagles into the first Red Flag games in Nevada and learned the hard way what they're dealing with when they started losing planes and killing pilots. They've quieted that down now, but it's still hellishly risky, considering the tough combat agenda out there. The Air Force is backed into a corner on this one."

Charlie Buldrigg turned away from the scheduling board and regarded his staffer with raised eyebrows. "What's involved? Management incompetence? Too much profit taking? Hanky-panky on the political scene?"

Fred Lightfoot shook his head. "It's not that simple. It never is. I haven't begun digging, you understand, not the way I'd like to, but the F100X engine deal poses some interesting questions. Like who in the Air Force approved the engines, since they apparently didn't pass the qualifying tests? I know there was some kind of decision at that point, because the F-15 program had hit a lot of delays from the beginning, and the Air Force was starting to sweat. The airframes had been ready for a couple of years, and Trueham still wasn't getting its act together with the engines. Then you have the political pressure, which was considerable. The Connecticut delegation in both houses wanted that engine contract for General Technologies; three of its subsidiaries, including Trueham, are located in the state. Connecticut and New England in general have been losing industry right and left in the past two decades—there's a big unemployment problem, high fuel costs, and a declining tax base. To make it worse, the only other major producer of military aircraft engines is General Electric, so you hardly have a competitive field. Then we have the special lobbies in Washington, and in this case the considerable contributions of one Bernard Gould and the Association of Aircraft and Aerospace Industries, of which he is the executive secretary—read 'lobbyist.' And that outfit, naturally, works hard to keep its military business alive and well. And some mention should be made of our friend Morty Glass of the Senate Armed Services Committee, who likes to think of himself as a military shaper and planner in the mold of the late Richard B. Russell, even though most of the time Morty construes this duty as promoting his— Morty's—pet projects. The F-15, need I add, was one of these. Taking all this into consideration, what we're talking about is big money, in the billions; these programs are getting so costly that we damned near can't afford them. It's an interesting situation. You can appreciate why the Air Force is nervous as hell about it—and about the real possibility of another fiasco like the F-111 and the C-5A."

While he listened, Charlie Buldrigg was mentally calculating the amount of advertising dollars Trueham Engines and the General Technologies conglomerate spent annually with *Finance* magazine. It was quite a sum; Trueham's advertising budget alone was substantial. But Charlie Buldrigg was less worried about negative advertiser reactions than he was over another factor: how to avoid conglomerate crossovers. Once, in the days of the magazine's own absorption by the large CARDCO conglomerate, *Finance* had published an article on tax manipulation and evasion by a group of mountain states corporations in which, all unknown, there had been a CARDCO-owned copper mine.

On his desk at that moment lay ten copies of the first press run of the August issue of *Finance*, already in mailing and distribution to vendors across the country. The cover story featured simultaneously by *Finance* and its newsweekly sister publication *Tempus* was an in-depth examination of the Administration's proposed Industrialization of Space program. The cover art depicted a stream of gold coins showering from a sky filled with solar energy platforms, the Space Shuttle, and, in the far background, the surface of the moon with a moon factory belching smoke. The cover lead asked: *SPACE—the Next Corporate Frontier?* On the inside, the lead article quoted remarks by heads of the nation's industry and members of Congress in support of the new bill—including its chief advocate in the Senate, the chairman of the Armed Services Committee, Senator Mortimer Glass of Virginia.

Fred Lightfoot looked down at his notes. He had been researching the subject of the worldwide economic impact of defense and aerospace programs, but most of the material he had gathered was outside the focus his managing editor had in mind for the Trueham Engine story.

But he said, "Well, there're always two sides, and there are a lot of suggestions in this area that are hopeful. For instance, some of the more enlightened industry heads have proposed an industrywide cost analysis of aircraft programs, really opening up everybody's books. Which means the defense industries might be getting a little worried, too. Some of them are realizing that the speed, range, and incredibly complicated electronic systems in these fighters are feeding on each other, increasing cost factors to the point where the companies are worrying about ability to maintain profit margins in the future. Projects like the Eagles, the Navy's F-18s, the experimental stuff they hope to get out of the labs—have been and are going to be so expensive, the taxpayers are beginning to balk, and the allied countries are beginning to back away. There's been a real reduction in military aircraft inventories in the free world because they're just so damned costly.

"In other words, our allies are being priced out of the market, too. The problem really applies to fighter jets; apparently there are some very hot projects ready to go in military research and development, but they're being held back because of the enormous sums involved to bring them on line. And I suppose we should recognize that political interest has really taken root in the prospect of all that funding. For one thing, hundreds of thousands of jobs are at stake with each new fighter model that comes up, and there are also important factors like balance of trade and national prestige. The issue that's not being faced right now, according to some informed observers, is that no country in the free world really has enough money to spend on this kind of arms race, and some hard choices will have to be made. How many fighters? How many supersonic bombers? How advanced do they have to be technologically—and how much is any country going to be able to invest in them, considering what they're going to get in return? That's a hell of a lot of money to put into stuff we're more or less committed to hoping we'll never have to use.

"At this point," Lightfoot continued, "the country really can't afford to distribute military contracts to industries that are not willing, or not able, to do a good job, simply because the work is needed to rescue a declining economic area. Or because some giant conglomerate can swing enough political clout to get a defense contract and bail out one of its marginal companies."

Charlie Buldrigg had not been listening. Now he turned his head and said, "What I can't understand is why the grass roots military people keep on flying these things. Hell, they're the ones going to get killed. Don't they complain? Don't they write letters to their Congressmen?"

Fred Lightfoot laughed. "That's not our Air Force. From what I saw in Nam, fighter jocks will fly anything; they defend the worst banged-up turkeys with their heart and soul. The only thing they don't want to have to do is stop flying. And besides, the Eagle jocks have elbowed their way through heavy competition to get a crack at flying the F-15s; they've got their flyboy mindsets locked on the challenge involved. They're *nuts,* as you and I would see it—but they wouldn't want to be into anything except the hottest, most advanced stuff going, even if it kills them. Which it does, sometimes."

"All right," Charlie Buldrigg said, "let's see what we've got." He went to the paneled bar disguised as a *cabinet de toilette,* opened the miniature refrigerator underneath, and took out a can of diet root beer. He held it up, offering some to his writer, but Lightfoot shook his head. "Okay, let's pull it together. I've got the Trueham Engine story chalked in for January, but we can move it around if it starts fleshing out." He poured the soft drink into a glass and stood sipping it thoughtfully. "I like the idea of getting people on the inside to talk to us. We ought to try to contact the test pilot from the aircraft manufacturer, maybe some aviation magazine people, see what rumors they've heard. And let's get some real user testimony. How about the Air Force pilots—will they talk to us, air any of their gripes, tell us what they feel and what happens when those engines give out?"

Fred Lightfoot flipped the pages of the notebook in his lap. "I've got a couple of names. One is getting out of the Air Force; he seems pretty pissed off."

"Well, somebody should be! Hell, this F-15 fighter was supposed to be a whizbang, wasn't it? The Russians have got the MIG 25 and the MIG 27, or something—and the F-15 was supposed to take care of that problem."

"There's something new coming down the line that's rumored to be a quantum leap beyond the F-15s, even, but nobody will talk to me about it."

"You see"—the managing editor pointed a finger for emphasis—"there you are. It just keeps right on. We've got the military on one side claiming they need all this new stuff to keep us from being fried in a nuclear war, and then the industrial establishment telling us we have to have big defense contracts to keep the country from going under economically. And hell, the taxpayers have a sneaking suspicion they're caught in a double-barreled rip-off. Is there a balance somewhere? If this is the way the country's got to go—an endless round of military defense production and technological wonders—what in hell are we doing with a deal like Trueham Engines? I thought the Air Force was supposed to ride herd on these production lines. They used to; find out why they don't now. See who gave the engine manufacturer all the winning cards—and why. Hell, if this was a deal for commercial engines for airliners, there'd be recalls, lawsuits—" Charlie Buldrigg stopped, struck by a sudden thought. "I thought Congress bought the F-15 program on the basis of fighting a conventional war. What's that all about? I thought the next war was going to be a finger war— our finger on the button against their finger on the button. What happened?"

Fred Lightfoot said, "Charlie, the last couple of wars were the Korean war and the war in Vietnam. They were conventional wars, limited conflicts. There's still Africa, the Middle

East, maybe Southeast Asia again. The finger war may be a long time in coming."

Charlie Buldrigg finished off the last of his root beer and left the empty glass on top of the bar for his secretary to take away.

"Okay, go ahead, and let me see what you've got in a week or so. The engine contract stinks; so does the bit about repairs; so, apparently, does the finished product. What's the good of these hot new fighters if they've got to be flown at half speed? Tell me where you're going to pick up on research."

"TAC headquarters first, to look up some of these names." Fred Lightfoot suddenly smiled. "I think I'm going to look up an old girl friend from Omaha. She's married to somebody in the Air Force down there."

Charlie Buldrigg grunted noncommittally. "Didn't we have a finder's fee on this story?"

Fred Lightfoot looked up. He'd almost forgotten Tony Meehan of the *National Globe*. And Meehan was not fondly remembered for his short stint with the *Tempus-Finance* organization.

"That fat redheaded son of a bitch," Charlie Buldrigg said. "I don't want that kind of slant on this story."

Fred Lightfoot remembered the years he had spent in Vietnam and the Saigon office he had shared with Meehan, who had been with the Associated Press there.

"I thought maybe five hundred."

Charlie Buldrigg growled. "Write a voucher on it, and turn it in downstairs."

In his office, Fred Lightfoot dialed the area code for Hampton, Virginia, and held open his address book with his thumb while he searched for the remainder of the number. It had been a long time. Candy McLemore. He corrected himself—Candy James. The Ak-Sar-Ben Ball was still clear in his mind after all the years. What a sight she'd been! Those magnificent legs, the great mop of chestnut curls swinging over her shoulders, the dimples, the unaffected air of pure sensuality. A nice girl, he told himself quickly, and vulnerable—something very sweet there in spite of all the beauty pageant claptrap. He'd been the reporter for the Omaha evening paper, and seeing her on the platform that night had knocked him for a loop. He'd taken her out a couple of times. He supposed she had a houseful of kids by now.

The telephone rang four long double rings before someone answered it. The first thing he heard was a low, murmured struggling noise and then a familiar voice that brought a smile to his face.

"Hello—hello?" the female voice said, with some apparent difficulty.

The muffled noises continued. Fred Lightfoot held the receiver away from his face for a moment, puzzled.

"Candy?" He wasn't sure, now, he'd recognized her voice. The telephone emitted a heavy, anxious breathing close in his ear. "I'm calling Candy James; this is Fred Lightfoot in New York. I don't know whether she—is this you, Candy? I don't know whether you remember me. Fred Lightfoot from Omaha."

The words were banal, but considering the distractions on the other end of the line, he was afraid he couldn't do any better.

"Oh, my God, Fred," the woman's voice said in a rush. "Yes, I certainly do remember you. My goodness, where are you? Where are you calling from?"

As quickly as he could, he explained that he was going to be in Hampton in a few days, and he thought he'd look her up. If her husband—his address book, he saw, didn't give the rank—was available, perhaps they could all have dinner somewhere.

The curious rustling in the background continued with what he thought were barely audible sounds of protest. Then Candy James's voice rushed on about how good it was to hear from him again, and my goodness, they certainly should get together, Topper would love it. Topper, Fred Lightfoot gathered, was the Air Force husband.

He gave her the name of the hotel where he could be reached, the Chamberlin, and the day of his arrival, and ended the conversation as quickly as possible. As he returned the receiver to its cradle he thought, What the devil, he was damned if he knew how to retrieve a situation like that. He'd sounded pretty clumsy. But considering what had obviously been going on, he didn't know why in hell they had bothered to answer the telephone.

* * *

"Oh, damn," Candy James said. She extended her arm and put the telephone back awkwardly on the night table. She was still shaking at the interruption. She pushed at the boy on top of her. From the living room where Emma was, the sounds of afternoon television, "Sesame Street," played at top volume.

"Oh, for God's sake! Rick—will you *leave me alone?*"

His body still lay on top of hers; he was gasping raggedly. She felt the warm seep of wet between her legs.

"I don't think that was *funny!*" Sudden silly tears of humiliation, exasperation, sprang to her eyes. To keep right on with it when she had a damned telephone call. It was something he'd think of, she told herself. It was getting out of hand. Everything. All of it.

"Aw, c'mon, Candy," he coaxed her; his mouth groped across her face. She heaved her body up violently, throwing him to one side, and had him grabbing for the edge of the mattress.

"Hey!" he yelped.

She jumped up, her knees quivering under her, and looked around for the towel. The sheets were wet now; the bed was a mess. Where's the damned towel? she thought, agonized.

The naked boy rolled over on his back and flung one arm behind his head; he lay there, staring at her. His penis was limp now; he seized it with his hand.

"When I tell you to leave me alone, I want you to leave me alone!" she cried. "Oh, God." She raked her wet hair back with one hand and looked about her distractedly. "Oh, God," she repeated.

"Hey, Candy," Rick said softly. His hand closed around his flesh and stroked it. "Hey, Candy, what's the matter?"

She picked up her shorts and lunged for the bathroom. She banged her shoulder painfully against the bathroom door.

I've got to stop it somehow, she told herself. It's only going to end in disaster. But her mind, her will, made no response. She stood shivering, her bare feet against the warm tiles of the bathroom floor, and groped for the shower faucets.

8

At 1500 hours Simon McAllister was killed.

As he was making a sixty-degree turn over Providence, Rhode Island, the computer flashed up the time of the kill, and the green-lighted lines on the display informed him that he had sustained a direct hit from an interceptor somewhere in the Boston perimeter, some defender unseen and undetected by the Eagle's radar systems. The only thing he could think of in that exact instant was that he'd been destroyed by a Navy fighter, probably some F-14 Tomcat equipped with the new TVSU, the Television Sighting Unit, which enabled the Tomcat to sit ten or twelve miles out of range of his own radar systems, identify him as the attacker, and fire a launch-and-leave Phoenix missile. He'd been zapped without knowing or seeing a thing. And the Navy Tomcat was probably halfway back to its base, having demonstrated what it was supposed to demonstrate—launch and leave.

The computer was telling McAllister that he had just turned into a blazing ball of fire. He stared glumly at the data on the display, full of the details of his death and destruction. He was informed that he hadn't even had time to eject. Well, I'll think about that, he told the computer. It was the second time that week he'd been killed in a series of sorties into the Boston and Otis Air Force Base vicinity, and the experience was not calculated to lift his spirits or renew his confidence in his combat skills. Damn, he thought. For some reason, he'd had a bad couple of weeks, and he didn't know what in hell was wrong.

Since there was no use in hanging around over Rhode Island, he cut off his ICS, which had been rendering him invisible to ground-based radar, and brought in the afterburners to kick the Eagle up to 1.8 Mach, bug-out rate. The Eagle went into a fast climb as he turned the nose in the direction of south, and Langley. As he swung in a screaming turn over Cape Cod, he could see that a thick, late-afternoon haze was closing down over the shoreline. There was nothing much visible from the tip of Long Island down to New York City, only a dimpled sheet of dirty gray steam that rose to almost 10,000 feet, fast closing its edges around the clear spots still showing inland in Connecticut. At Baltimore, he knew he would have to get a weather check on the Norfolk area. As the Eagle banked sharply at 59,000 feet, he looked down, getting a good view of the massive low-pressure system under him, a real summertime stewpot of unstable air. A stagnant warm front had overlapped the northeast and mid-Atlantic states for a little more than ten days and still gave no signs of moving off. He was reminded that if the weather was like this around Boston, it was bound to be bumpy farther south, particularly in the thunderstorm breeders that stalked the Chesapeake Bay and the confluence of the James and York Rivers.

The weather did nothing to make him happier. As far as he was concerned, it was enough for one day to be told that he'd been shot down by something he couldn't see and had no way of knowing was there, without the prospect of lousy weather coming home. He was not fond of being talked into Langley on radar Ground Controlled Approach through a Tidewater thunderbuster, and he couldn't think of anyone who was. Don't borrow trouble, he told himself, and tried to stop thinking about it.

He was leaving the rest of Topper flight in the Boston area, along with Dolph Bauernhauser's Dolphin flight—and the Navy, with their damned TVSUs. It wasn't necessary for him to make contact with Topper Leader; they'd all seen what had happened to him on their HUD systems. He wished them luck. It had all gone pretty well up to that point. Coming up the east coast, their Internal Countermeasures Systems had effectively rendered them invisible to ground radar detection, while their own computers, on time-sharing, had seen the whole bunch of ground threats working at them and had given them a blast of jamming. Topper and Dolphin flights had come in undetected over the Army Air Defense Nike and Hawk missiles located in the Washington perimeter and had neutralized the radar-jamming from a couple of Navy carriers located off the New Jersey coast. They had estimated, happily, that the Navy had blown a couple of fuses trying to outpower them. The Fleet Satellite Communications system hadn't been able to lock onto them, either—FLTSATCOM was probably still probing around overhead in its orbit, trying to find the Eagles on their coastwise strike. He hoped it was still a go situation around Boston, in spite of the F-14 Tomcat with the Television Sighting Unit. He thought: Hell, give the Eagles a break—they're still the hottest things going in spite of their troubles.

It was some small consolation that the Air Force was going to equip the F-15 squadrons with the Navy-developed TVSUs by fall. Then things should be a whole lot more interesting. Once they got into using the TVSUs, it would be an air war in which nobody saw anybody else and in which air combat would be even more dependent on computers and electronic systems. Including the one-second warning, if you were lucky, that you were just about to be eliminated.

But great stuff, he thought; the more really advanced systems involved the more fun there was. He had never been challenged by high-tech equipment; it fascinated him to pit his reaction times against some new whatsit and master it. Depending, of course, on whether the alleged genius who designed the thing had done his job right, and it wasn't full of bugs. Nobody could expect to win against malfunctioning junk.

Above the shriek of the engines, he thought he detected a faint, coughing noise, and he checked it out. The seat of his pants was advising him of some barely felt off-rhythm vibration. He didn't think it was anything to worry about, but he punched up a fuel systems analysis to be on the safe side. As the numbers rolled up, he frowned. He didn't know exactly what he was reading, but according to the panel, he was on Joker fuel and running away ahead of his fuel consumption rate. It was possible, he thought, that he had a fuel leak somewhere, but none of the sensors confirmed it. Don't give me any crap, he told the computer silently. He had drawn tail number Forty Thirty-three for the sortie to Boston, and he was well aware it was a crazy piece of equipment that only Linda

Criscio could make behave. He hoped she had worked her usual black magic on it.

The blanket of steam and smog broke a little at the western end of Long Island, exposing the ragged concrete teeth of lower Manhattan and the dull glint of the rivers. Philadelphia, ahead, seemed to be melting into a dingy bubble of smoke. The computer was showing an inertial fix, indicating a course change, and he slammed the stick to one side quickly. Too quickly, he saw. Running at almost Two Mach and at 60,000 feet, cutting a right angle, he felt his body lose its center of gravity and begin to drift. He went loose in the seat in spite of the straps. When he looked at it, the horizon was no help; like Philadelphia, it had disappeared in the undercast.

He checked his attitude indicator, saw it swing level, but his eyes and body refused to believe it. He hated days like this—it was no time for him to get a case of the "leans." He had a brief, disturbed feeling that all the elements of what had been a fairly rotten day might now be coming together to form an ominous whole: the poison-gray doldrums of the weather, the unaccountable kill at Boston, and now the potential insanities of tail number Forty Thirty-three's demon-ridden innards.

At a time when he should be enjoying himself. After all, he was alone in his supersonic bullet at the top of the sky, away from the problems that were usually dogging him, and ordinarily this, the time spent like this, was the best time of all. The voice of New York Center crackled in his ears, and he answered it. He swung his body into an angle his mind told him was leaning, not straight, and the queasy feeling of disorientation began to drain away. Straight it is, then, he observed, even if it doesn't feel like it.

Down on the ground, Philadelphia Area Traffic Control was seeing him as just a dot shooting high and fast above commercial air traffic lanes, just a small blip on somebody's radar screen. Ahead, Washington was coming up as a floating green and gray patch in a lake of smog. He gave Washington High Altitude Control his check. At almost twice the speed of sound, he was passing off Washington's screen in about the time it took them to acknowledge him. But they were watching. His invisibility screen, the ICS, was turned off, and the Navy was undoubtedly tracking him from their radar center at Patuxent, Maryland. And from Boston to New York Center to Washington, to Oceana at Norfolk, down to South Carolina and on to Jacksonville, the Army, Navy, Air Force and civilian defense centers—which had followed the Eagles' northward invasion earlier—were seeing him now as he returned, a casualty, pinning him in the web of electronic eyes on the East Coast of the United States and making sure he was as dead as the computer said he was.

In the past week, he had passed over Washington four times, and each time, thinking about Nancy, he'd picked a spot that he'd estimated was more or less Georgetown, on the western edge of the city. Twice he'd picked up Washington on moonless nights, and Georgetown had been an indistinguishable something down there, lost in the spangled lights of the megalopolis that spread from Boston in the north almost down to Richmond, Virginia. With the black dome of the sky overhead and the pinpoint lights of stars and without a moon, everything he saw closed in melding sameness. At high supersonic when vision begins to tunnel with sheer rate of speed, the night had a way of becoming a revolving fun house of dark and stars, lights and blackness, all dazzle and bright bits. The first night, he'd gone into a 180-degree turn over New York City, and it seemed as if the Milky Way had drifted over to the left side of the Eagle to stay there. After a second, he'd checked his instruments and realized it was no skyscape over him—hell, it was northern New Jersey! Even after he'd swung the Eagle back, he'd had an attack of the leans, disoriented as hell, and it had taken him awhile to get his head straightened out.

It bothered him more than a little, too, that he kept thinking of Nancy when his mind was supposed to be on flight procedures. After what had taken place in Washington the last time he was there, he had decided to let the matter drop for a while. The situation with Nancy seemed to be developing unnecessary complications, anyway; his position wasn't going to be too productive of anything if both Nancy and her father persisted in thinking of him as an opportunist concerned only with promoting his Air Force career toward test pilot school and eventually research and development. There certainly was more to it than that, and God knows he had tried to explain it. He felt he was due some credit: the proof of how he felt about Nancy was all the time he spent thinking about her.

It occurred to him that part of the current difficulty might

be that Nancy didn't really know what his life was like at the
moment, what motivated him to make certain career decisions,
or what was really at stake. But he could see that sometimes
he hadn't made the best impression. He could even allow that
Nancy had some reasons for seeing him as basically a manip-
ulative and self-seeking type (her own phrase), cultivating powerful friends who could help him along in the world. But she
certainly ought to realize that he wasn't stupid enough to base
a marriage on that alone. He could admit that there were times
he wasn't too damned subtle, but he saw himself as essentially
a decent person with the usual set of virtues. Hell—he couldn't
live with himself otherwise.

Still, he was considerably baffled as to why Nancy had
turned on him that night in Washington, saying what she did,
doing what she did. Damn, he told himself—even showing
him her father's secret papers and insisting that he read them!
He certainly hadn't wanted to read the report on the HTVs,
and it wasn't his fault that he hadn't been able to get it out of
his head since. Strange, the whole episode. And a strange girl,
Nancy, as he was beginning to find out. In the little time he'd
had to think it over since that night in Washington, he'd come
to wonder if perhaps he had projected his own idea of Nancy,
the girl he ought to marry, on what might be, just possibly,
an entirely different sort of person, and one largely unknown
to him. He didn't really see how that could have happened—
he credited himself with being smarter about women than
that—but he would admit it was possible. Even so, there was
no reason for the whole thing to fall apart so suddenly. No
telephone calls, no letters, no nothing. He had vowed he wasn't
going to be the one to make the first move this time. It was
damned inconvenient, though; if at any time he needed the
Senator's help, it was unavailable until he got things with
Nancy back on the right track.

Somewhat morosely he watched the fuel numbers telling
him that he was fast approaching bingo fuel, his go-to-home
reserves. He flipped the rotary switch to check the Eagle's fuel
tanks, mentally totaling each figure as it came up. He knew
he shouldn't be using fuel at the rate that was showing, but he
had to believe it. Out of fuel was out of fuel, even with Forty
Thirty-three and its crazy glitches.

He got Norfolk Area Traffic Control on the radio and advised them he was on minimum fuel.

"Right, Topper Three," Norfolk responded, "be advised weather in the area is thunderstorms, reduced visibility, rain, lightning, and heavy turbulence in all quadrants."

That certainly didn't leave anything out, he thought gloomily. He was buying a white-knuckle approach this time for sure. The fuel situation didn't leave him much choice. The Eagle was already into some turbulence and beginning to bounce around. Off to the west in the direction of Richmond, he could see one of the thunderstorm cells, a giant cottony pile reaching to 40,000 feet or more, the towering white heads blown apart by internal winds. Along the bottom of the monster storm, the lowered edge was flat and purple, heavy with rainwater. Lightning flickered inside the blue-white towers like the switching on and off of a battery of electric lamps. Inside the storm were winds that could seize the F-15, for all its speed and sophisticated systems, and toss it around like a tennis ball. An occasional ray of late afternoon sun sliced through the thunderheads like emergency warning beacons.

Then he saw it. The storm dead ahead, squatting over the peninsula and most of the city of Norfolk, made the thing over Richmond look like a playful summer shower. While he stared at it, it belched lightning ominously. Jesus, he thought, I don't believe it. He passed into a cloud, and his visibility suddenly became eighteen inches and no more, the world encompassed by canopy and cockpit, the fearsome Milk Bowl. He came out into the bright sunshine a moment later, bathed in sweat and relieved.

He took a deep breath and said, "Sorry about that, Norfolk; my fuel says you've got to bring me in now."

Norfolk was talking to Langley: "Langley, this is Norfolk Approach Control on the four-oh-seven Hot Line with a hand off."

Now the turbulence was coming hard and fast, hitting the Eagle like repeated blows. As McAllister dropped altitude, he went into heavy clouds again. He grabbed the handhold on the side of the canopy to brace himself. The Eagle moved from shock to shock, coming down in the sticky white mass reluctantly, boring its sleek supersonic body into a tunnel of cloud-like mattress stuffing. The Eagle slewed to one side and dropped rapidly. It seemed to fall a hell of a long way, and he waited for it to stop. When he looked at the altitude numbers, he blinked in disbelief. He had gone up several hundred feet, not down. He began to work frantically, trying to correct for altitude and attitude, his body drifting up and then slamming down in the seat as the fighter jet bounced around. Suddenly the Eagle staggered as if it had run into a stone wall. It recovered and slid forward uneasily. He gritted his teeth. He had bounced up so far that in spite of the restraining straps, his helmet had smacked into the canopy. Out of the corner of his eye, he saw the fuel numbers racing down.

"Roger, Langley," Norfolk was saying, "I've got Topper Three, an F-15, minimum fuel, fifteen miles east of Langley squawking four-two-five-one, heading one-eight-zero, at two thousand."

Well, you could call it two thousand, give or take a few hundred feet either side, he thought as turbulence battered him. Nobody knew how much he hated going in on Ground Controlled Approach, even in the best of times. It was a tense, powerless feeling to grope down blind on radar, guided only by the voice of some unseen airman controller down there in the GCA building on the north side of the runway. The ILS, the Instrument Landing System that he had some control over, was located at the east end of runway two-five. Since he had to keep the wind at his nose, he was out of luck. Ten minutes or so, he told himself, of pure unhappiness.

Norfolk said: "Topper Three, contact Langley GCA on this frequency now."

At that moment, he caught a wild updraft. The Eagle soared up into the thunderhead as though made of paper. He strained forward, trying to see. A sudden, searing light lit the inside of the Eagle, showing every dial and indicator in unnatural clarity, and blinded him.

Actually blinded him. He felt his eyes staring, trying to focus, trying to find something, somewhere. A second later, his vision returned to him, and he found he was looking into rain and whiteness. His eyes, his nervous system, every hair on his body stood at double alert. His face was dripping with sweat, running down into his eyebrows and streaming into the corners of his mouth. Against the roar of the rain beating on the canopy, he thought he heard the shaking snort of compressor stall. His mind turned all this over slowly. This couldn't be happening to him—it was suddenly some nightmarish class-room problem of his flight training days: *You're into a thunderstorm on radar ground controlled approach, low on fuel, and suddenly you detect compressor blade noises in your port engine. Your computer tells you—*

The computer was telling him he was on emergency fuel, and that he was having trouble in one engine.

"Roger, Langley," he said into his mask. He was amazed to find that he was not actually yelling; his voice in his own ears sounded fairly calm. The radar scope was probably show-ing him bouncing up and down like a cork. "This is Topper Three."

He was making contact with the Ground Controlled Ap-proach building down beside the Langley runway. There, in the perpetual twilight and air-conditioned cold necessary to see and maintain radar equipment, ground control personnel were bending over their lighted radar screens, trying to bring him home.

"Topper Three, you're loud and clear." This was the Pattern Controller, a firm male voice with a pronounced midwestern accent. "Position fourteen miles east of Langley."

The rain stopped abruptly. It was gray-dark now, and the brittle flare of lightning flashed all around the Eagle. A drop of sweat ran down inside his mask, dripped into his mouth saltily. His hands were wet. The net lining of the anti-G suit held his body, and he moved around in it greasily.

"Topper Three, turn right, heading two-two-zero, descend and maintain one thousand eight hundred."

He acknowledged the Langley Pattern Controller, his voice reflecting a confidence that, at the moment, he didn't exactly feel. The Eagle bucked, and he threw his free hand up against the canopy to brace himself. He eased back on the engines, hoping to cut some of the buffeting. It was going to be pure hell to stay on the glide path. A small voice in the back of his mind reminded him that he didn't need this screw-up right now; he needed everything to go smooth and easy, no trouble what-ever, right into test pilot school.

"Topper Three," a new voice said, "this is Langley Final Controller." The voice was soft and measured, almost intimate;

for a moment, he couldn't tell whether it was male or female. "How do you read me?"

The question was highly irrelevant. Garbled and scratchy, weak and wavering, loud and clear—no matter what the quality of the radio transmission, the computer was showing him he was out of fuel. There was no place to go but down.

In a few minutes, if both he and the Final Controller were lucky, he would emerge from the storm a few feet above the runway at Langley and settle the Eagle down on it. That is, if some sudden turbulence, some unforeseen gust of wind didn't plow him into the concrete at 150 miles an hour.

"You're loud and clear, Topper Three," the voice assured him softly.

You son of a bitch, he thought suddenly. If he needed something to hate at that moment, he supposed he could learn to hate that voice. It was too deep for a woman's; it belonged to some bastard down there in GCA, safe in a chair in front of a radar scope, away from life's turmoil and boiling dangers up in the clouds. By the tone of it, just doing a routine day's work.

"Topper Three," the voice went on, "be advised Langley weather four hundred, overcast with embedded thunderstorms, visibility less than one-half mile in locally heavy rain, and severe turbulence reported by a P-3 five minutes ago."

A big help, he thought. High winds all the way to ground level. Below in the radar building he imagined the GCA Supervisor had moved over to stand behind the Final Controller, watching what was going on. Big trouble got a silent, attentive audience down there.

The Eagle lurched from side to side as though trying to free itself from its wing and tail structures. What the hell is happening? he wondered. All the usual sense of the familiar had fled. Lightning flashed in his eyes. How big is big trouble, anyway? It was all going fast now; what was happening would be evaluated afterwards in seconds, not even minutes. Was there time to assess what's a matter of life and death, or do you only know it when everything's all over? His brain refused to answer him. It brought to his conscious mind instead the image of that quick, silent, unseen kill over Boston.

Sergeant Linda Criscio stood on the flight line, partly under the projecting wing of the last F-15 in the row, holding an olive drab poncho over her head. Lightning bored into the tops of the yellow pine trees in the fields beyond the runways. A low line of bulbous storm clouds emptied a sheet of rain down the row of fighter jets and swept on toward the Maintenance Debriefing Building. The figure of Master Sergeant Amos Schuld, as slope-shouldered as a gorilla, sloshed through the puddles toward the end of the flight line, his slicker streaming water. When he got close, he shouted, "It's coming in."

"There's been some trouble." Sergeant Criscio's words were barely audible above the rain.

Sergeant Schuld grunted. She meant the Eagle itself, not the pilot. Although, Sergeant Schuld knew, the pilot of Forty Thirty-three was having as much trouble right now as he could handle. What a strange girl, he thought, watching her. He bet she was right, too. Something or other had gone wrong with the flight, and she sensed it, had been fretting about it for the last half hour. He had just called the Langley control tower to ask a favor of Sergeant Tom Bullock, asking him to let him know when Forty Thirty-three made its approach, and Sergeant Bullock had advised him it had, at that very moment, been handed over to the Final Controller in GCA.

"It's that dumbass, the one they call Moonbird," Amos Schuld shouted.

To his surprise, the girl turned to him, frowning.

"He's not dumb," she said.

Then, with the abruptness Sergeant Schuld had come to expect of her, she lifted the poncho a little higher over her head, holding it tightly against the wind, and turned back to watch the runway.

In the Langley Traffic Control Tower, Airman Ronny Masarek picked up his binoculars and took a step toward the windows. It was a futile gesture; the rain was beating against the glass with a rattling noise, and visibility was near zero. Another burst of lightning cracked in the field across the way, followed by a rumble of thunder.

"Where is he now?" Airman Rosalie Tenchman asked.

The supervising Officer of Flying, Major Mattingly, said something too low to catch. An amber light blinked on Ronny Masarek's console, and he reached down to press the button, changing the light from blinking to steady. This was his seven-mile light, advising him that the Eagle with an emergency was only seven miles away from Langley tower, feeling its way down on radar approach emanating from the GCA building that Ronny Masarek could just make out in the driving rain across the runway. In his headset, the voice of the Final Controller was telling Topper Three: "Approaching glide path, wheels should be down." Airman Masarek waited expectantly. There was always a pause here. "Begin descent," the voice said.

Ronny Masarek wiped the perspiration from his upper lip with the back of his hand. There was no other air traffic at the moment. The massive belly of the thunderstorm lay over the western part of the Norfolk area, and all the flights that had not been rerouted were on hold. Only this hard-luck Eagle was coming in, short on fuel and unable to do anything else.

"On glide path," the voice of the Final Controller said. Down in the radar building, the Final Controller's scope was showing the tiny dot of the Eagle sliding down a radar beam to the final approach and the runway.

"Well above glide path," the voice said quickly. "Holding well above glide path," it repeated. "Below glide path," it warned. The Eagle, racked by turbulence, was hopping above and below the line on the radar screen. "Topper Three, confirm landing gear down and locked," the Final Controller said.

The response was, "Topper Three is gear checked."

Silently, Regina Murphy had come to stand beside Ronny Masarek. He heard the swift intake of her breath. There wasn't much for him to do yet, but he held his finger ready over the button of the green light—the four-mile light—waiting for it to start blinking so that he could punch the button and, acknowledging the signal, change it to steady. It flickered, and he hit it—hard.

"Cleared to land," Ronny Masarek said into his mike. His voice sounded surprisingly squeaky in his ears. He thought, God, we're assuming he *can* land.

"Cleared to land," Topper Three's voice echoed him. It cut off abruptly on the last consonant and the tower heard, "Ow—damn!"

Sergeant Murphy jumped. The Final Controller's voice said, suddenly fast, "You are well below glide path."

"He caught something," she muttered.

The Final Controller was saying, "Observe you correcting rapidly to glide path. You are well below glide path—you are well below glide path—"

There was a sudden chatter of voices. Airman Ronny Masarek leaned forward, balancing on his toes, staring out into the rain. A bulging cloud gusted along the runway, spilling a pale greenish light.

"Awarrr," Topper Three's radio said, drowning in static.

"You are well below glide path, too low for safe approach," the voice of the Final Controller said urgently in Ronny Masarek's ears. "If runway lights are not in sight, execute missed approach."

"Pull up, you jackass!" Sergeant Bullock barked from the other side of the tower.

Too low, too low! Ronny Masarek dove for the red wave-off light on his console. The binoculars fell from his hands and skittered across the table.

"Topper Three, go around!" he yelled into his mike. His voice and the voice of the Final Controller were both speaking at the same time, mixed with something Topper Three was trying to say.

"Tower clearance canceled!" Ronny Masarek cried. His voice mounted and cracked. "Tower clearance canceled, tower clearance canceled!"

"Topper Three, execute missed approach," the Final Controller droned.

Above them in the brawling center of the purple cloud, Simon McAllister bounded up in his seat, straining at his straps as the Eagle slammed into a giant burst of wind. The F-15 slid over to one side dispiritedly, losing headway, dragging its left wing. The power and the forward momentum dropped, and the engines wheezed to idle. Desperately, McAllister added back stick pressure to keep the nose high. The Eagle slid lower still, drooping its wing. Through a burst of rain, he glimpsed the concrete surface of the runway rolling over his head. Pull the nose *down*, not up! In an agonized second, as brilliant in his brain as the lightning which revealed the raindrops slanting up at him, he realized he had missed the cut to power. He had bitten down on his tongue in the last burst of turbulence, and the peculiarly thick dusty taste of blood filled his mouth. Voices babbled loudly in his earphones.

His left hand slammed the throttles to afterburners. He pushed forward on the controls to maintain negative Gs and the all-important climb attitude, forcing himself to do the opposite to what his instincts were telling. There was no goddamned way out; he was helpless until he gained some altitude off the murderous surface of the runway. He still wasn't clear— he had rolled over like a flipped pancake, and there was nothing to do but stay there and try to fight his way out of it.

I'm going to die, a small voice said in his head.

"My God," Sergeant Murphy breathed.

The thunderstorm cloud, blue-purple and split by lightning, parted as the F-15 emerged from it with landing gear stiffly topside, the bubble canopy beneath. It screamed out of the darkness in front of the control tower in a nightmare vision, twenty feet of flame streaming from its afterburners, and passed down the runway in front of them, still inverted as the pilot fought the controls to gain air speed and altitude. Straight and fiery as a Fourth of July firework it loomed up, filling the tower windows, then entered a rainsquall and disappeared.

"Holy Mother," Airman Masarek blurted into the open mike, "does that asshole know he's *upside down?*"

In the GCA building, the Final Controller was still intoning, "Missed approach, missed approach."

The Supervising Officer of Flying, Major Mattingly, grabbed the console microphone. "Topper Three, what happened?" he demanded of the now invisible Eagle.

There was no answer.

"He made it, he must have," someone whispered.

The SOF stood rigidly. "Topper Three, this is Eagle SOF. Come up on channel nineteen and tell me what happened."

For a moment there was only radio static and crackle on the speakers. Another bolt of lightning crashed in the fields across the runway.

Finally, the faraway voice of Topper Three said, "I executed a missed approach, dammit!"

Ronny Masarek licked his lips. He knew what he should say right now. He clutched the microphone button at his mouth. "Topper Three, are you requesting an emergency fuel approach?" he croaked.

Topper Three's voice suddenly blared in the tower speakers,

unbearably infuriated. "Shut the hell up, whoever you are—dammit, I've got it under control!" Then, "And tell that crew chief my fuel numbers are registering *normal* right now!"

From the darkness of the storm, from the radar building on the other side of the runways, the soft voice of the Final Controller said, "Roger, Topper Three. Are you rightside up or still upside down? State your intentions."

There was a strangled noise from the airwaves, full of fury.

"He's turning," Sergeant Bullock said across the tower.

They waited.

"Topper Three—" the voice of the Final Controller began.

"All right—all *right!* GCA, full stop! Request a precision radar approach to landing. What the hell."

The Pattern Controller came back on.

"Topper Three," the Pattern Controller said, "Turn left, heading two-five-zero, maintain eighteen hundred. Since you report sufficient fuel and are now upright"—there was the barest pause—"we'll do it over again."

9

"A damned stupid goof, right out of basic flight training."
Major Randolph Slyke stood up and walked around his desk.
He did not try to hide the satisfaction in his voice. "What did
I tell you? He thinks he's too damned good to keep his mind
on what he's doing!"

Topper decided to take another tack. "Randy, I've been
thinking about it," he began, "and there are a lot of things to
be taken into consideration."

"Doesn't matter. Hell, any fool can see it—the transcript
of the GCA Controller lays it all out. Not to mention the
eyewitness account of the kid on local position. He was wing-
down, then upside down right in front of the tower and smart-
mouthing all the way. That takes *brass*. Listen," Randy Slyke
said, "from what I can see, all he's got going for him at the
moment around here is that you claim he's the world's best
wingman. And that he keeps spreading it around that he's got
some kind of high-level political connection in Washington."

"His efficiency report—"

"Spotty."

"He's a brilliant—"

"No," Major Slyke said, "no, and no. I've had it. Hell, by
now I ought to know his type; God knows we get enough of
them. When they're in high school, somebody comes along
and kisses their asses and recruits them for some big college;
and when they're in college, somebody comes along and kisses
their asses and recruits them for the Air Force; and by the time

we get them here, they think their goddamned asses are golden! It's about time he learned differently."

Topper said nothing.

"I want him *out*. If he's swinging some big weight with a Senator's daughter, then let him use his brilliant brain to figure out what to do. But I tell you right now, I intend to make life so miserable for our aerospace genius that sooner or later he's going to get the message that he's marginal—damned *marginal* around here. It's as simple as that."

When Major James said nothing, the Flight Ops Officer added, "He blew it this time—boy, this one was a beaut! I'd like to see him get into test pilot school after this."

"Ah, come on, Randy. He was on minimum fuel—he didn't even know if he had enough for a second pass."

Randy Slyke jerked his head up sharply. "He wasn't on bingo fuel, there was nothing to indicate that; he was just grandstanding. And don't tell me he doesn't do that; I know better. He had some damned date he wanted to keep. He wanted to go home and look at his space movies. He wasn't going to be rerouted to Andrews until the weather cleared up—he was going to come in when *he* wanted to."

Whatever reading Moonbird's fuel gauges showed on approach, they were on normal supply when he touched down, and no subsequent testing came up with anything that showed differently. If it had been a fuel systems malfunction, there was no evidence to prove it. And the squadron ops officer rejected the idea that it was just another example of the demon-ridden systems in tail number Forty Thirty-three.

"Don't worry, I'm not going to do anything to his application to test flight. I don't have to do a damned thing. He's done it himself. Let him go see what his friend the Senator can do," Randy Slyke said.

Topper James stopped at the door of the squadron ready room on his way out for lunch. A small noisy group of off-duty crew chiefs and maintenance personnel were gathered around the dart board. Beyond them, and slumped disconsolately on the ready room couch, was the figure of Captain Simon McAllister, feet propped on the littered coffee table. Moonbird stared into nothingness with an expression of ineffable boredom. Or rather, Topper saw, his unfocused eyes actually rested on the ready room telephone that sat on the counter next to the coffee machine across the room.

Moonbird waited, as he had waited for the past week, for the next call from the sergeant on duty in the Flight Simulator Building which would tell him to drop what he was doing—which, under the circumstances, was nothing—and drive across the base for another hour of what Major Slyke had designated as flight retraining and re-evaluation. That was, another hour of the F-15 flight simulator. Time in the simulator was hard to get; it was always tightly booked, and Moonbird's sessions depended on cancellations. Which meant not getting too far from the telephone.

Grounded, Topper thought, and two weeks of it. That was pretty humiliating for someone of Moonbird's caliber. Punishment—there was no other word for it—applied on a flight student, juvenile level. The Flight Operations Officer made no bones about the motive.

Two weeks of flight simulator duty, on call at all times waiting for someone's last minute cancellation, was pretty rough. New pilots coming into the squadron routinely dreaded those first few hours of orientation in the flight simulator: the apprehension, even terror, of seeing the canopy of the machine come down and lock into place, leaving them in darkness, and the unnerving prospect of instrument flight with all errors inexorably recorded by the computer really raised a bad case of the sweats. They were always glad when it was over. But after the first few months of periodic checkouts required by regulations, the flight simulator became predictable, even boring. The simulator computer-generated programs seldom changed; the lost wingman scenarios, the hair-raising attacks by endless kinds and combinations of aggressor aircraft—even the famous interdiction situation where nuclear-armed threats penetrated continental early-warning defenses and headed straight for the country's heartland—all were ultimately not only anticipated, but even memorized. At that point, time spent in the flight simulator was regarded as just another professional chore; to be assigned two weeks' nonstop duty in it was definitely overkill.

In Topper's opinion, a royal chewing out in Roger Gazenove's office would have taken care of it; the worst part, the part that any one of them would dread, was, as Randy Slyke had pointed out, the business of trying to live it down. The story of Moonbird's inverted approach was already circulating on the gossip pipeline and was all over the base. And would be carried to every Air Force unit in the country eventually, especially where fighter jocks congregated and told their stories. As it was, Moonbird couldn't even eat lunch at the Officers' Club without heads turning, spreading smiles, and whispers: *Isn't that the one—*

Well, it made a pretty funny story, trying to fly a fighter jet into landing upside down; he gathered that was the version that was going around. It wasn't fair to the facts, but he could see how it would come out that way, and it was pretty hard to take. Topper had known men to go under for less. Piling simulator duty on top of it really blew it out of proportion.

The past week without his wingman had caused no end of tactical problems for Topper flight and had certainly built up the paperwork. But there was no doubt in Topper's mind that Moonbird's story about the fuel system malfunction was true. He had flown Forty Thirty-three many times himself and hated the damned thing. Its manifold troubles, coming and going like will-'o-the-wisps, never ceased to amaze him. There were others, he was sure, who believed the story, too. But fucking up was fucking up and difficult enough under any circumstance to justify. Moonbird, the consensus said, had it coming.

Dammit, he's my wingman, Topper thought. I've got blind faith in him—there're no other words to use. A good wingman was a gift from heaven, a bad one a disaster. He'd lost a good wingman in Nam, and his replacement, a kid who was always mysteriously off rhythm and worse—late—had nearly gotten them both killed. There had to be some element between pilots that, after hours of flying together, manifested itself in an eerie faculty for reading each other's minds; an ability to work with such intuitive feedback that you were always where your partner expected you to be—that you anticipated unfailingly split-second decisions, split-second dangers. You couldn't operate without it, especially in the hyperresponsive, greased-lightning Eagles of which it was said: this was equipment that flew you, rather than you it. You were two fighters moving with precision, depending on each other in that elemental faith that was closer, sweeter, than any lover's bond, because your lives depended on it.

He hated to see mortifying kid stuff punishments getting to Moonbird that might make him seek some way of getting out from under, that might cause him to give up hope of test flight school and want out—in fact, to *get* out, possibly by transfer to another unit in another section, or even out of the service entirely.

Topper was on his way off base to have lunch with an old friend. What Moonbird needed was cheering up, he told himself, to get out of the squadron ready room for a couple of hours. He decided to take Moonbird along.

The birthday party for Master Sergeant Amos Schuld was scheduled for 1300 hours, his regular lunchtime, and its hoped-for surprise effect depended on Sergeant Schuld's two friends, Master Sergeant Tom Bullock of Langley Air Traffic Control and Tech Sergeant Lew Alameda of the 94th TFS, who were to meet him at his office in the First Fighter Wing hangar and escort him to the Noncommissioned Officers' Club promptly and without arousing his suspicions. Sergeant Schuld was supposed to believe that he was being taken to lunch at the NCO Club and nothing more; at five minutes past the hour, and as Master Sergeant Schuld stepped through the doors of the small banquet room to the right of the main dining room, the fifty-odd co-workers of First Tactical Fighter Wing maintenance personnel and assembled friends on Base were to wheel forward—as they sang the happy birthday song—a large and elaborate mock-up of that bane of Sergeant Schuld's working hours, the F100X engine in the F-15 Eagle.

The turbofan jet engine pod, fabricated in the maintenance shop and looking remarkably like the real thing, had been mounted on a shop utility stand. Its innards contained an ancient washing machine motor donated by Sergeant Alameda which had, attached to its main shaft, a collar of welded iron flanges. When the electric motor was plugged in, the flanges engaged a collection of scrap metal and wires attached to its outer aluminum walls, producing a racket that had been compared, while it was being constructed, to the sound of a C-5 transport being attacked by an army of gnomes wielding electric hand drills. After a few moments of unbearable high-decibel uproar, the mock F100X was rigged to emit a cloud of gray-white smoke and, with a final scream of grinding surfaces, come to a shuddering stop. On practice runs, the effect had been magnificent. A real monument to that turkey, the F100X, they all agreed.

As Sergeant Linda Criscio got out of her car in the parking lot of the NCO Club, she could hear the laughter from the open windows of the banquet room and the sounds of Amos Schuld's birthday engine being started up again.

They're going to break it, she thought.

The mock-up was put together with spit and metal scraps and only worked because she had labored long at it; she hated to think of it being worn out before Amos Schuld ever got there. Or worse, at the moment of its being plugged in, nothing happening. Nothing at all. Not even the smoke.

She opened the door on the passenger's side of the car and got out the large white cardboard bakery box that contained Amos Schuld's birthday cake. She had opened the box before she put it into the car, and it was chocolate, his favorite, and covered with large pink and yellow roses fashioned of butter-cream icing which had already begun to soften in the muggy heat. But it was beautiful. Across the top of the cake was written *Happy Birthday Amos from All the Gang* in hard red candied lettering, and just under that was a cardboard replica of the seal of the United States Air Force.

She started across the parking lot with the box balanced in both hands, frowning a little at the continuing sounds of gaiety coming from the banquet room on that side of the building and the stuttering roar of the mock F100X. She wished whoever was in there would stop playing with it.

She had just stepped under the awning of the NCO Club when a car turned from the main base road into the driveway and squealed to a stop. She recognized the Porsche as the one belonging to Captain Moonbird McAllister. A second later, the familiar figure in the olive drab flight suit jumped out of the car, slammed the door, and hurried toward her.

"I have to talk to you," he announced. His expression was preoccupied, even harried. "I've been tied up. But I've been looking for you. I've got to talk to you about that crate of yours."

Sergeant Criscio's brows rose, slim and black over clear gray eyes. Suddenly distracted, Captain McAllister stared at Forty Thirty-three's crew chief in a summer dress. He became aware of the soft green and yellow fabric clinging to the outlines of her body, her dark hair, usually covered by an Air Force-blue baseball-type cap with the letters *17th TFS* across the front, spilling over shoulders and bare arms, the bright red lipstick on her mouth, and the definite wafting of perfume.

"Listen," he said finally. "I've got to get down to the nitty-gritty on what happened last week. They've got my ass over the fire—they tell me everything checks out, there's no fuel system malfunction, but I can't believe that. Something's got to show up. Even in Forty Thirty-three," he added broodingly.

Sergeant Criscio said nothing.

"I was already dragging one wing when that gust of wind hit me, and I—well, there was a delay in going to afterburners, I admit it. But the damned thing wouldn't have happened if I hadn't had to come in on a minimum fuel reading. The damned bottom line."

She said, "Could be a fuel probe."

"What?" he said, peering at her.

"It happens. They go out. Then they'll start functioning again."

"Jesus Christ, didn't you *tell* anybody about this? Why didn't you say something?"

She regarded him calmly. "It's in the report. But you can't prove it."

"Listen," he said, looking around him with the same harried air. "I'm on my way to lunch, and I'm late already. But I have to talk to you. Until this thing gets cleared up, I'm doing time in the simulator; my ass is on the line. I'll never get approved for test flight."

Another loud burst of noise came to them, and Linda Criscio turned her head. "I've got to go," she murmured.

He put out his hand. "Why don't I meet you somewhere tomorrow? Look, I'll take you out to dinner, how's that? I don't want to have to rush—trying to talk to you standing around in a hangar somewhere."

The moment he said this, Captain McAllister was reminded that Air Force regulations expressly prohibited the dating—or anything that would give the appearance of same—of enlisted personnel by commissioned officers.

"God, it's strictly business," he assured her. "What do you say?"

She looked at him for a moment, her grave, beautiful face unreadable.

"I'm off duty at four."

"Make it six o'clock. I'll call you."

"I'd like another bloody mary," Regina Murphy said loudly.

No one paid any attention. The Masareks, mother, father, and son, were too busy with what they were doing to hear her. Mr. and Mrs. Masarek, their heads close together and their shoulders touching, were conversing in Polish, absorbed in the soft-shelled crab which lay, surrounded by lettuce and French fries, on Mrs. Masarek's plate. Mr. Masarek reached over his wife's arm and with his fork laid back a portion of batter and crab shell for his wife's inspection. Mrs. Masarek bent her head close to the plate and seemed to sniff at it. She looked up doubtfully.

Ronny Masarek lifted himself on his elbows and stretched across the table, explaining in the same language that all parts of soft-shelled crabs were edible and that it was not necessary to open them up and clean them to prepare them for cooking.

"See, Ma," he said in English. He lifted a piece of crab from his own plate and stuffed it into his mouth. "It's good. It looks a little weird," he said with his mouth full, "but actually it's real *dobzhe.*"

His mother shook her head.

"Now, try, *try,*" Mr. Masarek urged her. His large good-natured face, crimson with sunburn, crinkled in a smile. "See, Ronny eats."

Mrs. Masarek shook her head again. With a decisive gesture, using the side of her thumb, she pushed the crab to the far side of her plate. Her heavy dark brows and prominent jawline were almost identical to her son's, as was the somewhat sulky look about the strong thin mouth.

"*Wygloda cmaczno, no nehce,*" Mrs. Masarek said. "*Dzekue bardzo.*"

Ronny and his father burst into loud laughter. But Regina Murphy repressed a shudder. She looked around the balcony of Harris's Restaurant with a small, strained smile that said for the benefit of anyone who might be looking that she certainly was not a party to all this, even though she might be sitting at the same table. Fortunately, Harris's was crowded; there were people waiting on the stairs for tables, and the flow of traffic was such that there was really not much room to see, or be seen. Regina Murphy watched as Mr. Masarek tucked his napkin under his chin and dished up a portion of his fried clams for his wife. He dumped the soft-shelled crab in the ashtray.

Coming to Harris's, she could see, was a mistake, but the past week had been full of them; she was glad the Masareks' visit was nearly over. The restaurant was one of Sergeant Murphy's favorite places; usually she adored having lunch on the quaint balcony upstairs under the green plants hanging from the oak beams, where one could watch the smartest crowds in Hampton in the Whaler Bar below. But it definitely was not right for Ronny's parents. You could see they didn't know a damned thing about seafood; they came from some place in Illinois, and she didn't know why they insisted on ordering it. Mrs. Masarek, Ronny had told her, had been sick on the stuffed flounder she had had the night before at the Strawberry Field Motel.

"They want to try everything," Ronny had said. "After all, this is the seashore. They don't want to go back home and tell everybody they blew the chance to load up on fish, do they?"

Regina Murphy sighed. If they just wouldn't do things like smell the *food,* she thought. A sense of her own superior upbringing obliged her to feel a little guilty at this, and she told herself that, well, their table manners were really not the worst, actually, but it didn't help that they kept doing such *foreign* embarrassing things. Mrs. Masarek actually crossed herself before she started her meal. She had seen her do it not once, but each and every time. And, of course, they kept speaking Polish.

She knew her own family, solid middle-class Irish people from Boston, would be definitely turned off at the way the Masareks behaved.

The elder Masarek, she had been told, was a Czech national who, for some complicated reason, had emigrated to Yugoslavia in time to be conscripted into the conquering German armies in World War II. After the war, he had been in a displaced persons' camp in Poland where he had met Mrs. Masarek, who had also been a DP. From there they had gone to Canada on some sort of quota, and they had lived in a log house that Mr. Masarek had built with his own hands. It was a terrible story, full of hardship, and she supposed they had all had a very hard time. It was certainly no wonder they had migrated again to the United States to join Mrs. Masarek's two brothers and sister in Illinois, where now Mr. Masarek worked in a steel mill, or something.

Mr. Masarek was wearing a brilliantly colored plaid sports jacket and sports shirt with open collar. His hair was gray, sweeping high above his forehead in a careful old-fashioned style. When he spoke, the gold caps on his bottom teeth were prominently displayed. Ronny didn't look much like his father, she had decided; he looked almost exactly like the rangy, black-browed woman opposite whose glance, when it rested on her at all, was covert and unyielding in its disapproval.

Regina Murphy knew that look. It wasn't hard to read. *Too old, too skinny, too smart*. Certainly not the nice Polish girl this mother would want for her son. Certainly not some red-headed green-eyed woman of thirty. And an Air Force Sergeant.

"Yeah, Ma," Ronny had told his mother, "she's my Sergeant. And I have to do what she says."

Well, don't worry, Regina Murphy thought; just don't bother yourselves about it at all. She knew what Ronny wanted them to think—he was getting the message across to his parents pretty clearly with all the handholding in front of them and the kiss, last night, when they got into his car. It was really sort of a comedy. Airman Masarek wanted his mother and father to think they were having a really serious relationship, maybe even thinking of marriage—when it certainly wasn't true— and he was getting a kick out of it. Showing off, she thought resentfully. *Sleeping together*, she saw in Mrs. Masarek's look.

Sergeant Murphy gave her head a disdainful toss. Well, they were all going to a lot of trouble about nothing, because that wasn't the way it was at *all*.

Not that Ronny wasn't a perfect doll—she couldn't resist a sidelong look at him, big and warm next to her, his arm resting on the table within reach of her hand. He was still talking Polish with his father. She watched his lips moving, the downcast movement of his eyes as he shoveled more food into his mouth, the thick, black lashes brushing his cheeks. Inwardly, Regina Murphy sighed again.

He was so *fantastic*, really; he had the most perfect lean, sexy body, and he knew more about making love than she had given him credit for. Sometimes she wondered where he had learned it all. But he was also terribly possessive and jealous, even in the tower when they were on duty, and this had begun to be worrisome. She didn't mind the gang knowing about it, but making an *issue* of it was something else again. He was still a kid, a big, sexy, passionate kid. But a kid, and that was the trouble.

"Try older men," Rosalie Tenchman had said once. "Honestly, Murphy, you can't keep robbing the cradle. You ought to find an older man, someone nearer your own age, you know."

Yes, but older men—

She always said: All the good ones are married.

Regina Murphy looked over the wooden railing of Harris's balcony into the lower level where the crowd had thinned out considerably after two o'clock. The bar itself was almost empty, and there was only a sprinkling of people still at the tables in the area decorated to resemble the saloon of a whaling schooner. With a start, she recognized the men sitting almost under the balcony overhang.

"Oh, look," she cried. She grabbed Ronny's arm. "Oh, look—there's Major James!"

She was unaccountably thrilled. She never got a chance to see him close up, and there he was! And, she marveled, so damned *good-looking*! You certainly couldn't miss that silvery blond hair or that handsome tanned face with a flash of big white teeth when he smiled or the *size* of him. Most of the fighter jocks were only medium-sized or even really small men, and Major James just sort of towered over them. The younger man with the thin sharp features sitting next to him was not bad-looking either, but Captain McAllister had a reputation for being hard to get along with, and he was currently in a lot of trouble over the bad approach he'd made a week ago. The small tough-looking man in glasses who seemed to be doing all of the talking, she didn't know at all. But oh, God—it really was Topper James down there!

"Oh, you should see him fly the Eagle in the Friday demonstration flights," she tried to tell the Masareks. "He's the best pilot in the Air Force! It's a—you know, a demonstration to show what the Eagle can do. It goes supersonic off the runway in two minutes in a vertical climb." She lifted her small hands in a scooping motion to show them. "The Eagle has this fantastic turn ratio—if an aggressor aircraft is on its tail, the Eagle can just cut a smaller arc, and the aggressor can't do that, so it has to overshoot. That is, in the MIG 21 class—nobody really knows what the MIG 25 or 23 capabilities would be." The Masareks were staring at her. "The first year," she faltered, "when the Eagles went operational, most of the tower crew had a hard time paying attention to traffic with Major James working out his flight ribbon pattern with the Mac Air test pilot." She looked around. "Oh, well," she said and shrugged.

The Masareks were silent, their eyes fixed on her.

She thought: they don't understand a word I'm saying. Even Ronny had half-turned in his seat, listening to her but smiling at her, waiting for her to finish.

Her Irish temper suddenly welled up, and she felt the blood rushing to her face. Holy Mother, she thought, how did I get myself into this, anyway? She was aware now that the atmosphere had shifted, that she was being caught up in the toils of something she found hard to define, much less fight against. If Ronny wanted her, she realized, his parents accepted her in spite of her obvious drawbacks. Now, their expressions said all too plainly, it did not become her to wave her hands about, express herself with such excitement about whatever it was—in a word, act silly. Mrs. Masarek bent that black-browed, uncomprehending look fully upon her.

They've got to be kidding, she told herself indignantly. They thought she was rattling on about nothing just because they were so ignorant themselves, because they had no knowledge whatsoever of a fascinating and exciting world, the Air Force, that was ten times more important than anything *they'd* ever come in contact with!

I've got to ditch him, she told herself.

Deliberately, even rudely, she turned and presented her left shoulder to them, resting her arm on the balcony railing. She was too angry to speak. But it's my own fault, she thought. She looked down at the table below and the three men just finishing their lunch. Captain McAllister looked sulky, as usual, but Major James appeared to be having a good time.

She studied his fair hair and the breadth of his shoulders, her anger fading. Major James was supposed to have a really beautiful wife. She hoped so—she would like to think he was happy. The burly little man in shirtsleeves gestured as he talked, and Major James listened attentively, lifting his head from time to time to nod.

Regina Murphy propped her cheek on her hand. They seemed to be having such a nice conversation. They seemed to be such assured, *interesting* people. She had a sudden, piercing sense of indefinable loss. The trouble with older men was that the good ones were always married.

The conversation, actually, was not going all that well. Sammy Durden was telling his famous eyewitness account of the fifteen Marine fighter pilots flying old Brewster trainers who had gone up at Midway to engage an attacking force of more than 150 Jap Zeros, and Topper had thought Moonbird would get a kick out of it, as he did himself, even though he had heard the story many times. But McAllister had gone out of his way to show that he was not only not entertained, but that he rejected everything the long account was supposed to illustrate. Topper had had to break in several times to save it; he wondered now what had prevailed upon him to invite Moonbird to lunch in his present mood.

Magnanimously Topper allowed that Moonbird had a right to be pissed off. It wasn't very smart, though, to take it out on Sammy Durden.

Topper knew a lot of people who would give a good deal to be able to sit at lunch with one of the top Marine aces of all times and listen to him spin his stories. Sammy was rated right under Gregory Boyington in the Pacific theater of operations, and best of all, he was a damned skillful analyst of fighter operations. He was now employed as an aeronautical engineer in the Advanced Tactical Aircraft Research Center at NASA, Langley—an award-winning designer of jet fighters and one of the few World War II aces who had gone on to preeminence in a nonmilitary profession. Certainly what Sammy could tell you about aerial combat—and not limited to piston-engine airplanes, either—was an education in itself. Not to mention, Topper thought, that vast, endlessly fascinating arena of the war in the Pacific, where men like the Marines at Midway had made the final, stunning gesture of sacrifice against hopeless odds.

"They were so brave," Durden said, shaking his head. His face, with the pale slick scars of burns still visible after thirty years over one eyebrow and in his reconstructed nose, twisted in a wry expression. "Brave sons of bitches, I'm glad it wasn't me. That was a ticket that had 'guaranteed suicide' stamped on it—there was no way you could do any good in those damned Brewsters up against the Japs' Zeros unless you were lucky. And you didn't get too damned lucky, outnumbered ten to one. On the other hand, there was no way that the Navy was going to let the Gyrenes sit on their asses and wait for a better day. So they went up at Midway as soon as the Japs moved their fleet in on them, and in fifteen minutes, maybe half an hour, it was all over. The fight went on—but there wasn't one damned Brewster left."

"Crap," McAllister said.

Durden raised one scarred eyebrow.

Topper said dispassionately, "Moonbird, shut up."

"No, hell—I mean it! But God, it makes a great war story, doesn't it? I don't know what in hell we'd do without our goddamned war stories—even if they only go to show how goddamned stupid the military is."

"Son, you don't make the rules at times like that," Durden said mildly. "A lot of orders don't make any sense; the point is—how're you going to carry them out? And the only answer to that is, with guts. You hope."

"Aw, hell, where's the waitress?" McAllister said. "I need another beer."

Topper said, "I'm not in favor of giving that type of order, like at Midway, unless there's a big gain apparent in it and the people involved know it. But Sammy's right, you sure as hell don't make the rules. In Nam," he said carefully, "we were up against stuff that really bothered us—orders not to initiate any engagement over the North Vietnam borders, and it sure as hell crippled us tactically. And caused losses that weren't worth it. In 1969, when I was flying F-4s out of Lon Nol, our orders were not to attack unless fired on—which gave the other side one hell of an advantage. He could get off one shot and eliminate you while you were waiting out the rules—and it only took that one shot, sometimes. That's a pretty crazy situation when you're supposed to be fighting a war. The thing is, we're trained to assume that orders are going to be logical, and it comes as a hell of a shock to find out some of them aren't. And it bothers you," he added. "It bothers you for years afterward, every damned time you think about it."

The waitress came up to take their order for another round of drinks. Topper waved her off. He didn't need any more—he was thinking about what he had just said, struck with the amount of truth still in it. He usually didn't like to think about the war. It *did* bother you for years afterward. And his words had suddenly conjured up the smell and feel of the southeast Asian jungle, even after so long a time. The country there, he was remembering, was amazingly beautiful, a paradise of green mountains and lush vegetation and a hell of an odd place to fight a war—it violated the sense of all that beautiful green country. The river crossings and mountain passes which had been heavily bombed were like open sores. Tough country, though, they had been warned—there were people down there who saw to it that you didn't walk out of the jungle alive.

There was the time they had had a rendezvous with an RF-4 from Thailand to go into the border area for some picture taking. No way of knowing what the target was, that mission; they were to meet the RF-4, escort it, and see that it got its pictures taken.

"You sure you don't want another?" Durden said.

Topper shook his head.

Radio transmissions were limited, as usual, since they were being monitored by the North Vietnamese, so they communicated mostly by hand signals. Near the border, the jungle was thicker. The RF-4 had said, "Going down," and nothing more, and it dove into an opening in the heavy cloud cover beneath them.

They took their F-4s into the hole after him, coming out at two thousand feet in a valley neither he nor his leader, Ruder, recognized. It was full of guns. What they didn't know was that it was armed with SAMs, too. There was still a heavy, steamy cover between them and the ground: they couldn't see anything coming up at them until it broke through all that murk. The RF-4 dove in, taking pictures down there, recording everything, whatever their mission was all about. Then his flight leader said suddenly, "Got a SAM low light." Then, very quickly, "SAM high, Top!"

"There are no guarantees in this life," Sammy Durden was saying, "and sure as hell not in the military. You're not going to stand there and argue with orders, for Chrissake. Oh, I mean, hell, yes, you can *argue—*"

McAllister said loudly, "Ah, come off it, will you? Jesus— 'God and England expects every man to do his duty,' right? But what you really want to realize is that the military never learns—it always trains for the next war the way it fought the last one. And we're still doing it! I don't believe all this limited, conventional war crap; listen, up in space is where it's at now. We're going to have to dump the brass's mindset about traditional tactics, how General MacArthur got back to Manila and all that jazz—all that stuff is outmoded."

"Son, space is nothing but the *high ground,*" Durden said.

For Topper, the sense and smell of the long-ago jungle was still perfectly intact; he could remember the look of the sheet of that covering, ominous mist as though he were still there. The ugly little tone in their headsets had switched to a higher frequency, telling them the surface-to-air missiles down there in the North Vietnamese launchers had just gone from "asleep" to "awake"—but not yet activated. They were not supposed to initiate an attack, though—just as the North Vietnamese were not supposed to have missile sites located so far south of the border. Coming up in that overcast, if they were going to do it, where you couldn't see them until the last split second was going to be tough as hell. The radio broke silence. *Pods on two—we've got a SAM high light. Better spread out.* The Phantoms, the RF-4 with them, slid farther apart.

Someone said, *Watch it—something's closing.* Just like that.

The next second it must have come up in the clouds under them, because there was a noise, the bright flash of explosion, and flame, and Ruder's F-4 disappeared.

You could blink your eyes, and it was all over.

It still struck Topper as singular that the flight leader, Ruder, an amiable little guy who hated Nam and wanted like hell to get back to his wife and kids in Las Cruces, New Mexico, should have been dead over ten long years. *Ten years,* he thought, turning it over and over in his mind, surprised. More than that. An now there was so damned little meaning in it. Now, looking around, sitting in a noisy lunchtime crowd in a restaurant in Hampton, Virginia, and after so much time had passed—in peacetime when people worried about taxes and gas shortages and inflation as they had never, apparently, worried about the Vietnam war—he remembered that afternoon over the jungle and could realize that Ruder's death made no difference whatsoever to this world. To his—Topper's— world, either. To anything.

He tugged at his ear, bemused. He realized Moonbird was gone.

"Where'd he go?" he asked Sammy Durden.

Durden lifted his glass and drained it. He gave him a quizzical look. The eye under Durden's scarred eyebrow had limited vision: he had to cock his head to see. "Your friend said he had to get back." Then, "You were faraway, Topper. What's on your mind these days?"

Topper shrugged. It was too complicated to explain, and he didn't know that he could. Fatigue was sneaking up on him lately; he was a little annoyed to think that he showed it. As for McAllister . . . Topper said, "He's not a bad kid, Sammy. And he's got his problems. He's got his back up this week."

"Oh, I heard about the inverted approach; hell, it's all over the place. That's going to take him time to live down."

"Yeah, well, that and a lot of other things." Topper got to his feet, and Durden pushed back his chair. Topper raised his voice over the clatter of dishes a busboy was loading. "And he's just broken up with his girl."

Durden stared at him thoughtfully.

"When you going to take your vacation, Top?"

He said, "I haven't even had time to think about it."

Topper thought about it going home. Sammy Durden's remarks, carefully juxtaposed, about having something on his mind lately and taking a vacation did not, he hoped, hint that he was showing the signs of the pressure that had been on all of them for the past few months.

Well, hell, what if it did? "Tired" had been the catchword for the past year. *Just tired,* he'd been telling himself all through June and July. But he wasn't particularly happy to find that that shrewd old fighter jock, Durden, thought he saw it in him.

As far as he knew, he hadn't been picking up any signals from Randy Slyke or, even more importantly, Topper flight. I've got to watch myself, he thought.

There wasn't going to be any immediate relief from their backbreaking schedule; but he could admit to himself in the privacy of his own thoughts that sometimes he felt as though he spent his life in the pressure cooker, the lid screwed on tight, simmering from one long day to the next. For too long to think about, he'd been turning in twelve-hour duty, beginning at 5 A.M., as regularly rotating Duty Officer—which meant that he worked like hell before the sun was even up making sure the F-15s scheduled were in operating condition, that the schedules themselves worked, that there was air space allotted for the day's flights. Which meant juggling tail numbers that were down for repairs against those that weren't and setting up the board by 10 A.M. And at least once a week, he had to hurry over in mid-morning to stand his three hours of rotated SOF duty in the control tower as Supervisor of Flying, and as flight leader, he briefed a flight of Eagles going out in the afternoon for area defense exercises, time on the missile range. He took them out, and got back in time to be on the ground at five-thirty, shutoff time for the twelve hours. And somewhere along the line, he had to complete the paperwork and intelligence updatings and briefings on the ever-changing, incredibly complicated instrumentation and systems.

A circus. A damned crushing merry-go-round that tried to beat out of you the only thing that made it worthwhile—God knows it wasn't the money, he told himself—and that was flying the F-15 Eagles. Eight years ago, coming back from Nam, he would have given anything to have known for certain that he would be where he was now, in the air superiority Eagles; with that perspective, it would have seemed the top of the world. Now, he thought, all he got out of it was having to tell himself he was just tired.

It was raining when he came out of the restaurant, a sudden tidewater thundersquall that slanted down in driving sheets, and he ran to the car. Talk about vacation—all he could get was time off in unplanned bits and pieces, when he could snatch them, to go home early and, if he was lucky, take a nap all afternoon. He remembered that he had forgotten to call home.

Candy was probably at the OC swimming pool with Emma, anyway, or in the snack bar, waiting for the rain to stop.

The storm caught up with him between Pembroke and Woodland Avenues, and Topper pulled the little Fiat over to the side of the road to wait it out. The rain came down heavily, hammering the sidewalks; the purple-black clouds in the direction of Buckroe Beach turned white with lightning flashes. He sat watching it. The steaming shallow neck of Chesapeake Bay that wended its way past the tidal flatlands of Virginia and Maryland was a prime weather breeder; he had never seen anything like it, not even in Vietnam. All during July and August, they had been taking the Eagles up in interminable V-sweeps in the same crazy weather, sweeping the air space with flights of four F-15s against Navy A-4s, simulating detect, intercept, and destroy against Soviet aggressors, both sides performing the same exercise, going at it like dogs, inter-service rivalry bust-a-gut. Storms all the way, equipment failures, and malfunctions keeping them company.

On Wednesday, shorthanded without Moonbird, they had been doing a straight high-altitude, high-speed intercept, running around 1.3 Mach, and Beeper had made a right-hand five-G turn when he caught the warning *Boom!* of compressor stall. Beeper looked down to find his indicators showing him that his left engine had stagnated. At that moment, he was coming right into a thunderhead, and he cautiously lowered the Eagle's nose. He pulled the left throttle off and accelerated to 450 knots with his good engine while his left spooled down; he was hoping to get it relit. A quick radio check showed he was okay, but inside the clouds, a lightning bolt hit Beeper's Eagle, and he got both his hands slapped. For about three minutes, his hands were paralyzed.

"I think I'll get it working," Beeper's voice kept assuring GCI.

But from the wrists down, he couldn't move a thing. His inertial navigation system was dumped, everything out, and they were loaded with fastpacks—every one of them conscious of Beeper sitting on a maximum fuel load and playing with lightning flashes. The second crash of lightning hit when Beeper was just getting some feeling back in his hands, this time numbing his right one. *To hell with it,* Beeper's voice said. He shut down his left engine completely and limped back to Langley alone on the remaining engine. . . .

The sky was showing a pale strip in the east, and the rain was slackening. A large black woman in a plastic raincoat, carrying a shopping bag, came down the sidewalk in the direction of the bus stop. Topper started the Fiat. The gutters were flooded, and down at the traffic light there was a lake that washed over the hubcaps. He turned the Fiat into the subdivision gates marked Pinecrest Manor.

He never passed through the entrance without remembering his father's phrase, "living beyond one's means." That certainly described it, Topper thought. The area was a nice place to invite guests; they were certainly impressed by the broad, flat streets, the moderate-to-expensive homes set back across grassy lawns, the correct, protected glossiness of good living. Ranch styles, old South plantation houses, Spanish haciendas, they were all like pages from the beautiful homes magazines. His own house on Magnolia Drive had been the model home in the development—the *all*-electric home, he reminded himself. From the corner of Pinecrest and Magnolia Drive he could see it, raising its Greek Revival columns imposingly halfway down the block. A gleaming white monument to utility bills. A mausoleum of Past Due reminders. He moved in a world of technological advances of staggering complexity, and he couldn't pay his light bills. There was some profundity there that escaped him.

The gutters were still running rivers. In front of his house, a naked little girl paddled happily in the flood.

"Damn," Topper muttered. He turned the Fiat carefully into the driveway and got out.

"Daddy, Daddy!" His daughter splashed toward him. "Emma swim!"

When he picked her up, she curled her wet legs around his waist. The water soaked through his uniform shirt.

"Dammit, where's your mother?" Emma was not only naked, it looked as though she had been out in the storm. Her hair still dripped.

He took her through the garage. The television set in the family room was blaring "Sesame Street." But no Candy. The kitchen cabinet doors were open, showing where Emma had climbed, and the counters were littered with open boxes. Cookies crunched underfoot as he walked.

"Coke," Emma demanded.

"Just wait," Topper told her.

Where the hell was Candy? he thought. She was pretty lax about Emma, but he had never found his daughter wandering around in the street before. His anger began to fade before an uneasy feeling. There were so many things that went on in supposedly safe neighborhoods. He opened the door to the basement, switched on the lights, and looked down there. Emma wound her arms around his neck.

He felt foolish. There had been no accidents in the basement, no Candy lying unconscious by the washing machine. He thought about Candy lying unconscious in the bathtub and started for the hall.

"Where's your mother?" he said. His voice rasped with fear.

The terrible dread rose up in him. Christ—you never knew what was going to happen—crazies that preyed on women and broke into houses in broad daylight, burglars, junkies desperate for money. Halfway down the hall, he heard struggling sounds, a woman's smothered cries. He broke into a run clumsily, holding Emma against his side. The doorknob to the bedroom wouldn't turn. He kicked the door open.

The bedroom was in twilight, the curtains drawn, the air chilled by the roaring air conditioner. His wife was struggling, squealing underneath someone on the bed. In no more time than it took to lunge into the room, the sight seared itself upon his brain. Naked muscular legs straining against her body, the convulsive thrusting of white buttocks as he shoved himself into her repeatedly.

He knew he would kill him. As Topper's momentum carried him against the bed, the tangle of thrashing flesh exploded, separated into Candy and a wild-eyed boy with long hair. Topper grabbed for him and missed. Candy screamed, a shriek that rose like skyrockets filling the room with sound. The rapist fell over the far side of the bed and disappeared. Candy bounded up in the bed, bands of naked white flesh against tanned skin, her face contorted.

"Oh—Top, no! Oh, my God—Topper, *wait!*"

And in Topper at that moment, muddled and almost blind with rage, the desire to kill was stopped, only for a fraction of an indrawn breath, to think, to say—not rape, not violence done.

"Topper!" Candy was screaming. "Don't—Topper, I *love* you! Topper, oh, God, I really love you, I really love you!" She bounced up and down in the middle of the bed with panicky shrieks, her breasts swaying.

It burst on him then that there had been no Candy lying dead or injured, nor yet pinned and mauled by some obscene attacker in the bedroom. The boy crouched against the wall on the far side of the bed, hands up in a gesture almost of supplication, his mouth ajar. Topper started toward him. The boy slid down the wall and disappeared under the bed.

The door to the master bath was open, and Candy ran to it, her long hair streaming, arms flailing, still shrieking madly. The boy came out from under the bed on the far side and got to his hands and knees and then to his feet and bolted for the bedroom door. Before Topper could get to him, he was in the hall. Running footsteps pounded through the house.

Topper charged after him. They raced through the kitchen. The naked figure careened off the wall in the family room, leaped the three steps down into the garage, and shot outside and onto the front lawn. Topper gained on him. They went around the corner of the house, water spraying under their feet from the storm-wet grass. The German shepherd from next door joined them, barking wildly, snapping at Topper's legs. The naked boy jumped over Emma's plastic swimming pool in a desperate bound and raced off through the grassy sward of the backyards of Magnolia Drive. In seconds, his brown and white body was out of sight.

Topper turned and ran back to his house, his ears filled with a thin wailing like a cat trapped somewhere. He slammed through the kitchen. Candy was in the hall outside the bedroom struggling into a bathrobe. When she saw him, she screamed again and ran back into the room. Topper lunged after, caught her before she could get inside the master bathroom and close the door on him. He slammed her up against the wall. He had to be careful, he knew. He was shaking all over. He was strong enough to kill her if he hit her. He had to be careful.

"The baby—" Candy howled. She flapped her hands.

The thin wailing was Emma, upside down under his arm.

"Goddamn you," Topper groaned.

His wife in bed with some kid. He still could not believe it. This was his own bedroom—his socks were still on the floor from morning; there was the torn and disordered bed, the clock radio playing on the night table. It had to be some dream. He set Emma carefully on her feet, and she staggered on her fat legs. She sat down, eyes glazed. Candy slumped weeping by the bathroom door.

The telephone rang.

It *was* the telephone bell, shrill and pure, clamoring in his head. He moved away. His hands were shaking as he picked up the receiver. As though programed, he said into the instrument, "What?"

Emma was screaming now full voice, and Candy wept loudly. He could hardly hear.

On the other end of the line, Fred Lightfoot said, "Could I speak to Mrs. James, please?"

The staff writer for *Finance* magazine recognized the sounds of mayhem he had come to associate with this particular number in the background.

"Say, is everything all right out there?" he wanted to know.

As he heard these words, everything was revealed to Topper in devastating clarity. He held the telephone receiver away from him and stared at it, at this mechanism of malevolence and betrayal.

"You son of a bitch," Topper roared into it. "What are you—number *two* in line for my bed—or goddamned number *ten?*"

The receiver clicked in his hand.

Part 3

/* ACCEPTABLE
                HAZARD */

10

At 11 P.M. on a Friday night in August, the flight line was almost deserted. The sky-splitting thunder of fighter jet traffic that punctured the daylight hours was stilled. The rows of F-15 Eagles parked on the concrete apron were inert, curiously remote silhouettes. A moonless dark lay over the airfield, broken by the blue and white beads of taxiway and runway lights and the bright glass bowl of the Langley Air Traffic Control tower hanging suspended in the distance. A few lights of late-working personnel showed in the 94th Tactical Fighter Squadron building just inside the gate marked "Fighter Country" and in the low, concrete structure across the darkened parking lot where the 27th and 17th squadrons shared quarters.

Beyond the squadron buildings and in the work area in front of the hangars, a battery of Light-Alls illuminated an F-15 and a ground crew working at its open panels. In spite of the hour, it was still hot and unpleasantly humid. The ground crews were in nonregulation shorts, and some of the men had stripped off their T-shirts.

Lieutenant Colonel Roger Gazenove came out of the rear door of the 17th Squadron building, followed by the tall figure of Major Topper James. The latter was in full flight gear and carried his helmet in one hand and a small DOP bag with personal effects in the other. Major James had just remarked that he had not yet received a copy of his TDYs, his Orders for Temporary Duty.

"They'll show up," Lieutenant Colonel Gazenove assured

him. "Somebody will find you and hand you your TDYs in the john, or at breakfast, or whenever it is you've just about forgotten them. It never fails."

As they passed to one side of the brightly lighted F-15 and the maintenance crews at work in its wire-filled belly, Roger Gazenove stole a glance at his flight leader. He was reminded of something that had bothered him a few moments before, as they were having a final cup of coffee in the squadron ready room. It was the proper time to take stock of small things, and, God knows, he thought, TDYs that came down the tube from Air Force General Staff, Pentagon, even those relayed quite informally by telephone as these had been, demanded a small last-minute flap about the pilot chosen and the potential quality of his performance. And there was something in Topper now and had been for the past week that was difficult to put your finger on, but it was there. Some loss of fine edge, he worried, that probably no one but himself would notice. Damn, he thought—it would have to be Topper. He couldn't think of anybody less approachable.

Lieutenant Colonel Gazenove hated signs of domestic problems. He didn't feel equipped to deal with them, even under a squadron commander's obligation to look after his people. It was a damned touchy area. Troubles at home that could lead to separation or divorce were, according to the strict interpretation of Air Force doctrine, a matter of a fighter pilot's fitness report. And the recommended procedure was to set the Flight Surgeon on the trail of the suspect for some covert observations, looking for loss of concentration, moodiness, difficulty in getting along with other squadron members, or anything that would reflect on combat ability. If there was trouble, it generated a verbal report by the Flight Surgeon to the Squadron Commander on the nature of the difficulty, its roots, and how it was affecting the individual's overall performance. Followed by a sit-down meeting with the psychiatrist—there was always one of those around—for advice about ventilating one's feelings and the dangers of suppressed emotional distress. Hell, Lieutenant Colonel Gazenove thought irritably, that sort of thing worked only in theory. Fighter jocks were prickly bastards. If they wanted to battle with their wives, if their personal lives were turning into pure hell as a result, it was their own damned business. And if you were fool enough to bring it up, you got the standard answer: I've got it under control, so don't worry.

It was never as simple as that. And with Topper James, even less so. His wife, Candy, was a nice girl; in Lieutenant Colonel Gazenove's opinion, not too bright, certainly too attractive for her own good, but nevertheless an amiable, appealing young thing. And there was a little girl, too. Topper was a hard man to know. The qualities which led a man to the top-rated position in the squadron—drive, concentration, near obsessive commitment to the job—were not necessarily those which contributed to a happy home life. Wives, the squadron commander well knew, got restless. And it was not only confined to the young and beautiful ones, either. Another man, Lieutenant Colonel Gazenove thought, might be more experienced where women were concerned, more perceptive—hell, it was hard to tell. But he was sure Topper's wife was crazy about him. Then what was it all about? he wondered testily. The question was rhetorical. He'd seen this sort of thing too many times before, not to know what it was.

The two men skirted the dark shape of the last F-15 on the last row of the flight line and started out into the undefined black of the taxiway area. The late hour, the dark, made their business all the more concealed. The squadron commander looked once more at his flight leader. The strain was still there, but once the temporary duty assignment was underway, he knew it would disappear. Topper had a remarkable quality, an ability to blank out under pressure everything but the business at hand. Probably all that was on his mind at the moment was a curiosity as to what in hell this summons to Washington was all about.

In the middle of Friday, the message had come in by telephone from the commander of the First Tactical Fighter Wing: "Don't make any plans, and call your wife. You have special TDY for the next few days." There would be a T-39 transport at Langley at 2300 hours. All flight gear required. Minimum personal effects—the shaving kit and a change of underwear kept ready in the DOP bag.

Ahead of them, the lights of a small transport descended to landing. The T-39 touched down and rolled to the end of the runway and taxied toward them. It finally rolled to a stop some distance away and shut down one engine to wait.

They quickened their steps, finally broke into a jog. They ran the two hundred yards or so to where the T-39 waited. As they got close, a door opened in the side, and an Air Force Sergeant, in a crisp summerweight uniform of shortsleeved shirt and blue trousers, jumped to the ground. He took Topper's DOP bag and threw it aboard. A small wind was blowing, stirring up the dust of the taxiway. The shriek of the idling engine made conversation impossible; Roger Gazenove clapped Topper on the back and saw him climb aboard. As he turned inside the door of the T-39 to look back, Lieutenant Colonel Gazenove, both hands held out before him, gave him the traditional thumbs-up salute in farewell. Topper's teeth flashed in the dark as he smiled.

Lucky bastard, Roger Gazenove thought. The TDY was something classified from the looks of it and bound to be interesting. He stepped back as the T-39 started its second engine. Wasting no time. In a roar of wind and noise, the transport started toward the active runway.

Thirty minutes later, the T-39 touched down at Andrews Air Force Base outside Washington, D.C. Late night traffic was heavy, and it was a good thirty minutes before the T-39 received clearance from ground control to move to its destination down what seemed like miles of secondary taxiways to a vast, darkened area of hangars and maintenance outbuildings. It rolled to a stop, and the Sergeant sprang out of his seat and prepared to open the door containing small portable steps. The Air Force Major at the controls of the T-39 shut down both engines; it was suddenly earsplittingly quiet. From somewhere in the dark came the night sounds of frogs. A staff car was parked not more than fifty feet away. A civilian in a light-colored business suit, carrying an attaché case, started toward the T-39, followed by a stocky man in an Air Force summer uniform with shoulder tabs which, when he was close enough, showed him to be a Lieutenant Colonel.

"Major," the civilian said, peering through the dark. His eyes found the nameplate on the flight suit. "Major James," he said. He was a thin man, and the light misting rain collected on his eyeglasses. "Welcome aboard. This," he said with a gesture of his hand, "is Lieutenant Colonel Bongo Irwin."

*　*　*

The ride in the staff car was short, bringing them to the side
of a giant hangar, its shape looming indistinctly in the darkness.
Lieutenant Colonel Irwin made use of the time by studying
Topper in silence. Once out of the staff car, they entered the
area around the hangar cordoned off with a red rope, denoting
a classified area. A security guard turned a flashlight on their
faces before waving them on. They climbed an open metal
staircase on the outside hangar wall that led to a brightly lighted
hallway. The Lieutenant Colonel led the way, opened an office
door, and gestured for them to pass in.

The office was blinding after the dark outside. It was large,
sparsely furnished with only a few chairs, a large standard-
issue gray metal desk, and a drafting board set against the far
wall. Two walls were covered with scale drawings of advanced-
design military aircraft: fighters with the new forward-swept
wings, bombers with X-shaped wing design to enable them to
achieve vertical takeoff and landing, strange objects that looked
like cruise missiles but that had cockpit pods for manned flight.
And there were photographs of the air superiority F-15 Eagle,
the single-engine F-16 fighter jet, the Navy's F-18, the SR-71
high-altitude spy plane, and several others that Topper, staring,
could not identify.

Another civilian rose from a chair as they came in, a tall
man in shirtsleeves with a tired air, his tie loosened against the
muggy Washington heat. The presence that dominated the office was, however, that of a natty Air Force full Colonel in
impeccable summer blues, a medium-sized man of almost over-
poweringly lean fitness. His face wore a pleasantly open expression. The Colonel stood with his weight balanced, leaning
slightly forward on the balls of his feet. When he saw Topper,
he smiled electrically.

"Major James." There was no hesitancy in this voice. He
stuck out his hand. "I'm Geordie Roos, SAMSO, Pentagon.
You've met"—he gestured—"Bongo Irwin, our Operations
Development Supervisor here. And John Rosewicz"—he in-
dicated the tall man in shirtsleeves—"engineer from Mc-
Donnell Douglas."

The civilian in the gray summerweight suit seated himself
unobtrusively in a chair in the corner of the office as though
he did not expect to be introduced. He folded his hands over
the top of the attaché case in his lap.

Colonel Roos's handshake was firm and abrupt. His eyes continued to appraise Topper openly. The Colonel from the Air Force Space and Missile Systems Organization strode to the desk and turned to face them, bracing his hands on its edge. He crossed his legs at the ankles and balanced delicately, tensely, on his narrow buttocks.

"I suppose," Colonel Roos began, "you're wondering why you're here." The well-worn words did not seem to bother him. He smiled again.

As though this was a cue, a small wiry man wearing Master Sergeant's stripes and heavy horn-rimmed glasses entered the office and placed a stack of papers at the Colonel's left hand as it rested on the desk edge. The Sergeant drew attentively to one side.

The Colonel went on, quickly replacing the engaging smile with an expression of penetrating gravity: "Well, Major, we've called you in for something we think you'll find very interesting." Without looking down, the Colonel's fingers touched the first paper on the stack beside him and the Sergeant deftly slipped it out and placed it in his hand. "What recommended you to us was first, your experience in the SR-71 as an instructor stateside in '70 and '71, plus your two Thailand-based overflights in the Blackbirds a year later. You liked them?" The words were less a question than a statement; the Colonel's head snapped up, looking for the response.

"Very much." The still-secret SR-71 spy planes had had a number of problems, in spite of their 80,000-foot cruise altitude and record-setting speeds of Mach Three. But, Topper thought, it was the Colonel's job to know that. And not his place to elaborate on past history just to show how smart he was.

There was a small silence, and Colonel Roos said approvingly, "Good. Good."

"How long were you in them?" Lieutenant Colonel Irwin wanted to know.

"Two years and some months."

"Why did you get out?"

"The war was winding down. And the F-15s were coming up."

Lieutenant Colonel Irwin raised his eyebrows but said nothing.

"Difficult times after the war," Colonel Roos said quickly.

"We lost a lot of good men going out of the service. Shifted around too many inside it, declining career horizons and so forth. I'm glad our computer updated your record for our use. Now," he said, "after your tour in Nam, you went into operational liaison with Mac Air test pilots on the F-15 demonstration flight. And I have your report"—the Sergeant quickly put a bound pamphlet into his outstretched hand—"entitled, 'Bringing the F-15 to Operational Readiness,' which you did with Captain James Wray in the First Tactical Fighter Wing. Outstanding job—*outstanding*," Colonel Roos said, putting it to one side.

Topper said carefully, "Thank you, sir."

"And I see you've had some limited contact with NASA scramjet development through Eagle-Intel."

The Colonel fixed Topper with his electric stare. Scramjets, Topper thought, surprised.

"You've done admirable work so far, Major. Ever consider applying for DARPA?"

"No, sir." The Air Force's Department of Advanced Research Projects had never really interested him. But Topper thought of Moonbird McAllister whiling away his time in the squadron ready room, waiting for the next call to the simulator. The breaks, he thought wryly.

The Colonel reached for the next paper, which the Sergeant placed in his hand. The tanned, youthful face surveyed the group in the room keenly.

"What we have for you is an F-15 Eagle with some interesting modifications, a dual propulsion system—specifically an afterburner incorporating the supersonic ram jet engine, NASA's scramjet—which goes operational at a defined altitude. The Eagle's current turbofan engine is capable of boosting it up to where we want it to go, say ninety thousand feet, and then computer functions will automatically make the transition to the SCRAMS. Our Eagle's been flight tested; we've got all the data we want from that phase. What we need now is an operational evaluation from someone who has both SR-71 experience in high-altitude, high-velocity flight and a knowledge of the Eagles' capabilities. We want evaluations of abnormalities, interesting reactions both pilotwise and equipmentwise—as much of the spectrum as you can give us."

"Presupposing there *are* abnormalities," the McDonnell Douglas engineer put in.

"You will find," Colonel Roos said crisply, "the next twenty-four hours will be unorthodox in more ways than one. We're going to require you to be extremely flexible. What we need is a generalist, and with your background, we believe you're our man."

There was a silence. Topper nodded.

Colonel Roos said, "Our demands are damned steep— you're going to have to be able to unplug from any current operational mindset and lock into an entirely new mode, one hundred percent, and with maximum mental and physical commitment. This is a low-visibility operation. I have to tell you that overall career perks will be, for the time being, minimal. But we're being watched by important eyes. Need I say more?"

The Sergeant held the next briefing paper ready, but the Colonel ignored it. His gaze rested intently on Major Topper James's face.

Topper said, after another small silence, "No, sir."

"Right," Colonel Roos responded quickly. "Now—one of the pressing concerns of the DoD right now is our capability for delivering rapid tactical air support to our NATO allies in the event of threatening movements emanating from and through the Iron Curtain countries. The buildup of the Soviet tank force in Eastern Europe is of major concern to NATO members, and we're constantly monitoring the situation. The United States wants to be able to guarantee our allies that we can support them, quickly and in strength, if the need arises. And our answer to this sort of challenge is rapid deployment of air superiority Eagles to reinforce NATO muscle. Which means—getting a strike force of F-15s to Europe in under two hours."

There was another silence. Topper finally said, "That sounds good."

Colonel Roos clapped his hands on his thighs emphatically. "Major, I like your attitude! It *is* good, damned good. And we're going to do it! And you're going to show that our Eagle force is operationally viable for our purposes. The modifications we've come up with are within the capability of current Air Force and industry effort without any consideration of radical design changes. We're just going to put some core and

intake conversions into the current afterburner systems in the
F-15 and go to SCRAMS. If you follow me. Now"—he turned
slightly to the Sergeant beside him—"Sergeant Bamberg here
has your familiarization and briefing material. You'll spend
some time studying the primary mission description ¯and
agenda. Tomorrow you'll do ground school with the Mac Air
engine team, and we've scheduled you for two hours before
lunch and two hours after lunch in the F-15 simulator here,
which has all our modifications. Bongo will give you all preflight and enroute material. Sunday 0500 hours is our time
target. Tomorrow at 1300 hours you'll go into the usual twelve-
hour rest, of which eight hours is, as usual, sleep time."

Colonel Roos stood away from the desk. Master Sergeant
Bamberg picked up Colonel Roos's raincoat and stood waiting.

"Fine. That's it!" Colonel Roos said dynamically. He
crossed the room, and as Topper quickly got to his feet, he put
his arm around Topper's shoulders. Colonel Roos was obliged
to reach up considerably, and the touch lingered only a second.
As his arm descended, Sergeant Bamberg slipped the raincoat
over his shoulders.

"Major, we're glad to have you aboard," the Colonel said.
"We have full confidence. John—Bongo—he's in your capable hands." He moved toward the door. "Sergeant Bamberg
will check in tomorrow and see what you need."

In a moment, Colonel Roos passed through the office door.
Sergeant Bamberg followed and closed it gently behind him.

Rosewicz, the McDonnell Douglas engineer, let out a groan
and then laughed.

Lieutenant Colonel Bongo Irwin crossed the office and sat
down in his chair behind the desk. He put his arms behind his
head and reached up and stretched. His swarthy face broke into
a smile.

"Relax, Major," he said. "The Second Coming isn't scheduled for another two or three weeks. By that time, you'll be
back at Langley."

The engineer stretched his legs out before him. "Bongo,"
he said with real interest, "what about that drink?"

Lieutenant Colonel Irwin picked up his telephone. The small
electric clock on the desk beside him showed the time, 1:35
A.M. "We can even have coffee if you want it." He looked at
Topper. "Major, what do you say?"

"Yes," Topper said. He felt the muscles at the back of his neck relax for the first time. "Scotch. Make it a double."

"Make it a triple, Major," the Mac Air man said. "They're going to cut you off in a couple of hours."

"I'll have a large bourbon and water," the Defense Department man said suddenly from the corner.

They went out into the hangar an hour later, feeling considerably more jovial, thanks to the drinks. The banks of overhead fluorescent lights filled the giant structure with a stale, late-night glare. An Air Force maintenance crewman was running a heavy-duty vacuum over the concrete floor in a routine foreign objects search, and the noise was deafening. Lieutenant Colonel Irwin yelled for him to shut it off.

"There it is," Rosewicz, the Mac Air engineer, said.

The Eagle sat in the center of the vast hangar surrounded by Light-Alls, portable generators, and the large metal boxes of air-conditioning units used to cool its electronic circuits while they were being worked on. The Eagle squatted like some huge bird of mythic, lightless dark.

"Damn, it's black," Topper James said.

"Meet Operation Nightwing." Lieutenant Colonel Irwin stood with his arms folded over his chest. "The antiradar covering replicates the SR-71's black, but like the SR-71, we can't guarantee that it's as effective as it should be. The problem here was to combine antiradar black with a light, semiporous element that we wanted to put to work for us. One that holds drag to a minimum but has some sloughing properties at high velocity. A little burnoff is useful in a pinch."

Topper touched the surface with his fingers. The texture of the Eagle's coating was like microscopically thin black styrofoam.

"And a pain in the ass," Lieutenant Colonel Irwin added. "You have no idea how much trouble putting a perfectly even coat of the stuff on this thing was. This is the third try. We had Blackbird specifications, but the spy planes are made of titanium. The Eagles are a mix of titanium and aluminum, so we weren't dealing with exactly the same kind of skin."

The Mac Air engineer was watching Topper. "One hundred thousand feet, the top of the atmospheric peel, will give you some burnoff under some conditions." He smiled. "The

Nightwing's not going to go suborbital, Major; we're not springing that on you," he said and laughed at the look on Topper's face. "But the Eagles are going to see some action as interim operational vehicles; that's the going idea." His hands moved together, struck, and bounced off with a clapping sound. "Although theoretically, intermittent propulsion from a scramjet mode could provide enough velocity to bounce it in and out."

"With another airframe," Lieutenant Colonel Irwin said shortly.

Topper gathered they were not talking at the moment about a rapid-tactical-air-support flight to some point in Europe.

"Am I going to be briefed on this?" he said.

The two men studied him. "Not exactly," Lieutenant Colonel Irwin said. "But it's not going to hurt. How much do you want to know?"

"Anything you want to tell me."

"Well, why not?" Bongo Irwin said. "We're going to go over all this in detail tomorrow, but I don't see why we can't have a little of the dog-and-pony show while we're at it." He looked at his watch. "I'll give you the short readout, so we can get you to bed pretty soon."

They went over the Nightwing Eagle thoroughly, climbing on its wings to look into the cockpit, mounting the crew chief's stand for a better look at the air intakes and the spikes that had been installed inside to close them at high altitudes, shutting down the turbofan system for the scramjet takeover. With the exception of new fuel gauges and readings and a boosted computer function, the Nightwing's cockpit was similar to that of squadron-operational Eagles. The canopy had a special sealer around its rim to insure the new pressurization system. The pilot was to wear a high-altitude pressure suit, nevertheless, as a backup.

The afterburners, Topper saw, were monsters. The tubes, extensions on the back of the Eagle's turbofan engines, provided additional power thrust when fuel was sprayed into them and ignited. The Nightwing's afterburners had been totally converted. They were longer, jutting three feet and more beyond the Nightwing's tail and encased in high-heat-resistant ceramic, the core lined with what the McDonnell Douglas engineer, Rosewicz, described as a layer of *inconel*.

"She's a little drag-ass," Lieutenant Colonel Irwin grunted. "You'll see when you get in the simulator."

The afterburners still functioned as afterburners at low altitudes, thanks to a computer-operated, dual-fuel override. At high altitudes, the computer switched to ram jet fuel for the SCRAM mode.

"Your afterburners are more or less auxiliary ram jet engines, anyway," Lieutenant Colonel Irwin said, "if you use the definition that a ram jet is a tube with fuel sprayed into it, with propulsion resulting from energy generated by gas blowing out the back end. As you know, afterburners are too damned fuel-energy-wasteful, except to use when your fighter needs a sudden kick of power. However, at high altitudes, the fuel being sprayed into a ram jet tube using the same principle is a hell of a lot more economical. The mix doesn't even need igniting—high air velocity does it for you. Since you've flown the SR-71 Blackbirds, you know we got a little bonus effect when the same thing happened—at their speeds, the air bypasses the compressors and starts functioning as simple rams. Which was a real find. However, don't think there weren't a million problems connected with our particular project." Lieutenant Colonel Irwin rubbed his chin ruefully. "Our first big problem was to provide two fuels, one for low-altitude air-density function and another when the tube is functioning as a supersonic ram jet, a SCRAM up where the air is thin. Fortunately, we started with a plus—the research labs at NASA had already developed a hydrogen mix that acts as a coolant for the extreme temperatures of the scramjets, as well as a fuel. What we came up with was a hydrogen-boron mix, although it was one long damned headache to work it out. Even with a principle as simple as spraying fuel into a tube to make it fly."

"Does it?" Topper said.

Bongo Irwin suddenly grinned. "Does a frog have a watertight ass? You bet it does. We've been through a year of test flights that say it really lays it on. The question is, *how* operational? Will it go up to ninety thousand feet and act like an Eagle? And shoot down nasty things the enemy has in orbit to frighten our Space Shuttle?"

"The hell you say," Topper said.

Lieutenant Colonel Irwin raised his eyebrows. "Why not? It's what we're basing our planning on. Our surveillance operations tell us the Soviet launch site at Plesetsk is still the busiest in the world—twenty-four orbiters this year and about six hundred twenty overall since they started putting them up. Tyuratam, the Kazakhstan site, checks in with twenty-six in the past twelve-month period, four hundred overall total. Compare that with the stuff the U.S. has shot into orbit—only fourteen from Vandenberg and Canaveral's only put up eighteen this year, and our overall total for all time is about seven hundred. Which puts us a respectable distance behind the Russians.

"Our intelligence breakdowns show military observation satellites account for most of the Soviet orbiters, but there was a sharp increase in store-dump communications hardware this year—those are your little beasts that pick up messages in one part of the world, record them and play them back on command later, your basic spy-in-the-sky function. But which can also serve as tactical real-time communicators in designated theaters of action—namely, war. To my way of thinking, the hard action is taking place up there. Our intel ops say they've identified six payloads the Russians have put up recently as 'A'- or 'C'-type rockets—electronic ferrets which go after anything they're ordered to. But we're really keeping a hard eye on their 'F'-class vehicle, which is a spin-off of their SS-9 missile. That one's being used exclusively for ocean surveillance, which means sub-hunting. There's some interceptor/destructors we wish we knew more about—especially since we seem to have lost some of our costly little spy orbiters rather mysteriously—and, of course, the well-known fractional bombardment stuff they have floating around. And we're still getting hot rumors that the Russians have got a space vehicle of their own ready to launch. We seem to be sweating that they may Sputnik us again before we can get the Space Shuttle's tiles glued on right.

"I can't tell you how unhappy that makes our R and D people—Geordie Roos got a report last month that a delta-wing orbiter, just like ours but not as large, had been undergoing drop tests from a Tu-95 Bear bomber over Siberia and that the Russians had a projected launch date of December. Everybody went into group therapy at NASA and nothing came of it, but they had a right to their breakdowns. It could happen. The

Soviets' Salyut-Soyuz series obviously set them up for some kind of competitive orbiter; that we know. It's going to be a damned busy place up there from now on, and God knows there's going to be a couple of surprises. Military Intel says the Russians are already using underground nuclear devices to power particle-beam weapons at their test site at Semipalatinsk. And we've just begun laser research."

Rosewicz, the Mac Air engineer, cleared his throat. "Well, what we have here is a proposal that the Eagles will go up to ninety thousand feet and launch antisatellite weapons at orbiting threats. The ASATS are the current hot stuff, miniature spacecraft with their own independent systems. The going model weighs only about thirty-five pounds, but it kills by sheer impact—ASAT velocity is anywhere from ten to forty thousand feet per second, depending upon how and where launched. But no warheads necessary."

"We're betting," Lieutenant Colonel Irwin said, "that the Nightwing Eagle can take the ASATs up, sustain altitude and speed, lock on target, and tell the ASAT to go get 'em. The key word right now is IOV—Interim Operational Vehicle, a role tailor-made for the F-15s if they test out. Hell, it's the logical move; once the Space Shuttle gets into orbit; we're going to have to scramble like hell to fill the gap between where we are now and where we'll be when the suborbitals— the Hot Victors—take over."

"Whole thing's Geordie Roos's baby." Rosewicz had carried his drink out into the hangar; now he lifted his paper cup and drained it. "Our Colonel figures, given the small size of the ASATs and their lethal potential, the Eagles have their dream payload."

"Don't worry," Lieutenant Colonel Irwin said; "you haven't got any ASATs loaded on the Nightwing. Just take it to France at nine-zero-zero altitude and give us a good report on it."

Topper looked from Rosewicz to Irwin and back again. "Which one?" he said.

Lieutenant Colonel Irwin laughed. "Hell, both of them, every damned thing—even when you feel like you have to go to potty. We need it all. The rapid tactical air support to NATO allies is only Geordie Roos's cover story. What we're really doing is seeing if the F-15 is a launch vehicle for our little satellite-killers." He paused. "What does Geordie Roos call it?" he asked the Mac Air engineer.

John Rosewicz lifted his empty cup and stared at it thoughtfully.

"I think he calls it killing two birds with one stone," he said.

Colonel George T. Roos's staff car passed out of the main gate of Andrews Air Force Base and into Suitland Parkway at a little past 1:30 A.M. After a short distance, Sergeant Bamberg turned the automobile into the entrance ramp of the Capital Beltway, heading for Colonel Roos's home in Arlington, Virginia. As soon as they were onto the nearly empty expressway, Colonel Roos reached up and switched on the staff car's overhead light. Sergeant Bamberg in front made a quick movement to adjust the rearview mirror and keep the reflected light out of his eyes.

Colonel Roos reached under the back seat and pulled out his leather briefcase. He put it in his lap and opened it and, from a deeply ingrained work habit rather than a desire to read anything at this hour of the morning, riffled through its contents. Sergeant Bamberg organized Colonel Roos's paperwork with admirable efficiency and neatness, with attention to order of importance: the top-most paper was a Department of Defense eyes-only report of DoD secret committee meetings on an alternate engine program for advanced tactical aircraft.

Oh, hell, Colonel Roos thought wearily. The Nightwing Eagle was ready to go, and here, he saw, was the DoD still wallowing in its seemingly endless troubles concerning the F100X engines.

By the wavering car light, Colonel Roos lifted the transcript of the committee meeting and started to skim it. He was halfway through the top-page summary when he was brought up short in surprise.

Now they've done it, Colonel Roos thought grimly. The Air Force, according to the transcript summary, was awarding an eighty-million-dollar contract to the General Electric Corporation for the prototype development of an alternate engine for both the Navy's F-14 Tomcat—which had major but somehow unpublicized troubles—and the Air Force's problem Trueham engines in the F-15 Eagles.

Colonel Roos reread the summary, frowning deeply. The Navy had done a good job of keeping its own engine disasters under wraps, thanks in part to powerful friends in Congress. But the troubles were bound to surface, since the TF30 engines in the Tomcat were racking up figures as bad as or worse than the Air Force's. And would—Colonel Roos knew—get even worse when the numbers came out on the Navy's not yet operational and brand-new F-18s. Nothing but bad news as far as super-advanced engines were concerned. Now he saw, reading the testimony of Dr. Richard W. Parsons, the Defense Department's Undersecretary for Research and Engineering, the DoD had out their patch-up kit—a whole new fighter engine program designated F101X which would be a marriage between the F101 engine developed for the late, lamented B-1 bomber program and the F404 engine developed for the Navy's new fighter, the F-18.

Colonel Roos snorted. Evidently somebody wasn't up on the latest reports on the Navy's F-18 problems. That looked as if it was shaping up as a lemon, too. The thing was too damned complicated for this sort of work, in his opinion. Although he was forced to admit they all had their backs to the wall on this one.

What these DoD secret committee meetings always failed to bring up front was that engines in fighter jets were chronic problems—fighters were damned tricky beasts built for speed and maneuverability, and their crotchets had to be evaluated as acceptable hazards. Hell, there was a long history of this sort of thing, Colonel Roos told himself, dating back to the first jet fighters of the late forties. The first of *those* things had a propensity for blowing up on the runway when the cartridges ignited the engines.

The pages of the report before him were filled with the usual testimony by Air Force experts as to what had gone wrong. Colonel Roos read them impatiently, stopping when he came to the name of General Almon Banks, head of Air Force Research Development and Acquisition. "Big Bird" Banks reported at length about durability and maintainability problems in the Eagles' engines which, unfortunately, had caused less aircraft availability, substantially reducing operational rates. In plain English, half the Eagles were on the ground at any given time for maintenance. "If a major problem were to crop up in the next few years in the F-15s' engines," General Banks was quoted as saying, "we would have to stand down our entire fighter force."

Now what the hell, Colonel Roos thought irritably. He didn't know what Big Bird Banks was trying to say; he couldn't take the fuzzy statement at face value. The engine troubles were, as Banks well knew, in the here and now, and no need to make statements implying that they might have to ground all their fighters at some indefinite time in the future. Colonel Roos was an ex-fighter pilot himself; he had a vast distaste for this sort of doubletalk, especially from Big Bird Banks, whose disappointment at not making head of NATO was well known.

General Banks had continued, "I think it's fair to say that maybe we've tried to go too far too fast, and we are now reaping the rewards." General Banks was also of the opinion, and so told the DoD committee, that aircraft engine production and management left much to be desired. It was time, Big Bird said, that the military got a better deal from industry.

Colonel Roos sat back in his seat and closed his eyes. He was not exceptionally tired; fatigue was a matter of what he would allow himself to feel in an hour or so when he finally got home and into bed. Right now he was simply pissed off. The higher levels of the military, by the very nature and demands of the structure, were full of politically minded assholes, nonleadership types whose staying powers—rather than talent or competence—propelled them toward command-decision circles. Plus the assets of nonchallenging mediocrity and influential friends. Colonel Roos had seen too much talent discouraged and lost not to believe it. Now here was Big Bird Banks, he thought, anxious as hell to get his ass out of the wringer in the matter of the Trueham contract he had, perhaps deliberately, let get by him. And from the looks of it, the Defense Department was in it with both feet, trying to fix things up by letting still another contract. Which could send them all down the tubes.

What was not written into the DoD committee meeting transcript, of course, was that General Banks was no particular friend of the Air Force's Space and Missile Systems Organization. General Banks was known to be very friendly with the Chairman of the Senate Armed Services Committee; the rumor pipeline had it that Senator Glass, along with other powerful figures in Congress and industry, were moving to promote a new agency within the Department of Defense to be called SPAD—Space Programs Support and Defense—which would oversee the development of future military space operations. And SPAD was a part of the newly proposed Industrialization of Space program and the Administration's attempt to rally the nation's industrial community behind a massive appropriation for space exploration and expansion. Which, the current economic picture being what it was, the taxpayers and Congress would otherwise balk at.

To Colonel Roos, the SPAD idea was that old demon "reorganization" again under a new guise—one proposed, it would seem, for the purpose of shifting military space weapons and development from SAMSO to SPAD and into a bigger sphere of political and big business influence. Under the Industrialization of Space program, it was reasonable to assume that big corporations would want maximum control for their money—but any fool, Colonel Roos thought, could see there was a real danger in a lot of military departments being swallowed whole in the process. And there was too much at stake for SAMSO, at least, to struggle through months, even years, of attempted co-option, with the not unlikely prospect of ending up under Big Bird Banks's command.

No way, Colonel Roos told himself.

What was shaping up, as much as he could gather from the DoD committee report, was an eventual leak of some pretty nasty problems with hot new military fighters that were sure to make the public howl. He couldn't understand why whatever it was couldn't be worked on quietly, as these problems had been in the past. There had been the same engine problems with the F-4s, which had gone on to become the reliable workhorses of fighter operations. Of course, that had been a Navy program, and the Navy had a way of carrying out its programs successfully in spite of bobbles. The Air Force, as with the F-111s, had never been so lucky.

Ultimately, Colonel Roos knew, part of the glory of being a fighter jock was mastering your damned volatile, unpredictable, high-performance equipment. But the figures—if true—on maintainability were pretty bad. That was going to make them all suffer.

If the SPAD program got off the ground, if Congress shaped

up on the whole Industrialization of Space bill, he could see that his own SAMSO department was going to have to plan accordingly. Fortunately, SAMSO was in a position of strength, its projects a testimony to its ongoing effectiveness: ASATs, the projected manned orbiting military posts, lasers and particle beam generators, unmanned space vehicles—the catalogue was crammed full. And virtually unassailable. Barring, of course, the unpredictable, sometimes quixotic actions of a Congress which often set itself perversely to upset the military's best-planned apple cart. No one in the Air Force had forgotten the B-1 bomber debacle.

The problem was that the struggle for dominance in space had been quietly heating up in recent months. The Soviets had their own ASAT systems now, and Soviet antisatellite weapons were a very real threat to anything the U.S. had in orbit. When the Space Shuttle went up, it would be highly vulnerable. Which raised an interesting point, Colonel Roos knew: since, under current international agreements, the destruction of any satellite would not be an act of war, the United States—theoretically, at least—would have little recourse if the Soviets used their ASATs to shoot down U.S. orbiters. Until the Space Shuttle got up there, it would be hard to determine what U.S. satellites were being picked off and by what. Although it wouldn't be too damned hard to guess.

At the moment, SAMSO was still in good shape and continuing with its impressive agenda of missiles and space systems, Colonel Roos consoled himself. Operation Nightwing, under the direction of SAMSO's energetic and resourceful Brigadier General Latimer Holmes, was going to come up with results that would hopefully push offstage the current DoD hysteria and ass-covering about engine shortfalls. Operation Nightwing couldn't refute all the hard facts of a billion-dollar engine goof—which was Big Bird Banks's domain, anyway—but it would help.

Colonel Roos's hopes, at the moment, were pinned on Major Eric James of the USAF 17th Tactical Fighter Squadron.

Strange son of a bitch, Colonel Roos thought suddenly. There was something at work there under that handsome, stone-cold surface that might be—just *might* be—unaccounted for. But phenomenal ability, to judge from his computer profile. Top-rated. And a fastburner, to make major at thirty-three.

Colonel Roos shrugged. As long as he can fly like his ass is on fire, he told himself.

The third time Emma screamed, Candy James stumbled from bed, too sleepy to come awake instantly as she had the first few times. She careened clumsily out into the hall between the bedrooms. She heard the choking noises of Emma vomiting, broken by piercing shrieks when Emma could get her breath.

"Oh, my God, oh, my God," Candy cried, hurrying into Emma's room.

She lifted her exhausted, wailing daughter from the crib and wiped her face with the clean sheet she had put on just an hour ago. She carried Emma into the bathroom, turned on the light, and, holding the child on her hip, bent to turn on the bathtub taps. Emma threw up again, spattering the floor and the wash-basin. Candy managed to get a struggling Emma into the tub. It was a virus, some virulent summer thing, and Candy herself had been sick with it the day before. Emma, screaming, thrashed around in her grip, her fine yellow hair in sticky ringlets full of regurgitated food. Candy tried to sponge Emma's hair with a washcloth, but her daughter only grabbed at her hands and screamed louder.

"Oh, *damn*," Candy said. Emma's belly sucked in tensely with her howls. Her hands were clenched, her body wracked with shivering. "Oh, honey, don't," Candy pleaded.

She picked up her daughter, wrapped her in a bath towel, and carried her into her bedroom. She put Emma on the bed. Emma sat hunched, hiccuping. The room smelled of vomit, and it was cold. Candy couldn't face putting Emma back in bed with her.

"Mamma," Emma said. She reached up and locked her arms around Candy's neck.

"Oh, sweetie—if you just didn't smell so bad." Candy's own stomach was still not in good shape.

She carried Emma out of the bedroom, into the hallway, and through the living room. It was still dark, although a faint light showed through the living room windows. The house was breathless and hot.

Candy unlocked the screen door with one hand and carried Emma outside. The flat-topped pine trees that edged the marsh-lands were showing their shapes against a lightening sky. Candy sat down on the front steps, holding Emma in her arms. The mimosa trees on the lawn of the house across the way were in bloom, their fuzzy blossoms spots of pale color against the massed shadows of leaves. A faint mist drifted over green lawns. The pretty, comfortable homes of Pinecrest subdivision rested in postcard neatness among winding streets, shade trees, the bright plots of flower beds.

"Mamma," Emma said. She curled wetly against Candy. The warmth of her body came through Candy's thin nightdress. Emma put her mouth in Candy's neck. "Emma sick," her voice said, muffled.

Candy sighed. She didn't feel very well herself. A sense of curious desolation enveloped her, compounded by the empty house, the empty street, the silence. "It's a mean old virus," she told her daughter. And the standard reassurance: "It's all better now, hon."

Across the street, the screen door of the brick ranch-style house opened, and Mrs. Tomlinson stepped out, looking for the morning paper. Candy rested her chin on top of Emma's head and watched her neighbor. Mrs. Tomlinson gave no sign that she saw Candy. She stared fixedly into the street. Then she turned and went back inside, and the screen door closed.

Candy's lips trembled. At any other time, Mrs. Tomlinson would have rushed across the street in quick sympathy, wanting to know what was the matter. But everybody on Magnolia Drive had seen Rick coming and going for weeks, had made note of it, had known what was going on. All the neighbors had seen, or at least heard, the horrible row. Knew of Rick's flight, naked, through their backyards.

I must have been crazy, Candy thought in a rush of misery.

"Daddy *gone,*" Emma said, against her throat.

Candy choked back a desire to cry. "He'll be back, sweetheart," she said finally. "Daddy's gone on TDY."

She considered the words, Daddy's gone on TDY. Air Force children grew up learning the catchword for Temporary Duty before they could understand it. Mamma. Daddy. TDY. For a brief second, Candy felt the sobs rising. The depths of her suffering astonished her. She had never in her whole life imagined she could be so desperately unhappy. Topper had said, "When I come back, we're going to have to work something out." *Separation, divorce,* her mind told her.

Maybe Topper will forgive you, her mother had said.

Forgive me, Candy thought. The idea, even now, seemed eminently unfair.

Emma had gone to sleep. Candy looked down at her daughter. There are women, she told herself, who get divorced every day. They rented apartments, got jobs, hired babysitters, entered whole new lifestyles. They claimed they were happier. But, she thought, they just seemed to drop out of life; no one saw them anymore; they entered shells of loneliness, otherness. She had been married almost ten years. Almost a third of her life spent with Topper, sleeping in the same bed with him, talking to him, waiting for him. What will I do? she asked herself.

A car turned into the street. It was the first of the early rides, the car pool collecting its members for the first shift at Langley and NASA. The birds had begun to sing loudly, detecting dawn light in the trees. A large collie dog came ambling down from the direction of Pinecrest Road. It paused and lifted its leg beside some azalea bushes. The car passed slowly. The faces inside turned to stare at her.

Candy drew Emma closer and bent her head to her daughter's wet, smelly curls, hiding her face.

11

Major Topper James opened the door of the refrigerator and reached for a can of Miller's *Lite*. There were four kinds of beer to choose from, including two imported varieties, but Topper elected to stay with a low calorie Miller's. The absence of any hard liquor was apparent, but there was enough food in the refrigerator to keep him happy for a week: pizza and sandwich steaks in the freezer, cheese, cold cuts, and a bowl of fruit prettily arranged underneath. There were several plastic pitchers of fruit juice and a half gallon of Tang, "the astronauts' drink."

Topper closed the refrigerator and went back to the living room with his can of beer. The crew quarters assigned to him in the research hangar at Andrews Air Force Base were, by military norms, quite luxurious. *Outstanding*, he thought, and had to smile. The apartment consisted of a sitting room, bedroom, and combined kitchen-dinette, furnished in cheerful orange and blue Motel Modern down to the familiar lithographed copy of the New York skyline at dusk over the sitting room couch.

What one didn't notice—at least at first—was that the rooms were soundproofed, air-conditioned, windowless, completely sealed off from the rest of the world. And a uniformed Air Force security guard stood at the door outside.

Topper looked at his watch. He had gone into crew rest at Andrews at 1500 hours on a hot, sunny August afternoon just as the Red Sox and the New York Yankees were beginning their game on television. Lieutenant Colonel Bongo Irwin's schedule had been half an hour late all day, beginning with the delay in getting into the flight simulator that morning due to computer-programming difficulties; otherwise, things were rolling smoothly. Most of the credit went to Bongo Irwin. The Research Operations Officer had demonstrated that he ran his domain with an efficient, if iron hand.

Dinner had arrived on a wheeled cart outside the door promptly at five-thirty, an excellent meal of prime ribs of beef, baked potato, and salad, and he had finished it off in the company of Lieutenant Colonel Irwin, Rosewicz, the Mac Air engineer, and two members of the engine crew from McDonnell Douglas who had worked, and were still working, on the Nightwing Eagles' modifications. They had reviewed the briefing material again while he was eating his dinner, updating it all from the notes taken through the ground school sessions and the four hours he had spent before and after lunch in the flight simulator. The pile of briefing papers was scattered now on the coffee table, and some of them spilled over onto the couch: descriptions of the boron-hydrogen fuel which would supply the ram jet system; the cockpit computer displays and computerized systems checks he would have to monitor in flight, talking into the compactly designed tape recorder which had been provided for him; preflight checklists; and at least and literally a hundred other items. A good part of the evening's work had been spent familiarizing him with the tape recorder. The mike button would be taped to his throat and automatically bypassed the radio transmission mike in his oxygen mask by a series of complicated sensors which determined whether or not Topper was using the radio.

"We want a record of everything that's going on," Bongo Irwin had said. "Just think out loud all the way into Cherbourg."

Topper stood in the middle of the living room in the bathrobe which had been provided for him, sipping at his can of beer and watching the television screen. The Yankee-Red Sox game had ended, and now the "CBS Evening News" was on, the set filled with the voice and face of Dan Rather. There was nothing more for him to do that he could think of; the last go-through of briefing papers had been scrupulously thorough. The pressure suit he would put on at 3 A.M., a mylar and nomex maze of air tubes and heating circuits, was laid out carefully on a stand in the bedroom, along with his helmet, jock strap, and urine bag. Thinking of the latter, he was reminded of all he had had to eat for dinner and the inevitable steak and egg breakfast in the morning. Not exactly a low-residue diet, especially in the quantities consumed. He would have to make sure his bowels moved before going to bed and again in the morning. Tomorrow he would be in no place to be distracted by a sudden call of nature.

Topper sat down in a chair before the television set, holding his beer. He watched Dan Rather make an announcement of a CBS News Special at eight on the Space Shuttle, now only weeks away from a launch date. The screen flashed to an artist's animated simulation of the Space Shuttle in flight. The spaceship rotated around the earth against a deep blue sky filled with unblinking stars.

The meaning of Lieutenant Colonel Irwin's words as they had inspected the Nightwing Eagle in the hangar a little over thirteen hours ago came back to him. Colonel Geordie Roos had said the flight's function was to demonstrate the feasibility of rapid tactical air support for NATO allies. But the operations officer and the Mac Air engineer had made it plain that Topper was taking the Nightwing up in a high-altitude, high-velocity test that would show the Nightwing's capability to go operational just inside the earth's atmosphere and launch antisatellite weapons against any threat the Soviets might put in orbit, such as communications jamming satellites, manned military space stations, nuclear-armed satellites. Rumors, Topper knew, said the last were already there.

Deliberately, cautiously, he let himself think: Christ! I'm part of all this.

The two years he had spent with the supersecret spy planes, the SR-71s, the first year spent bringing the new F-15 Eagles operational—all that paled by comparison with what he was about to do. After tomorrow, it was not unreasonable to assume that his name would be down forever in Air Force Flight Research: *"On August 20th, Major Eric T. James took a specially modified F-15 Eagle equipped with a dual propulsion system, consisting of turbofan and supersonic ram jet (scramjet) engines, in a transatlantic flight from Andrews Air Force Base, Washington, D.C., to Cherbourg, France. Attaining cruise altitudes of 90,000 feet under normal turbofan power, Major*

*James then converted to supersonic ram jets, achieving a re-
cord velocity for the F-15s of—"*

He was attacked by a sudden feeling of apprehension; even
thinking that sort of thing was dangerous. He told himself:
Write your own press releases when it's over.

Topper stood up abruptly. He turned off the television and
started for the bathroom and then bed. In fifteen minutes, he
would be asleep.

Master Sergeant Arthur Bamberg, Administrative Assistant
to Colonel George P. Roos, Deputy Administrator of the Air
Force Space and Missiles System Organization (SAMSO),
Development Coordination Division, entered the Pentagon at
11:30 P.M., showed his pass to the guard at the east entrance,
and walked to the elevators. Even late on Saturday night, there
was considerable traffic in the Pentagon corridors, mostly Navy
Commanders and Army and Air Force Lieutenant Colonels,
the common denominator of the Pentagon population. Sergeant
Bamberg threw them a meticulously refined half-salute, half-
curt wave of the hand developed over many years of Pentagon
general staff service that filled regulations, yet gave the barest
possible recognition of what was, in his estimation, a very
insignificant ranking. Sergeant Bamberg was aware that, in his
present capacity as Administrative Assistant to Colonel Geordie
Roos attending the supersecret work of the Development Coordination Division of SAMSO, his job was more demanding
of skill and experience—not to mention native intelligence—
than that of a thousand Pentagon field grade briefcase carriers.

Sergeant Bamberg left the elevators at the fourth floor,
walking briskly down the corridors of a building that, as he
often reflected, was not only the size of a small city, but as
intricately laid out as the tunnels of an ant's nest. His key
opened the door marked SAMSO, *Colonel Roos,* and he quickly
switched on the lights of the outer office. The room beyond,
the secretary's quarters, opened into a hall with another door.
Into this door Sergeant Bamberg inserted a metal stub on his
key ring and waited for the computer lock to release. Once
inside, he threw on the overhead lights, revealing the room
where Colonel Roos, at 0430 hours, would come to monitor
the tracking of Operation Nightwing, destination Cherbourg.

Several computer display screens were mounted on desks

to the right and left of the conference room. The far wall was covered with a screen for three-dimensional color displays effected by software and programming controls. The large screen would not be needed, Sergeant Bamberg knew. He moved a chair in front of it, facing away, and carried a small coffee table with ashtray to set beside it. The command display arrangement at the table in the middle of the room was the only one to be used. Captain Voerner, Colonel Roos's aide, would be monitoring Andrews Air Force Base Traffic Control during takeoff, and then Washington Center's radar and the Navy installation at Patuxent, as well as Air Force radar eyes into and beyond New York Area Air Traffic Control Center, once Nightwing had achieved cruise altitude.

Sergeant Bamberg checked the floor plugs of the three telephones located on Captain Voerner's desk to make sure they were connected. Then he went into the outer office and collected pads and pencils, more ashtrays, a water carafe and glasses and brought them into the conference room. Colonel Roos would be carrying his own papers on Operation Nightwing with him, as would Captain Voerner. And Tech Sergeant Patsy Hamilton, Captain Voerner's assistant, would show up, hopefully, before 0300 hours. Sergeant Bamberg looked at his wristwatch. In a few minutes, he intended to go downstairs to the Pentagon coffee shop and order a hearty breakfast. You never knew when these things were going to give you time to eat, and he had no intention of being hungry as hell by daybreak.

At 4 A.M., he would start the automatic-drip coffee machine in the conference room, using a blend of Kivu and Brazilian coffee beans that Colonel Roos liked, ground to order in Colonel Roos's favorite Georgetown specialty food shop. By four-thirty when Colonel Roos arrived, the coffee would be hot and fresh, ready to serve with the Danish pastry Sergeant Bamberg had picked up from Colonel Roos's favorite French bakery.

Sergeant Bamberg brought in a model of the F-15 Eagle on a lucite stand from the outer office and put it on the coffee table beside the ashtray. Colonel Roos liked to meditate on the visible evidence of his months' planning when that particular operation was underway.

Sergeant Bamberg looked at the small plastic model of the Eagle, nose up, sweeping gracefully into the air from its plastic base, and realized something was wrong. Black, he thought.

He had been so rushed in the last few weeks on the planning for Operation Nightwing that he had overlooked this detail.

Sergeant Bamberg went back into the outer office and opened the drawer of his file cabinet. The compartment held a model of the F-111G, the updated version of what had once been the Air Force's skeleton in the closet and which was now, with its new canard design, the shape and promise of a renewed, glorious future beyond all expectations. Sergeant Bamberg picked up the ghost-gray camouflaged shape of the F-111G and put it in the drawer above. The special mission involving the F-111G simulation of a Soviet Su-19, code name Fencer, had been over months ago. Wrapped in tissue paper below the place where the F-111G model had been was the triangular shape of the XF-19, the prototype of the first suborbital Hot Victor. Sergeant Bamberg moved it gently to one side. SAMSO had not yet determined from the Advanced Research Projects Administration whether this would be the final structural shape or not; from what they had heard, the test flights had been uniformly poor, indicating major design revisions. Sergeant Bamberg's fingers found what he was looking for: small bottles of acrylic paint. He held one up to the light, assuring himself that it was black and not dark blue.

Sergeant Bamberg carried his bottle of paint and a sheet of typing paper back to the conference room and slid the paper under the model of the F-15 Eagle on its lucite stalk. It would take but a few minutes to turn the F-15 into Nightwing Eagle, and the paint would dry quickly. When it was finished, it would be ready for Colonel Roos to gaze at, as the real Nightwing made its way across the ocean and just under the limits of the earth's atmosphere, traveling at three times the speed of sound.

The mike button of the tape recorder was held to Topper James's throat and to the left side of his larynx by a wide piece of surgical tape. The connecting wire and jack dangled across the front of the high-altitude pressure suit as he walked. The damned thing itched, he found.

"Any airframe reaction abnormalities," Bongo Irwin was reading from the flight sheet. "And"—he looked up—"that's about it."

The actual tape recorder to be used was already installed in the Nightwing Eagle's cockpit. The one Topper had used for practice had been left back on the coffee table in crew rest quarters. Topper glanced at the stocky figure beside him. Lieutenant Colonel Irwin was haggard, and he needed a shave. His summer uniform looked to be the same one he had worn at the dinnertime briefing. Lieutenant Colonel Irwin had had some sleep somewhere in the hangar, but its effects were not visible. John Rosewicz had been up all night working with the engine crews, but his air was one of perpetually rumpled durability.

The weather reports showed everything north of Boston good—a bright, late August day coming up, right into Cherbourg. But the flight line at Andrews was thick with ground fog at 4:30 A.M. as they walked out. The air was hot and wet. The Mac Air people and the Air Force ground crew greeted them wearily.

"Will it work?" John Rosewicz called to them.

There was a cheerful chorus of boos and catcalls. They all extended their hands, thumbs up, grinning.

There was no conversation as they walked out to the waiting F-15. It loomed suddenly out of the dark, its radar-absorptive coating making it almost invisible until they were right on it. Topper shook hands with both men. The crew chief held the ladder; and he mounted it and carefully folded himself into the cockpit. The crew chief's head appeared at the top of the ladder for the run-through of the cockpit checklist. The crew chief's face shone with sweat. Topper plugged in his pressure suit hoses and checked the heating circuits.

"Okay, Major," the crew chief said finally. "One more thing."

With the canopy open, the cockpit was full of condensed moisture from the ground fog. The crew chief produced two clean lintless rags and gave one to Topper. Together they wiped the instrument panel and the cockpit as dry as they could make them. The crew chief's head disappeared down the ladder, and then the ladder itself moved away.

The flight line was deliberately dark. Lieutenant Colonel Irwin, the McDonnell Douglas engineer, the ground crew were only indistinct shapes in front of the black bulk of the hangar. The crew chief on the ground raised his arm and gave a circling motion, two fingers raised—the signal for number-two engine start.

Topper pulled the jet-starter fuel handle which activated the automatic light-off, the small electric motor that ignited the turbofan jets. He watched his indicators; when number two had risen to 18 percent rpm, he moved the throttle to idle. Number-two engine whined, rose to a growl, and then broke into a screaming roar. Below him, the hand of the crew chief signaled again, one finger for engine number one. The automatic light-off raised number one, and the air reverberated with an avalanche of sound. The small green light on the Eagle's engine control panel went out, showing the JFS had turned itself off.

For a moment, Topper rested his left hand on the throttles, the massive bellowing roar of the jet engines surging under him, watching the indicators show their messages. The crew chief was giving him the thumbs-up signal with both hands, emphatically. *Goodbye. Good luck.* Topper returned it with one hand, then pushed the canopy handle and watched it lower, the sealants making a peculiar sucking noise as they joined. For a brief moment he checked his own responses; found he was doing fine, concentration sharp and easy, everything clicking.

"Andrews Ground, Operation Nightwing taxi," he said.

He checked his brakes and nosewheel steering and then began the Eagle on a slow roll to the taxiway. Two security jeeps moved ahead of the Eagle, their taillights covered with cat's-eye blinders. Two more security vehicles came up behind.

Andrews Air Force Base was shut down to air traffic for the Nightwing takeoff. The bowl of the lighted control tower hung on the edge of darkness, and voices crackled in his headset. "Operation Nightwing, taxi to runway zero-one right."

"Roger, Andrews, Nightwing's taxiing to runway zero-one right," he responded.

The night was fine; slight streamers of fog drifted away at the edge of the apron and showed the dark sky clear and full of stars. He brought the Nightwing to a stop while figures appeared out of the dark with flashlights. He waited while the ground crew completed the EOR, the end-of-runway check, looking for hydraulic leaks, inspecting the tires, making sure all the pins had been pulled out of the landing gear. The flashlights drifted down the Nightwing's sides, determining all panels were secure.

Topper said, "Andrews tower, Nightwing's number one for takeoff."

"Nightwing, taxi into position and hold," the tower said.

The trucks and security vehicles pulled away. The Eagle taxied slowly onto the end of the runway. It vibrated slightly, restless in all its parts. *A little drag-ass,* Bongo Irwin had said, *watch it on takeoff.* Topper reviewed the rpm, the engine temps, and the fuel flow. The computer was trimming the nozzles in the turbofans. Air density was good, humidity okay, the mix optimized, hydraulic pressure normal.

"Roger, Andrews," he said. His heart began to beat slowly and heavily. "This is Nightwing ready for takeoff."

He watched the computer roll down the seconds. When it hit zero point ten seconds, he advanced both engines to 80 percent rpm and kept his eyes on the instruments. The numbers kept rolling down. One banana—two banana—the method for verbally counting off the seconds ran through his head. When the numbers hit exactly 0500 hours, he stabilized the Nightwing at military power for a one-banana count, then plugged in the afterburners, slammed the throttles forward to maximum power.

He told himself: *Firewall coming up.*

The Eagle did not roll forward down the runway. Rather, with its magnificent capacity for climb, it thrust itself ahead with a gravity-defying jump, its nose pointed to the stars. He was braced for it, but it was still like being in a giant catapult. Maximum power pushed him back in the seat. His ears filled with the bellow of afterburners filtering through the canopy and his helmet. It was gut-instinct time, the seconds running together with no space for him to think. The Eagle howled into a straight vertical climb, having used up only less than a tenth of the runway on takeoff. He worked like hell in those first few moments, getting his landing gear and flaps up and gaining control of the flight. He was at .85 Mach in the time it took him to get his breath. The flight profile was directing him to go to Mach One. He sat with his knees in the air, facing the dark sky.

He twisted the Nightwing into a five-G half-loop. At five times normal gravity, the air pressed hard; his face sagged and his belly felt as though it was hanging in his lap; a force stirred heavily, uncomfortably, in his bowels. He began to see the edge of darkness closing at the back of his eyes, narrowing his vision. He was coming out of Washington in an incredible spiral, straight up and accelerating.

At one-banana count, he pushed the Nightwing to 1.2 Mach.

Through the Defense Department, SAMSO was braced to handle the complaints of the residents in the Washington area who at that moment were being jolted from their beds as he came through the sound barrier. He wondered what National, Dulles, and Andrews were telling them as the switchboards lit up—*mysterious noises over the East Coast, probably caused by unknown atmospheric conditions*. He grinned into the mask.

He turned the Nightwing into the second half-loop of the climb, now heading north, reaching for 2.5 Mach. Only two minutes had rolled by on the computer clock. The envelope of his spiral was unbelievably small, less than six miles. He was inside that invisible tube now and climbing at twice the speed of sound. The voice of Andrews was advising him of a handoff to the Washington High Altitude Controller.

"We have positive identification, Nightwing," Washington Center said promptly, "and see you coming up. We have you on course. Call when level."

A trickle of sweat ran down Topper's forehead and dripped into his eyes. He had taken Eagles up in accelerating climbs at full power before, but it still had a way of shaking you down to the core. If, as Bongo Irwin maintained, the Nightwing was measurably tail heavy with the weight of the scramjets, it sure as hell hadn't shown it.

"Nightwing," Washington Center was saying, "you're cleared right turn to zero-six-zero degrees."

The strain on his body was easing. And the Nightwing was leveling smoothly at 90,000 feet. He looked out of the canopy and down; in the night darkness spread under him, he could see, all at once, the cities of Philadelphia, New York, Providence, and Boston. The coast of the eastern United States shrank rapidly in a definitive line of lights. As he watched, they separated themselves into bright clumps like distant galaxies. There was water below, the Atlantic, and the intermittent sparks were ships.

The voice of the Washington Center High Altitude Controller said, "Nightwing, contact New York Center on frequency three-two-five point eight." It paused and added, "Good luck!"

He couldn't respond. He was on limited radio transmission as a classified flight, and at that moment he was also busy checking out his instruments and watching the computer readout of engine sensors. The Nightwing Eagle bored into the night, the turbofans laboring a little in the thin air of high altitudes. But it was a small, powerful bullet, nevertheless—how small, he thought, you had only to realize where he was. There was barely enough room to move his arms, even less room for his legs.

"New York Center," he said into the mask, "this is Nightwing level at cruise altitude."

New York Center said, "Roger, Nightwing, we have contact. Be advised there is nothing above you to conflict with your course."

For security reasons, the careful words of the High Altitude Controller in New York gave no more than minimal information. New York Center was now locked onto his radar Selective Identification System, and soon Canada would lock onto the SIF, if it hadn't already done so. There was nothing around the Nightwing as far as he could tell, except maybe a Concorde or two passing 40,000 feet below. He had achieved his cruise altitude of 90,000 feet in those short moments of climb over Washington.

Topper pushed the button on the tape recorder that cut radio transmission when he spoke. He cleared his throat and said, "Level at nine-zero-zero, showing two point five-five Mach. Nice and smooth, no evidence of tail drag in climb. Engine instruments normal. Twenty minutes away from SCRAM transition."

At this speed, he lifted in the straps with a slight floating sensation. Also, he was pretty cold in spite of the pressure suit heating elements. And there was that strange sense of ghostly, diffused attention centered on the Nightwing as it passed high above the eastern edge of the landmass of North America: Canada defense radar now tracked him as he approached Nova Scotia, and behind him the United States civilian and military networks were locked on. To them, he knew, he was just another early morning exercise to be speculated on briefly, then logged. As soon as he passed Newfoundland, advance-warning bases at Thule would pick him up, lock onto the Nightwing's SIF, identify him, and pass him on to NATO radar on the other

side of Greenland. And overhead, he was being watched by
satellites, particularly Soviet military intelligence orbiters.
Right now, someone in Moscow was collecting the computer
readout of the Nightwing data and passing it on to processing
centers in Soviet command. According to his chart, it was
eleven-thirteen in Moscow. Lunchtime coming up.

His own feeling of the hour and distance traveled was that
of the Nightwing, and it seemed that he had only been in the
air a few minutes. But it was different—time rolled backward
and forward in flight; the saying was that going east you lost
four hours the minute your landing gear left the runway. Racing
ahead, clocks were speeding up; when he arrived in France,
it would be only a little past noon and still another measurement
of time, different also from that of the Russians evaluating his
course on the other side of the polar ice cap. The man-made
force of the Nightwing's jets that propelled him high above the
revolving ball of the earth now surrendered him to another,
infinitely mysterious affect of reality, that which was defined
as light-bound existence; as time; as velocity.

He said into the tape recorder: "Initiating SCRAM automatic
transition."

At this point the computer program was activated, and the
scramjet throttles moved out of shutoff détente. The computer
was programmed to synchronize the shutdown of the turbofan
engines and initiate the ram jets, adjusting temperatures and
velocity and the fuel and air for both systems. Shut down one;
cut to the other. Smoothly, he hoped. He pushed the ready
button on the computer. There was a loud thump and whine
as the wind-driven powerpack was deployed. There was another
thump as the spikes in the turbofan air intakes moved forward
to lock shut. The turbofans moaned loudly, an eerie *whoo* as
they spooled down. He was slammed forward with the sudden
deceleration. His helmeted head rolled like a bowling ball.

"Shit!" he exclaimed. He felt the harness that held him in
the seat stretch as though it was made of rubber bands.

For seconds, only seconds, the Nightwing Eagle was in
limbo. He could hear the sound of the slipstream and the auxiliary powerpack generator keeping the Nightwing's systems
alive. A little uneasily, he watched the computer gradually
lower the Nightwing's nose as the airspeed fell. In the rear
mirror, he saw the air-intake scoops for the ram jets slowly

rising out of the afterburner section. As the air at that supersonic speed rushed into the intakes, the SCRAMS ignited and caught with the feel of a suddenly activated earthquake. It took him unawares. He slammed back in the seat violently, his head snapping back. His teeth cracked together, catching his lower lip. His knees, always cramped, caught under the edge of the instrument panel.

Holy Christ! he thought. For a moment he was sure he had lost control of the Nightwing. But now the nose was coming back up to recover lost altitude. His hands had scrabbled for the controls, only to find the computer already making the corrections in attitude. His back hurt where it had sledgehammered against the seat. And his neck felt as though it had come within an inch of being dislocated.

"SCRAM transition complete," he said into the recorder. He made an effort to edit out his first reactions and substitute a more professional assessment. "Seems to have a lot of power, although Nightwing shows evidence of slight mushiness at this altitude. I'm getting a stability limit warning light flicker every now and then."

His flight level showed 90,000 feet on the nose. His speed was at 2.8 Mach and for some reason increasing. He stared at the figures, waiting for the computer to make some adjustment of the scramjets for speed reduction, but there was no response. That wasn't the only thing bothering him—the Stability Augmentation System warning lights kept flickering. At 90,000 feet, there just wasn't that much air to hold the Nightwing steady. It had a tendency to drift. And at the speed it was traveling, it could very possibly develop a roll, first on one wing area and then the other—the dreaded Dutch roll of high altitudes—shifting the strain back and forth on its aerodynamic surfaces until it was battering wildly. Until it eventually tore itself apart. He swallowed the blood in his mouth from his split lip. He hated like hell just to sit there. His hands itched to seize the controls and override the computer.

"Number-two engine," he said into the recorder, "still shows a little rotation, otherwise a clean shutdown. That was a rough transition, though—pulling the plug on the turbofans could use some moderating. Going to SCRAMS wasn't much better. It really threw things around."

He read the data the computer was showing into the tape

recorder, even though the flight systems were being monitored and recorded in the black boxes behind the cockpit. It was something to do; showed he was alert and minding the store. The Nightwing continued to vibrate. Maybe it's not there, he told himself. There was no deviant reading in the data. The drifting seemed to be easing off as the computer trimmed the Nightwing's movement.

Damn, I still don't like it, he thought. The transition from turbofans to scramjets had been far too rough the way the computer handled it. He couldn't help wondering how it would go manually.

Deliberately, consciously, he relaxed the muscles in his sore arms and shoulders. He had been through some hairy test flights in the SR-71 Blackbirds, and what he remembered of those times came back to him now with surprising clarity, especially that it was axiomatic that disorders which were almost imperceptible at first developed very fast into major crises. Some whisper of some malfunctioning system would suddenly become impending disaster with only a second in which to wonder, *What in hell is it?* before you had to react. And up where he was, at 90,000 feet, it was useless to grab for the ejection handle.

He was over Newfoundland now, the lights of Halifax, Nova Scotia, slipping away. And he was beginning to hear the transatlantic chatter of other air traffic on VHF frequencies. One voice identified itself as a French Concorde, calling New York Center at 47,000 feet. When the Concorde gave its position, 120 miles east of St. John's, he figured it was somewhere right beneath him. The computer showed the Nightwing just past the 1,000-mile mark. He was now forty-five minutes out of Washington, and it didn't seem like half that much. Aer Lingus, with a pronounced Irish brogue, came on, asking for weather in Boston. Traffic eastbound like himself but down at 30,000 feet in commercial air traffic lanes was busy with conversation. BOAC flight 478 was correcting its course, picking up a fellow "speedbird" going into Heathrow.

The Nightwing Eagle passed over them all in radio silence, a black-painted shadow on the roof of the world. On UHF, a military voice identified itself as the U.S. Aircraft Carrier *Nimitz*, 503 nautical miles south of Iceland, and switched to a code transmission.

After a while the voices faded, and there was nothing much going on. The ocean stretched out below in impenetrable darkness. He waited about ten minutes before he said into the recorder, "I think I see a little false dawn on the horizon."

He was still feeling cold, and he found he was thirsty. "We'll get real dawn in a little while when Nightwing catches the sun. I'm at fourteen-zero-nine nautical miles, on course, feeling good. No disorientation. I've got some soreness from being banged around during scramjet transition, but otherwise okay. Fuel consumption running at normal according to the figures, scramjet temperatures good. I've got about forty feet of bright blue flame back there from the SCRAMS, and the light is somewhat distracting in the cockpit. But SCRAMS working well."

Suddenly a voice came on in his ears, scratchy and faraway. "Nightwing, this is New York Center. Your routes are deconflicted and cleared. Contact France Control, three-six-four point zero, when able."

He was almost beyond New York's reach. He was 1,500 miles out of Washington at the halfway point now, and the first light was showing on a cloudless horizon. As he watched, the sun quickly appeared as a bright red rim, then as a glorious, slowly rising orange ball, full of light and joy. Sunrise at 0600 hours, right on the nose. He was running at 3.2 Mach, and the computer was holding the Nightwing steady at that speed. He couldn't believe it. He read the observation into the tape recorder, trying to keep the irritation out of his voice.

In the early morning light, there was time to look around. The sky was a deep midnight blue, and the stars were out. At right about this sector and cruising at three times the speed of sound, the Nightwing Eagle was capable of launching lethal little ASATs at anything the enemy might have orbiting above. It works, he told himself, damned if it doesn't.

"France Control," he said, "France Control, this is Nightwing level at cruise altitude."

Another distant elfin voice whispered, "Confirm, Nightwing, this is France Control." The English words were accented and pleasant. "We have positive radar contact and have you on course. Call when you begin your descent."

In twenty-four minutes, the computer told him, he would be a hundred miles south of Cork, Ireland, his letdown point.

And exactly 2,300 miles from Washington. The computer showed his time in the air had been 1 hour, 5 minutes, 2 seconds. Underneath, there was only dawn light and water.

"Level at nine-zero-zero," he recorded. "Three point two Mach. Fuel consumption within limits. Temps and pressures in the green. Course coming around south. I need a drink of water. And there's the sun."

Sunlight was streaming full into his eyes, and he reached up and lowered the visor of his helmet. The sky was almost black at that altitude, not blue. And the earth burst into radiant light under him in a vista of clouds and ocean.

He said into the recorder: "I've still got the intermittent SAS lights, which means the yaw dampers are working pretty hard. I'm not very happy with computer control; I think it appears to be overcompensating, which is worse than not doing anything at all. Maybe. Ireland is just visible now, coming up down there like a green spot. A beautiful day. I've got some fatigue in back and legs. I do have some minimal hearing loss after an hour of scramjet noise transmitted through the airframe. Put it down to audial nerve fatigue."

In spite of an occasional, almost undetectable shiver, the Nightwing was riding smoothly. It was still pushing too much speed, thanks to computer management of the SCRAMS, and he was considering what to do about it when beginning descent if it didn't modify. He put the figures into the computer and frowned when he saw how much speed he would have to drop and within what length of time before the turbofans cut back in. Cork city was coming up, and there was the tip of England visible ahead.

"Land's End at eleven o'clock," he said into the mask. "Top of letdown." He made a sudden decision. "I'm disengaging computer management now. SCRAM transition was way too rough before. I'm going to relight the turbofans on manual mode."

He retarded the SCRAM thrust levers for descent and de-selected the dash-thrust. He was now using the manual scramjet control head installed at his left knee, but it felt as though he had lost all momentum with just a slight reduction in power setting. He felt sweat break out on his face. He swung sharply forward in the straps as the Nightwing turned nose-down. For the first time he saw sparks, almost invisible in the bright sunlight, flicking off the Nightwing's black skin.

Quickly he told France Control, "Nightwing is departing cruise altitude for descent to landing."

The silence after the scramjets shut down was deafening. Nightwing was, the HUD display told him, nose-down by four degrees.

"SCRAM fuel is shut off," he recorded.

Land's End and the Isle of Wight were covered with the puffy cumulus clouds of summer. He heard himself swallow loudly against the hum of the slipstream and the whine of the auxiliary power unit. *Now comes the hard part*.

"Scramjet air intakes stowed," he noted. He was still nose-down, slowing to 2.5 Mach. The turbofans were unspiked and open, and he noticed the computer showing him the engine rotation figures. His airstart data were 28,000 feet altitude, 23 percent rpm. The auxiliary powerpack that had seen him through the engine transition automatically stowed itself with a loud *clunk!* that startled him.

He reviewed the steps that computer management would have taken if he hadn't bypassed it:

SCRAM thrust levers to cutoff.

Stow ram jet air-intake scoops.

Check for engine rotation. At 23 percent rpm, move throttles out of "off" to "idle."

Fuel flow, rpm, turbine temperature, check.

Move throttles into intermediate flight setting.

Hydraulic pressure, generators, check. Engine instruments, air-speed, and rate of descent appropriate for flight plan.

All present and accounted for.

Finally he said, "Level at two-eight-zero," into the recorder. He had stopped sweating. The surge of the Nightwing's turbofan jets roared under him. Transition complete. He was in the clear. "The switch from scramjets back to turbofans went smoothly. Although I held the shutoff mode a little longer than we had discussed in the event of a manual. But I had to get airspeed down." No credit to computer management, he thought. "Nightwing is at two Mach. Starting letdown procedures for Cherbourg."

The manual transition control was going to come as something of a surprise back at Andrews. But the computer-controlled scramjet sequence was a bust, as far as he was concerned. Not to mention the way it had handled stability and airspeed. The latter particularly bothered him. Obviously, the Nightwing could go up to 3.2 Mach and stay there, but he suspected this was an arbitrary figure, probably brought about by the computer not adjusting for some variable. Or maybe just hung up in the tail-weight factor. There had been little to indicate, on this flight, at least, that the Nightwing had an overdose of tail drag. But there was the possibility that the computer was programmed to compensate for it and somehow couldn't adjust back down. He warmed to the thought that in the final analysis, you needed a human being in the cockpit. Fighter jock theory, he told himself, and smiled into the mask.

He pushed the bypass button on the tape recorder.

"France Control," he said, "this is Nightwing on a straight-in visual approach."

France Control responded: "Nightwing, we observe you descending through two-four-zero. You are cleared for a straight-in approach and landing on runway one-one. Contact Cherbourg approach on frequency three-one-seven point eight."

Now there were only minutes left. The rocky coast of Brittany was in view, with Cherbourg off to the north.

"Roger, France Control. Nightwing's going three-one-seven point eight."

He switched over to the Cherbourg radio frequency, and the computer locked his tactical air navigation system onto Cherbourg's TACAN channel 72, CGB. He remembered to review his letdown plate quickly, as he was not familiar with Cherbourg: single runway eleven-twenty-nine, 8,000 feet long by 148 feet wide, elevation 456 feet.

The Nightwing was descending rapidly. He was on priority landing status, courtesy of the French government by request of SAMSO. All traffic was cleared. But suddenly he saw two blips on his radar screen closing fast.

He stared at them. What the hell? he thought. He had an estimated three minutes left on approach and no time to do anything but get Nightwing into Cherbourg, and here were two Mirage 4000s coming in on his nose. For a moment, he was baffled. He had a visual now; the Mirages were jazzy brightly painted deltawings, looking like spaceships with the canards on the upper body. One Mirage was silver and blue in a thunderbolt design; the other was neon-red and purple. He couldn't keep back a snort of laughter. Just like a space movie. The French advertised the Mirages as their answer to the F-15 Eagles.

The pair of Mirages moved in boldly, hanging at his wingtips, giving him a thorough looking-over.

Take your time, he told them. He was busy with what he was doing. And not all that impressed, even as he saw them tighten up at his wings. It occurred to him that the somber black shadow of the Nightwing in its antiradar paint probably looked, in those minutes over Cherbourg, like a sinister funeral director being escorted by two showgirls.

A few months ago, an F-15 had come into the French Flight Test Center at Istres a few miles to the south, and the same sort of thing had happened: two fancy Mirage 4000s had come up as a welcoming party to crowd the F-15's wings. The Eagle pilot's response had been to lower his airspeed and lower it some more and keep lowering it until the Mirages, unable to do that particular trick, were falling all over themselves and had to pull ahead.

He brought the Nightwing into Cherbourg, ignoring his glittering escort, the tower's heavy French accent in his ears. The Nightwing dropped to the runway smoothly and rolled to a stop. As soon as he got clearance from Cherbourg tower, he turned off into the taxiway, and immediately a United States Air Force truck raced up and pulled ahead of him to show the message on its tailgate: FOLLOW ME. It was ten fifty-six in the morning in Cherbourg by the computer clock, making the total time for the flight from Andrews one hour fifty-eight minutes and seventeen seconds. And that, he told himself, was not bad. If Andrews was looking for speed—and he gathered that was part of it—they ought to be ecstatic.

He followed the USAF truck down several intersecting concrete pathways, finally rolling the Nightwing to a stop in front of a large unmarked hangar. The ground crew quickly pulled a ladder up to the Nightwing's cockpit, and Topper climbed down. A French Air Force Colonel and a USAF Lieutenant Colonel were waiting for him in the bright morning sunshine. The American officer was carrying a blue nylon hang-up bag over his shoulder.

"Good to see you, Major," the Lieutenant Colonel greeted

him. "I've got a shower waiting and a change of uniform. I bet you could use it—and, oh, yes—"

He handed Topper an envelope. Inside was a Xerox copy of Air Force Form 626, his Orders for Temporary Duty.

Twenty minutes later, Topper James emerged from a shower stall in crew quarters in the back of the hangar at Cherbourg and was handed a summerweight Class B uniform and nylon windbreaker which the Lieutenant Colonel took from the hangup bag. He found with some surprise that the clothes fit him perfectly; then he remembered Bongo Irwin's efficient operation at Andrews. Everything, he thought, right down to the last detail.

The Lieutenant Colonel had stood right outside the shower door while Topper was inside, and now he vetoed the time it would take for a shave. There was a KC-135 waiting on the flight line to return Major James to Washington.

As he followed the Lieutenant Colonel back through the hangar, Topper tried to adjust to the feeling of being on the ground briefly and then promptly making a turnaround flight of five or six hours. Not that he had expected to spend any time at Cherbourg, but he had at least anticipated a debriefing. He was still thirsty. All he could think of was a tall, cold glass of orange juice. And he had been looking forward to some sort of food—lunch, breakfast, dinner—whatever was appropriate to his compressed time schedule.

As they emerged from the hangar into the bright, hot sunshine, he saw that the ground crews were dismantling the Nightwing Eagle and towing parts of it into the belly of a giant C-5 transport that stood waiting on the hangar apron. He stopped, amazed at the speed of the operation. At the rate the ground crew was going at it, he estimated the Nightwing would be tucked into the C-5 and on its way back to the United States at about the same time his own flight was taking off. The Lieutenant Colonel took his arm and hurried him on.

As they made their way out to the taxiway, they were trailed by quite a crowd of assorted French Air Force ground personnel, including a handful of Mirage fighter pilots in their bright orange jump suits. The latter sauntered along behind them within earshot.

"We've got company," Topper observed.

The Lieutenant Colonel turned to look, not breaking his stride. "Oh, that—you get used to it. This is Jealous Country."

The KC-135 was ahead of them, the two starboard engines idling. The French pilots followed all the way to the steps. A civilian in a dark three-piece suit stood at the doorway of the transport.

"Major James, it's good to see you." He shook Topper's hand as Topper climbed aboard. "I'm Greensmith, DoD liaison to SAMSO staff. Nice piece of work."

A Major and a Captain in the cockpit, the pilot and copilot, turned to lift their hands in greeting and congratulation. Topper muttered an acknowledgment. All he wanted, and he found that he lusted for it with all his soul, was to stretch out somewhere and ease the soreness in his back and legs. The scramjet transition had been rougher than he'd first thought, and the shaking-up had produced a hammering headache.

As he followed the DoD man into the main cabin, he realized he wanted to get the whole thing over with, sleep the six hours' transatlantic time and wake up at Andrews. He thought longingly of breakfast at home in the kitchen of the house on Magnolia Drive. *Home*. Mentally he adjusted the picture to a bowl of cornflakes, having first fished the bowl out of the sink and washed it. But he yearned for the pleasant sight of the sun shining through the sycamore trees in the backyard. And Emma at his knee, pestering him for something or other. And Candy.

The thought was so clear and sharp, so sudden in its piercing misery, that he was stunned. He stopped short and looked around him.

The DoD man stopped, too. "Everything okay, Major?" he wanted to know.

Topper nodded. The thing had taken him by surprise. Just tired, he told himself.

"There's a general officer aboard," the DoD liaison said. "Just take a seat in the compartment."

The KC-135 was one obviously used to transport VIPs and Air Force brass. It was filled with leather lounge chairs and covered with Air Force blue carpeting with the service insignia woven into it halfway down the aisle. Midway in the cabin, a heavy floor-to-ceiling curtain had been pulled to make a fairly large private area. The DoD man held the curtain aside.

A small portable table had been set up within, and the

surface was covered with papers. The cockpit tape recorder from the Nightwing Eagle lay to one side. The air was blue with smoke from a pipe that lay in a large glass ashtray. A brigadier with the insignia of SAMSO on his collar points looked up. The brigadier was young, taut-faced, and vibrantly assured. Topper was reminded of Colonel Roos. Jesus, he thought.

The brigadier smiled.

"At ease, Major," he said, reading Topper's thoughts. *"I* am your debriefing."

12

Senator Mortimer Glass left his car at the intersection of Sixth Street and Pennsylvania Avenue with instructions for George, his driver, to bring it along to the Senate garage and struck out briskly in the direction of Capitol Hill. The morning was that rarity in summertime Washington, dry and crystal clear, with a light breeze blowing from the Potomac River. The hour was early, only a few minutes past eight, and, since Congress was adjourned for the month of August, the streets around Union Station and Capitol Hill were fairly empty.

Although he was not fond of walking, the Senator had been prompted by the fineness of the weather and the absence of traffic to get more of that daily exercise increasingly recommended by his doctor at his annual checkup. Mortimer Glass was a big man, and the weight he carried was well distributed and not yet unmanageable, but the warnings had been clear: walk, not ride—and fewer martinis before dinner. Considering the all-too-familiar rate of cardiac incidents among his colleagues in the Senate, Senator Glass had opted for the ounce of prevention recommended by his internist.

As he crossed into the park on the Capitol's southwest side and made his way up the inclined path, the Senator's full, handsome face noticeably deepened in color; he squared his shoulders and made an effort to breathe more deeply and regularly and not give way to an obvious puffing as he went. He was not particularly pleased, however, to see the junior Senator from Connecticut, Vincent Mastracchio, angling across the park from the railway station to join him.

It was an awkward moment. The hill was steeper than the Senator had anticipated, and he desired to avoid any early morning conversation with anyone, much less junior Senators. Senator Mastracchio commuted from his home in Maryland, and his path from the train station took him through the park on his way to the Capitol; it was impossible to avoid him. Some civility was in order; Mastracchio was a member of Senator Glass's own Senate Armed Services Committee.

At the Connecticut Senator's eager hail, Senator Glass nodded curtly. He was not particularly impressed with Mastracchio's style. The first-term member of the Senate was not aware—and probably never would be, given the limits of his background and education (some third-rate law school, Senator Glass told himself)—of the fine technique of distancing practiced by a preeminent and very senior member, the Chairman of one of the Senate's most prestigious committees and an acknowledged Congressional power. Senator Mortimer Glass of Virginia was accustomed to being regarded—by junior Senators first and foremost—as awesomely unapproachable as Mount Everest and certainly as frigidly hostile to the presumptuously inexperienced. That was not to say, though, that Senator Glass had not availed himself of the opportunity to know a great deal about his junior committee member and his political connections in his home state, part of an area kept alive economically by defense industry contracts.

As the younger man fell into step beside him, Senator Glass noted out of the corner of his eye the considerable changes for the better in Mastracchio's appearance. The ready-made suits in attention-getting colors and designs of the past year had given way to a modest gray summerweight outfit, buttoned over a simple white shirt and striped tie. Mastracchio's thick black hair showed the effects of a thirty-dollar hairstyling— well shaped and neither too short nor too long—and there was the tasteful shine of gold links in the French shirt cuffs above Mastracchio's hairy wrists. The junior Senator carried an English leather attaché case in his hand—a twin to the Senator's own Hamilton-Marx.

It was fairly obvious to Senator Glass that someone had taken Mastracchio in hand, and he was fairly certain who that might be. Young Vincent Mastracchio was the political protégé of the House of Representatives' Budget Committee Chairman and longtime delegate from Connecticut's eastern industrial district, Thomas Biaggio. Representative Biaggio, it was generally known, served the extensive interests of the organized crime families that flourished in the state's Italian-American communities from Bridgeport to Providence in Rhode Island and controlled, among other things, dog-racing and jai-alai franchises and southern New England's powerful labor unions.

Senator Glass had entered the Senate at a time, some twenty years ago, when the infamous Southern demagogues still retained a good bit of Senatorial power, particularly as senior members of key committees; as a Southerner himself, and a not particularly liberal one, he had nevertheless been embarrassed on more than one occasion by the deportment and often incomprehensible voting records of those members of Congress he personally regarded as the mistakes of deluded and backward constituencies; he had been glad to see the Southern bloc's numbers and influence decline over the years. Now, he had become increasingly aware, a new faction represented by men like young Mastracchio was making an appearance, worrisome because of the persistent rumors of links to organized crime syndicates. The presence of Mastracchio on his own committee had, from time to time, made him vaguely uneasy—although he had to admit that so far the junior Senator had given him no cause for unease.

Bernie Gould of the aviation and aerospace industries lobby had, quite unexpectedly in Senator Glass's view, been an advocate of Mastracchio's appointment to the Armed Services Committee, citing Mastracchio's close association with labor union leaders in his state. It had been nothing more than that— a friendly recommendation from an experienced Washington hand—but the implications, when the Senator cared to think about them, were certainly interesting.

Senator Glass's own dealings with Bernie Gould and the AAASI had always been scrupulously correct, in his own view. His personal political philosophy was that of his own conservative state, and over the years he had voted a straight record for the rights of private enterprise. The extension of this applied to the defense industry's right to reasonable and necessary profit taking in a field of rising costs and often extravagant labor

demands, occasionally complicated by Congress's own investigations. Certainly Senator Glass had proven that he ascribed
to a tolerant and pragmatic line as regards the multibillion-
dollar business of defense acquisition; he found no quarrel with
corporate profits as long as they did not impair what he saw
as the basic issue: the delivery to the nation of sufficient and
workable weapons for the preservation of the country's freedom. He defended that viewpoint vigorously, and it had been
his experience that, barring occasional scandals and some few
inexcusable bungles, the system worked. The ultimate proof
that it worked was that the nation's taxpayers—at least those
who bothered to concern themselves, and they were not
many—readily accepted the premise that it was necessary for
the federal government to pay, and pay exorbitantly, for the
guns and planes needed for its well-being. And the end result
of that was, in spite of billion-dollar cost overruns and some
catastrophes of corporate dealing, the United States still had
the best military system in the world and by far the most
advanced weaponry.

Senator Glass turned into First Street, and Senator Mastracchio, talking animatedly about his view of upcoming bills
in the fall session, broke into a trot to keep up with him. The
young man's chatter was innocuous, most of it calculated to
impress the Senate's august senior member with his talent and
industry and pleasure at being able to serve on his committee—
the usual stuff, Senator Glass told himself crossly.

Senator Glass was aware that where they were, in front of
the Capitol, there were plenty of eyes to observe them, and he
had no particular desire to be seen with Mastracchio. The
impression might be, as the junior Senator no doubt hoped it
would, that Senator Glass encouraged Mastracchio's company
and that some sponsorship existed.

If it had been anyone else, Senator Glass would have made
it all too clear that he wanted to finish his walk as he started
it—in solitude. But he was also considering that it might not
be wise to cut Representative Tom Biaggio's political ward at
that time; there were favors passed back and forth between the
House Budget Committee and the Senate Armed Services Committee, particularly at appropriations time, that were invaluable.

Senator Glass gave way.

"All right," he said abruptly, "let's slow down. I'm getting a damned pain in my chest."

He was not in a good mood when he entered his offices in the Russell Senate Office Building, and the immediate demands of his staff, gathering around him as soon as he passed the door of the reception room, did nothing to improve it.

"My God," he growled, "don't you people know Congress is on vacation?"

There were a few dutiful smiles. His staff was hardworking, and they wanted him to be reminded of it; their early morning energy was calculated to let him know they were on the job and were, in fact, there well ahead of him. His administrative assistant, Gus Yoder, followed him into the paneled inner office trailed by the Senator's secretary, the two summer interns from the University of Virginia Law School, and the office researcher-file clerk. Senator Glass threw his attaché case down on the desk.

Gus Yoder said promptly, "Jerry O'Brien called about seven-thirty; that's last night." The administrative assistant worked late; taking a call at that hour was not unusual. "He's been stumping the youth summer conference circuit back home, and he's come up with a startling discovery, he says. He claims youth is interested in space. That and jobs. He wants to know how many jobs you think the Space Shuttle program will provide in the future."

Senator O'Brien was a western states representative whose support for the Administration's proposed Industrialization of Space bill was important.

"Hell, we're not the Department of Labor," Senator Glass snapped. "All right, pack up the breakdowns on careers in the aerospace field and send it to him," he told Yoder.

"He mentioned the Industro-Space bill, too. He wants you to call him."

Senator Glass took the typewritten sheet with the telephone number of Senator O'Brien's law offices in Bismarck, North Dakota, and put it on top of his desk calendar where he could find it later.

The Congressional interns, a boy and a girl, couldn't wait to tell him their news. At a quarter to eight that morning—the interns came in early and left early for Capitol duty—Grigori had strolled into the outer office. And he certainly must have known there wasn't going to be anyone around at that hour.

Senator Glass was skimming his messages. He looked up. Grigori Ilyushin was the KGB attaché at the Soviet Embassy. He had every legal right to come into the office and did, but his presence never failed to infuriate the summer interns.

"Well, what did he want?"

"Oh, the usual," the girl said. "All the Armed Services hearings transcripts, everything we've got printed. I know he's supposed to get them, Gus warned me, but he was just *sneaking around*, I'm not exaggerating. He asked me if we had anything on some hearing about aircraft engines."

"Morty"—his secretary of twenty years always used the familiar—"Dr. Parsons called. He said he tried to get you at home, but your daughter told him you'd already left."

Senator Glass stopped what he was doing.

The Undersecretary of Defense for Research and Engineering often started his workday early in the August doldrums when one could, at least in the upper levels of the DoD, make an early quitting time. But this was unusual.

Senator Glass reached for his private line and looked at his staff significantly. Without a word, they filed out and closed the door.

The Department of Defense Undersecretary answered his telephone himself.

"Hello, Dick," Morty Glass said cheerfully, "what's on your mind so early in the morning?"

"Can I talk?" Dr. Parsons' voice was deliberate, conveying some strain. "Are you on your red line number?"

"No other. Go ahead."

"Well," the Undersecretary said slowly, "I'd like to pass on some information to you very, very informally, strictly off the record, but I'm soliciting your input. Mort, I think we're in a little difficulty."

"Okay," Senator Glass said. He swiveled his desk chair around to face his office windows which looked down on the Mall and the needle of the Washington Monument in the distance. He braced himself for whatever was coming.

"Mort, we have sources in New York that tell us that *Finance* magazine is setting up a story right now for fall publication that might cause us a good bit of worry. And any hopes we might have of getting a decent break on the Trueham engine product in our current advanced tactical fighter series are, we're told, pretty well negated by the writer they've assigned to the story and the way they're going to develop it."

"Dick, I gather somebody's going to do a story on the F100X engine in the Eagles," Senator Glass said. "What's the problem?"

"Uh—well, uh, *that* is the problem. I'm told they're going to title the thing 'The F100X Engine—Trueham's Problem Child' and go on to lay it all out—stall stagnation, fuel systems breakdowns, high maintenance and repair ratio—practically all the data we evaluated over here last month. We suspect some kind of leak."

Senator Glass considered the news, which was not good. His first thoughts were for Bernie Gould and whether he had gotten it yet on his pipeline. But his tone to the Undersecretary was unalarmed.

"*Finance* is strictly business-oriented," Senator Glass said. "I don't think they're going to come down too hard on that kind of thing, Dick—it's counter to their interests. I really don't think this is going to blow up into anything we need to worry about. Look, we're not at war like we were ten years ago; people are fretting about inflation and the gas shortage, not about some military fighter jet engine. We've come," Senator Glass said persuasively, "a long way from the days of the F-111 mess, Dick. It's not the same kind of ball game."

"Mort, the writer on this is *Fred Lightfoot*," the Undersecretary responded, raising his voice. "He was a thorn in our sides when he was in Vietnam with Associated Press—he did a story on the Black Virgin Mountain campaign fiasco that won a Pulitzer Prize, remember?"

Senator Glass did not remember, but he assured the Undersecretary he would take his word for it.

"*Finance* has been doing some tough coverage lately," Dr. Parsons went on. "They've found that their readership likes a little heavy investigative stuff in with the marketing statistics. Mort, government spending is a sore spot in a lot of places. There are a lot of citizens action groups that could pick up on this, to say nothing of your antimilitary block over there on the Hill. Of course, I'm going to admit to you that I think we made a mistake in sitting on the bad news about the F100X;

I'm afraid we waited a little too long on it before going public. But the Air Force was reluctant as hell to admit anything for months, even internally, and I guess you know why. That Trueham contract really stuck them for millions in repair; they dumped a lot of money trying to get the bugs out and still haven't succeeded. And you know as well as I do that when Congress blows a lot of money on a project like the F-15 Eagles—and those engines, Mort, are a real disappointment— then all you people start worrying about your voting records and what your constituents are going to remember about them. Nobody loves a goof—and if there's any place on earth that's true, it's Capitol Hill."

"We haven't proved it's a goof yet," Senator Glass said. "You have to give these things a little time."

"Wait, Mort, there's more bad news." The Undersecretary dropped his voice confidentially. "The Space Shuttle is having problems; it needs about eight million more in the current fiscal year and about two hundred million in the near future. That's on top of the one-hundred-eighty-five-million increase which was passed by the Senate and the House last season. We're going to have to go back to Congress. Put the two together, Mort, and you can see we're going to have a lot of negative impact coming up next month."

There was silence for a moment, and then Senator Glass said, "When in hell did you find this out?"

"Wait—there's more. NASA's going to get the Space Shuttle money; we can't call off the show at this point, but those damned thermal tiles on the Shuttle skin are coming up fast as our next big problem. The current application rate on those tiles is about three hundred a week—that averages out to just a little more than one tile per man each week. Rockwell is going nuts. I spent all day last Thursday listening to the Rockwell International rep try to explain it to me. The tiles have to be held under pressure while the epoxy glue sets, and it takes six or seven hours for that process. Then the gaps between the tiles have to be maintained at point eight millimeters; if they're less than that, there isn't room for thermal expansion on re-entry. And too big a gap allows heat to penetrate the Shuttle's skin. There're thousands and thousands of tiles, Mort, and I don't think any of them are worth a damn. If you want my projection on it, I think they're going to have to rip them all off and start over again."

The Senator frowned. The implications of the cost involved were bad enough, but the between-the-lines reading was worse. Tiles falling off the underbelly of the world's first—and it was not an exaggeration to call it that—spaceship was downright ludicrous. It was hard to maintain the public's confidence with that sort of thing going on.

"Mort," the Undersecretary of Defense said, "your Industrialization of Space program is going to go down the tubes this session, and I don't see much hope for the next couple of years. We've hit too many snags."

"Oh, come now, Dick, it's not as bad as all that," Senator Glass said heartily. "We're not just talking about a lot of money—we're talking about the *future of this country*."

In spite of the Undersecretary's exceptional early morning call and a conversation that was, as Dr. Parsons himself had defined it, very, very informal, Senator Glass was beginning to see the outlines of a possible trade-off. While he worked mentally to assess what was implied in all this, he kept talking.

"Let me tell you something, Dick," he said. "Seventy-five years from now, the internal combustion engine will have reached the same status as the horse—okay in small numbers and good for races, and that's about all. Our whole society is going to undergo a radical change; people are going to own personal transportation machines, fully automated, that will go anywhere by air, just like you see in space movies. There's going to be unmanned supersonic cargo transports delivering the earth's goods from continent to continent and from earth to moon and back. We're going to have beam-energy-powered flight from our space platforms that will eliminate the need for individual propulsion systems; solar energy stations are going to be orbiting the earth, and all of the Space Shuttles—the Challenger, the Discovery, the Columbia, the Enterprise—will be on regular schedules like Greyhound buses, coming and going in space. And we're going to have private industry on the moon developing profitable mining operations—hell, it's all there in the Industrialization of Space bill, Dick; you've read it! We'll be training welders and pipe fitters to work in orbit, hanging off cranes in their space suits—"

"Just a minute, Mort," the Undersecretary interrupted, "I've got to answer the other telephone."

When Dr. Parsons came back on the line, Senator Glass had had his moment to think. "Look," he said abruptly, "what's the proposal?"

"Morty, there was some discussion here last night about having somebody pick up the ball on this Trueham engine thing. We kicked around the idea of how to anticipate the *Finance* story impact and any follow-through in the media. Television kills us, Mort. It could be bad."

Senator Glass leaned back in his chair. "We're talking about subcommittee open hearings."

"I'm glad you mentioned that," the Undersecretary said promptly. "Actually, we felt you might want to contribute what you could to get some of the pressure off in sensitive areas. We all know the Industro-Space bill represents a big commitment on your part, Mort—"

"Dick, we could use some support from DoD on the bill," Senator Glass broke in. "Not that I would ask you people to do any arm-twisting, but I think you know what a goddamned uphill job this Industrialization of Space thing has been. Also, I want to tell you right now that some of your people over there seem to think that the opening up of space development to private enterprise is somehow going to jeopardize your operations. But the SPAD program is a forward-looking opportunity for DoD—you all just can't see the forest for the trees."

The Undersecretary waited a moment before he said, "Come on, Mort, you pushed those F100X engines pretty hard when it was clear they weren't going to pass Air Force acceptance tests, don't forget. It's in your best interests to see we don't take too much of a beating on this. Now I·like your idea of a subcommittee public hearing, but remember, it's going to take a lot of careful planning. You want me to be frank, don't you? Well, we know we're not going to come up smelling like roses—all we want to do is get up front with our side of the story before *Finance* comes out with their version. I just want you to understand that. There's no cover-up, believe me."

Senator Glass went on imperturbably, "There's a lot of opposition over in your territory to the SPAD program. And I'm definitely getting negative feedback from the crowd at SAMSO."

Another silence fell, and then the Undersecretary said, "Mort, I'd be glad to sit down with you and rework our thinking on it, if that's what you want. But remember, my area is limited as hell. I can't promise you anything."

Senator Glass chuckled. "Hell, Dick, I'm not trying to drive you to the wall on anything, am I? You have my sympathies, believe me. I told you the Space Shuttle program was going to cost a bundle; I warned you about it right from the start, but your analysis is correct. You're not in any trouble in Congress—the money will have to come, that's all. Don't worry about it."

But Senator Glass was considering his options, and they were few. A subcommittee hearing was a lot of work, more than he could take on at this particular time with the fall session coming up, but it was vastly better, he knew, to be in control of the problem when it broke in the press than to have no way at all of getting a good, substantial rebuttal before the public.

"Can you set it up by October?" the Undersecretary wanted to know. "Say the first week in October? Actually, we'd like it even earlier than that if we could get it—we don't know the exact date of the *Finance* piece."

Senator Glass consulted his desk calendar, flipping through the pages to October. "That looks tough, Dick. My staff is pretty overloaded; I don't see how in hell we could get the paperwork together."

"I think we could help you on that," Dr. Parsons said cautiously. "You have access to our hearing transcripts, don't you? If not, I'll send them all over to you."

Mortimer Glass suddenly remembered Senator Vincent Mastracchio. The Senator was already on the subcommittee for military space research and development and was not exactly overworked, as he understood it. And Mastracchio's *consigliero*, Congressman Biaggio, had seen to it that the Senator had been set up with an excellent staff: a smart young Jewish boy was Mastracchio's administrative assistant, and one of the best on the Hill. Senator Glass knew where to find a bright young counsel who knew how to ask the right questions—and the right questions, in this sort of thing, were more important than the answers.

"I think we might be able to put something together," Senator Glass said finally. "There's a junior Senator on my committee who can pick up on this thing; he needs some exposure right now, and I think his heart would be in it. I'll get Gus Yoder to rough up a list of witnesses. But I want to hold down the testimony by the military brass; they'll scream, but you know as well as I do, Dick, that they don't come off on TV, not the way they think they do. Let's stick to some engineering types, young earnest ones; they have a high level of credibility. And I think we ought to do some front-line user testimony. I'm thinking of some Air Force fighter pilots, the men who know what it's like to handle the F-15s and keep them flying. They're always gung-ho for their equipment—any equipment—and they project a hell of a good image. I know we're going to have to use the maintenance and availability figures, and they're pretty bad, but I'm thinking we could balance them out with some actual user comparison to other programs. The F-4s were riddled with problems when they first went operational, but they served us well in Vietnam. Stuff like that is very reassuring to the public."

"I don't know," the Undersecretary said. "Mort, we don't want to leak any horror stories inadvertently about engine stall and having to ditch a fifteen-million-dollar F-15 into the ocean. No strong, off-the-cuff stuff—and no kid who's going to freeze up on camera, either, and look as though he's been through some military brainwash. That won't fool anybody. Look, why don't you get Latimer Holmes over at SAMSO to carry the ball? He's young and good-looking; so's the guy who works with him, Roos. They've been doing something big with an F-15 converted to ram jets that's turning out very, very well."

Senator Glass started to say something, then thought better of it. He assumed his hearty voice. "Dick, Latimer Holmes and Big Bird Banks are *both* going to have their say; I give you my word on it. But it wouldn't hurt to get some of our young warriors out on this thing; it would keep a good image of the peacetime military up front with the taxpayers. Look how the public went for the astronauts. We could use some of that. Those F-15 pilots are smart boys, sterling types, superb physical specimens—we can project that image right into the subject of space programs and score a few points. It's certainly got sales appeal."

* * *

Major Topper James stood in the doorway wearing only a drunken gargoyle grin and his combat boots. His fair-skinned torso gleamed palely in the half light, and a dark girl, also naked, swung from his flexed right arm like a monkey from a tree branch, her knees lifted, trying to bear him to the floor by sheer weight. On Topper's left, another girl in nothing but a sequined brassiere attempted to shinny up his back. Both girls kept up a playful, high-pitched squealing. Topper opened his mouth, seemed to say something, but his voice was drowned out by the racket of the party going on below.

"Beeper!" Simon McAllister yelled.

They both lunged for the door, but a second too late. One of the girls kicked it shut, and they heard the lock snap.

"Aw, *hell*," Nizzard said disgustedly.

They heard the sound of something falling inside the bedroom and a muffled clatter, followed by the low thread of Topper's voice. Simon leaned his head against the door and tried the knob. It was really locked.

"Hey, Top," he called, "can I speak to you a minute?"

There was no answer.

Nizzard said, "C'mon, Moonbird, we've got to get the hell out of here. We've got an early-go in the morning, and I gotta sober up."

He couldn't leave his Porsche. Couldn't leave Topper, the way he was. Simon shook his head.

It had been Nizzard's idea to leave the Officers' Club bar and follow the Egyptian crowd out here. They were all still in their flight suits, still a little loaded from Happy Hour which had been a hell of a long time ago. Topper had been drunker than anybody, which was one reason they wanted to get out of the OC bar, but it had been a stupid idea to take Topper anywhere when he was drunk. They also—all of them—knew enough to stay away from the Middle Eastern crowd and their parties. If they hadn't been boozed up at the time, if Topper hadn't been getting into his bit about biting the sides out of beer cans in the OC bar, they never would have given it a second thought. None of them had a clear idea where they were, exactly, even now. Just somewhere in a house at Virginia Beach.

One of the Egyptian pilots standing on the stairs said, "Too much noise will make the police come."

Simon doubted it. If that was true, the police would have been there by now. The house was jumping. Cars came and went in the driveway with a screeching of tires, and people were yelling and running around out there. Whoever had the place probably had some arrangement with the local gendarmes, like the Saudis did at their place farther down.

Beeper said, "Damn, I wonder how old those women are."

"Old enough to take care of themselves." He wasn't going to worry about anything like that. He wasn't worried about the girls as much as he was worried about Topper. Damn Candy, he thought.

A faint odor like sweet burning hay drifted up the stairwell. A few minutes ago, when he had been going through the house looking for Topper, the two belly dancers had been doing their thing on the coffee table in the living room, and he had found the sun porch full of humping couples. A fat man was wandering around in his underwear, carrying a water pipe. So he wasn't exactly worried about proprieties. The only thing that surprised him was how fast Topper had managed to gather up the girls and talk them into whatever it was they were doing behind those locked doors in the bedroom.

He hadn't been to a party like this since his college days.

And he was not exactly happy to find himself here, now that he had sobered up a little. It bothered him. There were at least a hundred people in the house, and hardly anybody seemed to know anybody else.

"Look," he said to Nizzard, "do me a favor, will you, and go find somebody who's got a key. What do these girls speak? Do they speak English?" Nobody seemed to know, not even the Egyptian hanging around on the stairs. "Well, look around down there and see if anybody's in charge. Get somebody to come up here and open the door so we can get Topper out of there."

But Nizzard said, "Moonbird, why don't we try to keep it quiet? You know, I'd just as soon get the hell out of here without anybody knowing it. Because I'm drunk, man, and Beeper ain't too damned sober, either. Besides, I think we're the only damned Americans in here. You know that?"

Simon had had enough to drink to give him a headache. He rubbed his forehead. "Jesus, it's too damned late to think about that."

If the girls in there with Topper were after money, they were going to be greatly disappointed, because Topper didn't have any. Topper was always broke. And he realized he didn't have much cash with him, either, only credit cards. He wondered how you said American Express in Arabic. He hoped to hell Topper was getting it out of his system.

"We could break the door down," Beeper said.

Simon sat down at the top of the stairs. He put his head in his hands and said, not looking up, "Nizzard, take Beeper out before he falls down, will you? And for Chrissake, don't let him drive."

Nizzard said, "Moonbird, I hate to leave you here with all these crazy Arabs. I'll break the door down, like Beeper said."

"No—hell!" he yelled at him. None of them had any sense.

If Topper was anybody's responsibility, he supposed he was his. He was caught up in it whether he liked it or not, in the classic game, the myth, the all-military brotherhood-of-the-skies scenario. But nobody knew how much he hated these messy, free-form, uncontrolled situations.

"Just get the hell out of here," he told them. He sat there, fighting his creeping headache-hangover. "I'll just sit here. I'll figure out some way to get him out of there."

13

Major Adolphus Bauernhauser dropped Captain Bob DeVol off at DeVol's house in Hampton and started for his own home off the Williamsburg highway, ten miles away. It was still early, and in ten or fifteen minutes, Major Bauernhauser estimated, he would be in his own living room and—if his wife was still up—in time for a nightcap and a little end-of-the-day conversation. It was a comfortable thought.

The killing heat of the late August afternoon had gradually given way after dark to the damp, oppressive cool of the Tidewater night. The low stretches of Mercury Boulevard at the John Glenn and Gus Grissom Bridges were thick with fog wraiths; the side and rear windows of the Ford were thoroughly misted over. He stopped at the Shell station just before the Route 64 fly-over and got out to wipe them off with the contents of a box of facial tissues his wife always kept in the car. When he finished, he was as dew-drenched himself as though he had been standing in an open field. He wiped his hands on his trousers and then took off the crimson and yellow neckerchief of his Senior Boy Scout Leader uniform and threw it in the back with the tissue box. As always, the Boy Scout regalia attracted more attention in Hampton than any military uniform: the handful of youths in the glass cage of the Shell service station seemed fascinated, and one boy came to the door to watch him as he got back into his car.

Dolph Bauernhauser had enough years in scouting so that his Senior Leader's uniform, covered with jamboree badges and ribbons denoting length of area and regional council service, was indeed a magnificent thing, far more impressive than his Air Force blues with the modest row of Vietnam decorations. He had worn it enough so that the initial feeling, that of being a field marshal of paper drives and campouts, had lost its faint embarrassment. The scout uniform hadn't really been required for the area council meeting he and DeVol had just attended, but since he was tuned to the formality of the staff meetings of the military, he had found it easy enough to dress for it; one uniform was much like another, once you got used to routine. And he was aware that his spare, muscular body, trained for years in uniform wearing, did more justice to the senior leader's gear than did those of other council members, civilians who were developing unleader-like potbellies of middle age.

Captain Bob DeVol, whose youngest boy had just gone into Cub Scouting, had been impressed if somewhat surprised to see that Dolph Bauernhauser still maintained an active interest in scouting, especially since Dolph's own two boys were no longer interested—Tom, the older, a junior in high school, had discovered girls, and Gus Junior was involved with the electric guitar. As DeVol had commented, what Dolph was doing was now largely for the benefit of other people's offspring; to continue with scouting when one's own kids no longer took part— to continue to make the sacrifice of time and energy under the unyielding pressures of military life and particularly those of an F-15 Eagle squadron—well, Captain DeVol had said, it certainly indicated a real commitment to community service. But Bob DeVol hadn't been impressed with the area council meeting, which had dragged on tediously over the nomination of officers for the coming year.

Thinking about it, Dolph Bauernhauser had to admit that the endemic struggles between the Newport News Senior Scout Leaders—the longtime, stable community, as they saw themselves—and the scouting representatives from the mobile military population of Hampton was bound to be discouraging to someone like DeVol, at least at first. He knew the unspoken question in Captain DeVol's mind after an evening of observing the area council's wrangling: Considering the time all this took and which encroached on the already eroded amount available for one's wife and family, was it, then, really worth it?

Major Bauernhauser's answer, given jokingly, was that one got to see one's picture in the Tactical Air Command Journal every year when the annual Community Leadership Awards were announced.

But the real answer was, he supposed, that one did what one as a father was compelled to do in response to the pressure that was on all of them to maintain what was known as A Normal Family Life, trying conscientiously for the near impossible goal of Caring Father and Good Family Man in spite of, or perhaps because of, the often schizophrenic pressures of their peculiar profession. More than once—although he had not bothered to mention it to DeVol—Major Bauernhauser had spent the day in simulated combat scenarios or interdictions at maximum altitudes and speeds in his F-15, covering a good part of the United States, and then had driven home at breakneck speed from Langley to shower and change into jeans and pick up seven little boys (or eight, or nine, or ten)—and on *time*, by God!—for some Troop 157 overnight campout. Or bowling game. Or woodcraft competition with Troop 401.

It could be done; they all did it, in some form or other. Roger Gazenove, the squadron commander, had flown back on a commercial airline during a weekend break at the Red Flag war games in Nevada to be at his daughter's high school graduation. Boots Gatland had juggled his night flying schedule all during the spring, so as not to miss any of the Lamaze natural childbirth classes he was attending with his pregnant wife. *Normalcy* was the key—the commitment, whether they accepted it or not with any great faith, to something other than the obsessive world of tactical fighter squadrons. Dolph Bauernhauser had found that he had no basic quarrel with it; the long years in scouting had been enjoyable, had given a different sense of accomplishment. And as he had told Bob DeVol, it got your picture in the papers once a year.

Once on the Williamsburg highway, Major Bauernhauser stepped on the gas, urging the Ford up to sixty-five, then seventy. The moon was out, large and pale over the dense flatland forest, and the road was almost empty of traffic. The highway headed north straight as a die, drifted over in spots with tags of mist from the woods. It was easy to see speeders in this long straight stretch; the headlights hit his rearview mirror first as bright pinpoints, then as rapidly growing white holes in the blackness. Dolph moved over to the right lane and let the Ford drop down to sixty miles an hour, giving the speeder coming up plenty of room.

But the rapidly closing headlights had a wavering echo of light behind them—another car. As he watched them in the mirror, he judged they were not only coming up fast, but taking up most of the two northbound lanes as they did so. The moonlight was bright; he could make out the unmistakable beetle shape of an old Volkswagen. The car behind it appeared to be much larger, the size of a Dodge or a Pontiac, although he couldn't be sure. There was something odd in the weaving all over the road, a purpose that was hardly playful, not like the game of "chicken" played by the local dragsters. The Volkswagen swerved; it looked as if the larger car was aiming at its front bumpers.

"What the devil," Dolph Bauernhauser muttered. He pulled his Ford as close to the shoulder as he could without actually running off the highway.

The Volkswagen, its high beams glaring, passed him doing around eighty. As the car following pulled abreast of him, he saw the driver was a young man, might even be wearing some sort of military uniform; that wasn't unusual around Hampton. Dolph squinted. Surely nobody would be that stupid, he told himself. The Virginia State Highway Patrol was always around; Route 64 was a popular dragstrip after dark. To be caught in uniform—

He watched the taillights gyrating wildly down the highway in front of him. Drunk or high on something, he thought—but there was skillful driving going on if they were.

Ahead of him, the highway dipped slightly and turned to the left for the Patrick Henry Airport cloverleaf. When he came up to the crest of the rise beyond, the two cars were no longer in sight. He felt a strong sense of relief. It was none of his business; he hoped they were gone safely, eliminating the prospect of his coming upon some gory wreck. He reached down and turned on the car radio. He was still turning the dial when he saw both cars ahead, pulled over on the shoulder. He groaned inwardly. If something had happened—as he had the feeling it had—he knew he should stop. The way the automobiles were angled on the dirt gave fair warning.

It was the Volkswagen, all right—he supposed there wasn't

more than one bright yellow VW on Route 64 at that hour. The vehicles had just come to a stop, he was sure; there was a sense that whatever had happened, had happened just seconds before. As he slowed the Ford and tried to estimate the situation, a young man in an Air Force uniform threw open the door of his car and ran toward the Volkswagen.

Dolph slowed and pulled the Ford to the side of the road. As he did so, the airman dragged someone out of the VW. What happened next was violent and confused—two figures fell against the car in the bright moonlight, struggling fiercely. He thought the second figure was that of a woman. Dolph Bauernhauser yanked the gearshift into reverse and started backing up rapidly.

He stopped some feet away from them and jumped out. The moment he did, the figures broke apart, and the man ran for his car. The girl was screaming. The other driver started his engine, backed up with a squeal of tires, and lurched onto the highway. The car passed and sped off.

He found the girl slumped by the side of the Volkswagen, howling with what he hoped was more rage than pain. He had to haul her upright. He couldn't tell at once whether she was seriously hurt, but he discovered she, too, was in Air Force uniform. She wore Sergeant's stripes. She was, he saw, a tiny thing, freckle-faced in the moonlight, her hair a mass of red curls. She kept howling. She threw herself against him, grabbing the front of his shirt.

"He tried to kill me!" she shrieked. "He's a *lunatic*—he really wants to *kill* me!" The thought seemed to overpower her. She stamped her feet. He felt her fingernails through his Scout Leader's blouse. He took her wrists quickly and held them.

"Now calm down," he told her. "Are you hurt?" She had a smear of blood on her cheek, he saw. "Did he hit you?"

"He's crazy—*crazy!*" she screamed. "I'm not going to marry him—I wouldn't marry him, for God's sake! He tried to wreck my car! He's really crazy—he said I was *pregnant* and going to get an *abortion* so I wouldn't have to marry him! I don't know where he gets these crazy ideas!" She clutched her red curls with both hands. "Oh, my God, he's going to kill me, and nobody will ever find out! He's *Catholic* and crazy, crazy, crazy—he actually chased me in his damned car and ran me off the road! You saw it, didn't you? And then he punched me——" She gave another piercing shriek. "I've got to get out of here, he's out of his *mind!*"

"Sergeant," Major Bauernhauser said firmly. He hoped his use of her rank would penetrate. "Are you stationed at Langley?" He gave her a little shake. "I'm Major Dolph Bauernhauser with the First TFW. Now calm down and tell me what's the matter."

He thought he was catching on now——a lovers' quarrel in the middle of Route 64. And both of them in uniform. Subject to disciplinary action as a consequence. Creating a public disorder.

The headlights of a car passing in the southbound lanes caught them in a white glare for an instant and then roared on. For the first time, Dolph was aware how they both must look—— the distraught girl in Air Force uniform, the cars pulled off the road at crazy angles, the ridiculous Boy Scout regalia he wore.

He told her gruffly, "I think we ought to get off the road. You can come sit in my car until you calm down." He took her by the arm and steered her toward the Ford. He supposed her assailant was gone, but if he was still around, she'd be safer there.

As soon as the girl got into the front seat, she burst into nervous tears and a tirade directed, he gathered, toward the airman who had chased her in his car and roughed her up. He listened uncomfortably for a few moments, mindful of the late hour and the fact that his wife was expecting him.

Finally she wiped her eyes with one hand and looked up at him. She peered at him in the darkness. "Major who?" she said doubtfully, eyeing the Senior Leader's resplendent blouse.

He got out his wallet and showed her his military ID. He explained that he was in Scout uniform because he was coming back from a meeting. And he was sure he recognized her now—— the little redheaded air traffic controller from the Langley tower; he'd seen her before when he'd had SOF duty——with great flirty brown eyes and a manner to match and, according to tower gossip, something of a man-eater. Murphy, he told himself. They called her Murph.

She wiped the tearstained face with the back of her hand, angrily. Some of the pertness returned. She straightened up and looked around, her face puffy under the sprinkling of freckles.

"You haven't got a cigarette, have you?" she asked him. "Oh, well, never mind. I'll get one later." She touched her cheek and winced. "God, he really banged me around! I didn't know what I was getting myself into this time. You should see his family—ignorant, all of them! Well, fat chance—I'm not going to give up what I've worked for, for that sort of thing!"

By now, Dolph Bauernhauser thought, his wife had probably called Bob DeVol to see what had happened to him.

"Sergeant, you've been lucky tonight," he said severely. "It's a wonder the police didn't pick you up. I don't exactly understand what this is all about, but I gather you're having some trouble with your boyfriend, and he's in uniform, too, from what I saw. I don't know what in hell you two thought you were doing out here—"

"Oh, Jesus—tomorrow!" she exclaimed. "We've got duty together. I mean, he's on duty tomorrow and so am I, right there in local position." She broke into a furious wail. "I'm *training* him! Oh, what am I going to do about that!"

Well, she did have herself in a mess, he thought. The plot thickens. "Who's your supervisor?" he asked.

Sergeant Murphy, now that she had regained some of her composure, was very much aware of him. Dimples flashed at the corners of her mouth when she spoke. She crossed her legs and leaned one elbow on her knees, turning sidewise to look at him.

"Master Sergeant Tom Bullock—and, oh, I don't want him to know about this! That would really throw things FUBAR."

The word, he remembered, was tower slang for "fucked up beyond all recognition." He started to say something, but she continued, "I've got to do something about Ronny, but I don't know what it's going to be. I've never had anything like this happen to me before. I mean, most guys have some *sense*. Marry him," she said indignantly. "I'm not going to give up my Air Force career to get married and raise a whole bunch of kids. I should think *not!*"

Her voice, her face, were comical; he said sternly, "Sergeant, what career are you talking about? It seems to me you don't mind indulging in some pretty unmilitary behavior. I gather you're involved with someone on your own shift who, you claim, is trying to kill you or marry you—I'm sorry, but I don't seem to be able to understand what's going on. But you're open to discipline on a number of counts, if what happened here tonight is any indication of what's going on."

She bristled. "That's a hell of a remark for you to make. I'm a career Air Force person."

Pointedly he got out his car keys and put them in the ignition. "All right, Sergeant; I'll take your word for it."

"I *am*. I think you're prejudiced, Major. About women, that is."

Inwardly he sighed. That again. "Listen," he said, "I'm not going to argue with you, but if you want it straight—yes, I think women in the Air Force are a big mistake, and I think you've just demonstrated why. You had no business getting involved with this guy if you're training him. That's the difference right there. An all-male military, or at least one that's ninety percent—"

"Hey, wait a minute!" She turned to face him indignantly. "I really appreciate your coming along when you did; I owe you a big thanks, but I really don't have to take the rest of it, do I? That it's probably all my fault? You just listen—if I was a *male* Sergeant, and you saw some woman chasing me in her car, and she ran me off the road—I'm a man, now, remember—and she got out of her car and started screaming and pounding on me, maybe beating me over the head with her pocketbook, you'd just think I'd gotten myself into some little male-type problem, right? And I don't know about you, because I really don't know you, Major, but if this woman made some sort of trouble for me on base—and I know what I'm talking about, I've actually seen this happen—maybe you'd be a good buddy and help me get it straightened out, cover up for me if it wasn't too much trouble. But you wouldn't think I'd asked for it, would you? But oh, boy—is it ever different when I'm a woman! That's not career Air Force *then*, is it?"

She glared at him. The choice, Dolph Bauernhauser knew, was between responding in kind or being good-humored. He smiled.

"Well, I'm glad to know you feel strongly about the service," he said. "That's in your favor."

"You bet your boots I do," she said emphatically.

Now he had to laugh. "Okay, Sergeant, you win. I respect your goals; don't get me wrong. But if you value your Air Force career, I think you'd better start looking after it. Let me give you the usual 'male solution' to this problem; if I were in your place, I'd start thinking about transferring out."

The indignation faded from the pixyish face, and she turned suddenly thoughtful.

"Well," she said. Then she murmured, almost to herself, "Gee, I've got such great quarters here; Rosalie and I just finished fixing them up—we've bought such a lot of stuff. And all my friends are here." She sighed loudly. "That's the thing to do, isn't it, transfer out? It really solves a lot of problems. But it takes months for a transfer, even if I could get it approved."

The sadness was genuine, and Dolph was reluctantly impressed—she was not kidding about her career.

On impulse he said, "Sergeant, who's your CO in Communications—Tom Shoffel?"

She nodded.

He was well aware of the risks in inserting himself in the matter, but he rationalized that it might save Tom Shoffel a lot of future trouble.

"I think you ought to talk to him and lay it all out," he said. "I know Tom—I think it might be possible for him to put this thing on some sort of priority basis if he understood what was involved." He hesitated. Then he said, "I'll put in a good word for you."

She looked up abruptly and broke into a grin, bringing all the dimples into play. "Oh, say, *would* you? Oh, that's really *nice* of you! You're such a doll, Major! Jeepers, do you think I could really get priority on a transfer?"

Sobered, he said, "Well, if you think you're in any danger—"

She bounced in the seat. "Oh, God, that solves all my problems! It's not going to work out in the tower with Ronny there because I can't explain it to Tom Bullock, I mean, ask Tom to put me on another shift. Because he'd still be around! Yes, right now I'd take *anywhere*—Mountain Home, Tinker—I don't care if it's the boondocks, I just want to get away from him!" She put her hand on the door handle. "Major, you don't have to follow me in your car, I'm all right; I'm going back to the base, anyway. But I really want to thank you!"

"I can't promise you anything—" he began.

"You can do it, I know," she assured him. "Just don't forget, will you? Just don't forget to speak to Major Shoffel." She looked at him meltingly. "I could give you a great big kiss, Major; you're really an angel." She saw his involuntary movement and laughed. "I'm only kidding!"

But she bounced out of the car and wheeled to face him. To his surprise and amusement, she shot him a very sharp and snappy salute and then turned to walk back to her car.

It was still early, not yet midnight, when Simon McAllister drove the Porsche into a Seven-Eleven store at Virginia Beach to get Topper some coffee. He was as tired as if he had been up for two days' combat sorties without sleep. And he was not too sober himself. They had done a lot of drinking, both in the OC bar in the afternoon and later at the weird party at the Middle Easterners' house; from time to time during what he now regarded as an interminable evening, he had cursed the easy socializing which was one of the hazards of military life. It began, usually, with a few drinks in the OC bar, getting slightly looped, then often went on to a boozed-up dinner somewhere with drunken diehards or a surprise visit to somebody's house for a few more in the kitchen—pursuing the notion of deserved hell-raising, living it up to dissipate the pressures of the fighter jock profession.

Which was all right, he supposed; he certainly wasn't against it, except that too much good-timing increased his uneasiness with the inherent disorganization of life, a disruption of that orderliness that, considering his education and his interests, was a fundamental part of his makeup. If nothing else, the Air Force brought out a solitariness in him; it wasn't the first time, during such an evening, that about midnight he had wished to hell he was home in his own apartment with the sound system and the space movies turned on, fixing himself a can of hot soup to taper off the booze. This other aspect of his life was really getting in his hair.

He had a hard time keeping Topper in the car and out of the store in the few minutes it took to get a container of coffee. On their way back from the party, Topper had gotten out of the car at every stoplight and wandered around in the intersections, hailing other cars and trying to hitch rides. Since they were still in their flight suits, illegal off base, and in an area crawling with Navy shore patrols, this was not especially funny.

On the Norfolk-Virginia Beach expressway, Topper became interested in the idea that it was a great place for mooning cars, and only the fact that he was too drunk to get the zipper of his flight suit pulled down kept him from doing it.

Topper, he was finding, was a pain in the ass when drunk. The cool, quietly superconfident flight leader had, some hours ago, been magically replaced by a red-eyed monster of powerful whims that would not be denied, right in the fighter jock tradition of rugged individualism and mayhem, the stuff of stories. Great to hear once they were enshrined in myth, but pure hell to have to deal with in the flesh.

On the turnoff to Highway 64 north, Topper vomited up the coffee. In a matter of seconds, it was all over the inside of the Porsche, even the windshield, and Topper looked as though he had taken a bath in it. It wasn't just coffee, either. A lot of other stuff came up.

"Aw, God, Topper," Simon said.

Topper leaned forward, shoulders hunched, and pressed his head against the dashboard. "Look what I did," he said.

Simon thought it was possible to feel sympathy for Topper, especially after what Candy had done to him, but all he could think of at the moment was that he could have used Beeper and Nizzard around.

Topper bored his head into the glove compartment, his body bent in two, hands hanging at the tops of his boots. "I'm fucking up, Moonbird," he said hollowly.

"Yeah, Top." He was thinking that he had to get the Porsche off the expressway and do something about getting it cleaned up. The stink was driving him crazy. My damned car, he thought.

"No, I mean it," Topper said. "It just started." Bent over, his voice was muffled. "I never saw anything like it. I mean, *damn*, Moonbird—I never fuck up, everybody knows that."

"Everything's cool, Top," he told him.

"The hell it is." Topper lurched forward, grinding his head against the radio knobs. "I never fucked up before. It's the end, Moonbird—you know that?"

He found it painful to listen to. He knew all about this, the superstition of fighter jocks, that you had only so much luck allotted to you, and when it ran out, it ran out. He was amazed that Topper, of all people, seemed to believe it.

God, he's drunk, he told himself.

Topper lifted his head suddenly, looked around with an expression of dim distaste. He wiped his hands on the front of the nomex flight suit. "Hell, your car's full of crap, Moonbird," he observed. "Why'n the hell don't you clean it up?"

"Ah, shut up, Topper," he said.

Simon turned the Porsche off the highway and into Northampton Boulevard. The night was warm and sticky, and a full moon was rising. He remembered a long open beachfront at Ocean View. Topper was too drunk to try to check into a motel, even one of the riding academies down at the far end of East Ocean View Avenue, but somewhere, sometime, they had to get fixed up. They were due on the flight line in about five hours.

The road stretched through the coastal flatlands, mist rising from the marshes. The indistinct lights of housing developments for military personnel and their families swept by, glowing from oblong concrete shapes surrounded by chain link fence. He wasn't sure where they were, but he knew they had left Northampton Boulevard and were on some road near the beach. He could hear the sound of surf. He made several right turns, passed some new construction, and kept going. Finally he turned the car onto an unpaved road lined with dunes and grass and drove down to the end. He saw the water. The sea was smooth under a moon which paved a triangle path of light toward the horizon.

With difficulty, he managed to get Topper out of the front seat and down to the beach. Topper fell down several times but got back up, coated with sand. He maneuvered Topper down to the water's edge and threw him in unceremoniously. It was shallow, the tide was in, soft waves curled over his feet. He rolled Topper around in the water and pulled off his flight suit and left him there, wearing only his boots. He was too tired to try to get him out of those.

Simon sat down on the sand a few feet away to keep an eye on him. He threw Topper's wet flight suit up on the beach behind him. It was a hell of a place, he thought, looking around. And then the humor of it struck him—Topper drunk out of his mind, and he—he had been now and all evening playing the faithful wingman, the one who looks after his leader. The inevitable extension of what they were in the air, that dependent and trusting relationship, had continued; for whatever it was worth, he found he could not go off and leave him. Topper was actually in pretty poor shape.

Earlier in the evening, Topper had said, "I came home— well, hell, you know what happened, they were in bed."

As a matter of fact, he *didn't* know what had happened. There had been talk about it in the squadron—everything went through the squadron eventually—and he had heard one version which sounded bad but believable.

"They were in bed. The kid was right there in my bed. You could hear them all over the house. I thought he was killing her—a rapist, or something."

The worst part of it all was that Topper, who could deal with everything, could not deal with this, nor, apparently, leave it alone.

"Moonbird, the only thing I do good is fly. And even that's getting fucked up. The brigadier didn't say I fucked up, but he didn't have to. When they say computer-managed, they mean it, and that means no override, no manual."

He'd had no idea what that was all about.

He heard Topper climbing out of the water, grunting, crawling on his hands and knees up the beach. Simon lifted himself on one elbow, watched Topper sprawl out flat on the sand.

There were practical considerations to where they were and what they were doing, he reminded himself. It was better for Topper to sleep it off on the beach; God knows he wasn't capable of dragging him anywhere else; it took two men to do that. And if he could stay awake, by four or five o'clock he could probably get Topper on his feet, get him back to his apartment where they could shower and get something to eat. The key to the whole thing was to try and stay awake. If he went to sleep on the beach, he'd never wake up, and he knew Topper wouldn't.

The moon, small and cold now, bathed the beach in a hard white light. He saw a fiddler crab scurrying away, tangled in its black shadow. He lay back against the sand. There was a difference in being alone and being lonesome, and he pondered why the thought had occurred to him just then.

He stared at the moon. Then he looked for Arcturus, for Nunki, other navigational points and couldn't find them. He thought about Nancy, about Linda Criscio and made himself stop thinking about that. He heard Topper snoring. The waves lapped at the beach.

The mission was programmed by data link from Denver. What wasn't done in the HTV simulator buildings—as it was 90 percent of the time—was done flying atmospheric, still attached to Hot Victor's airbreathing booster, flying mock intercepts. Or doing laser-beam practice at carefully identified pieces of earth-orbiting junk. There was enough of it up there where they had been surreptitiously picking off each other's satellites.

He got into his robotlike silver pressure suit, and his airman spaceflight assistant zipped and Velcroed him up like a mummy. The last item was the bubble helmet attached to the portable life-support boxes. The airman escorted him carefully down the hall from the equipment room, carrying the all-important computer program card to be attached to his sleeve by a plastic chain just before he got into the cockpit. The chain was vital—if he dropped the program slip when he was inside the Hot Victor, he was so bundled up in the pressure suit he would never be able to bend over enough to find it.

He rode with his spaceflight assistant out to the flight line in a special self-propelled cart, standing up to protect his gear. The still experimental Hot Victor XF-20, armed not only with lasers but the new particle-beam cannon, was the first in line, designated Charlie Two. He looked at it with immense satisfaction. It sat there, exhaling cold steam from the umbilical cords feeding liquid oxygen and liquid hydrogen into its belly. Charlie Two's titanium skin had not yet been covered with antidetection coating; it gleamed polished silver, a sharp deltawing with three airbreathing engines which almost overshadowed the rocket engines that would take over once the HTV was clear of the earth's atmosphere.

His spaceflight airman helped him up the ladder into Charlie Two's high cockpit. The final check was already done, and flight orders were relayed after takeoff in the instantaneous computer-processed translation from the data-link center in Colorado.

Slowly, careful of his wiring, he eased into the cockpit, guided by the airman's voice over the portable intercom. The spaceflight assistant inspected his hose and wiring connections and plugged him in, checking to see that all the lights were lit on the inboard computers, signifying proper contact. The airman stepped back, motioning for him to close the canopy, two inches of tempered, fused quartz shutting down over his head.

The umbilicals dropped from the hybrid tactical vehicle's belly. Air traffic control was being put into the local computer, sent to Colorado where it was encoded to binary calculations, then sent to a satellite in geosynchronous orbit, relayed back to earth to his microwave receiver in the Hot Victor, decoded by his cockpit computer, and the voice reconstructed for his own ears. And after all that, all that emerged was a little Donald Duck voice checking out his clearance.

He threw the switches, and one after another the three air-breathing jet engines roared into life. His computer flashed the message: CK FIN OK in red letters on the bottom of the main CRT display, meaning the cockpit computer had done the thousand or so items on the pretakeoff checklist and was telling him now that the HTV was flight-ready.

"Moonbird Charlie Two, you up?" the tower wanted to know.

"Affirmative."

"Moonbird Charlie Two, this is Edwards. Taxi to runway two-eight, cleared for takeoff. No conflicting traffic."

That was it. All other flight information would be coming on board from satellite data transmission after takeoff, giving him all he needed on his course, altitude, airspeed, and further traffic information.

He lined up Hot Victor Charlie Two on the runway. He was surrounded by a cloud, the steamlike vapor of liquid hydrogen and oxygen escaping from the vents as it bled off enough to keep the fuel cool and liquid.

He moved the three toggle switches for the airbreathing engines forward. The toggles were at his left for controlling thrust; two toggle switches were on the right for control of pitch and roll. The computer did everything else and told him what it was doing in the little red-lighted code words of the display on the visor of the helmet just in front of his eyes.

As he held the toggles forward, the airbreathing engines spooled up in a mounting crescendo. The display said /* TO * THST */ He relaxed the switch back to center position. The

Hot Victor Charlie Two moved slowly, lumbered down the runway, roaring and shivering like some storybook dragon about to be released. He braced himself for the slam of Gs on takeoff. The numbers on his computer display counted down to zero next to a red VR .

Delicately, with one finger, he pulled back on the toggle switch, and the nose wheel jumped off the runway. There was a resounding blast, a contained explosion.

He counted two seconds and hit the computer button for the flight program. The computer lit up with its cryptic notations informing him that it had just completed its computer feed from Colorado via satellite and was ready. It banked Hot Victor Charlie Two sharply in the air and began a full power climb, thirty degrees nose-up, in a maximum performance drill.

Which suited him just fine. This was the moment he had damned well lived his whole life for. Except that now he had gotten the thing in the air, he was not sure what he wanted to do with it. On a test flight, anyway. Below him on the beach, Topper was snoring enough to simulate hypersonic ram jets.

Or he could have his computer spelling out the acronym SCATANA , the code for national emergency for commercial air traffic. His cockpit computer would spell out MISSION PROFILE SUB ORB * SKIP CAPETOWN WPT * ENG LO ORB & TYPE 1 BAL CONSOV...

On the other hand, what was he doing in a combat mode? His business was test flight. . . .

A jeep or truck came roaring out of nothingness, cutting down the beach close to the waterline where the sand was hard; there was a powerful searchlight mounted on it, boring a blinding white beam straight at him. He raised on one elbow and flung his arm over his face.

The thing came to a stop. Out of the blackness behind the searchlight, a voice said, "Okay, you guys, this is government property."

He sat all the way up. *Government property?* With one arm still over his face, eyes shrinking, blinded in the spotlight, he reached for his breast pocket and his ID.

They were standing over him.

Another voice said, "Jesus—this one here's buck nekkid." One of the shadows trained a flashlight on his knees, then back up to rest on the nameplate over the pocket of the flight suit.

"What are you—Air Force?"

A second voice said, "Captain, this is Little Creek Amphibious Base, and you are trespassing. I hope you got some military identification on you."

The *Navy*.

"Oh, shit," he said.

The limousine of the Saudi Arabian Ambassador had just rolled away down the main drive of the White House, headed for Pennsylvania Avenue, when the President's National Security Advisor, Professor Barrington Wojniak, stepped from his automobile on the west side in front of the small entrance which led directly to the Oval Office. It was late, and only one lamp was lighted under the portico. Professor Wojniak moved carefully, remembering the several steps there. The President's executive administrator, Dale Byers, was waiting right inside the door.

"Good timing, Bart," Byers said, keeping his voice low. "Our Saudi friends just left." The President's chief of White House staff was a fattish young man with an officious manner, which he carefully moderated now for the National Security Advisor. "This thing sort of took us by surprise. They called at eight and wanted a priority appointment right away, tonight. The President canceled his movie so he could get right on it."

Barrington Wojniak nodded. He had had his car wait at the West Gate until White House security called down to say the Saudis were leaving; then he had told his driver to proceed to the small private entrance to the Oval Office.

Professor Wojniak followed Dale Byers down the narrow corridor that led to the President's office. As they entered, the figure behind the desk got up and came around it to greet him. The President's expression was one of unflagging cheerfulness.

"Bart, I'm sorry we dragged you away from the ball game. What's the score?"

Barrington Wojniak placed his briefcase on a chair and murmured something to the effect that when he'd left home, it was the top of the ninth and the Orioles were ahead, three to two. But he lifted his arm and looked pointedly at his wristwatch. It was almost midnight. From what Byers had told him on the telephone, the President's unscheduled meeting with the Saudi Arabian Ambassador had begun at a little past nine.

"This must have been important," he said.

The President turned and walked toward the curve of bay windows behind his desk. The drapes were still open, and the floodlit obelisk of the Washington Monument, a quarter of a mile away, raised its shape against the black summer sky, somewhat distorted by the inch-thick bulletproof glass. Two Secret Service agents stood in plain view on the lighted gravel path beyond.

The President scratched his ear thoughtfully. "Well, yes and no. I got the usual lecture on oil conservation. The Prince wants us to know that the United States Congress isn't doing its job and that our image continues to be that of profligate wasters of limited world resources—the Ambassador's got a set speech on that subject these days. It varies a little from visit to visit, but the content's always the same."

Barrington Wojniak waited patiently. Israeli warplanes had attacked southern Lebanon again that afternoon—he'd received the dispatch from NSA just as he was leaving his office. Dale Byers gathered up the copies now and offered him the sheaf of briefing papers, but Professor Wojniak shook his head, no. He was familiar with what little information they contained.

Byers said in an undertone: "The Israelis claim two MIGs shot down."

"Dale—" The President turned from the window. "We'll get to that. What Ambassador Massaouimi's got on his mind right now is the delivery schedule of the Saudi F-15s. He's pressing for some assurance that the delivery date hasn't been moved back again."

Barrington Wojniak sat down in the chair nearest the President's desk and took out a crumpled pack of cigarettes. "At this time of night?"

"Well, our friends are concerned about their delivery of F-15s. The new fighters are a prestige item, and right now the Saudis are complaining that they're not getting much prestige these days out of their alignment with the United States. We've already given the Israelis their F-15s, and they're operational—*too* operational, to judge from today's news—and that makes the Saudis very unhappy. Massaouimi is convinced we're going to continue to drag our feet on their delivery schedule. God

knows, every time the Israelis go over the border and engage
Syrian MIGs, the Ambassador hotfoots it right over here to
demand their Eagles. Massaouimi keeps reminding me that
we've not only failed to decrease our imports and do anything
about the decline of the dollar abroad, but that we sold those
F-15s to the Israelis with the tacit understanding that they were
never to be used offensively, only to defend Israel's borders.
He can recite chapter and verse on the agreement just as Congress approved it."

The President's voice had grown fretful. Professor Wojniak
looked about him for an ashtray. While Byers was bringing
him a servidor from the other side of the room, the door opened
and a White House waiter came in, pushing a wheeled cart
with a large silver service.

"Yes, good," the President said, "here's our coffee. It's
decaffeinated, Bart; you don't have to worry."

Professor Wojniak said wryly, "It's not the coffee around
here that keeps me awake."

The National Security Advisor was not an authority on the
Arab world; his area of expertise was the Soviet bloc of Eastern
Europe. But he had become accustomed to being consulted on
a wide variety of subjects; "advisor" meant, to this particularly
literal-minded chief executive, a source of nearly limitless
wisdom and knowledge, not to mention the considerable bonds
of intimate friendship. The business of the sale of the F-15
Eagles to both Israel and Saudi Arabia—with the Saudis waiting impatiently for their delivery—was complicated by the fact
that the United States Defense Department was keenly interested in the combat performance of the Eagles against the
Syrian-based MIG 23s and MIG 21s. No amount of simulated
aerial combat stateside could produce these vital operational
evaluations; nothing could—outside of a fighting war with the
Russians. But it was a rather unpleasant either/or situation in
international politics: the DoD was hopefully trading off a
feigned ignorance of the Israelis' use of the F-15s in Lebanon
in return for performance data that was invaluable. Meanwhile,
the Saudis fumed. And not the least at stake was the awk-
wardness of the Saudi position in a sea of growing anti-U.S.
feeling in the Arab world.

Professor Wojniak said, "I hope you told the Ambassador

that the Secretary of State has filed a strong protest with the Israeli government over the illegal use of the F-15s."

The President snorted. "Oh, Bart, they don't fall for that anymore. That gesture is just a damned embarrassment. They know what's up."

The President put his coffee cup down on his desk and walked back to the bank of windows. He stood there for a long moment, his hands clasped behind his back.

"The Saudi Ambassador," he said slowly, "tells me they've heard we're having more than the usual problems with the engines in the new F-15s. What do we know about that?"

Professor Wojniak raised his eyebrows. "The Israelis don't seem to be having any difficulty."

"That we are," the President continued, "about to break into the nationwide media with it, even a Congressional subcommittee hearing."

Professor Wojniak and Dale Byers exchanged looks.

Wojniak said cautiously, "Something about the maintainability figures being pretty bad. Didn't Dale give you the report from the Defense Department meeting last month?"

"Did he?" the President said.

Byers said quickly, "The Air Force is spending six hundred million on a Component Improvement Program they say will take care of their problems. If you want to wait a minute, I'll get you the outline from the office."

"No, no." The President looked around. "Is it as bad as all that? Is the press picking up on it, as Massaouimi says? I hope not. We're getting a lot of bad news on the Space Shuttle; we don't need anything else right now. It only makes for tough sledding on Congress on other things, the Induspace bill for one. Has anybody talked to Morty Glass?"

Professor Wojniak said, "What I want to know is, where are they getting their information? Saudi intelligence isn't good enough to predict a media break on engine problems in our new tactical fighters. The Saudis have gotten a leak from Mossad. Israeli intelligence usually knows what toilet's being flushed here before we can get out of the john. What's Comverse doing?" He referred to the White House press secretary. "Has he checked this out with his press people?"

Byers said, shrugging, "Larry doesn't know anything about it."

They were all silent for a long moment.

"I would say," Byers suggested, "if the media's going to raise a major issue on anything, it's going to be on the Space Shuttle. We could go from bad to worse on that item very easily."

The President said, "ABC News did a whole story on the problems with the Shuttle thermal tiles Tuesday night and the Shuttle engine problems, too. I saw a video replay of it. Did you see it, Bart?"

Professor Wojniak shook his head.

"Reynolds quoted some source as predicting the Shuttle will last only one trip."

"Well, will it?"

"We are," the President said firmly, "keeping to our current launch date."

Wojniak smiled. "We'll keep our fingers crossed."

"What NASA wants to do now is schedule a space walk for the astronauts to inspect the thermal tiles before re-entry, in the event some of them have to be replaced."

In spite of himself, Professor Wojniak had to laugh. It was late, and he was tired; but the laughter, he saw, was not well received. He said quickly, "Sorry—I was merely hoping they wouldn't have to stay up there until they got the spares glued on. The reaction—"

"Is one," the President said glumly, "that a lot of people are having, Bart. I don't discount it. We've been over a barrel on this one too damned long, and all we need is for the Russians to get something up there before we do. Don't think intelligence hasn't been watching them like hawks. We're sticking to our launch schedule; we really haven't much choice." He turned and sat down at his desk and drummed his fingers on the surface. "It's hurting the Induspace bill, there's no doubt about it—Morty Glass is taking a beating. Congress knows the cost overruns on the Shuttle are way beyond acceptability limits, and they're tired of voting more money. Now the F-15s are coming up with the same thing—six hundred million dollars is not going to create a viable climate for anything."

Byers said, "I think the public realizes these things are costly. Besides, six hundred and sixty-five million, which is the actual cost of the CIP, includes not only repair and modification on the Air Force's F-15s, but the fixes on the same engines in the F-16s and the Navy's problems with—"

The President interrupted to ask, "What's our last evaluation—are the Eagles still rated above the MIGs?"

Wojniak and Byers looked at each other. Byers shrugged.

Professor Wojniak said, "I haven't heard any differently."

More positively, Byers said, "With what the Israelis are doing with them against the Syrians, yes—the Eagles are way out ahead."

"Then we ought to be able to figure some way to capitalize on that." The President paced across the room. "How about goodwill tours?"

"That costs a lot of money. But the Saudis—"

"Might respond to it," Professor Wojniak said. "It's a nice gesture of concern. They should understand that."

"Can the Air Force get—what—a squadron there and back in good order?" the President wanted to know.

Professor Wojniak said, "We're in trouble if they can't."

14

The first yellow leaf, stirred by a fairly brisk breeze from the tidal creek known as Southwest Branch, detached itself from the sweet gum tree and sideslipped its way to come to rest on the asphalt surface of the driveway. It lay against the black like a leathery gold star.

It was not the first sign of autumn, Amy Gazenove knew, although in the heat of September, one looked eagerly for it; the gum trees were still green, and the crepe myrtles raised thick, ragged red blooms at the creekside—even the leaf still showed bright verdant veins against its yellow. But the change of seasons in the flatlands began this way: not with a vibrant clash of color, but a dim, hot fading; the exhaustion of summer imperceptibly melded into mild, russet days and cool, damp nights. One hardly noticed it.

Only the calendar marked the movement of true time—that and the emptiness of the house again after the brief rush of activity in getting the children back from their summer jobs and off to college once more.

Amy Gazenove picked up the fallen leaf, lifted the lid of the garbage can, and dropped it inside. Then she undid the neck of the green plastic trash sack she had dragged from the den and began taking out the empty bottles. She dropped them one by one into the garbage can, listening to them crash against each other as they fell to the bottom.

It was not as though her husband could not take out his empty whiskey bottles and dispose of them himself; on the contrary, he was, like most military men, trained to neatness and order. But for the past few months, he had put his empties back into the liquor cabinet, letting them accumulate, knowing that she would find them when she cleaned—all these dumb, drained witnesses to his unhappiness with the state of things.

He had drunk his way through the bonded scotch, the two bottles of bourbon, the vodka—there was even an empty sherry bottle. Amy Gazenove lifted it and stared at the label. Sandeman's Cream Sherry. She had bought it for the Wing Commander's wife at New Year's; as far as she knew, Alice Kelley was the only one who drank Sandeman's on the rocks. But she had heard Roger stirring downstairs Sunday night; she supposed he had gone through most of the stuff in the liquor cabinet by then, and she hadn't bought any liquor for weeks. So it must have been this, or start on the Kahlua.

She had to smile.

He would never allow himself to be comforted, this tough, ardent, irascible man; mentally she put her arms around him, small as a bantam, not even as tall as she was, and kissed him consolingly and smoothed his hair with her hands and pressed lovingly against him. And the mental picture of Lieutenant Colonel Gazenove, touched to the quick, snarled, *For Chrissake, Amy*—and stalked off.

She folded the empty trash bag carefully and carried it back through the garage and into the kitchen. The message was meant for her. *You know I'm suffering.* During the two weeks the children had been home, he hadn't drunk very much and then only at night in the nocturnal prowling, the sitting up before television. And never during the week. Never when he was flying. The old pattern.

She turned on the water at the sink and got the bag of carrots out of the refrigerator and placed them under the tap. Beef stew was his favorite: the strange solace of all those hard years of struggle when they ate stew and swore when the good times came they would never eat it again, they would have steak seven times a week. The tap, turned on full, trickled to a thin stream, and Amy watched it with dismay. There was trouble with the water pressure again. The city had raised the tax assessments on Commodore Drive with the promise of new water lines, but nothing had happened. *Ye Gods,* she thought. She was not unhappy over the prospect of living in an apartment, even in crowded Washington. This house was getting too large and too empty now that the kids were in college. She disliked cutting the grass when Roger couldn't get around to it, and the neighborhood boys were unreliable. The house was hard to clean—it was, after all, only a house in that twenty-year parade of places lived in because they were available near the bases where you were assigned. In the beginning, she had consoled herself with the thought that someday, *someday*, she would find one she really liked, or that they would stay in one place long enough to build. But you get over that. After the first years, one house became very much like another; you worried about finding the right schools first and foremost and commuting time to the flight line and the equity on hand to put into the next. And, of course, how much your housing allowance was going to be. Only at the bottom of the long list of necessities did you come to the luxury of whether you liked it or not. She had lost all feeling about houses, she told herself, looking around the kitchen. Once she had longed for a wall oven, one of the really nice ones—had actually had it in Louisiana when they had scrimped and saved for it and Roger had installed it himself. And that had been left behind, too, when he went up to Lieutenant Colonel and squadron commander and was reassigned. Now, she knew, she didn't really give a damn.

I have suffered, too, she told herself. *I just don't leave empty booze bottles around to let you know it.*

Nothing lasts, if that was any consolation. She paused, the cold water running over her hands. It was so unfair—it was a world where they all grew old too soon, and he was so certain of retirement. He was still young, and too vital, too handsome to have a daughter in college; it was what everyone told him. Both of us, she thought watching her reflection in the window over the sink. A pretty woman looked back, still slim and pretty and attractive. A year at the Pentagon and then out, he had said. He never talked about it.

She had been faraway; the chimes of the front doorbell were ringing. She put the carrots back into the colander and turned off the water. She was in shorts and an old T-shirt—whoever it was at the front door would find her dressed for cleaning house. She looked around for her sandals. She had slipped them off and left them somewhere. Oh, well, she told herself.

She wiped her hands on a towel and padded barefoot down the hall to the front door. Halfway there, she recognized the figures silhouetted against the screen. It was Candy James and her little daughter Emma. Oh, no, she thought with a sinking feeling. Candy's face was full of tragedy and woe.

Damn, Amy Gazenove thought, this was going to be trouble. She had heard what was happening to Topper and Candy, and she was not sure she wanted any part of it. A sudden resentment filled her. How many times have I done this? she asked herself. I have given up my houses, my life, my wall oven—yes, even my husband for all this, these moments when some unhappy squadron wife appears at my door with those fatal words— *Amy, I've got to talk to somebody.*

Candy's eyes were brimming with tears. As she pushed the door open, the tears spilled over and coursed down Candy's cheeks. The girl made a sudden convulsive movement toward her.

"Amy," Candy wailed, "I just can't go on like this any longer! Oh, Amy—I—I've *got* to talk to you!"

The resentment vanished at the sight of Candy—poor forlorn Candy—and her little girl. That imp, Amy Gazenove thought, with Topper's porcelain blue eyes and funny iron jaw.

"Oh, Candy, honey," Amy Gazenove murmured from the depths of her warm heart. She put her arms around her. "Ah, love—don't *cry.*"

"Okay, you already know something about this. Here's your big tin can of a turbofan engine, the F100X." With his index finger, Simon McAllister traced out the shape of it against the bare skin of the girl's belly. "From the last figures I've seen, about eighty percent of the big stall stagnation trouble occurs when you go to afterburners, and most of the stall takes place in the upper lefthand corner of the flight envelope—at high altitude and low speed. For instance, you might develop a dose of stall stagnation when you're driving the Eagle at about four hundred thirty KT and forty thousand feet. That's a poor environment for stable afterburner combustion, and when you hit the afterburners hard, they're going to snuff out sometimes. Now, the mist of the unburned fuel left in the afterburner by the blowout is ignited by the hot gasses still in the turbine part of the engine, making a powerful pressure pulse travel *forward* through the fan duct. Keep this in mind as a sort of backing-up effect. So as a result, the fan blades lose their bite on the air being drawn into the engine. The *fan* stalls. It no longer pumps air into the compressor."

Simon looked at the girl's face. It followed him raptly—with a look he hadn't seen even when they were making love. He drew his nail lightly along her flesh.

"And inside the compressor, what air's left in there thins and slows down. The *compressor* stalls now—and the compressor stops pumping air and slows down. But the compressed air stored downstream in the diffuser and combustor surges forward through the compressor, clearing the stall. When the surge is over, the engine tries to pick up normal speed again. But as pressures climb in the *afterburner* where the trouble started in the first place, the unburned fuel is ignited again by our friends, the heating turbine gases."

"Which starts it all over again," Linda Criscio said.

"It's called 'bang, gasp, burp, and speed-up' by engineers. In aggravated conditions, it repeats itself about seven times a second until the pilot can establish stable afterburner combustion. Which is just one of those little problems."

She frowned. "You lose airspeed."

"Now watch," he told her. "Stall stagnation starts as a normal surge, but the engine thrust drops down to a few hundred pounds. The compressor remains partially stalled, and rotor speed drops. When the airflow is starved off, the combustor flame sputters and delivers unburned fuel to the turbine, where it ignites. Then your turbine starts getting hot. What you have to do there is throttle *back*—not forward, that's only going to make the problem worse as it dumps more bad stuff into the system—and shut off the flow of fuel to the engine. Once your compressor slows down below 'idle,' the engine unstagnates and can be restarted. That is, providing you haven't chewed up or burned up some of the turbine blades during the overheating."

"Wh—" she began.

"Wait. It isn't new—in the early days of military turbojets, it was called 'hung stall,' and it could be taken care of by providing enough diffuser and combustor volume to provide a good surge after you hit the compressor stall. But that isn't enough for these advanced turbofans."

"The air—"

"No." He shook his head emphatically. "I don't care what Awful Amos has been telling you, it's not airflow at the intake lip or anything like that; it's improper flow as a result of afterburner troubles. But you're on the right track. The problem apparently is in the space between the fan and the compressor inlet. Look—if a negative pressure impulse strikes the inlet while the compressor is trying to recover from a normal surge, a rotating stall develops."

He looked at her and she nodded quickly.

"Okay, think of it as a bubble of dead air that moves along with the blades. There are really two sources of negative pressure pulse. If, during a surge, the fan unstalls an instant before the compressor, it starts pumping air and builds up pressure in front of the compressor intake. When the compressor clears out in a few seconds, the accumulated pressure drops, and the compressor intake gets a strong negative pressure pulse. Also, repeated engine surging at low altitudes can trigger stall stagnation, but that's another can of worms."

"Hey," he said. His hand moved up to cover her breast. "I really like talking to you, you know that?"

She looked at him thoughtfully. The small pale mouth curved delightfully.

"I wish I could go up."

"Jesus—" He made a gesture of exasperation. "I don't see why in hell you people aren't briefed on this. *You* can understand it. But they've got their damned management-assembly line system worked out; they yank out the engines and put in new pods and cart the busted ones away to engine repair, but I don't see how a little theory on the flight line is going to hurt anybody. Hell, I think you people ought to be trained as advanced technicians—I think you ought to be going to school all the time, learning everything. If the Air Force had any sense, it would be scheduling every ground crew member for an orientation and personal-bonding flight in the Eagles every three or four months. Instead of waiting until they're going to check out of the service and then give it to them like a booby prize."

She caught his hand and held it.

"Okay," she said.

"No, it's not okay. Damn, you don't know how much the

Air Force pisses me off. They give those rides to VIPs and politicians when they ought to take everybody up who works on the Eagles, the ground crews, the weapons loaders—that's the only thing that makes sense—to lock you people into close identification with the equipment, to let you know how much the fighter jock depends on you. But the military does everything ass-backwards; they're still living in the past. The Air Force ought to dump it. The clubs for officers only, the clubs for NCOs, the clubs for enlisted, the caste system. It went out with horse-drawn artillery. Listen, some day—" He pulled his hand away. *"Some day* every goddamn body is going to be involved with outer space operations, working out there, and there's not going to be any time for this crap. You know that? The technician is going to be as important as the guy who climbs into the cockpit—more important. Instead, look what we've got."

"What?" she said. She reached up and smoothed his hair from his forehead.

"Well," he said, distracted. "Well, half the Eagles are sitting on the ground at any given time while the maintenance crews are working their butts off ten, twelve hours a day with everybody on their ass about it, nothing but pressure coming down from the top to get things moving. But you can't operate that way anymore. Ground crews are not a bunch of grease monkeys. Hell, I don't know why they don't all quit. The equipment is enough to make you sick—the Air Force chickenshit makes it worse. Look at the way the senior NCOs are bugging out. They take their early retirement, and to hell with it."

Splashes of late morning sunlight fell across the bed where they lay. In the parking lot below, someone was cranking up a car. A lazy warmth drifted in the room. Linda Criscio rested her hand against his ribs. The feel of her hand was firm, tender. He put his hand over hers.

"Why don't you?"

"What?" The lucent eyes, rimmed in black lashes, looked up at him.

"Quit. Look at you—you don't have any time for a social life, any time to make friends. How many overtime hours have you pulled this month?"

She frowned. "I have friends."

"Who, Awful Amos? Christ, I didn't know he could talk. What does he speak—Mad Gorilla?"

He thought it was funny. He could see from her face that it wasn't.

"Why don't *you?*"

He considered this soberly. "I've thought about it. Since I've been on the squadron shit list, I've thought about it. Getting all the way out. But you know what that would mean—dumping two whole years, my fifteen hundred hours that I sweated to get in that crazy tactical zoo, my application to test flight school, everything. My chance to fly experimental stuff, the important stuff. Everything I really want to do. Hell—I want to get into *space*."

She sat up abruptly, swept her dark hair from her shoulders with one hand. She bent forward, away from him, her hands on her knees.

He took a handful of her hair between his hands and pulled it toward him. He still marveled at how long it was. "You know," he said, "once you're inside the Air Force, once you accept the promises, the opportunities they keep telling you are there, it just fades away. You find you're stuck on a damned treadmill, jostling for elbow room like everybody else. But hell, Linda, I'm not aimed up the squadron ladder, up the big systems ladder with the rest of the career military—I wish somebody would realize that! If I had to be a fighter jock the rest of my life—if I had to be a goddamned *General*—"

She moved her head, pulled her hair out of his hands.

"Nobody," he said morosely, "will even tell me if my application to test pilot school has been rejected, or what. I swear to God, I think they've lost it. That's one thing I've learned about the military. They're always *losing* things in the damned system."

She shrugged. The muscles in her smooth gold-colored back rose and fell.

"I like it."

He considered this for a moment. "Linda, you're strange," he murmured. "You really like it, don't you? A woman who likes fighter jets—*loves* fighter jets. As good-looking as you are—"

She turned quickly, and he threw up his hands to defend himself. "Okay," he yelled, "okay!"

She picked up the pillow and threw it over his face and held it there. He wrenched it away. He tried to grab her around the waist, but she eluded him deftly.

"Okay, Linda, but don't kid yourself—they're not going to let you open up one of those engines and mess around. They're not going to listen to any theories. You just try to work your way up in the system and see what happens. Listen," he said, "did you go to bed with me just to get me to explain to you about compressor stall?" He sat there. "C'mere."

She curled her feet under her, sat facing him crosslegged in the bed.

"Yes."

"Damn, I believe you."

She said solemnly, "They're going to get them fixed. They're issuing borescopes to the crews. Fiberoptic borescopes. To look inside the engines. Fifty-hour checks to inspect the turbine blades for damage."

"Okay." He patted the pillow. "Hey, Linda, just come over here for a minute."

"Major James came out to look at them."

He didn't want to talk about Topper. "Topper wouldn't know the inside of a turbofan if he had to wear it. All he knows is flying. With his ability, he could be making fifty–sixty thousand a year with TWA. Instead, he can't even pay his bills at the OC." He said, "Come lie down a minute, will you? It's early yet."

She frowned. "He's been boozing," she said.

"Right," he said. "Who's going to fix lunch, you or me?"

"You can smell it on him."

Now he scowled. Fucking-up was catching. Was she trying to tell him the flight lines knew about it?

She sat before him, unselfconsciously naked, one of the most beautiful women he had ever seen and, he saw even now, with a curious air of containment. Mysterious. He had made love to her; it had been totally satisfactory—he remembered very vividly what it had been like—but he was not at all certain that they were ever going to do it again.

"Listen, Linda," he said, "we've got something going for us, haven't we?"

She was totally fascinating; he really enjoyed talking to her. The conversation was completely unlike that of conversations with other women: engines, advanced electronic systems, how he had managed to get messed up on the inverted approach back in August. Everything. He could see the situation had a lot to recommend it. He saw that she watched him coolly, thoughtfully.

"He's really your friend, isn't he?"

"Nobody's my friend," he said shortly. "Ask them, they'll tell you." He threw back the covers. "I'll fix lunch. I make a great Mexican omelette with *jalapeños* that'll make your eyeballs turn blue. Guaranteed."

She slid out of the far side of the bed and stood there for a moment. She lifted her hair with both hands and started to twist it into a rope.

"They say you cover for him."

That annoyed him. "Bullshit. Hey, where are you going? What are you doing?"

"I have to go in."

He jumped out of bed, naked as she. "You haven't got duty today. It's Saturday. Hey, Linda?" He followed her into the bathroom.

"I have to go in for FOD."

On Saturday, the duty maintenance crews did the Foreign Object Detail at noon, lining up on the concrete apron of the flight line to walk shoulder to shoulder picking up trash, pebbles, anything else that could be sucked into the air intakes of the jets.

She pushed him out of the bathroom, shut the door in his face.

"No, you don't," he said.

He heard the water running.

"I always go in on Saturday."

There it was again.

She came back out. He watched her step into her uniform skirt, zip it up. She picked up her blouse. He stared at her. It was the first time a woman had ever left him to go on *duty*. What the hell, he told himself. She sat down on the bed to put on her shoes.

She said, "Why don't you patch it up with your girl friend?"

He was dumbfounded. He wondered where she had heard about Nancy. The damned flight line must be a sewer of gossip. He watched as she stood up, wound her hair around her hand

and began to pin it up. She held the bobby pins between her teeth.

"I was married once," she said around the bobby pins. "We never talked."

He could believe that. "We talk," he told her. "We've been talking all night. And making love," he added significantly. He followed her helplessly.

She smiled. "You're really a nice guy," she said.

"Sure, great," he said. He tried to get in front of her in the hallway, to block her way to the door. "Listen, Linda, say something. It's not the officer-enlisted thing, is it? I don't give a damn about that; I know you don't. Hell, I've been taking you out—"

She looked up at him with those great sea-gray eyes. She smiled. The lips curved up enigmatically. "It's not you, it's me." She put her hand on his arm. "But we're alike. It's sort of funny." It was a long speech for her. "Maybe we don't like anybody a whole lot. Not like other people. I mean *love*." She shrugged. "Maybe someday."

"Now what does that mean?" he said.

She kept smiling. She opened the door and went out.

He stood there for a moment, baffled. He was surprised that he wasn't really angry. That had never happened before. Unwillingly, he had to admire her. He thought, She just walked out on me.

"Oh, Christ," he said aloud.

Naked, he went into the kitchen with the intention of getting something to eat. The sink was full of dirty dishes. It was warm, a hot summer day. He turned on the burner on the stove and took the frying pan down from its hook. He set it to one side. He sat down at the counter, moving his arm away from the heat of the flames roaring up from the gas burner.

He put his elbow on the counter and ran his fingers through his hair. He was tired of the life he was living. A woman had just walked out on him when he thought things were going good. The hell of it was, he didn't really care all that much. She was a smart girl, that Linda. What was wrong? Well, no need to worry about it, he told himself. He picked up an empty potato chip bag from a plate and crushed it and tossed it over his shoulder to the floor.

He was going to have to make the first move. And he had

promised himself he wouldn't. He took the wall telephone from its hook.

He started to dial the area code for Washington.

"Dammit, I don't want to look at it," Master Sergeant Schuld said, "take it away."

He was holding a styrofoam cup of hot coffee in his right hand. Casually, so as not to draw attention to it, he covered the stack of papers on his desk with his left forearm. But the color of the top sheet, which was the pale blue used for Air Force personnel business, was still plainly visible.

He had heard Staff Sergeant Alec Bonsomme coming across the concrete floor of the hangar outside, Bonsomme putting his feet down briskly, heels hard, *bap, bap, bap,* and that had been fair warning. From the sound, Sergeant Schuld figured it was either Bonsomme or Airman Lynwood from the Squadron Ops Office. Both walked on cement like they were stamping out cockroaches. Bonsomme had appeared carrying a newspaper, wanting him to read something in it.

"It's Saturday; I'm not working," Sergeant Schuld growled. "I'm not even here. Get the hell out."

Staff Sergeant Bonsomme, a large gangling young man with an eager expression, was not deterred; he knew from the state of Chief Schuld's desk that he was working and working hard, even though Saturday was, for him, a nonduty day. The top of Chief Schuld's desk was covered with well-thumbed Aircraft Status Sheets which, divided into columns, showed those Squadron F-15s that were mission-capable, those that were somewhat ambiguously designated "partially mission-capable," those needing maintenance in varying degrees, those needing parts, and in the last column, the most aggravated cases—those needing both maintenance and parts. The last columns on every sheet were heavily penciled in Sergeant Schuld's handwriting; parallel to the tail numbers were the ominous block letters written in red crayon pencil: K-Ball—denoting the F-15s so far gone in the maintenance circuit that they were being cannibalized for parts.

"Hey, that looks bad," Staff Sergeant Bonsomme observed. He craned his neck to read upside down. "Fifteen million per, just for parts? We're doing it the hard way, Chief. Hey, Eighty-ten—that's a new one; that's not going to the boneyard already, is it?"

Eighty-ten was dogged with persistent fuel line breaks, a problem—for once—not connected with engines. The last mission flown, the fuel line rupture had been spectacular, bringing the pilot home in a Class One emergency sitting in a cockpit full of kerosene to his knees.

Master Sergeant Schuld moved the Aircraft Maintenance Sheet from under Staff Sergeant Bonsomme's gaze and slipped it over the sheet he was hiding with his arm.

"Hell, they're all new. But we need the damned parts," he admitted, "you know that. Now they tell me there's a strike going on in some place that makes turbine bearings, and they think it's going to be a long one. The company says it can hold out for six months if it has to. The hell of it is, we can't. Right now, I'd K-Ball my own grandmother if she could grow turbine blades."

Staff Sergeant Bonsomme had seen the blue personnel form under Master Sergeant Schuld's hand when he came in, and he was not particularly alarmed. It had been off and on Chief Schuld's desk all summer, and its presence was no secret on the flight line; there was another like it on the desk of the 94th Squadron's production supervisor, Chief "Roaring George" Parker. Only Roaring George, the rumors said, had already filled his out, even to the target date for his retirement, and kept it ready to send on to the First Wing OIC of Maintenance, Colonel Drugge, the first time Chief George felt like he wanted to quit.

Staff Sergeant Bonsomme doubted that Chief Schuld would really put through his retirement papers. Sergeant Bonsomme had a hundred-dollar bet with Lieutenant Borlund, the 17th Maintenance OIC, that Awful Amos wouldn't put through his retirement this year or next, even though the Sergeant's birthday last month had made him eligible to retire at full scale. And even though the dissatisfaction of the senior NCOs these days was pretty well known. At lunch break, most of the chiefs gathered in Roaring George's office down in the 94th area to air their gripes about the never-ending problems with the F-15 equipment, the resulting long hours their wives and families were raising hell about, the high prices at the Base Exchange, the erosion of traditional NCO privileges and benefits brought about by an economy-minded Congress, and all the grievances with the system contained in the words, "damned little job satisfaction." It was the usual stuff, what NCOs were prone to from time to time, but, Staff Sergeant Bonsomme was aware, with a new note to it now under the pressures of a Command itself under pressures in Washington about engine performance.

But Staff Sergeant Bonsomme was betting the Chief wouldn't leave. Hell, Awful Amos was a fixture, an Air Force Legend, an old-time ramrod, and damned near indispensable. The 17th ground crews busted their asses for him, and the 17th had the best maintenance record on the Eagles in the Eastern area—even though the figures were nothing that any of them took any particular pride in quoting.

"Here, Chief," Staff Sergeant Bonsomme said, spreading the paper out in front of Sergeant Schuld. "How about some good news for a change?"

Sergeant Schuld lifted an eyebrow. "What in hell is that?"

"Come on, Chief, don't you read the newspapers? They're going to hold a hearing in Congress on our problems. Look right there."

On the lower right-hand side of the front page of the Washington *Post,* a headline announced:

SENATE SUBCOMMITTEE TO HEAR TROUBLES IN NEW AIR FORCE FIGHTER

"Jesus," Sergeant Schuld said under his breath.

A special subcommittee hearing will explore the admission by government officials that the nation's newest fighter jet, the F-15, is in deep trouble, it was announced today by Senator Mortimer Glass (R, Va.), Chairman of the Senate Armed Services Committee.

The engines already built for the F-15 Eagles are breaking down frequently, grounding the widely heralded "air superiority" fighters, and new engines are going to be delivered late, due to strikes at plants supplying engine parts.

"The engine problems," said Senator Anselm Foutts (D, Ark.) of the Senate special investigating committee, "leave us in a potentially dangerous position with the

F-15s. The entire matter is an embarrassment for the Air Force and its hottest new fighter."

Each F-15 is powered by two Trueham Engine Company F100X engines. Foutts said that because of persistent engine problems, only half the Air Force F-15s can fly at one time. Air Force leaders admitted in closed hearings held at the Defense Department last July that they erred in stressing performance over reliability in setting down the requirements for the F100X engine.

The engine runs so hot, to cite one major problem, that its metal turbine blades sometimes burn up, causing breakdowns. The Air Force is short of parts for fixing the F100X engines already on hand. The service is also faced with delays in deliveries of new engines. Strikes among several companies building engine parts are being blamed for delivery delays.

The House Appropriations Committee, in its report on the fiscal defense budget, recommended last month that the Pentagon reform its engine buying practices. The committee called for more testing of engines before they go into production and more competition among engine companies for contracts.

"Well, what do you think of that?" Sergeant Bonsomme said. "Congress is going to get on the ball; I bet we see some changes made. What do you think they're going to do about it?"

Sergeant Schuld scowled at the copy of the Washington *Post* in front of him. A goddamned witch-hunt—the F-111 thing all over again, if they didn't watch out. Which was a damned shame. Staff Sergeant Bonsomme was probably too young to remember any of that; all Sergeant Bonsomme saw now were the F-111Gs that flew in and out of Langley, beautiful birds living up to all the good in them which had been there all the time. Sergeant Schuld doubted young Bonsomme would believe him even if he told him. With great deliberation, Sergeant Schuld pushed the newspaper away from him and indicated to Sergeant Bonsomme that he was through with it.

"I think you ought to get the hell out of here," he said, "and let me finish what I was doing."

Surprised, crestfallen, Sergeant Bonsomme picked up the paper.

"I thought it was going to do some good," he said.

Sergeant Schuld burst out suddenly, wrathfully, "Good? Damn, did you ever know politicians to do the military any *good?* Son, you haven't been in the service too damned long or you'd know better than that! Listen, you ever see those Eagles *fly*—I mean, you ever take time to stand right out there on the flight line and watch them? They're so damned far out ahead of everything else any military force in the world's got— Hell, when you been around as long as I have, you have to learn that all the new shit's got problems; nobody knows what in hell it can do until it's been around awhile and tested operationally, until the fighter jocks get some sense about how hard and fast to push it, and that goes for the brass, too. And until the brass quits wetting its pants when it hits a big problem. And son, they *all* hit big problems, all the new stuff; that's what it's all about; that's the tough titty in advanced equipment. The Eagles' little lightweight engines were made to go like scalded cats; they're light and they run hot, and I'm damned sick and tired of working my ass off on them. But you take my word for it—they're not shitpots, no matter how many people you got running around right now shooting their mouths off about it." Sergeant Schuld paused for breath, looked around him as though judging that he might, perhaps, be wasting his time restating the obvious. He glowered at Sergeant Bonsomme. "Well, we got a damned expensive Component Improvement Program going to fix them up; I don't see what all the bitching is about. They'll work, if we can just get everybody off our backs. And Christ, no—I don't think the U.S. Congress is going to help. I been through that kind of goddamned flap before—I sure as hell don't want to be around if that crap starts up again!"

"Hey, Chief," Sergeant Bonsomme said mildly. *"Okay.* You don't have to make a federal case out of it. It's just that everybody—"

"Goddamn everybody!" Chief Schuld roared. *"Everybody* screws things up, kid, because everybody only knows what they read in the goddamned newspapers, and the goddamned newspapers don't know what in hell they're talking about! You ever seen anybody from the newspapers come out here and ask *me* about those engines?"

"No, Chief," Sergeant Bonsomme admitted. "But that

would be a good idea, I guess. No, honestly, somebody like you—"

"Aw, get the hell out of here," Sergeant Schuld said.

Sergeant Bonsomme swallowed, then shrugged in a gesture that said his intentions had been of the best and he didn't see that any of this was his fault and beat a hasty retreat through the office door and into the hangar.

Sergeant Schuld continued to stare after him for some minutes. Sergeant Schuld was damned if he could understand why Bonsomme had thought he was bringing him good news. Evidently Sergeant Bonsomme was the type who earnestly and truly believed in the powers of the U.S. Congress and that its attention would shed some light on their problems. Sergeant Schuld knew differently. If the Air Force General Staff reacted the way it usually did to the prospect of a Congressional subcommittee hearing, there would be a sudden rush of orders culminating in the mainly useless and frustrating round of activity designed for the purpose of at least *looking* like they were doing something about something: another round of Inspector General's visitations, a tightening up on the flight lines and scurrying around in squadron operations with a review of every procedure, an accounting for and probing of every difficulty, no matter how minor—and no matter whether it had just been probed and reviewed several times before—that would drive them all to the wall in an excess of explaining, verification, and hours more of work.

Dumbass, Sergeant Schuld told himself.

Sergeant Bonsomme and others like him were part and parcel of yet another, equally insoluble problem, as far as Sergeant Schuld was concerned.

Sergeant Schuld lifted his arm slightly and pulled out the blue Air Force personnel processing sheet from under it. Attached to the form by a clip was the notification that Master Sergeant Amos A. Schuld, Maintenance Production Supervisor, 17th TFS, 1st Tactical Fighter Wing, Langley B, Va., was required to enroll in Special Noncommissioned Officers School, Mountain Home AFB, Idaho, for a period of three months, to acquire the rating of Certified Technologist.

Amos Schuld lay the notification of special NCO school in front of him. After over twenty years of service, new Air Force regulations were requiring him to be certified under what was loosely referred to as the *new technologist program*. And personnel like Staff Sergeant Bonsomme were largely the reason, or at least Air Force philosophy regarding young men like Staff Sergeant Bonsomme and his qualifications was a contributing factor. Staff Sergeant Bonsomme, fitting the Air Force's newly designed recruitment goals, had had two years of college. It was true, the two years had been spent at some modest educational institution in southwest Kansas, and Sergeant Bonsomme's area of interest had been political science; still, Sergeant Bonsomme was, as the Air Force saw it, a worthwhile addition to the ranks of prospective *new technologists,* recommended by his studies at a college level to enter and improve the ranks of noncommissioned personnel who kept the country's new space-age equipment flying.

Such new material, as represented by Staff Sergeant Bonsomme, and the consequent upgrading of the field, presented something of a problem in relation to current and senior NCOs like Sergeant Schuld. Therefore, a real effort was being made to bring things up to date and mindful of goals in the form of certification in special NCO schools.

One of the courses at the NCO school in Idaho, Sergeant Schuld had heard, was something called Short-Term English Improvement, aimed at ironing out the grammatical structures of senior NCOs and generally improving their verbal and written communications.

Son of a bitch, Sergeant Schuld thought. If the rumor was true, he was against it. Most of the verbal and written communications of senior chiefs were, as anybody in his right mind knew, sheer masterpieces—if you hadn't learned the art of improved communication after twenty years, you sure as hell wouldn't make chief.

Since the notice of Special NCO School had come across his desk, Sergeant Schuld had mulled it over with considerable resentment and resistance; in his opinion, it was some damned crackpot idea some personnel whiz in the Pentagon had come up with who didn't have anything else to do; it undermined the authority and immeasurable achievements of the backbone of the service, the senior NCOs, questioned their qualifications, and struck at the vital heart of what was the invested power of any military—the experience with both men and equipment that NCOs had in the day-to-day school of hard knocks and that kept the damned system functioning.

But somebody up there in Washington, Sergeant Schuld knew, had dreamed this one up, the upgrading of Chief to new technologists—a stainless steel image of some new, infinitely better breed that did away forever with the old-time seniors who, when the chips were down, could be found anytime in the course of their duties in the pouring winter rain and sleet with their bitching, overworked crews, devoting themselves to some cranky piece of equipment that somebody had to fly and fly two hours ago and which got fixed, thanks to senior NCOs knowing *how* and *when* to do it. And there was go goddamned new technology in that.

Amos Schuld had already decided he was not going to haul his ass out to Mountain Home in Idaho for three months to have his twenty years and more of experience certified by the Air Force. It was time for him to get the hell out.

As he reached for the form which was his notice of desire to terminate service, the telephone rang. Sergeant Schuld picked it up.

A voice said familiarly, "Hell, I knew I'd find you in on Saturday. What the hell you doin'?"

"Who the hell wants to know?" Sergeant Schuld responded.

He thought he recognized the voice. Chief Master Sergeant Herman Wakes, who had gone to general administrative staff in the Pentagon after two tours in Vietnam, had a WATS line in Department T-7B.

"Well, *I* do, dammit!" There was a pause, and the voice on the other end of the line said, "Sergeant, we got a report up here you been selling spare engine parts. But it won't do you any good—they don't fit anything the Russians've got."

"Some one of these days," Sergeant Schuld said, "somebody's going to be listening in on that wire up at GS—then what're you going to do?"

The voice in Washington said, "Shut down your rotor, Amos; I got some good news for you."

More good news, Sergeant Schuld was certain, would wreck his day.

"No, hell, Amos, settle down—it's the straight poop; you'll be getting it through channels Monday. We're waiting on final clearance from State; I'm typing it now."

In a few brief words, Chief Master Sergeant Wakes told Sergeant Schuld what was in the papers he was processing for Air Force General Staff.

"Purple-ass Jesus," Sergeant Schuld said with real interest. "I get it, but I don't know what in hell that's supposed to do, except bust our balls."

In a swift movement, with the telephone held clamped between his chin and shoulder, Amos Schuld drew the blue sheet of his retirement request form off the top of the stack of papers before him, opened the bottom drawer of his desk, and dropped it in.

"Hell, yes," he said in response to Sergeant Wakes's question, "I like it. I like it a lot—it beats anything else we're doing, doesn't it? Who said I wouldn't like it?"

15

Senator Anselm Foutts of Arkansas leaned across Senator DeLean of Kentucky to speak in a portentous undertone to the subcommittee presiding officer, Senator Vincent Mastracchio of Connecticut. The bright floodlights required for the television cameras lit the subcommittee members with a relentless glare, and it was hot. The Arkansas senator mopped his head and face with a large white handkerchief.

Senator Foutts murmured, "Vinnie, I've got to take a leak. You think I can slip out of here for a few minutes?"

The special subcommittee hearing had only been underway for a bare half hour, but Senator Foutts's prostate trouble, which aggravated his bladder condition, was well known on the Hill; Senator Mastracchio nodded and murmured his assent with equal gravity. For those watching in the committee room, they were, for all intents and purposes, discussing a point of order or perhaps some element in the testimony of Undersecretary Richard Parsons of the Defense Department now before the subcommittee microphones. As Senator Foutts slipped away from the table in an awkward crouch that would, hopefully, keep him from the view of the nation's millions, Senator Mastracchio turned his attention back to Dr. Parsons.

"Well, yes, in answer to your question, Senator," Dr. Parsons was saying, "I have had some real experience in this. I got a very interesting personal exposure to the problems of the reliability of the engines we are now talking about when I went up a few months ago to go on a flight in the new F-16s, the single-engine fighter we're putting these F100X engines into next and which, as you know, have not yet gone operational. On the trip to Edwards, I read through a volume of reports we have on the F100X engine problems—I do not plan at this time to review those statistics to you, but my prepared statement is before the subcommittee—and I do want to call your attention to one which aroused my interest in a very profound way. Because I was on my way for a flight in the F-16, and I could envision landing minus one engine in the F-15, but I had a lot of trouble imagining that in the single-engine F-16. So when I got to Edwards, I asked the test pilot who was about to take me up whether this stall stagnation problem had been solved and, indeed, whether he had experienced that sort of thing in the single-engine F-16. And he went on to tell me not to worry, that they had had about ten instances of stall stagnation in the F-16 in the development test flights to that date. He went on to explain that that had happened when he had been flying outside the ordinary envelope. He was probing the outer limits of the performance of the F-16 at that time, and he did not plan to probe the outer limits while I was riding with him. The flight turned out to be very interesting and noneventful. I was unable to gather any new data on stall stagnation because none occurred while I was up in flight. The point though, and the serious point of it is that an engine with that rate of failure in a single-engine fighter is unacceptable. In a two-engine fighter, it is enough of a problem. It certainly cannot be accepted in a single-engine fighter. And I think that's what some of the countries participating in the F-16 program in Europe are complaining about. They have heard about the F100X engine performance in the F-15s, and they are very, very worried about using it in the upcoming F-16s."

The Undersecretary paused for a moment very deliberately and looked down at his notes.

"So, in a sense, I am deviating from the usual approach to the hearing here. I want to start off right now by acknowledging some problems which I consider significant. I would like, then, to spend the rest of my discussion describing to you how I think we got into this particular box and what actions I think we should take to get out of it."

The counsel for the special subcommittee, Garland Blitzstein, leaned back in his chair, extended his arm across the back of Senator DeLean's chair, and touched Senator Mastracchio on the arm. When Mastracchio turned, Blitzstein said, "Parsons didn't say anything to *us* about changing his testimony. How much is he going to change it?"

Senator Mastracchio silently mouthed, *It's okay*, to the subcommittee counsel. The Undersecretary's testimony was getting off to a slow start, but he supposed, remembering some of his own court pleading, he could see the reason for it. Cautiously and meticulously was the best way to put something potentially explosive in the right perspective. The personal story wasn't bad, either. It was just, Senator Mastracchio thought, that the Undersecretary's whole manner seemed a little on the down side. He expected, hopefully, it would improve.

Senator Mastracchio's attention was suddenly diverted by a television camera dollying up for a close-in shot of the Senators seated at the subcommittee head table, and he broke away from Blitzstein—rather, they broke simultaneously—and turned to put his elbow back among the papers, assuming an attentive expression.

Undersecretary Parsons continued, "Now, the new Component Improvement Program, which is designed to supply needed modifications to the current engine design, is performed while the engine is in the operational F-15. And so we go into production on this fighter, we deliver it to operational tactical fighter units in the Air Force, but all the time we're doing that, we are continuing the maturity testing on the unit itself. And because we have tried to introduce this fifty percent improvement in performance this way, we are finding a fair number of problems. We are finding problems that are induced by this increase in temperature from—" Here the Undersecretary used a figure that he requested be deleted from the published transcript as it was classified, and the deletion was noted. "We are having problems with the increase in pressure from a range of thirteen up to numbers in excess of twenty. In retrospect," Dr. Parsons said thoughtfully, "it would probably have been a wiser decision to hold the engine back from operation until this testing had been further along and until it achieved a degree of maturity. In any event, what I'm describing to you here is a set of decisions that have been made over the last decade and a half about developing something like the F-15, and how those decisions have gotten us into the situation where we have an engine whose performance we're satisfied with, but which has unsatisfactory maturity relative to reliability and relative to maintainability."

Counsel Blitzstein said, after a pause, "Then you believe the Component Improvement Program, the CIP, is the answer?"

The Undersecretary considered this. "Well, I would say that the problem resulted from an underestimation of the reliability and maintainability problems that would be caused by the introduction of advanced high performance features in the engine. And a solution to the problem has been to try and improve the engine in the operational F-15s through the Component Improvement Program, yes. I would like to point out to you that the CIP could very well be considered a part of the engine development cycle. In retrospect, that might have been a better way of doing it—to have performed at least the first half of the CIP as part of the developmental cycle, rather than performing it after the F-15s were in operational squadrons."

Quickly Senator DeLean of Kentucky broke in. "So what we're in effect trying to do is fix an engine that's already operational?"

"Well, yes, you can say that, but only in the context that this is part of the overall development of the engine itself. The goal of the CIP program is to reduce stall stagnation rate from its present factor of two point two failures per thousand engine flight hours to point fifteen. In other words, we are looking towards an improvement here of considerably better than a factor of ten. We do not have a program yet where we envision the stall stagnation rate going down to zero. We have not approved the fix yet. But we have those objectives."

Senator Foutts had returned to his seat, and now he said, "Isn't that a pretty high rate of failure in those new engines?"

The Undersecretary looked inscrutable. "Yes, I consider it to be a high rate. Let me give you the actual statistics on that." He turned to the Air Force Director of Research Development and Acquisition, General Almon Banks, and said, "Al, do you have a number?"

General Banks said, "Yes, sir. We will provide that for you right now. We have had forty-seven turbine failures as of right now, sir. We have about three hundred thousand engine operating hours. We do consider this to be a high rate, and as Dr. Parsons suggested, we are using the Component Improvement Program of fixes to bring that down. We have had forty-seven turbine failures."

Senator DeLean asked if all turbine failures were alike.

"No, sir, they are not all alike," General Banks responded. "There are some differences. We are finding failures back in the hot section, behind the combustor where the flow of gas first comes into the rotor disc of the high-pressure turbine. We are having some failures in what we call the second-stage vanes and the second-stage rotor blades. What is happening is that these blades are burning up sooner than we had anticipated. Part of the problem is the stall stagnation which makes the temperature in there get very hot. Some of those blades and vanes in the second stage are burning up. What happens is that a blade will break apart and can damage the entire engine case; it can even penetrate the airframe skin. They are different in the sense that there are both blades and vanes that are failing."

"The vanes burn up, or just the rotor blades?"

"Both of them are having problems, sir. The second-stage vane back there, a fixed vane, redirects the gases and is the one that seems to be failing first, thus causing the second-stage rotor blade to break up under high pressure and heat."

"The second-stage rotor is behind the vane?" Senator DeLean pursued.

"Yes, sir, exactly."

"Then when the vane breaks up, it goes into the blade?"

"Yes, sir, we have had forty-seven of these failures out of four hundred fifty F-15s operational. I guess my answer would be, more correctly, that there are similarities. Those are the kinds of things that are happening."

"The second objective," Dr. Parsons put in quickly, "of the CIP is to greatly improve the maintainability of the F-15 and to state that goal and objective in quantitative terms. The program is not exactly inexpensive. For the F100X engine, for instance, we expect to spend more than six hundred million dollars through this year. So the CIP is a program of nearly equal magnitude to the development of the engine itself, but it is clearly the most significant factor today that will allow us to deal with the problems we have with these engines and give us reliable engines and reliable fighters and give us engines that have reasonable maintainability costs associated with them."

While Dr. Parsons spoke, the television camera swung to pick him up in profile. The Undersecretary's intense, self-contained expression, his long nose and shock of sandy hair rising from a high, sloping forehead, looked positively melancholy—the technologist-public servant conveying the bad news. Behind the camera, the television unit director could see that the eye and mind of the viewer tended to drift away from this somber spectacle in search of something else: the fidgeting hands of the Defense Department assistant on the Undersecretary's left, the large black mole at the corner of General Banks's strong, thin-lipped mouth, the refracted spark of light shooting whitely from Dr. Parsons's tie clip.

The camera moved to eliminate the light blip and swung for a panned shot of the crowd in the committee room. Unfortunately, there was a lack of drama there, too. In the rows of the press corps squeezed between the subcommittee Senators and the camera dolly, the correspondent from the Los Angeles *Times-Mirror* syndicate was surreptitiously picking his teeth. The camera quickly swung back to the Defense Undersecretary's profile.

The television director held the head shot of the Undersecretary, wondering mildly what he could do next to liven up the picture. It was, he thought, the usual problem with Congressional committee coverage—all it amounted to, when you came right down to it, was Talking Heads. Unless the daytime audience was unusually focused on what was happening—which he doubted—and had a burning interest in the problems of military aviation engines—which was unlikely—the subcommittee television coverage was total boredom, even for PBS. A Washington affiliate was feeding the subcommittee hearing in a joint television pool that included the major networks, which were taping it for possible highlights on the evening news; the Public Broadcasting System was taking it live. But not live enough, the director thought. He yawned. If it kept on like this, he doubted they would bother with a second day.

In his earphones, a voice said, "Hey, Bob—hey, Bob, this is Charlie. Are you with me?"

The voice was that of the ABC affiliate director in the control room of the studio in northwest Washington, monitoring the remote telecast on his screens.

The unit director moved behind the cameraman and the dolly, tucking himself between it and the end of the witness table. He cupped his hand carefully over the mike button at his mouth. "Okay, Charlie," he murmured.

"Ah, Bob," the voice went on, "we think we have a cutaway coming up in ten minutes. We will drop live coverage there and cut to a local feed from Cape Canaveral for an announcement. PBS goes live on this, so stand by."

This was the fourth announcement of an announcement from the space center on the Cape in the last forty-eight hours, and each one of the bulletins had, in due time, been canceled.

"Will advise," the control room director said. "They may announce launch this time. Ten minutes; stand by."

Looking around the committee room, the unit director thought that the proceedings would break for lunch on time. If the Cape finally got to a countdown on the Space Shuttle, it was possible they wouldn't return for the afternoon telecast, even for taping. Which was all right with him; he might be able to get in some tennis.

On camera, General Banks was showing a chart of comparative engine improvement figures and pointing out each category: Qualified by Military; Engine Manufacturer; Maximum Thrust (in Pounds); Thrust to Weight Ratio; Turbine Inlet Temperature (Fahrenheit); Bypass Ratio; Pressure/Ratio Stages. The numbers were too small for the television camera to pick up, and General Banks was asking that the figures for the F-15 and the canceled B-1 bomber under Maximum Thrust (Pounds) be deleted from the published transcript, as well as the figures for the same engines under Turbine Inlet Pressure (Fahrenheit) and Pressure/Ratio Stages, as they were classified. The subcommittee noted and agreed.

The voice of the director in the affiliate control room suddenly came back on the earphones.

"Ah, Bob," it said, "false alarm on the Space Shuttle announcement. The Cape's canceled out for the rest of the week."

The unit director watched as General "Big Bird" Banks struggled to prop up another cardboard-mounted chart on the other side of the table microphone. The Defense Department aide got up and came around the witness table and relieved the General of the chart, holding it up for the Senators to see. In this quick movement, the aide blocked the camera, filling up the television screen with the dark, muddled blot of his thigh and hip. The cameraman backed hurriedly, pressing the director up against the committee room wall.

"We're not doing too damned good over here, either," the unit director said into his mouthpiece.

Flight Operations Officer Major Randolph Slyke let himself into the 17th Squadron Building at 7 A.M., noting that Staff Sergeant Kevin Johnson was already on duty at the operations desk in the lobby. Staff Sergeant Johnson greeted Major Slyke with what was openly and pointedly a churlish lack of enthusiasm, although Major Slyke was glad to see that Staff Sergeant Johnson appeared to be merely sleepy, rather than, as was sometimes the case, actively resentful. It was necessary to remember, Major Slyke told himself, that Staff Sergeant Johnson on the hot spot of the Ops Desk was probably as deeply and continuously tired as he was himself; their once open and enjoyable camaraderie had disappeared under the crush of work several months ago.

Randy Slyke checked the status of the squadron's complement of twenty-six F-15s which the Squadron Duty Officer had copied from the maintenance board in the hangar onto the greenboard behind the operations counter, designating which Eagles were currently operational and those that were not. Below the seventeen F-15s listed as operational—including, Major Slyke noted with an involuntary grimace, number Forty Thirty-three—were the flying schedules and the pilots assigned to the various tail numbers and the missions to be flown for that day. Everything, he saw, looked okay. Overloaded but okay.

Randy Slyke gave particular attention to the interdiction exercise for Topper flight that had been rescheduled. The first mission had been a real mess-up, not like Topper flight at all, although, he supposed, the basic problem there was unresolved. How long to go along with it without some sort of action was the problem. If it kept up at its current rate, Topper James's flight would shortly make full transit from first place to the bottom—and that he would not have believed a few months ago.

Randy Slyke read the weather report posted on the greenboard and spent a moment putting the elements together in his head, making a quick estimate of what the day's flying schedule would look like. Remembering Topper flight, he mentally moved tail number Forty Thirty-three to another flight. There were days when it was best not to tempt the odds.

Once in his office, Major Slyke sat down at his desk and flung his cap into a drawer. He could see that his in-basket was filled to overflowing, a monument to a creeping backlog of work. And someone had put a neatly folded newspaper in the middle of his desk, a back issue of the Washington *Post*.

Randy Slyke bent for a moment and rested his head in his hands. Outside, the early morning fog was burning off the runways. The sky-cracking roar of F-106s, one right after another on takeoff, shook the squadron building. The day was there, he told himself, and beginning, whether one wanted it or not.

He lifted his head and reached to shuffle through the in-basket papers. The basket was full of accumulated correspondence, the notice of a Squadron Assistance Visit—a euphemism for three Wing-level pilots coming in for quarterly inspection—a stack of TDY orders for two flights going cross-country the next day, and the paperwork for the semiannual assignment of the 17th Squadron to the Air Force Red Flag tactical war games at Nellis AFB, Nevada, in less than a week.

Randy Slyke got up and took his coffee cup and headed for the percolator in the ready room, and as he did so, the telephone rang. He turned back to answer it, and an unidentified voice on the other end demanded to speak to someone in charge. The voice turned out to be someone in the Office of the Deputy Commander of Operations wanting flying schedule information for the 17th Squadron. As he gave it, Randy Slyke picked up a pencil and wrote a note to himself to review the gun camera film from yesterday's missions. He made another note to remind himself, while he was at it, of his SOF duty in the Langley traffic control tower from 11 A.M. to 1 P.M. Mentally, he eliminated the prospect of lunch. At 2 P.M., he was due in squadron briefing for the air-to-air mission in which he would be leader of the combined Dolphin and Bullet flights in a Sidewinder exercise off the South Carolina coast.

When this had been done and he had hung up the telephone, he sat down again, forgetting his coffee. In front of him and clipped to the Saturday edition of the Washington *Post* was a memo from Squadron Commander Lieutenant Colonel Roger Gazenove. The note did not quite cover the headline on the front page, lower right, which said: SENATE SUBCOMMITTEE TO HEAR TROUBLES IN NEW AIR FORCE FIGHTER. Randy Slyke sighed.

Lieutenant Colonel Gazenove's note, perhaps not irrelevantly, was apropos a Friday afternoon conversation with Colonel Strathmore, the Commanding General's aide, and concerned itself with General Couch's thoughts on professionalism.

Professionalism, Colonel Strathmore's telephone conversation with Lieutenant Colonel Gazenove had conveyed by way of General Couch's ruminations on the subject, was not demonstrated by the following behavior in the OC at Friday Happy Hour, to wit: mashing beer cans on forehead at the bar; excessive use of *"Klingons!"* in the OC television lounge (in this instance, Major Slyke knew, one read "excessive" as "any"); eating two dozen roses out of the centerpiece on table in OC banquet room set up for the Wing Adjutant's twentieth wedding anniversary dinner. The note went on: "See *Directive on Tactical Call Signs* to follow."

Without meaning to, Randy Slyke sighed again. He had already been advised of the tactical call signs directive and knew some way would have to be found to facilitate that already notorious document, although he was not hopeful of the outcome. From now on and as a forward step in the Air Force's continuing effort to promote a clearer image of professionalism, the use of tactical call signs was to be immediately discontinued. If referred to at all (and in no way, repeat no way, during tactical combat exercise radio transmissions), tactical call signs were to be employed only as nicknames. Beginning immediately, a suggested list of professional call signs by flights only would go into use. Examples of such professional call signs, selected by the Command Office, would be: Conqueror, Rocket, Victor, Hunter, Winner, Destroyer, Challenger, etc., to be combined with the numbers one through four, the complement of each flight.

One of the unexplored problems inherent in the tactical call signs directive, Major Slyke knew, was that nomenclature was usually rotated daily, so that Winner flight or Conqueror flight became, on the following day, Rocket flight or Victor flight. Or sometimes Conqueror or Winner again.

A bare three days before while on duty in the Langley tower as Supervisor of Flying, Randy Slyke had heard the results of the new tactical call signs directive from a Langley flight maneuvering over Delaware: "Gopher, I have a visual—F-14s at two o'clock." With the response, "Goblin three, I am *Goblin One*—now use it!" Followed by, "Gopher, I'm *Wildcat* Three, and you're *Wildcat* One—and I've still got a visual on those F-14s closing fast!" "I see them. And you're not Wildcat Three, you're *Goblin* Three." And quickly, "Gopher, I wrote it down on the back of my hand. I'm *Wildcat* Three today!" And a third voice had said, "He's right, and I don't know who I am, but I just got a tally."

Major Slyke detached Lieutenant Colonel Gazenove's note from the front page of the Saturday edition of the Washington *Post* and dropped the newspaper in the wastebasket. He opened the top drawer of the desk and put the note with General Couch's thoughts on professionalism and what one did, in part, to achieve it on top of the confidential report of the wing psychiatrist on the incident of a crew chief's attempted suicide in the hangar last Monday. Suicidal psychotic was the wing psychiatrist's diagnosis. The crew chief had just transferred in from Eglin AFB; Major Slyke was beginning to discern the reasons, even with the glowing fitness reports, for the switch. Under this thorny and as yet unresolved matter was another personnel problem, the latest in a series of infrequent but nonetheless potentially grave reports concerning the youngest—it was always the youngest, Randy Slyke told himself—members of the Maintenance Office known to be indulging in occasional joints of prohibited substances, detectable by their fragrance in the hangar toilet. And under all these evidences of the perplexing and insoluble problems which he, if not actually able to dispose of, was somehow to satisfactorily compromise, lay the notification from Navy Interservice Communications, NAVOPSEC, NAS, Norfolk, citing charges of trespassing in restricted areas [Navy Amphibious Base, Sector 12G, Little Creek, VA.] by USAF Major Eric T. James, ser. no. 45622-01-933, 1st TFW, 17th TFS, Langley AFB, Va., and USAF Captain Simon R. McAllister, ser. no. 33165-11-056, 1st TFW, 17th TFS, Langley AFB, Va., date: 9/11, hrs: 0130; specifically: entering Sector 12G Restricted, Navy Amphibious Base, Little Creek, Va.; illegal uniform, etc., etc. Further In-

formation Requested: route to: Lt. L. B. Andrews, NAVOP-
SEC, NAS, Norfolk, 467825 G3 NAV-4.

Randy Slyke slammed the desk drawer shut.

On the wall directly in front of his desk he had hung a large
poster which he considered to be his guide *in extremis*—in
day-to-day decisions and responses of Flight Operations—and
which he had come to regard as the outer wall of his defenses:

> *We're already doing this . . .*
> *We're well into an approach that looks even better . . .*
> *If you had our classified data, you'd understand why*
>   *we're doing it our way . . .*
> *It doesn't fit into any of our service jurisdictions (Try*
>   *the Navy) . . .*
> *It won't work under combat conditions . . .*
> *It might work, but our allies would never agree to it . . .*
> *Determined adversaries will find a way to thwart it . . .*
> *The advantage you claim for your approach will be*
>   *quickly lost when our experts review it . . .*

Out of the corner of his eye, Randy Slyke became aware
of a sudden speedy movement in the hallway, and the next
second Lieutenant Colonel Roger Gazenove shot into the office.
The short, wiry figure in the green nomex flight coverall radiated a potent cheerfulness, an exuberance that the flight ops
officer had not seen in months. The squadron commander was
frowning purposefully.

"Randy," Lieutenant Colonel Gazenove barked, "we're
going to Saudi Arabia. Just came down the line EAT, hustle-
hustle, Wing Command Post."

Major Slyke stared at Lieutenant Colonel Gazenove. Cautiously he said, "Rog, we're going to Red Flag."

"I know that. We're on standby, but we have deployment
date, time—a complement of twelve. What's left goes to Red
Flag." Lieutenant Colonel Gazenove wheeled and started for
the door. "Meeting in the main briefing room in ten minutes.
Alert the mobility officer—flight alignment—general recall."

Randy Slyke reached for the telephone.

Senator Mortimer Glass, seated at lunch in his Georgetown
dining room, watched the Senate special subcommittee recess

on the screen of the portable television set wheeled in by his houseman.

"Dammit," Senator Glass said aloud.

The television screen showed the committee room emptying, the Senators filing out the rear door which led to the hallway of the Richard Russell Senate Office Building. Senator Glass knew the committee room well; in a few minutes, Senator Mastracchio would take the nearby elevators to his office on the second floor. Senator Glass shoveled the rest of the cottage cheese on his plate into his mouth and washed it down with bourbon and water.

The morning's testimony had been, by any standards, a far cry from what they had originally planned. First of all, Mastracchio had showed his inexperience by not letting his smart young counsel, Blitzstein, guide the questioning, and as a consequence the Defense Undersecretary and Big Bird had had the field all to themselves—and had gone on forever about those damned engine temperatures and burned-up turbine blades, a subject, they had agreed on earlier, they would try to get through without making too much of. But what had gone on, Senator Glass was well aware, was too consistent not to be deliberate; he detected a subtle, measurable shift in the wind as he watched the Undersecretary suddenly convert the agreed-on Positive Stance to that of Bad News—and imminent ass-covering. Senator Glass was not surprised; twenty years in the Senate had inured him to that sort of thing. He had, however, no intention of dancing to the Defense Undersecretary's change of tune.

"George," Senator Glass shouted. He cut into his lamb chop viciously. "Bring me the telephone."

When the extension was placed before him, Senator Glass dialed Senator Mastracchio's office. The Senator, he was informed, was on his way; he was, in fact, talking to reporters in the hall outside. Senator Glass waited. Finally Senator Mastracchio came on the line.

"Hello, Vinnie, Morty Glass here," Senator Glass said jovially. "I'm watching you on television." Then, "What seems to be the problem?"

There was a pause as if, at the other end, Senator Mastracchio was considering for the first time that he might have a problem and what it could be.

"Oh, Senator, hello. Listen, Senator, we're just getting started—I don't know how it looks on TV; I haven't been able to talk to my staff, yet, and they've been monitoring the set in the office—but I thought it was going—"

"Listen, Vinnie," Senator Glass said kindly, "Richie Parsons isn't the best speaker in the world; I just wanted to tell you in case you had any doubts about it. And all Banks is doing, from what I can see, is projecting a Pentagon-size anxiety attack. But we sort of anticipated that, didn't we?" Senator Glass laughed ruefully. "Now, I know things are going to pick up, that we're going to get out of these people what we want to get out of them sooner or later, but television is a tricky thing— the public out there is watching, Vinnie, mainly because they want to be *reassured* about those fighters, and we don't want to lose track of that. If you don't mind my saying so, I think you ought to try to speed things up this afternoon and keep DeLean out of it as much as possible. He's got a tough election coming up out there in Kentucky, and he's going to try and show his constituents that he hasn't been sitting on his ass the last two years, that he's been doing something really important. It's a little late, but he wouldn't mind latching onto something he thinks will get big publicity. Hell," Senator Glass chuckled, "if the Russians are tuned in, they must be counting their blessings. The way DeLean's going, they'll think we're going to ground all the F-15s and call the whole thing off."

"I didn't get the impression anything like that was coming across," Senator Mastracchio said, a trifle defensively. "After all, as I said before, the hearing's just getting started. I've been sitting there listening to every word—"

"Now, Vinnie, I'm just giving you my impressions," Senator Glass said, "but I think you ought to give some thought to bringing out these positive aspects pretty soon, don't you? I mean, after lunch wouldn't be too soon to start. I don't know what in hell's gotten into Parsons and Banks, but they aren't doing us any good. How about the crowd from Trueham Engines, the young engineers? Those boys have worked like hell on the engines in the F-15s; they know how good they are, what a quantum leap—"

"Senator, I hate to disagree with you, but I think things have been going pretty smoothly so far. As I said before, we're just getting started. And I want you to realize that this thing's been a lot of work." There was a new, detectably petulant note in Senator Mastracchio's voice. "My staff is limited, and we didn't exactly expect to get into anything this big so early in the year. Handling those Air Force people hasn't been easy. As for instance, General Holmes from SAMSO says he wants to go on this afternoon, especially since General Banks was on this morning, although I still haven't got a clear idea of what he wants to say. He tells me he can't talk about the Nightwing Eagle flight, since all that's still classified and he hasn't been able to get it unclassified. And if he doesn't talk about *that*, I don't know what he thinks he can contribute— SAMSO's not really in on any part of this. But he says he's got to be at Cape Canaveral tonight, and he doesn't know whether he'll be available later this week. I'd like to drop him; I think he makes a very good impression, probably better than General Banks, but I can't see how we're going to use him if he can't talk about that Nightwing thing."

"Well, go ahead and put him on," Senator Glass said agreeably, "this afternoon, if he wants it, and make him keep it short. We certainly don't want him to think he couldn't get equal time. Just put the rest of Parsons's speech over to tomorrow and get Banks to say something good about the F-15s, like they're being used in stuff so secret he can't talk about them, but they're performing well. Get as much as you can out of it. But we still need some fresh faces in there, Vinnie— what about that good-looking young fighter pilot TAC was going to send us? He show up yet?"

Mastracchio's voice altered. "Senator, that's one of the things I did want to talk to you about. Listen, the fighter pilot they sent us from Langley is sort of—well, first of all, he's not a Captain as we anticipated; I mean, he's not so *young*— actually, he's a Lieutenant Colonel. He looks all right, but he looks—did you ever see a movie called *The Green Berets?* Actually, I wouldn't say he has any expression at all, if you follow me. Actually, he's a very difficult man to talk to. My staff's been working with him up here in my office because, well, actually, he has a prepared statement he wants to read."

"He wants to *read?*" Senator Glass said.

"Yes, sir. I get the impression, although he doesn't come right out and say so, that the Air Force doesn't let anybody under the rank of Brigadier General come right out and talk extemporaneously. He says he has to read it."

"Oh, *hell*," Senator Glass said.

John McGillicuddy remained in his seat after the crowd in the Senate committee room had filed out. He held his briefcase on his knees, watching the television crew secure their equipment and move it toward the side door and the anteroom.

The small delegation from Trueham Engine Company that had been seated in the third row of the witness section had, with the exception of the field engineer, already left the committee room, anxious to find a restaurant and lunch. The subcommittee would not reconvene until two-thirty, which gave them plenty of time, as the assistant engine program manager had put it, to realign their stress loads.

John McGillicuddy had had no particular desire to join the crowd from the Connecticut plant. He had a sandwich in his briefcase that his wife had packed that morning, and he had set aside the lunch hour for a stroll in the park in front of the Capitol and some sightseeing on the Hill. There was small chance now, a committee aide had informed the Trueham people, that any of them would be called that afternoon; they would not, he estimated, be called until Wednesday—if then. None of them had really anticipated that sort of delay. Cassell, the man from the public relations office, had decided to call the home plant to see if they should schedule an indefinite stay in Washington or fly back to get in a few days' work.

Now, looking around the empty committee room, John McGillicuddy was glad to have a few moments for himself. He hadn't slept well the night before. His plane flight up from Florida had been rushed, with some last-minute doubt about his reservations, and he was still reacting to his surprise at being where he was, with the rather sketchy explanations given him. As he understood it, he was to testify before the Senate subcommittee investigating Trueham Engine Company's troublesome new product, the F100X turbofans—a job usually delegated to company vice presidents assisted by a battery of legal counsel and production experts, and not low-level field research engineers like himself. It sounded crazy. He didn't even know if he had enough information at his fingertips to be able to do it. Nobody had explained to him fully because, he sensed, they didn't know enough about what was wanted to explain it. But the company had rushed them all to Washington to testify.

The actual committee room was, he saw, rather plain and unpretentious, not at all what he had expected, considering they were being watched by millions through the medium of television. The actual number of people in the room that morning could not have been over a hundred. He had been reminded of some college investigating board looking into exam irregularities, rather than an assembly of some of the country's most powerful legislators probing the complexities of a possible military and economic fiasco.

So this is how it's done, he thought.

From what he understood of the hasty briefing given him by the field research control office in Florida and the lengthier but more confusing conference he'd had with the central operations public relations man in Washington, his part in all this—if he was called at all—was to tell a convincing account of the laborious, loving work that had gone into the development and particularly the testing of the F100X, and some of the dedication felt by men like himself who had sweated out so many hours on the program. An account that would be, hopefully, a fleshing-out of the picture of the joint development by Trueham and the Air Force Department of Research Development of the incredibly intricate, partly experimental—at least in its early stages—high-bypass, hot-running, 3,000-pound lightweight F100X with its stupendous, innovative thrust.

Give us some of the drama involved out there in the Everglades, the company PR man had said.

He didn't know that he was going to be particularly good at that. There was a saying among engineers—let somebody else talk, you show the drawings. Still, all morning long as he had sat in the committee room, what came to mind was a lot he'd found he'd like to say—technical details that he knew no one was going to get on record. That if, for instance, some Air Force fighter pilot misses the light on the afterburners, it will put a hell of a jolt into the fans. And why. And that, he knew, would be stepping on a lot of toes.

He had spent all morning there, well aware that it was a hell of a long way from the months, years, he had spent in the swamps of Florida, buried off some dirt road in the Everglades at a supersecret test site he had to commute to from a motel in some backwater town, hundreds of miles away from his wife and family. And where, they had all assured themselves during all those months, it was tough but worth it to be working on something hot, a project that was a real breakthrough, the culmination of years of pure research that had sat waiting for something to put it into, and which they would now see get practical use, by God—would see it *fly!*

Now it all had come to this, he thought. In spite of the ins and outs of the matter, and the truth of the figures, which were pretty bad, and the claims and counter-claims of the people who had gotten up before the subcommittee to speak their pieces, he could not help thinking what a damned shame it was. He was not himself and never had been a defender of the corporate conglomerate structure or the necessity of precisely calculated profit formulas that made the wheels go around; but there were some fairly simple factors that even someone like himself could see. That there was the risk of millions of dollars that Trueham Engines had had to lay on the line for design and retooling which, if the project misfired, was likely to drop them to their knees financially. Even the preliminary stages, the development of a prototype to submit for competition, constituted a gamble that might well leave a company without a financial margin for recovery.

He didn't exactly know why he was sitting there thinking about it. He was only a field research engineer from the Florida boondocks. He told himself: you're getting star-struck; you want to get up there and shoot your mouth off like everybody else. And a voice answered: Yeah, but just once—just once—

He had to remind himself that anything he could say would contribute nothing new, perhaps jeopardize his job. He had heard about subcommittee hearings; they were a fact of life, as predictable in the aviation industry as the production of any item. And whatever he wanted to say had been testified to, probably in this very committee room, over and over again in years past.

The only question that remained was: Why do we have to keep saying it?

He felt a touch on his shoulder and roused himself. A Senate security guard was standing there, waiting politely.

The guard said, "Sir—I guess you're going to have to leave now. This committee room here has to be cleared during recess."

John McGillicuddy grabbed his briefcase and stood up. "Sorry," he apologized. "Just sitting and thinking."

The guard's black face broke into a sudden grin. "Well, that's all right. We could use some of that around here."

Captain Pete Michaud hurried across the expanse of B hangar, swearing to himself. The telex which had come from USAF General Staff, Pentagon, Washington, and which the First Tactical Fighter Wing duty controller had carried, uncoded, to the wing commander in operations, had been broken out on the view graph for the hurriedly assembled major elements of local command, namely the vice wing commander, the chief of maintenance, the chief of resources, the base commander, the deputy chief of operations, the chief of plans, and the wing intelligence officer upon whom rested the decisions relating to the deployment of twelve F-15s to Saudi Arabia as per request of the State Department. The resulting final computerized flight plan, configurations, and vital data were then processed and forwarded to the commander of the 17th Tactical Fighter Squadron, Lieutenant Colonel Roger Gazenove, and had finally come to rest, with considerable impact, upon Captain Michaud's shoulders as squadron mobility officer. And Captain Michaud was looking for Staff Sergeant Florence Walters, who had charge of squadron administration office files and who was, in spite of the frantic activity of that day and hour, still at lunch. In his hand, Captain Michaud carried Sergeant Walters's Con Ex forms for containers for files and typewriters to be loaded on a waiting C-5 transport, destination, Saudi Arabia by way of the Azores. As he approached Master Sergeant Amos Schuld and Chief Master Sergeant Porschner, the First Wing maintenance superintendent, in front of Sergeant Schuld's office, Captain Michaud opened his mouth to ask if they had seen Sergeant Walters, but his words were drowned by the sudden bellow of jet engines being tested out on the flight line. Defeated, Captain Michaud shook his head and hurried on.

Sergeant Schuld and Chief Porschner regarded the obviously harassed mobility officer incuriously; their expressions said they had problems of their own.

Chief Porschner said, shouting over the engine noise: "Amos, there's no damned good way to pick out people; it makes for evaluations right out in the open that you just can't avoid—good, medium, and what's left, and there's no way around it. Sure, somebody's feelings are going to get stepped on. Sure, somebody's going to find out they're down on the bottom of the list. But there's no way to avoid what we got. Which is, take the best off the top, and the rejects go to Red Flag."

Sergeant Schuld growled something.

"Amos," Chief Porschner shouted, "we got tough logistics on this one—the Azores stop, eleven-twelve hours unbroken fly-time each way. We need all good hands. No argument."

Sergeant Schuld and Chief Porschner had just ended a meeting with squadron maintenance NCOs to determine the allocation of ground crew personnel for the Saudi mission. And Amos Schuld was not happy with the decision to split Sergeant Linda Criscio from tail number Forty Thirty-three and send her with the Saudi crew. Which left that notorious hangar queen of hers for deployment to Red Flag and in the care of a fairly inexperienced maintenance junior, an E/5 who was totally unfamiliar with Forty Thirty-three's uncanny and even bizarre capacity for breakdowns.

"Linda Criscio goes because she's an A-one resource," Chief Porschner declared. "With her expertise, she'd be top of the list, anyway. Now, you say her hog is down and won't go. It's a waste of talent to keep her here just for that. You get somebody else to get that tail number fixed up; they can do it. You're going to need it to fill the square on Red Flag."

Sergeant Schuld yelled back, "Spearman can't take care of it. Out at Red Flag—"

"Amos, I got a hell of a lot of other things to worry about right now. Spearman's in charge of that Red Flag crew; he'll just have to do the best he can. Go tell him what you want him to do."

Sergeant Schuld stamped angrily away from the hangar. After a few feet, he turned and shouted: "Porsch—I'm telling you; Spearman's got to keep a hard eye on that bird."

Chief Master Sergeant Porschner said, "Amos, *you* tell him."

The orders had already been given that all local flying be stopped. On the flight line, the F-15s selected for the Saudi mission were being tested, checked, and refueled, and the attendant noise penetrated even the concrete walls of the squadron building as a low, consistent thundering. Thirty days' clothing and effects were in possession of all squadron personnel. In the ready room, half a dozen officers had dumped out their mobility bags on the floor and busied themselves sorting out dirty underwear, the required three flight suits, civilian clothes, and DOP kits. The NCOs manning the flight ops counter in the lobby checked out the mobility board, telephoning a general recall to all squadron personnel not on duty. Orders had been relayed prohibiting off-base trips. A pilot briefing was scheduled for 1500 hours.

On Lieutenant Colonel Roger Gazenove's desk, an accumulation of memoranda covering clearance of personnel immunization records, dog tags, leave and earning statements, TDY orders to be cut, and advance pay sifted over neatly clipped lists of names and telephone numbers.

"Make it Dolphin flight," Major Randolph Slyke said.

Major Adolphus Bauernhauser, leader of Dolphin flight, was back in the ready room, waiting around in anticipation of something of the sort. Under other circumstances, Dolphin flight would be assigned to the Saudi Arabian mission, but Major Slyke was opting for some respectable show of strength at Red Flag. And Dolphin flight would balance it out.

Lieutenant Colonel Gazenove muttered, "Damn, Randy, I never thought I'd have to do this. Topper's flight has been in one continuous drop since August—that's what you get for letting things slide. What the hell's the matter, anyway?" The question was rhetorical, as was the implied accusation; the squadron commander knew full well what had happened. "Did we," Lieutenant Colonel Gazenove wanted to know, "ever have the flight surgeon talk to him?"

Major Slyke waited.

"Well, Jesus God, it beats me." Lieutenant Colonel Gazenove rubbed his mouth peevishly, then pinched the end of his nose while he considered it. "I can't figure it out. What in hell's holding them together?"

Major Slyke laid down his pencil with obvious patience.

"God moves in wondrous ways his miracles to perform."

Lieutenant Colonel Gazenove lifted his head and glared. "What in hell does *that* mean?"

"It means," Major Slyke said with great deliberation, "that he picks him up in the morning and takes him somewhere and pumps him full of coffee and sees that he eats a hearty breakfast. Somewhere off base, so that hopefully nobody will see them. Then he brings him in on time and does his paperwork for him and lines up his flying schedule."

Lieutenant Colonel Gazenove groaned. "Christ, that can't go on. How long's this been happening?"

Major Slyke said, "Even so, he's operable. Good days, he's even up to par, which—par for Topper—isn't bad at all."

"Well, hell." Lieutenant Colonel Gazenove pinched his nose again. "We've got to have the flight surgeon look him over when he gets back. Make a note of it." He said, aggravated, "Is Topper going to hold up as detachment commander at Red Flag? I don't want to give it to Dolph."

Major Slyke said, "Rog, it's right there on your list."

Lieutenant Colonel Gazenove picked up a list at random and stared at it. It was not the list he wanted, being an account of off-duty officers still not contacted by telephone by the Flight Ops desk. He started to put it down, then held it up. He kept reading it.

"General recall," he said absently. "How did we get this many people out of town? Moose is in Tennessee. Get somebody to call his family out there. McAllister went up to see his girl in Washington; that's his usual leave, isn't it?" He frowned. He reread the line, then looked up. "Where in hell is Topper?" he demanded. "Now what?"

"We'll find him," Major Slyke said soothingly. "It's early yet."

16

The telephone kept ringing.

Major Topper James lay in bed holding the cold, slightly sweating can of beer on his stomach, his right hand behind his head so as to raise it enough to see the piece of paper on the bureau dresser. The letter rested against an aerosol can of Christmas cologne that he seldom used, held upright by the small brass box containing his uniform lapel insignia. After he had read the letter, he had carefully put it back where he had found it. And it had stayed there ever since.

At the angle at which he lay, he could see the flat edge of the bureau and the layer of dust there. It surprised him that so much dust could collect in just a week. Not, he was reminded, that his wife was any great shakes as a housekeeper—no one could accuse Candy of that—but it was amazing how dirty everything had become without her. And how fast.

It puzzled him. He was finding that he did not exactly know what to do with the house, a whole house with nobody in it now but himself. After a few days had passed, it was as though he had been left the custody of some reluctant presence, thrown together with it in mutual solitude, that needed looking after; that required of him something that neither he, nor it, could define. And that wound down, little by little, into dust and emptiness and, finally, a complete and curiously expiring silence. If not dead—then at least sunk in deep coma.

When he thought about it, when he allowed himself to think about it, he was aware that he missed the sounds of breathing life—the washing machine in the basement, the voices of the neighborhood children who came to the back door looking for Emma, even the television. The damned television that was always going full blast in the family room, even when there was no one around to watch it.

Only the telephone rang.

When it wasn't ringing, there was a humming stillness in the air. It was strange, but there was actually an audible silence. The house was filled with it. And with bright sunshine. And with dust, which danced in the air like specks of light.

The letter on the bureau was the first thing he saw in the morning, the last thing at night before he turned out the bedside lamp: a piece of paper covered with Candy's large, rounded, straggling script.

I guess I'd just better say that I don't think I can go on like this, at least I can't live in a place where people don't talk to each other anymore. Even if there's no love or meaning anymore there has to be some sort of communication. I know I did this to us, it's all my fault, isn't it. But I never meant to hurt you. I know that sounds crazy, I suppose it's too late to say that now and I know you won't believe it but I never meant to. I must have been out of my mind, some sort of temporary mental illness. That's possible. I don't want you to worry about where we're going so I'm going to tell you that we're going to my mothers.

That, he told himself, was that. You had to face it.

It was, God knows, what he had trained himself to recognize and accept as just another loss sustained. It was a phrase he found meaningful and profound; he had looked up *sustained* in the dictionary years ago and it meant: "to carry or withstand; to bear up under"—and therefore, by this definition somehow realizable, reduced to terms capable of being absorbed and dismissed. That was it. The only way to deal with it. Otherwise the pain kept returning, and, as he had learned, you couldn't live with that.

The telephone stopped ringing.

The dancing motes in the shaft of sunlight turned to small, flashing lights—some optical illusion, he told himself, and was unalarmed. After a while, he saw them drift slowly upward, the ceiling become a brilliant canopy of reflected light, the bits and pieces hanging there like burning, floating fragments. They shimmered before his eyes, and he blinked. It was too early in the morning to be so drunk. He was lying in sunshine, painlessly. The light smelled green and moist like the jungle, the smell of mud and trees. He told himself that he was flat on his back in his own bed and full of beer and not hanging upside down, swaying in the trees over warm, wet, brown mud, under a roof of trees. Like a bird caught and pinned in the branches.

There was not a damned thing you could do about a loss sustained. It had taken him a while to learn that, to get it through his head. There was no chute down below after Ruder dropped, so, sustaining a loss, you go on. No Search and Rescue to be initiated. Just get the hell out of the area.

The sun was shining brightly on the overcast below, and he was on his way out, trying to get well above the clouds and stay there, when he heard the warning tone down there change to a higher frequency, which, since the RF-4 had disappeared in the mist, meant he was the primary target. He started to climb, and the SAM broke out of the overcast under him. It was one of those split-second things as usual—he had barely enough time to slam his F-4 into a hard turn when the missile exploded under him. There were two explosions in the F-4's airframe, one right after another. He lost the hydraulics system, the right engine spooled down, everything went out. When he ejected, when the charge propelled him up and out of the F-4 and clear and the sky went around like a Ferris wheel, he was thinking that unless he was lucky this time, there would be two losses to sustain, he and Ruder, over the brown-yellow river there below. And that even if he got down, there were people who weren't friendly. From what he had heard they did to you when they found you, it was better to die, perhaps, than come down in the jungle.

His hand relaxed, and the can of beer fell over on his chest. It was half full, and the cold liquid dripped over his ribs.

When unconsciousness faded and he came to—when his eyes opened—it was, curiously, the same stillness in the jungle, the same dancing motes of dust in the streaked sunlight breaking through the clouds and trees. Somewhere, the only thing in all that silence, a bird squawked. He was hanging upside down in a tree looking at the mud and green leaves far below, hanging by his parachute shrouds. Upside down because a branch had caught his foot as he descended, and his ankle was broken, the pain already a screaming agony, tangled in the shrouds. But upside down. Head down. In all that strange buzzing silence and broken sunlight. He could see the light down on the lower canopy of leaves. Eventually, maybe hours, maybe days later, he heard the faraway chatter of the SAR helicopter looking for him in the overcast above the jungle trees.

He told himself—

He forgot what he was telling himself, to pick up the edge of the sheet and wipe away the dripping beer.

After a while he thought: It was fair to call that one loss "sustained." His flight leader, Ruder, anyway.

The telephone began to ring.

Senator Glass said, "Well, Captain, I wish to hell we'd had you in Washington this past week."

The Senator pulled an opened bottle of champagne from one of the ice-filled buckets on the tailgate of the station wagon and, with a brief jerking motion that signaled Simon McAllister to hold his paper cup ready, filled it to the brim and a little over. The liquid foamed up, and Simon stepped back, holding it away from him gingerly. The Senator's houseman, George, who had been setting out the picnic lunch, quickly grabbed a folded napkin and came forward to wipe the bottom of the dripping cup. George was wearing a red hunt coat with brass buttons; his expression said that he was enjoying the day and acting his part to the fullest.

"There now, Cap'n," he said unctuously.

Senator Glass went on: "To tell you the truth, I was thinking about someone like you; I couldn't ask for you specifically, you understand—the military being what it is, putting it into channels wouldn't have been a good idea. But some smart type who could give good user testimony on what it's like to fly the new Eagles, get in some of the romance of the space age, the challenge of advanced technology, split-second thinking— dammit, George," the Senator broke off, "don't flap that thing at me! Get some of that ham and biscuits and pass them around."

The last event of the morning, the Children's Equitation Class of the Middleburg Horse Show, was being announced over the loudspeakers, and the Senator paused, waiting for the amplified bellow to die away. Through the opened gate of the horse ring, a single file of little girls in bright red coats and English-style hunt caps, mounted on fat ponies, cantered inside. The crowd, the inner edge of which was composed of uniformly handsome young couples in jeans and tweed hacking jackets— the interested parents—pressed to the rail. The sunshine of a clear autumn day illuminated a scene which was studiedly un-pretentious, considering the enormous wealth represented: the casually dressed spectators, the ring of station wagons and pickup trucks parked on the show grounds and the adjacent grassy field, the children and horses milling everywhere. The ring of low-lying hills that enclosed the town of Middleburg was brilliant with the scarlet and yellow of turning trees. Around most of the trucks and station wagons, black servants in white coats prepared for the noontime tailgate lunches, laying out Virginia ham and chicken and buckets of champagne and beer. The loudspeaker rumbled something incomprehensible, then broke into a recorded waltz. The children, faces set, intent under their black-billed caps, their chests decorated with large cardboard signs carrying their event numbers, urged their ponies to a slow trot.

The Senator lifted his voice above the music. "What we ended up with was some damned crewcut lobotomy case from Langley, some Lieutenant Colonel—you know a Hardesty down there?—with a statement he said he had to read, *read*, dammit, in spite of what we told the Air Force, and he wouldn't turn it loose. Subcommittee counsel practically had to pry it out of his hand to make a xerox. Even then, it didn't say a damned thing; some General rewrote it when their PR people got through with it; that's the way it always goes. Didn't mention the engines or stall stagnation. Waste of time to put him on. Didn't try."

George returned with a plate of miniature biscuits stuffed with ham. The Senator took one absently and put it in his mouth and held out his paper cup for more champagne.

Simon McAllister smiled politely. He could see the Senator

was getting a little oiled, and he was surprised and more than a little flattered. The Senator was definitely letting his hair down among friends, and Simon was included in that circle. The Senator was also going at his drinking pretty steadily; he'd been into the champagne ever since they'd gotten to the show grounds, had broken off to have a couple of quick shots of bourbon when Nancy had taken a fall in the steeplechase event, and he must have had at least two or three eye-openers during breakfast. Now he was showing it. The Senator's large and florid features had taken on a rosy flush; there was a waxy melding of facial flesh that did not reflect his usual healthy, vigorous look. In spite of the booze, there might be some signs of strain.

The last few months had been hard on Nancy's father. Simon hadn't kept up with the state of the Industrialization of Space bill in Congress, nor with the new subcommittee hearings on the F100X engines, but there was a *Finance* magazine issue out with an article on the Eagles and their engine problems that had penetrated even the squadron. He had been involved pretty much in his own problems lately. He was aware of how the Air Force absorbed all his time these days; it was a realization that didn't make him too happy.

But for some reason which he was not immediately able to fathom, the Senator was making himself extraordinarily accessible, even friendly, this trip. Since Nancy hadn't been around much of the time—busy preparing for the horse show—the Senator's interest hadn't been exactly unwelcome. But Simon didn't know why he had risen so suddenly in the Senator's estimation; whatever it was, he told himself, he certainly was going to take full advantage of it.

Naturally, Nancy reacted the way she usually did. According to some rule she laid down, it was impossible to be on good terms with Nancy and her father at the same time. When the Senator had his ear, which had been a good part of the time, Nancy was sulking somewhere. And the choosing up of sides was still going on. That morning, when Nancy had taken a header off her horse in the women's steeplechase and he had gone out on the field to see if she was all right, she had shaken him off, stalked away, wouldn't even let him take her to the medical tent. And right out where a hundred or more people could hear her, she had told him to go back to what he was doing, which was sucking up to her father, and leave her alone. She had gone off to the car to drive herself up to the house, limping, her face bleeding, stubborn as hell.

So much for getting back together again, he told himself. That was the way it was with Nancy—he had decided half a dozen times during the weekend to throw the whole thing up, get the hell out of there, that he was better off with it over and done. Except that the Senator had managed to step in, take over, engage him in some sort of conversation until he calmed down.

He still wasn't sure, though. Seeing Nancy this time had been something of a surprise. There had been a considerable change in her, although he had reminded himself that Nancy was never what you might call a really pretty girl; she had always been more than casual about her looks and her clothes. But this visit he had found her even more so—not just uncared-for, indifferent, but almost *vengefully* sloppy, as though she wanted to call attention to it. He wondered if the Senator was even aware of it. It had occurred to him that the way Nancy was acting might not only be directed at the Senator but also at himself, although he was damned if he could see any reason for that. Still, it was annoying to see her walking around with a gray face, no makeup, sullen and grubby. In the steeplechase event, she had ridden as if she wanted to break her neck or kill her horse or both. Acting like a kid. And she was too old for that.

With all this, and with the time he had spent in the Senator's company the last few days, he was beginning to wonder if Nancy's stories about her father were totally reliable. At first, listening to Nancy, he had assumed there was some truth in her accusations about collusion and kickbacks; this was nothing new in Washington, but the more he thought about it and the more he remembered what he had heard about it, the more it seemed to him that Nancy's complaints fit the standard radical counterculture line in the colleges a few years back and the crowd she used to run around with. It was hard to admit that Nancy might be presenting the case as she wanted to see it, but he was telling himself there was no other conclusion you could come to.

He had thought there had to be some truth in what Nancy said, because it was directed against her own father. According to the way he looked at it, the seriousness of such charges demanded some truth in them; he knew he wouldn't say anything like that about his own father unless he knew it was true. Now he was not so sure. Once he'd been able to get a little distance from Nancy, once he'd had the opportunity to talk to the Senator as he'd been doing and form his own judgments, he found he was getting a different side of things entirely.

Not, he told himself quickly that the Senator wasn't a pretty tough case—he'd been in Congress a long time, and politics, as he let you know, were an old game to him. Senator Glass made no effort to hide the fact that he was cynically assured of his power and what made it work. But, Simon thought, if now he had to render a verdict on whether there were, or ever had been, any connections between the Senator in his capacity as Chairman of the Senate Armed Services Committee and Bernie Gould and defense industry contracts, he would have to say he didn't know. There had probably been nothing *outstandingly* illegal or unethical—he found that easy to believe once you got to know the man. Ultimately, perhaps, you had to give Senator Glass due credit; he had done a masterful job of building the country's armed forces in the years following Vietnam, when public support had been almost nonexistent— and, to hear Senator Glass tell it, he had done it almost singlehandedly. Whatever else one could say, or what Nancy did say, the Senator had a burning commitment to space exploration and development as demonstrated in his work on the Industrialization of Space bill. That program was something NASA had tried, unsuccessfully, to get through Congress for years, and the Senator was, in the Senator's own words, now laying his twenty-year career on the line for something that did not look too promising. From what the Senator had said, his long-time political supporters seemed to be falling away from him in recent weeks, dismayed over the problems with the Space Shuttle and the controversy over the engines in the F-15s.

It was no wonder, he told himself, that Senator Glass was showing signs of strain.

"What it boils down to," the Senator was saying, "is that the Air Force doesn't have any goddamned finesse. Listen, son, in all the years I've been dealing with them—and hell, that was even before there was an Air Force; it was part of the Army—I've learned you can count on the Air Force dropping the ball just when you're depending on them not to. It's the youngest branch of the service, right out front with growth and expansion, and you'd think they'd be on their damned toes. But I'm willing to bet you—" The Senator interrupted himself to turn and shout, "George, open up that champagne bottle there! We're running dry." The Senator looked around. "Yes, well, as I was saying, they freeze up at the worst damned times, haven't learned to stand up to it. They've got to learn that."

George came around the tailgate of the station wagon, selected a bottle of champagne from the ice bucket, twisted the wire open, and popped the cork expertly. The crowd around the ring was dispersing; it was the hour for lunch. Some passersby spoke to the Senator, but he appeared not to hear them. He was watching the stream of champagne flowing from the bottle into his cup.

The houseman looked up covertly at Simon. George's face was smooth, solicitous, even amused. The look said that between them, it was obvious the Senator was feeling no pain, that he was indulging himself in some well-deserved relaxation. If he wanted to tie one on, that was all right. And the Captain was supposed to be both tolerant and discreet. Which meant listening patiently to the Senator's stories and keeping his mouth shut later.

Simon understood. Not all of it, for it was impossible to encompass everything in that look; but it included going along with the Senator for now, perhaps even helping him back to the house later, if it came to that.

He took a deep breath. Where they were standing, here in this spot in the foothills of the Blue Ridge in Virginia, was a select and extraordinary environment, a casual congregation of the nation's wealthiest and most powerful people. Nothing in it could be compared to his own background, which most people assumed to be eminently affluent and privileged. But his father was only a corporation lawyer, and he had been telling himself all morning that the horse show in Wilton, Connecticut, where his own sisters rode was several hundred social layers below this one in Middleburg. One of the judges during the morning's competitions was a daughter of the Mellons; one of the Rockefellers had ridden in the hunter class. Hidden in the trees beyond the town were private airfields located on estates whose entrances were deliberately unmarked. Lear jets had been passing over the show grounds all morning, taking visitors away from the long weekend, returning them to the highest circles in government, to the power bases of Boston, New York, and San Francisco; the horses would be flown back later in their own jet transports.

The Senator's presence there was no mistake. The Senator's house in Middleburg, where it cost a fortune to live in that modest, understated township, his house in Georgetown, the expensively restored family home in Lynchburg all gave evidence of the Senator's profitable connections somewhere, sometime, in all this. But that didn't mean, he told himself, that he believed Nancy's wild stories, either. The truth was probably somewhere in the middle, but certainly not the way she had once put it.

He didn't know why it kept bothering him.

Standing by the Senator's station wagon in the warm sun, listening to the flow of words and not paying attention, particularly, to the Senator's familiar observations on the shortcomings of the military, he found his whole perspective changing. Without even realizing it, he was, he supposed, developing a sense of *laissez-faire* about how the world was run. Nothing worked right, when you came right down to it; at any other time, in any other year, he supposed he would have had some pretty definite reactions, would have known the solution to a lot of things, but now he felt a sense of world-weariness. The Senator, that all-powerful, charismatic figure, was imprudently tying one on right in front of him like any other middle-aged, stress-filled human being, rambling on without his usual charm. And, he couldn't help reminding himself, the best person he had ever known in his life, the one person not to buckle or turn unpredictable—Topper—was doing just that. Or almost that. And as for himself, right now his career in the Air Force was stalemated, lost in inertia and frustration. And Nancy—

"The Air Force could learn a hell of a lot from the Navy," the Senator was saying. He leaned forward for emphasis, and some of the champagne in his cup dribbled down the front of his trousers. "Son, you have to take dinner aboard an aircraft carrier—now *that's* an experience; the Navy has it down to an art. All this interservice rivalry costs the taxpayers a bundle—don't you believe it doesn't—but what the Navy does is sheer *art*. Marine Corps is good, but a bunch of friendly cannibals—don't get happy until they get out their knives and start playing games."

The Senator waved away the houseman's offer of the champagne bottle. He said heavily, "But get any one of them into a committee room, and it all falls apart. It's like a damned confessional—*mea culpa*—they can't wait to get the last negative number off their chests. Just wait until the damn Defense Undersecretary resumes his testimony. They tell me he's turned full circle, decided to make a clean breast of it and plead guilty that we made an enormous blunder with the F-15s. Got the military stampeded since they saw that *Finance* magazine piece. Real hatchet job. What about you?" the Senator said suddenly. "Air Force all you want?"

He hadn't been listening. Now the sudden question left him adrift. "Sir?" he said.

The Senator frowned. "You happy being a fighter pilot?"

Those canny eyes fixed on him, not so drunk now. Narrowed, regarded him.

"Ah," he said, "no, sir. I—I thought Nancy told you—I have an application in now, some months now, for experimental test flight school." He swallowed, said, "My goal is to get into advanced research projects. I want—I have degrees in physics and aerospace engineering, Senator. I hope eventually to get into test flight in advanced tactical research." He didn't know how much he wanted to say. "Some of the new stuff coming along—the suborbitals."

The Senator said nothing for a moment but continued to stare at him. "What's the matter, qualifications not good enough?"

"Oh, no, sir, it's not that. From what they tell me, from the response I've gotten from my inquiries, I think I'm in the top ten. But it's a slow process. There are thousands of applications, and only a few slots coming open at test flight school every year."

There was a prolonged silence, and he began to think the Senator had lost interest. The Senator stood with his head thrust forward, the ring, the tailgate parties around them. A small wind blew across the field, raised a dust devil among the polished pickup trucks and horse vans, and then subsided.

The Senator said deliberately, "Well, it ought not to be so hard to do something about that."

The words fell into stunned silence. He was not sure he had even heard them correctly; he thought that he might have misunderstood. He knew you could make an awful mistake by picking up on that sort of thing too quickly. But on the other hand, he might be on the verge—something might be coming into his grasp at last if what appeared to be happening was really happening.

George came between them with a plate of fried chicken. The Senator took a piece. Simon took a breast of chicken and held it in his hand. After a minute or two he was able to say, "I certainly could use some help on it, sir."

The Senator did not answer. He bit into a chicken leg, gnawing it thoroughly. When he had eaten it down to the bone with relish, he put it carefully on a paper plate the houseman had placed on the tailgate. He wiped his hands on a paper napkin.

"Yes, but you've got to be damned sure, committed—damned committed. I like people who know what they want." The eyes pinned him, small and hard in the red, puffed face. "Now, you take my daughter. She's not very happy. If you could put your finger on the trouble there, I suppose you could say my daughter doesn't know what in hell she wants. It's gone on for a long time—I don't see that it's getting any better; it might be getting worse. A damned disease of our times, not knowing what you want."

At that moment, Simon could think of several retorts. He sifted through his mind for the better ones, not able to decide. He supposed the Senator was right. Nobody knew what Nancy really wanted, probably not even Nancy herself. He was relieved that the Senator could see that.

He said, "Yes, sir."

The Senator looked away over the treetops.

"At the moment, as you can see, she's pretty damned unhappy. And unhappy, I gather, over you. Mystery to me—she might need a strong hand, sense of commitment, something of the sort. Doesn't have much of her own."

With a sinking sense of dismay, Simon realized he hadn't been sharp enough to discover until that moment what was going on, what the conversation was, in effect, all about.

Dumb, he thought. It would be a mistake to need the Senator to lay it all out for him in detail.

Through stiff lips he said, "Sir, I'd like to ask your permission to marry—to get engaged to your daughter."

It was easier than he'd thought it would be. And in that instant as the fatal words hung—fell—into the air, forever spoken and noted, a vista opened up to him of actuality, of decisions that, finally made, would stand. He was going to get engaged, he was probably going to get married, and he was going to test flight school. Somewhere along the line in this amazing but not unwished-for chain of events, he would become the son-in-law of the Chairman of the Senate Armed Services Committee. He was positive he could deal with that condition productively, modestly, honorably; he saw the possibility of trouble with Nancy on the first two items, but the third was—hell, practically a certainty.

The Senator only said, "Well have you asked her?"

He thought about that for a moment. "We've talked about it, sir."

The Senator was watching something behind him.

"Well, it looks as if you're going to have a chance to talk it over with her. Here she comes."

He turned. Nancy was limping across the field toward them. She was still in jodhpurs and hunt jacket, and there was a Band-Aid above her left eye. Not friendly—but there was something pathetic and appealing about her now. The Senator's remark, that Nancy was unhappy because of him, had astounded him. What had he done? Was it possible, unbelievably enough, that she really loved him? And that he had given her the impression that he didn't love her back?

He started toward her. He wanted to say something to her. He felt a sudden rush of tenderness and protectiveness. She was his *girl*—that's what the whole thing was about, wasn't it? He supposed he had always intended to marry her. What he had to do now was get her to agree to it.

But he could see, even as he hurried toward her, that she braced herself, that she turned her head to one side, looking away.

"Hey, Nancy," he said.

He resisted the impulse to put his arms around her in front

of the Senator and everybody. That would be too much. He knew her well enough to know that.

She said, not looking up, "You have a telephone call at the house. They want you to call right back. It's urgent."

He took her hand. "Honey"—he said.

She shook him off. "Right now. It's your *squadron*. They said to tell you it's a general recall."

General recall? He stared at her. The first thing he thought was that she didn't know what she'd said. Then he knew she'd gotten it right. But that might mean war—anything! He grabbed her hand, started dragging her in the direction of the car. She limped along slowly.

"Christ, hurry up, will you, Nan?" he told her. "Give me the car keys. I'll drive."

On the telephone, Randy Slyke said, "You get it all when you get here. Just get here. When's that going to be?"

"Make it three hours," Simon said. He was in the Blue Ridge foothills at Middleburg. It would take three hours to get back to the Virginia coast. Then he thought of the Porsche. "Make it less," he said.

Randy Slyke's voice dropped. "Moonbird," he began. To Simon's surprise there was, in the Ops Officer's altered tone and for the second time that day, an implied intimacy. "I need to find Topper. You usually know where he is. I need to find him quick and easy, no flap."

He stood by the telephone in the hallway of the Senator's house and stared at the wall in front of him, knowing what trouble they were in if Topper had gone missing. He understood. He also understood that Randy Slyke had asked him, because there was nobody else who could do it.

"No sweat," he said. He kept his voice down. "I know a couple of places. I'll take care of it; don't worry about it."

When he hung up, he saw Nancy standing there. He ran his fingers through his hair, feeling suddenly harried, preoccupied. He was thinking of where to look for Topper. He might have known this would happen if he went out of town.

Nancy, he thought. There she was, right in front of him. Christ, he had forgotten all about her!

Part 4

/* Real Time */

REF   TACR 51—2 *BFM * ACM * ROE
1. INSURE:
    A.   ALL PILOTS WILL NOT BE SCHEDULED
            FOR SORTIES*MANEUVERS BEYOND
            THEIR ABILITY.
    B.   MISSION WILL BE BRIEFED IAW * TACR
            * 51—2 IF DAC SORTIE.
2. RULES OF ENGAGEMENT:
    A.   THE DEFENDER MUST ASSUME AN
            AIRCRAFT CHASING HIM INTO THE
            SUN HAS LOST VISUAL CONTACT AND
            HE IS RESPONSIBLE FOR MAINTAINING
            SEPARATION.
    B.   IF VISUAL CONTACT IS LOST DURING
            SET-UPS FOR ENGAGEMENTS, THE
            FLIGHT LEAD WILL ASSURE THAT
            ALTITUDE SEPARATION IS PROVIDED
            UNTIL TALLYHO.
    C.   IF TWO AIRCRAFT APPROACH HEAD-ON,
            EACH FIGHTER WILL CLEAR TO THE
            RIGHT AND THE FIGHTER WITH THE
            HIGHER NOSE POSITION WILL
            ATTEMPT TO GO ABOVE THE
            OPPONENT.

"Unless it's Topper," Nizzard said. "Topper still thinks he's fighting in fucking Vietnam."

Simon McAllister looked for a place to hang his clothes in the room, and there was none. He said, "We're doing all right for rejects. Don't knock it."

"I never ran into anybody," Topper said.

    D.   FRONT QUARTER GUN ATTACKS ARE
            NOT AUTHORIZED.
    E.   ALL REAR QUARTER ATTACKS WILL BE
            INITIATED AGAINST THE TRAILING
            WINGMAN IN AN ELEMENT. ATTACKS
            MAY BE INITIATED AGAINST ANY
            ELEMENT.

F.   ANY FLIGHT MEMBER CAN
     TERMINATE THE ENGAGEMENT BY
     TRANSMITTING "KNOCK IT OFF" AT
     WHICH TIME ALL PARTICIPANTS WILL
     CEASE MANEUVERING AND
     ACKNOWLEDGE WITH CALL SIGN, SUCH
     AS "RED ONE—KNOCK IT OFF."

G.   FIGHTERS CONDUCTING SEPARATE
     ATTACKS WILL MAINTAIN A MINIMUM
     OF 1000 FEET ALTITUDE SEPARATION
     ON ANY TARGET UNTIL TALLYHO. ALL
     AIRCRAFT WILL HAVE THIS ALTITUDE
     SEPARATION WITHIN 10 NAUTICAL
     MILES. FIGHTERS MAY TRANSIT
     TARGET BEYOND 10 NAUTICAL MILES.

"It's that damned stupid tallyho," Simon complained. "That's a British fox-hunting expression, for God's sake. You'd think they'd find some other word."

Beeper said, "We got it from the RAF."

"Screw the RAF, too."

H.   TERMINATION WILL BE
     ACCOMPLISHED WHEN ONE OF THE
     FOLLOWING SITUATIONS OCCURS:
     [1] IF THE BATTLE DRIFTS TO THE
         BORDER OF THE AUTHORIZED
         AREA.
     [2] IF AN UNBRIEFED*UNSCHEDULED
         FLIGHT ENTERS THE ACM WORK
         AREA AND IS A FACTOR
         DETRIMENTAL TO THE SAFE
         CONDUCT OF THE MISSION.
     [3] IF VISUAL CONTACT IS LOST BY
         THE ATTACKING AIRCRAFT
         WITHIN ONE NAUTICAL MILE, AND
         CONVERGING VECTORS EXIST OR
         SAFE SEPARATION CANNOT BE
         ASSURED.
     [4] WHEN THE DESIRED LEARNING
         OBJECTIVE IS ACHIEVED
     [5] IF STALEMATE OCCURS.
     [6] IF ANY AIRCRAFT ROCKS ITS
         WINGS.

[7] IF BINGO FUEL IS REACHED.

[8] IF A DANGEROUS SITUATION IS DEVELOPING.

[9] IF MINIMUM ALTITUDE OR CLOUDS ARE APPROACHED.

[10] IF RADIO FAILURE OCCURS.

[11] IF COMMUNICATIONS DETERIORATE TO A POINT THAT INDIVIDUAL AIRCRAFT CANNOT RECEIVE ALL RADIO TRANSMISSIONS PERTINENT TO THE ENGAGEMENT.

[12] AT 500 FEET SLANT RANGE FROM THE TARGET.

[13] IF SITUATION AWARENESS IS LOST [DISORIENTATION].

[14] IF ANY MEMBER CALLS "KNOCK IT OFF."

"Jesus Christ, doesn't anybody wear anything but dirty underwear around here? You smell like a goddamned billy goat, Nizzard." He made a face. *"I'm going to find myself some other VOQ billet."*

"There are no other VOQs at Nellis."

"Christ, I'll go live in a tent! Your feet stink, too."

Topper said patiently, "I want you two to knock it off."

NOTE: THE ABOVE PROCEDURES OF ENGAGEMENT APPLY ONLY TO MISSIONS WHERE THE INTENT IS TO CONDUCT BFM * ACM * ACT TRAINING. FOR PURE AIR DEFENSE INTERCEPT TRAINING SEE JM 55-200 AND THE TAC CHAPTER 4 THERETO.

GENERAL:

A. TRAINING WILL BE ACCOMPLISHED ONLY IN DESIGNATED AND AUTHORIZED ACM AND*OR AEROBATIC AREAS.

B. ACT ENGAGEMENTS WILL NOT BE CONDUCTED BETWEEN TWO OVERCAST LAYERS OF CLOUDS WHEN THE VERTICAL DISTANCE BETWEEN THE

LAYERS IS LESS THAN 15000 FEET.
MANEUVERS WILL BE A MINIMUM OF
2000 FEET FROM A CLOUD. FLIGHT
VISIBILITY WILL BE AT LEAST 3
NAUTICAL MILES IN THE AREA OF
ENGAGEMENTS.

C.   AN "OPS CHECK" IS REQUIRED AFTER
     EACH ENGAGEMENT.

D.   SEPARATION FUEL WILL BE JOKER
     FUEL STATE. AT FIRST JOKER CALL,
     THAT AIRCRAFT*ELEMENT WILL
     ATTEMPT AN ACTUAL SEPARATION.

At 2 A.M., Beeper was still telling his Nellis OC bar jokes. He had been into Las Vegas with Dolphin flight, playing black-jack, and he had won some money. He was still wide awake.

"Hell, what do you have to do to get some sleep around here?" Topper said.

"So this Indian kid says to his father: 'Pop, I don't want to go to school anymore; they keep making fun of our Indian names.' So the father said, 'Son, let me explain that to you. When your mother was getting ready to have your older brother, she went into the teepee, and we all went with her to sing the old songs and help her along, and when the baby came, we opened the flap of the teepee, and we saw this beautiful deer running across the valley floor. So we named your brother "Running Deer." And when your little sister was born, and after everything was all over, we went to the flap of the teepee and opened it, and it was this beautiful autumn day with a big blue sky and clouds, so we named your little sister "White Cloud." So you see, you shouldn't be ashamed of our Indian names, Two Dogs Fucking, because—'"

Nizzard jumped out of bed, naked and howling. "I'm going to punch you right in the mouth, man! Don't you know I'm one-quarter Cherokee?"

E.   INITIAL RADIO CONTACT ON A
     PREBRIEFED COMMON FREQUENCY
     MUST BE ESTABLISHED PRIOR TO
     ENGAGEMENT. FLIGHTS WILL NOT
     OPERATE ON SEPARATE RADIO
     FREQUENCIES FOR ANY MISSIONS.
     EXCEPTION: ENGAGING FLIGHTS MAY

REMAIN ON DISCRETE FREQUENCIES
PROVIDED A POSITIVE GCU MONITOR
IS ESTABLISHED AND WEAPON
CONTROLLERS ARE MONITORING THE
ASSIGNED FREQUENCIES.

F. ATTACKS ON AIRCRAFT BELOW 5000
    AGL ARE AUTHORIZED WITH THE
    FOLLOWING LIMITATIONS:

    [1] ATTACKERS: THE ATTACK MAY
        COMMENCE FROM ABOVE OR BELOW
        5000 FEET AGL AND WILL
        TERMINATE NO LATER THAN
        MINIMUM GUN RANGE IF ANY
        MEMBER OF THE FLIGHT
        ACKNOWLEDGES THE ATTACK, OR
        IF THE ATTACK FLIGHT BEGINS
        WEAPONS DELIVERY [POP-UP].

    [2] DEFENDERS WILL ACKNOWLEDGE
        THE ATTACK BY A RADIO
        TRANSMISSION [IF SAME
        FREQUENCY], A WING ROCK, A
        LEVEL*CLIMBING DEFENSIVE TURN
        TERMINATING WITH A WING ROCK
        AND RETURN TO COURSE [AS A
        GUIDE, DEFENSIVE TURNS WILL
        NOT EXCEED 90 DEGREES].
        DEFENDERS WILL NOT MANEUVER
        COUNTER-OFFENSIVELY AGAINST
        AN ATTACK.

When it was dark and quiet again except for the thunder
of F-4s taking off from the runway on a night CAP mission,
he said, "Hey, if it makes you feel any better, the rest of the
squadron's not doing so damned good. Walter Cronkite said
tonight that some Congressmen were questioning whether it
was worth the time and money to send unarmed F-15s to Saudi
Arabia on a Show the Flag Mission."

Beeper said, "No kidding, Nizzard, are you really one-
quarter Indian?"

Topper rose up on one elbow. "Hey, what's going on,
anyway? I said, KNOCK IT OFF."

"Hell, yeah," Nizzard said. "Us Indians don't lie."

17

In February of that year, a Major Howland out of Eglin Air Force Base in Florida was killed when his F-15 Eagle crashed fifty miles southeast of Tonopah on the Nellis Red Flag range.

In the same month and during the same Red Flag exercises, Captain Boomer Rose of the 488th Tactical Fighter Wing at Luke in Arizona was killed when his F-104 jet crashed in the snow-covered mountains eighty miles south of Tonopah.

The first week of March, two fighter pilots in a two-seater F-4D Phantom crashed 115 miles north of Las Vegas on the Red Flag range.

In July, Major Lenny Heyse was killed when his A7-D fighter slammed into mountains thirty miles southeast of Tonopah on the Red Flag range. Ten days later, Lieutenant Colonel Arthur McFadden in an F-106 Delta Dart collided in midair with an A-7D over the Red Flag range, but both pilots escaped injury: Lieutenant Colonel McFadden's F-106 was damaged only slightly, and the A-7D crashed after its pilot had ejected.

In the next to last Red Flag of the year, Captain William Phillipson and Captain Jonathan Bright were killed when their Strategic Air Command F-111 crashed in rugged mountains forty miles north of Pioche on the Red Flag range.

In all, the most realistic combat-training exercises of any military in the world produced losses that were, it was claimed, mostly due to pilot error; the rationale was that Red Flag would have no training value for the aircrews involved without realism and the accompanying danger.

Topper had been to Red Flag year after year since it began and had a coffee cup someone had presented to him in the OC bar which said, across one side: Survivor.

Topper flight was billeted in a wooden World War II barracks at the far end of Nellis Air Force Base, a fifteen-minute walk to the flight line, more than that to the OC to get breakfast in the morning. They were the worst visiting officers' quarters on base. The only other people in the barracks were Air Force engineers working with a construction crew of Desert Rats, repairing the simulated airfields and missile sites out on the Red Flag range that somebody or other blew apart each day. Although they couldn't get anyone at the billeting office to admit it, they figured they had drawn the worst VOQ because they were odd numbers, a detachment of rejects selected out for Red Flag while the rest of the 17th Squadron went to Saudi. Since the squadron's mission was in the newspapers and on television, it was no secret; they were known everywhere as the 17th's rejects.

The beds in the room that all four members of Topper flight shared were so close together, they had to climb over them to get into them at night. Also, Simon McAllister noted right away, there was no desk, not even a table. Since he had put himself on a schedule to write Nancy every night whether she answered his letters or not, he had to walk over to the Nellis base library each evening and find a table where he could get it done. The library, at least, was rewarding: it had a fine collection of technical monographs on space-related areas in among the usual copies of *Aviation Week* and *Astronautics and Aeronautics*, especially a Royal Aircraft Establishment (Farnborough) report on "Reheater Design of Hypersonic Turbofan Engines for Tactical Purposes" and a NASA paper on "Inertial Coupling Stability Problems Affecting Design of Lifting Body Re-entry Vehicles" that kept him busy for a few evenings, taking notes.

On the walk back from the base library, he usually stopped at the Officers' Club to get Topper out of the bar. Otherwise, as he well knew, Topper would close it up.

It was hard, under these circumstances, to get a good night's sleep. The day's routine, as always at Red Flag, was fighter-jocking at its most competitive and punishing, and none of them had much energy, at least the first week, to do more than early sack time. But with all of them billeted in one creaky wooden room, it was impossible not to lie awake some nights, listening to Topper talking in his sleep about eternal dogfights or Nizzard grinding his teeth. And while doing so, to remind himself that this was the last Red Flag—that he wasn't coming back to this sort of life anymore.

Dolph Bauernhauser's Dolphin flight was billeted next door. Dolphin flight coped with the bad VOQ by staying away from it as much as possible. Dolph took his crowd into Las Vegas and the Strip every other night; they came back late, feeling good, slamming the doors, making a lot of noise to show their high level of the don't-give-a-shit factor as it was affected by being at Red Flag this time as the squadron's rejects.

And this Red Flag was tough. The war games were designed originally to be the fighter pilot's ongoing certification—a postgraduate course in tactical combat flying, even though it had to be repeated every year and it had been more or less demonstrated that it was not humanly possible to respond to that deliberately generated level of competitiveness with any kind of self-renewing maximum response, except, as Simon saw it, to keep from getting killed. Or perhaps, as he had begun to feel, to get out in front of everybody else performance-wise just to show that it could be done, after all, violating all logical limits and restrictions—as a sort of personal gesture to the military mindset.

Red Flag had always been, in his opinion, the kind of thing the armed services had to think up when there wasn't a real war going on. Naturally, nobody agreed with him. But he could see that it gave meaning and purpose to a variety of operations that were, perhaps, essentially meaningless and unpurposeful: it kept generals busy; it made for high visibility where it counted—all the visiting Congressional VIPs and newspaper and magazine writers at every Red Flag testified to that. In addition, as their daily briefings stressed, Red Flag combined an opportunity for unmatched advanced combat training, tactics development for the future, operational testing of equipment on hand, and above all and generating a mountain of paperwork, the analytical studies. It was, in all, as near to a real war as time and money could produce. Providing, of course, a real war was held in and over a shovel-shaped piece of desert some forty miles north of the city of Las Vegas, Nevada, bordered on its western edge by a national desert wildlife preserve and to some extent the tourist areas of Lake Mead and Boulder Dam, enclosed on three sides south, west, and east not only by the Interstate Highways of 95 to California and north and 93 to Salt Lake City, but also, in the air, by the major commercial flight vectors from Las Vegas, controlled by the FAA at Los Angeles Area Traffic Control Center.

It was a simulated war ostensibly based on the lessons learned in Vietnam, that the survivability rate of fighter pilots and their equipment rose in geometric proportion to the number of combat missions flown. The first ten missions, it had been ascertained, were the critical ones, and Red Flag provided those first ten missions under maximum learning environment. The environment so far had been particularly tense, as the problems in the F100X engines in the new Eagles were currently under scrutiny in a Senate Armed Services subcommittee hearing. The Eagles had revolutionized modern combat tactics, but the exploration of what they could do had just begun. None of them were happy to find, when they arrived, that a thick book of revised combat directives had been issued for the F-15s at Red Flag and that a select commission from the Air Force Inspector General's office was on base as their special observer.

At dawn each morning, the Nellis airstrip was crowded with sixty to seventy military aircraft from the continental United States and overseas: Navy F-14 Tomcats from San Diego; Marine attack A-6Es from Cherry Point, North Carolina; Vulcans with their RAF crews out of Bawtry, England; a detachment of Royal Netherlands Air Force in the new single-engine F-16 light fighters; FB-111s from the fighter base at Plattsburgh, New York; F-4s from Kanehoe Bay, Hawaii; F-105 Thunderchiefs from George in southern California; antitank A-10s from Myrtle Beach, South Carolina; and the Eagles, the F-15s from Langley and Holloman in New Mexico. These were the Blue Force, the good guys.

Against them, the Tactical Air Command had specially trained squadrons of F-5s that simulated MIG 21s, the Aggressors, who studied Soviet fighter tactics; they also brought in F-111s from Mountain Home in Idaho to act as Soviet sweptwing Su-19s, code name Fencer. Or B-52s called out of North Dakota and Texas to fill in scenarios as nuclear-threat-delivering Soviet Bear or Bison bombers.

At first real light, as the rays of the sun lit up the bare slopes of Sunrise Mountain like a beacon over Nellis airfield and the sky glow of the Vegas Strip receded, the war began.

Each day, twice a day, they were given their missions from

an assortment of tactical assignments: Suppression of Enemy Air Defenses—usually air-to-air combat, MAC escort—meeting and protecting the Military Air Command's C-141s. Interdiction—interception and destruction of simulated missiles sent over the North Pole. Or F-111s acting as Soviet Fencers on nuclear strikes. Or Close Air Support of troop movements coordinated sometimes with Army maneuvers over in Death Valley. Or Combat Air Patrol. Or Composite Operations—a mix of everything—or Search and Rescue, the all-important SAR detection and recovery of downed airmen.

Every year at Red Flag, there were more electronic detectors and assists added to the command control centers at the base, where giant computerized screens tracked and tape-recorded the war. More Wild Weasel aircraft were added with their radar ferreting systems; more airborne AWACS were used—big Boeing 707s with sixty-foot radar dishes suspended above their airframes which painted the area, issued warnings of enemy activity, and relayed them simultaneously to the fighters in the vicinity and to the radar screens and computers at Red Flag control. Recently, the Blue Force team had been getting the help—when it worked—of a military communications satellite in geosynchronous orbit which locked on its systems over the American desert and sent its observations of what was taking place there back to the computers on the surface of the earth.

As always, and as in real wars, the aberrant, the unexpected, the unplanned-for happened. The first week they were there, the central computer in Red Flag control went down for two days. Operations went on, but it was like World War II—nobody knew what was going on except for radio transmissions and the daily mass debriefing when the several hundred pilots assembled in the Red Flag auditorium. Then the assigned Red Flag SAR team and, later the regular Nellis Search and Rescue, failed to find an F-105 fighter pilot who had bailed out in the sector around Black Mountain; helicopters and then motorized ground units swept the desert in mounting degrees of class B and then class A emergency for two days, until the pilot finally straggled to Highway 95 on his own, hailed a State of Nevada Highway Maintenance truck, and rode back into Nellis—carrying in his plastic map case a small striped tarantula he'd picked up on his way in as a congratulatory gift for the non-success of combined SAR teams. The Navy squadron of F-14s from San Diego was so short of its new launch-and-leave

TVSU systems that its ground crews worked through the night in secret, switching them from one Tomcat to the other. An F-111 squadron commander and his operations officer, nerves rubbed raw over a series of errors and their growing hatred of each other, drove down to a bar in Boulder City in civilian clothes, had a few drinks, and then fought it out. Four Royal Netherlands Air Force F-16 pilots jumped an F-15 captain from Eglin behind the Nellis Officers' Club, held him down and stripped him of his flight suit, and carried it off for a souvenir. The Eagle pilot was picked up by Nellis security after he was found wandering drunkenly in front of VIP quarters in his underwear. An AWACS assisting a combat air patrol exercise over the far northwest corner of the Red Flag range developed a fire in its radar dome and returned to base on full class A emergency, the crew abandoning it at the end of the runway where it burst into soaring flames and burned to a multimillion dollar ruin. An F-15 pilot, returning from a night sortie and on final approach, responded to his flight leader's transmission with: "Following you, on course," and then crashed to his death on the mountain behind the Nellis control tower. An F-4 crew chief slipped on a spot of grease on the cockpit ladder during a routine check and fell to the concrete below, fracturing his skull.

And, it was rumored, two Marine F-4 pilots from Cherry Point won over two thousand dollars at the crap table at the Desert Inn in Las Vegas, then lost it in the next hour at blackjack.

Simon McAllister had planned to stick close to Topper during Red Flag, as it was getting so he didn't know what Topper would do next. For one thing, there were days when Topper didn't talk at all. He had sat through the first few nights at dinner in the Nellis OC without Topper saying a word. On Wednesday, he borrowed a car from the Desert Rats in the barracks and took Topper into Las Vegas to see a rerun of *Star Wars* at a theater in a shopping center off Tropicana Boulevard. When they got there, they found the theater was crowded, standing room only, full of fighter jocks from Nellis.

At night, after writing his letter to Nancy in the base library, he went to the OC bar to pick up Topper. At eleven-thirty, Topper went back to the barracks to change into some old clothes he'd brought to run in, and he jogged out in the streets near the flight line. After that, Topper went to their sector on

the flight line and stayed with the ground crews for a while,
giving the kids a little help in holding things together.

On Thursday night, Topper came back from the flight line
at one in the morning, turned on the overhead lights, and
announced, "Okay, I think we're going to make it."

The ground crews had stopped going to their billets in the hotels
on the Vegas Strip and were sleeping out on the flight line, in spite
of the cold. The word had gotten out that Topper flight was getting
hot. Team spirit was up. And they had more maintenance work
than virtually any other detachment as they flew Eagles, and they
had brought the demon Forty Thirty-three with them.

Theoretically, there was no way for any maintenance crew to
know their flight's simulated-combat ratings. There was no formal scoring at Red Flag, only the mass debriefings of assembled
pilots in the auditorium at the end of each day, when the flight leaders came up to the platform to reveal their assigned scenarios and
whether their unit had won the war or not. Ground crews were supposed to know no more or less than what they picked up on the
flight line or what their own pilots told them. But the usual gossip
pipeline operated at Nellis as everywhere else; in spite of the fact
that there were several hundred maintenance personnel from
bases scattered all over the country and a sprinkling of foreign
groups, the military poop channels were set up and operating by
the time they had arrived. There might not be any official running
score at Nellis, but there was a fantastic system among the maintenance crews. It was the first time, for sure, that Topper flight
knew what their standing was. Good, and getting better. Coming
up.

Topper brought Spearman, the E/5 acting production chief
for Red Flag, a bottle of Courvoisier and told him to give the
kids a drink and get them off the flight line and back to their
hotels before they all caught pneumonia. Spearman gave the
bottle back to him, saying there would be plenty of time to
celebrate when Red Flag was over. They had to work all night
on Forty Thirty-three to see if they could get it combat-ready
sometime while they were there.

It was time, though, to be critical of the way they handled
the equipment—even Topper—and Simon tried to tell them
so. There was a lot to be desired, especially at Red Flag, but
Simon was told to stop interrupting the briefings, stop lecturing

about it. Beeper asked him why he didn't go over to Baron Control and play with the computers and stay out of their hair.

So he said, "Okay, I just want to know what you thought you were doing when you came in on hydraulic systems emergency again."

Beeper, putting down the ROE he was reading from, said: "I don't know, and I don't give a shit," wearily.

Nizzard said, "Hell, let him finish the briefing for once, Moonbird."

"Well, you ought to," he told him, "because you keep doing the same thing, one of these times you might just go ahead and kill yourself. Let me explain it to you," he said, not caring whether they liked it or not. "When you initiate landing gear 'down' and you're pulling zero or slight negative Gs, it's going to put a small bubble in that hydraulic system every time—there's nearly always one in there anyway, but when the *pump* gets the bubble as a result of your not watching what you're doing, it begins to cavitate, and your trouble starts. The solution is to resume normal one G, shut down your hydraulic system, and start it up again, instead of calling everybody out on the field with a class B emergency. If you'd watch your G numbers when you put your gear down, you'd save yourself all this crap."

He told himself he didn't give a shit, either. But he wasn't kidding about Beeper getting himself killed. Beeper was always pulling hydraulic systems failures.

Topper, sitting there, watching, listening, said coldly, "I thought you two had cut this out."

Airborne, everything changed. The friction and fooling around that drained off boredom and tension and which they used deliberately, aggressively against each other was instantly dropped; they froze to the precise and icy skills of their business. Time in the air was real, the only thing real to many of them, and at Red Flag it was more real than anywhere else. In the cockpit, Nizzard metamorphosed into a controlled, maximum-risk-taker of prodigious concentration and nerve, a coordination of man and machine whose effect on adversaries was apparent after the first few passes. Beeper was, like Topper, an instinctive split-second reactor, but essentially a hunter; Beeper used his weapons to optimum envelope and had a feeling for cannon, especially, and an unending bag of tricks. Of them all, it was always Beeper who consistently scored the most difficult shots.

Topper went over to C Building, looking for a bathtub so he could soak his hemorrhoids. A lot of the Vietnam jocks had hemorrhoids from years of pulling Gs.

On Wednesday, Topper flight engaged seven of the special Aggressor squadron over the desert and Mount Helen, killing three of the F-5s simulating MIGs, firing Sidewinder missiles, and using their cannon. They ran the Aggressors out of gas in a supersonic dogfight. Topper snatched his Eagle through max-performance turns, punishing his engines; in the end, he caught a case of stall stagnation and had to shut down his engines and relight. But the Aggressors limped home, defeated.

The following morning, Nizzard and Beeper drove a strike package of Aggressors off target at a missile site made of oil drums out at Tonopah. Acting alone, as an element, the two of them forced the MIGs into so many defensive turns, the Aggressors ran out of gas before they could get anywhere near the missile site.

After the mass debriefing in the afternoon, the Aggressor leader came up to Dolph Bauernhauser and said, "I thought you people were supposed to be the 17th's rejects."

At 2 A.M., Topper came in and switched on the overhead lights. He had been out on the flight line with the ground crews; his face was red with cold.

"Where the hell's everybody?"

Simon raised up on one elbow and blinked.

"For God's sake, Topper, it's Friday night." He lifted his wristwatch to his eyes and squinted at it. "Beeper and Nizzard went to Vegas. Go to bed."

But Topper sat down on the edge of his bed and began talking about keeping it all together, the more so since they were going good. The importance, for instance, when Topper flight cleared the runway for takeoff, of the last check—everybody coming in on the channel to sing off one-two-three-four-five-six-seven-eight—that since everybody at Nellis was listening, how important it was to look sharp and be in good military order. The striving for perfection, all the canopies clicking shut at the same time. It was what Topper always said.

In the harsh light, Topper's blue eyes were as clear as glass.
"Yeah, Top," he told him.

He knew Topper was crazy. There were, he told himself, mild forms of craziness like kleptomania, monomania, and so forth. They were *all* crazy. He rolled over in the bed and pulled the covers up around his head.

But Topper roamed around the room.

"You write your girl?"

He burrowed under the covers to get away from the light. He wanted to tell Topper that as far as he was concerned, none of this mattered anymore. That he was practically assured that in not too long a time, he'd be out of it, on his way to test flight. Only right now, he couldn't explain the details.

Under the covers he said, "Goddammit, Top, go to bed."

They were stationed out on the edge of the Red Flag perimeter at Cactus Peak on combat air patrol when they engaged a mixed gaggle of Aggressor F-5s and Navy F-4s. Topper split to take the Aggressors, and Simon took the Phantoms. As the fight developed, they switched from one pack to another and then back again so that their opponents lost track, couldn't get themselves together. The result was mass disorder among the adversaries. The final score was three F-5 kills, five Navy F-4 kills. No Eagles lost.

"Not bad," Topper said, satisfied.

The next sortie, they escorted three B-52 bombers across the north ranges unmolested. The Aggressors had caught on.

"We'll catch hell on Monday," Dolph Bauernhauser predicted.

The next Monday, they did night sorties. The mission was escort for a SAC attack, rendezvousing with the B-52s in the northwest corner of the range at Tonopah. Finding the bombers was their first problem. The B-52s came thundering along in the night among the desert peaks at 500-feet altitude and maximum speed, half a Mach, running with their lights out in the moonless dark. Real war mode. No AWACS was available to help them out, and Blue Force at Nellis—as was usual at night—could only get an occasional fix. The mission was labeled all-weather night fighter training, but the primary idea was not to run into the B-52s or have the B-52s run into them. The big eight-engine bombers roared along the desert floor, shaking the earth, scattering the sheep out of the foothills. The B-52 pod leader was glad to see the Eagle escort, even gladder to find they were some distance off his wing. The exercise was primitive, almost blind—their radar painted incomprehensible ground signals most of the time, and they relied on visuals and their radio, straining their eyes to make out dim silhouettes against the night sky. It was nearly impossible to establish a fighter weave above the bombers or much of a sweep out in front with any safety, and the commander of the lead pod told them not to sweat it.

The F-4s that were supposed to jump them couldn't even find them in the dark. Never did find them—they sneaked in under the radar cover, dumped the big SAC bombs, and kept on going.

As Simon was doing his final cockpit check on Friday, the crew chief climbed up the ladder to talk to him. The crew chief was a redheaded boy with big teeth who had just transferred into the squadron a few days before they left Langley and was, therefore, a reject by default. His pocket tab said R. Woodruff.

Woodruff leaned in on him confidentially and said, "They say you're going to get the Robbie Risman trophy, Moonbird. The whole flight line says. No kidding—best fighter jock of the year."

"Topper," he said automatically. He was busy trying to get out of his straps.

The kid shook his head. "No. Major James got it twice already, didn't he? They say *you.*"

For once, he couldn't think of anything to say. He knew the crew chief must have been joking. Woodruff went back down the ladder again, and he sat there, staring at the empty radar screens, the gauges and indicators, without seeing them. Thinking about it.

Saturday before dinner, he went over to the Officers' Club. Dolph Bauernhauser's wingman, Hollis, had carried the message back to the barracks that Topper had been in the bar all afternoon, and it was time somebody came and got him out.

It was about six o'clock and Happy Hour and things were just warming up Half of Red Flag was there especially the half that didn't have the money to go to Vegas and blow it on the Strip. The bar was dark as a pit and wall to wall with fighter jocks. The weekend go-go dancer was in her regular place behind the bar where the customers couldn't grab at her. Two Marines, Second Lieutenants, hung by their knees from the overhead beams in the snack bar. It was so noisy, the go-go dancer complained she couldn't hear her music.

He couldn't find Topper in the crowd, but he located Beeper at the near end of the bar with some Canadians. Beeper pushed through the jam, carrying a bottle of beer.

Beeper yelled in his ear, "He's out in the telephone booth."

When they came out into the lobby, Beeper said, "He's been trying to call his wife all week. Comes in here, has a couple of drinks, then goes into the pay telephones there." He steered him toward the last booth in the line. "It's going to be hell to get him out; he's sort of slid down on his knees in there. And he's so damned big, he's jammed in."

He couldn't believe it. "Trying to call Candy?"

Beeper shrugged. "Yeah. I guess nobody knows where the hell she is."

18

Topper drew Forty Thirty-three the last morning at Red Flag. His regular number, Ten-Eighteen, was down with radar trouble. Last-minute switches on the flight line were nothing out of the ordinary, but to hear that Forty Thirty-three was combat-ready was something of a surprise. They hadn't had it up since they had flown it into Nellis. Spearman, their acting chief, told them that Forty Thirty-three had checked out the night before and was ready to go.

"I'll never believe that," Simon said. "It's never been ready to go. I'll drive it."

Topper turned and stared at him.

"No kidding, Top, I can do it as well as—" he began.

"Oh, I don't doubt that," Topper said and strolled away.

Beeper came up and wanted to know what the trouble was.

There were over fifty aircraft of all sizes warming up on the flight line and the taxiway. The ground crews were wearing their ear protectors. They could hardly make themselves heard.

"Nothing," he yelled at Beeper; "everything's just great."

There was a steady wind blowing, stirring up the dust. They couldn't see it in the dark, but they could taste it. He felt jumpy. The sky was just beginning to lighten in the east.

"Don't worry," Spearman told him, his mouth against his ear. "I checked it out myself."

That was only part of the trouble. Forty Thirty-three. The rest was Topper. He was the only one who saw it. If he tried to explain it, he'd just be wasting his time.

"Everything's just great," he told Spearman.

They went on station over the desert at Quartzite Mountain at 0600 hours, taking up position at loiter speed. The combined Dolphin and Topper flights circled like lazing hawks, keeping their eyes alternately on their radar headings and the horizon. There was still too much wind, noticeable at low altitudes.

Simon watched Topper as they circled, saw Topper turn to watch him from time to time, the gray of Topper's helmet turning to black as the dark visor of the HUD swung in his direction. They maintained maximum radio silence.

The last day, they'd drawn an Area Defense mission over a simulated airfield on the desert floor, behind an invisible political border drawn roughly from Reveille Peak in the north, through Kawich Valley, down to the Belted Range of mountains in the sector marked 9° on their charts. South and east of that sector there was Dreamland, the Class One restricted area of the Atomic Energy Commission. He was with Topper in low forward CAP position at 500 feet, Beeper and Nizzard on the right, and Dolphin flight five miles to the rear on CAP at 20,000 feet—which gave Dolphin a good chance of sighting anything coming across. The airfield beneath them looked amazingly like the real thing, even down to the pockmarks where it had been hit with live ordnance earlier in the week.

At 6 A.M., the desert sky still held the dawn colors of green and rose and amber. The bald mountains were painted gold in the rising sun. Facing east, though, the light was in their eyes, which was no advantage. The valley floor around Quartzite was scattered with the upright posts of eroded 7,000-foot peaks. They called it the pinball machine. Hard to fly in and out of at 500 feet.

They waited.

After fifteen minutes, Topper broke radio silence to check air warning and control, their Blue Force AWACS airborne somewhere north of their position. The AWACS was hooked into several scenarios going at the same time in as many sectors. Its sixty-foot radar dome, like a flattened salad bowl atop the Boeing 707 airframe, painted the desert for miles, looking for attackers.

The sky turned pale blue, and still they waited. It was hunting time for the small predators; the mountains were full of hawks, even a few eagles, and they could climb, some of them, as high as 10,000 feet. And get sucked into the air intakes of the jets, if you didn't watch it. On the radio, Topper asked for a fuel check. Loiter at low altitude used up their gas. Behind them, on CAP, Dolph Bauernhauser did the same.

The waiting dragged on. They wondered if somebody had forgotten them and knew they hadn't. The advantage of an early-go, routed out in the dark to make a 4:30 A.M. briefing, was that the day was over early. The last debriefings on the last day at Red Flag wound up by four o'clock. They wanted to do it and get it over with.

Simon watched the desert floor slide by at 500 feet, a brown blur. He watched the brown sand turn as the Eagle bit into the far curve, then slid straight again. The longer they waited, the harder it got. All hell would break loose when the strike came, but after two weeks of it, the anticipation of all hell breaking loose no longer set the adrenalin pumping. He saw Topper looking at him. When's it going to start?

They sat and waited. They turned, down on the desert and turned again.

In his earphones, Topper called the AWACS.

"Dragnet, this is Topper One." Topper's quiet, even voice. "How's it going, Dragnet?"

And AWACS responding, businesslike: "Negative contacts, Topper One. We're looking."

Keep your shirt on.

Slowly the sky brightened to a pale white glare. A mile away, Topper turned. Three miles away, Beeper and Nizzard did the same. Waiting.

Their intelligence briefing had hypothesized an attack by the Aggressor over Iron Curtain countries to strike a number of targets, airfields, and missile sites supposedly located somewhere in eastern Europe. So as of the hour, some alert was supposedly in effect, the Eagles out looking and waiting for the strike. But not too long—logistically, the problem was to stay fueled up and ready. And that meant a trip to the KC-135 tanker was upcoming, northwest of Tonopah sixty miles away.

Coming into Red Flag range at the entry point over Highway 93, they had passed over Skull Mountain and the Shoshone hills where the Desert Rats of the engineer corps were already at work cleaning up around the imitation trains and plywood truck convoys. A little farther on, the trucks were clumped around the simulated missile site at Tolicha that Dolphin flight had struck the day before. The desert down there was plenty forbidding. It took the Desert Rats a couple of days to truck into some sites on the Red Flag range, and once in, they pitched tent cities while they rebuilt the targets. Down there with the scorpions and snakes.

The first year at Red Flag, Simon had been the lucky bail-out for a Search and Rescue training exercise. He had been dumped down there with survival gear to find out what it was like. And he had found out—it was the emptiest damned place in the world. He had gone miles and miles on foot in flight gear and had prayed, after a while, that somebody would spot him pretty quick and get it over with. By dark, he was talking out loud to keep himself company. He had kept walking. It was either keep walking or lie down in the dark and find, when you woke up, that some desert rattler had crawled into your flight suit to keep warm. Great stuff.

Topper's voice came on the radio asking for another gas check.

It was getting late. The computer clock said 0641 hours. His nose began to itch. His HUD visor was down, his mouth and nose clamped by the masks, and his face felt as though a fly was walking on it.

He listened to Topper again checking out with Dolphin flight on the state of their fuel.

Next year, they had been told, the Eagle's systems at Red Flag would be hooked into the Intel-Seven Satellite. Then the airborne AWACS would interface with the satellite, setting up a three-way input from datalink to AWACS to the Eagles' computers and back again that would provide a cosmic overview—any size pictured from a couple of F-15s mixing it up with a flight of Aggressors to an entire war. And instead of holding radio transmission to a minimum, they could communicate from the cockpit via satellite, voiceout and cryptic.

"Moonbird," Topper's voice said, "check gas."

Great advantages, great progress—as long as somebody didn't run out of gas. The weak link in the whole thing was still a simple engineering problem, their dependency on their fuel gauges. In the Eagles, they had revolutionary equipment that would fight, maneuver like a streak of light, climb supersonic in a furious thrust—and had to scamper off to the tanker every forty-five minutes to refuel.

To have something to do, Simon punched up the computer for the BIT tests. When bored, check your systems. The computer went to work, testing them and lining them out on the display.

ICS—the radar jamming internal countermeasures—check. The
little red mark popped up. Missile status on the load of Sidewinder
and Sparrow missiles—the digital display printed out a whole line
of checks: tuned, on standby-ready, all electronic circuits operational. The built-in tests started on the HUD systems in his helmet.
On the range scales: max range—check. Min range—check. Radar BIT—check. Suddenly he yawned convulsively. TACAN
range to Topper's Eagle a mile away—check.

The wait, on the last day, dragged on. When he got into
test flight, there would be other, different problems, but good
ones, solid ones. No fighter jocking. No more fake wars.

He strained to look beyond the Eagle's acrylic bubble to the
horizon. He wanted the Aggressor to come barreling in, a hell
of a fight, a blaze of glory—all of them winners over everything they threw at them.

It was the last damned time at Red Flag.

"Mein Gott," the President's National Security Advisor
muttered under his breath. It was a rare slip; Professor Wojniak
seldom spoke German, much less his native tongue, Czech.
But he seemed genuinely confounded.

He picked up his morning cup of tea and came around his
desk to stand in front of the office television set. His secretary,
stapling press releases at a large mahogany table, looked up,
saw what it was, and then went back to his stapling. The
television screen was running a videotape piped through one
of the White House closed circuits of the Senate Armed Services subcommittee hearing on the F100X engines. The secretary had seen it live—or at least parts of it—the day before.

The Chairman of the House Defense Appropriations Committee came to stand beside Professor Barrington Wojniak. The
House Budget Committee Chairman, Representative Biaggio,
remained at the far end of the office, by a partly opened window, finishing the last of one of his notoriously rank cigars.

"Incredible," Professor Wojniak muttered. And then to himself, "What is this film?"

As if in answer to his question, the words *Riyadh, Saudi
Arabia* appeared across the bottom of the screen. On camera,
a line of sleek winged shapes rolled onto a taxiway and posi-
tioned themselves for the runway and takeoff. At some signal,
the F-15s aligned themselves in pairs, roared in the grasshopper

jump of full military power, afterburners glowing, and hurled into the sky. The words at the bottom of the television screen changed to: *17th Tactical Fighter Squadron, USAF.*

Over the sound of the jet engines, the voice of Senator DeLean said, "Well, there, ah, haven't been any problems in this flight, no troubles with the engines, then, I take it? That is, nonstop over the ocean and so forth."

As the camera followed the flight of Eagles into the sky, another voice said, "As far as I know—as far as it is apparent to any of us—and I think you'd have to go to the Department of Defense or the Air Force for the actual figures, I would say, yes, this has been a trouble-free sortie. The Eagles have performed as desired. In fact, I would say the host countries have been impressed."

Professor Wojniak said, without taking his eyes from the screen, "Who is that?"

The House Defense Appropriations Committee Chairman, who had also seen the live telecast the day before, said, *sotto voce,* "Herrenman, from the Middle East desk at State."

Professor Wojniak shook his head ponderously. "Films? Why is the State Department before this committee? They are supposed to be investigating the troubles with these engines."

The Congressman said, "I suppose it's pertinent, Bart. About sending them to Saudi and back without any breakdowns."

The screen dropped the F-15 film and returned to a shot of the committee room and the State Department witness at the microphone, a balding man with a rather lofty, almost disdainful expression.

From across the room, Representative Biaggio said, "Well, Morty Glass had to have some sort of counter to that *Finance* story—it raked over the engine problems pretty hard. The idea was to get some big guns to bear on positive testimony. After all, the F-15 program was Morty's baby from the start."

"That's ass-covering," the Defense Appropriations Committee Chairman said, "and pretty obvious, don't you think?"

Representative Biaggio shrugged. "Better now than later was the idea."

"The Saudi Arabian trip has nothing to do with any of this," Professor Wojniak said. "It was not designed for this—to show that the Eagle engines are reliable."

The voice of the State Department man was saying, "Initially, yes, there was some question of admitting the female

Air Force personnel attached to the squadron, but this was not an actual problem. I believe a woman crew chief and, um, some of the ground crew were delayed in the Azores until permission was granted by the Saudi Arabian government. The Saudi Arabian armed services do not have female enlisted personnel. Unfortunately, we had to deal with this under pressure of last-minute advisements by the Saudi Arabian Foreign Office. Although clearance was arranged very quickly."

The voice of Senator Foutts said quickly, "I understand the Saudi government had to declare the women in the ground crews honorary men."

There was a ripple of off-camera laughter.

The State Department witness said, "There wasn't any problem, Senator. If you mean, did the presence of women enlisted personnel on this trip interfere in any way with the initial purpose of the deployment of this detachment of F-15s, which was to afford friendly Middle Eastern countries a chance to observe F-15 maximum performance, the answer is, no."

Professor Wojniak growled in his throat.

"I mean," Senator DeLean was saying, "there was a lot of discussion in the European press about sending these new fighters over there *unarmed*. Now, these new fighters represent a very advanced, even aggressive military posture—don't you think this sort of thing is confusing, that—"

The camera moved to a tight shot of Senator Anselm Foutts of Arkansas, who was saying, "—unless the whole idea of this trip was to put the F-15s into the air and take them over there just to prove they can fly. Don't you think that might reflect a pretty compromising position, I mean that the reliability of these engines is in such doubt that we have to resort to something like this? And I can't say that the Saudi Arabian government reacted with any great enthusiasm, from the reports I've heard—that is, these F-15s going over there and not carrying any armaments. What the Saudis want, as I understand it, is their shipment of F-15s we've promised them. Not an air show." Senator Foutts swung his head slightly to inquire of his colleagues in a stagy aside, "They still want to buy them, don't they?"

There was a burst of voices in the committee room. Over them, the State Department man said, "Senator, I can't honestly answer that. About the engines, that is. That's a question you will have to put before someone from the Defense Department."

"Ouch," the Defense Appropriations Committee Chairman said to Professor Wojniak.

From the other side of the office, Representative Biaggio said, "That's a great statement, isn't it? Now, who's going to clear that up?"

"At least he could have hedged. What the hell gets into these State people? We're up in Canada this week trying to get the Canadians to stick to their order on the F-16s; doesn't he know that?"

"—the same engines in the new F-16s," a voice on television went on, "which, being the new single-engine fighters, forces us to focus on some of the problems centered on the F100X engine used in both."

"He should have waited," the Defense Appropriations Committee Chairman murmured. "That's one of the problems with Morty; he's run that committee so long—"

The telephone on the desk rang, and the secretary moved to answer it.

Professor Wojniak fingered his lower lip thoughtfully, frowning. "Is it off the point? It is off the point, definitely. What is this subcommittee doing with all these films, which concern another matter entirely?"

"—that he thinks it's his domain. Of course, Morty's been out in front for the Air Force since Vietnam; he's worked hard in a vacuum, with a lot of public apathy, after all."

"The Navy's not too happy with him," Representative Biaggio put in.

The Congressman shrugged. "The Navy gets their slice. I admit Morty's pro-Air Force, but you've got to consider that the demand's been on him for most of the advanced aviation programs—and now the Industro-Space bill. With that sort of commitment, the art becomes the lifestyle, doesn't it? Hell, if we're dealing with a little overreach—"

Professor Wojniak inclined his head to the secretary, who said something.

"I agree with Bart," Congressman Biaggio said, not without some satisfaction. "They're all over the place with this one. They should start thinking of some sort of windup. I don't think Morty's been watching the tapes."

"Come," Professor Wojniak interrupted. "The Oval Office is ready now. I think we should go."

The secretary picked up the press releases, copies of the

President's remarks to be made shortly on the morning's long-awaited launch of the Space Shuttle, and handed two to the Congressmen. Professor Wojniak waved his copy away a trifle impatiently. He was familiar with it; he had helped write much of it, including the paragraph hailing the United States' return to the leadership in space exploration and development after a nearly ten-year hiatus in that field.

The House Defense Appropriations Committee Chairman said in a carefully lowered voice, "What's the status on the tiles, Bart? Are we still scheduling a space walk to check them out?"

Professor Wojniak's mind was on something else. He said, "I will look at those subcommittee transcripts. What is this focus, anyway? The focus should be positive, very positive."

As they moved toward the door of the National Security Advisor's office, the House Defense Appropriations Committee Chairman smoothed his hair quickly with one hand. There would be photographers at the press conference. "Well, thank God we're into a whole new ball game," he said absently.

Representative Biaggio said, "How about a giant step forward for all mankind, Fred?"

"Hell, for what the Shuttle's costing us—" He laughed. "Don't knock it, we can use another one. We need to get back on top again."

The secretary held the door open for them. As they passed out into the hallway, they joined a group of Congressmen and dignitaries also on their way to the press conference in the Oval Office. A group of reporters, burdened with flash cameras and tape recorders, clumped behind. At the forefront of the first group, Senator Mortimer Glass's broad shoulders and graying mane were visible slightly behind the Secretary of Defense and the Speaker of the House. The final countdown had just been announced. The reporters shoved a little, eager to get inside and stake out a good position.

Smoothly, the President's National Security Advisor quickened his pace and, taking the path of least resistance along the wall of the corridor, came abreast of Senator Glass. Smiling, he took the Senator's arm.

"Morty, it's good to see you," he began.

* * *

Topper was just positioning under the tanker for refueling when the first strike came.

The voice of the AWACS saw it first and said tersely "Topper flight—we're picking up some tracks

From where he was, on the KC-135 tanker's left wing, Simon McAllister could look down and see Topper below him The refueling boom in the tail of the tanker dropped down, and the probe came out and down, feeling for the F-15 under it. In the belly of the tanker, the boom operator was lying on his stomach, looking down through a small window, controlling the refueling boom with its small wings attached, literally flying it home to the F-15's fuel intake. The long metal probe passed over the canopy of Forty Thirty-three and Topper's helmeted head, reaching for the intake neatly; a nice hookup, right on the apple, as Topper always did it The F-15 held steady on the end of the refueling probe, riding a slight air turbulence. Linked, the KC-135 and the Eagle circled at 500 miles an hour at 30,000 feet, simultaneously maintaining the miles-long pattern of the racetrack oval

They were caught—they were not only on tanker, they were sixty miles away. Whatever it was that was coming now over the political border to hit the airfield would be there and gone by the time they got back. The best they could hope for was to refuel and get back to catch a few trailers

He wondered what Topper was thinking They were holding minimum radio transmission, and their radar systems were shut off to protect the tanker crew from being radiated with high-energy transmission. All they could do was sit there and listen

Somebody squawked: "We show a couple of bogies!"—picking up something on their radar

The voice of the tanker boomer said businesslike, "Gas Can Two-niner, contact."

And the AWACS, out of their area but sweeping it with the big airborne radar dish, came on. "Topper Three low altitude tracks—multiple targets, westbound

He looked down at Topper coming under the tanker. Poor Top. He was still in position himself off the tanker's left wing, waiting for Topper to complete refueling Beneath the transparent plastic canopy, he could see Topper s head bent, watching the fuel counter, probably cursing. At best Topper had three to four minutes on the tanker, and then he was next maybe eight minutes to go, an eternity in the air. The strike would be coming in at near supersonic.

The radio blared, "Dolphin—we're committed!" Beeper's voice. "And going in."

It hurt just to sit there listening. He wished them well. He twisted around and craned to look through the bubble. He saw only sharp-edged mountains like brown wrinkles from that altitude and the glaring morning sun.

They heard, as the defenders barreled out to meet the attackers:

"Nizzard, say your position—"

"Roger, I have a visual—smokers!"

"Coming to support, Topper Three."

That was Dolphin flight, coming down from the 20,000-foot CAP.

"F-4s! F-4s! I see smokers a long way out!"

Another voice: "Dolph, experiencing music."

Radar Dolph Bauernhauser's voice: "Roger, same-o."

"Check gas! Check gas!"

Dolphin flight was low on fuel. It had been their turn next on tanker.

"Roger, tallyho—go for guns. Will try snapshot. Keep going north."

Somebody was out of missiles already. In spite of himself, Simon tensed in the straps, moving restlessly. He knew Topper was going nuts down there on the end of the refueling boom. He could see Topper's head wagging from side to side, talking to himself. Topper kept up a stream of conversation with himself all during air combat.

There had been a couple of kills. He didn't hear Nizzard's radio anymore. The problem at Red Flag was always who shot whom, even with all the electronic scoring. They would argue about it later in debriefing. But only the ACMI computer tapes knew for sure.

The voices snapped on and off the air. *Rrrrrarr. Squeak.* A piercing high-pitched tone when two tried to transmit at the same time.

"Check slightly high—eight o'clock!"

"Break right—he's on your *tail!*"

Some of the flight had been jumped by F-4s—the "smokers" of the earlier visual with their heavy jet exhaust. It sounded like Dolphin flight was being eaten alive by F-4s and F-5s. In his mind's eye, he saw Beeper and Nizzard out in front at 500 feet and Dolphin flight slamming down from 20,000 to join in. The palms of his hands sweated. He could visualize the chase over the desert down there, afterburners cooking, grunting as they pulled Gs, twisting and cork-screwing to position on the tails of the attackers and get a missile shot up the tubes. On the ground, it was pretty incomprehensible, bits of supersonic metal snapping across the air like pieces of an explosion—three-dimensional chaos, only three master moves: out of the sun, at a high angle of attack, and fast as hell

Topper was signaling to come off the boom Simon found his teeth were clenched; his jaw muscles ached. As for Topper—he told himself moodily that it was not that he didn't trust Topper anymore, although that was part of it.

It took him a little over four minutes for his own fuel. As soon as he was through, Topper turned on his radar He said, "Moonbird, go spread."

Simon moved away from the tanker Above him, Topper peeled off in a hell of a hurry, slicing the air, standing Forty Thirty-three on one wing.

Topper said to Oakland Center: "Topper One and Two, request present position direct to restricted area."

Back to the fight.

Oakland Control came on. "Roger Topper, you're cleared for restricted area entry."

He moved out after Topper, keeping up with him. Topper was in a hurry, he pushed airspeed up to .98 Mach. Tonopah came up, sliding under them fast. Then Stonewall Mountain to the right, Mount Helen on the right under their nose. Going through Mach One. He thought, *Topper, take it easy.*

Topper's voice said, "Moonbird, go to button fourteen."

He switched frequencies "Two," he responded. His neck and jaws had gone rigid. They were at 30,000 feet, and the fight at the airfield was mostly down on the desert floor.

They were on Baron Control now, at Nellis, getting clearance to come in

"Arm up," Topper said

He punched up the ready light for the Sidewinders and Sparrows

"Two s up," he said into the mask

Their radar was picking up something now, down there and ahead. Locked on, it showed multiple targets coming in from the east like a swarm of bees, jinking and angling off the brown desert ridges, hugging the terrain. He stared at the radar scope and swallowed, the sound loud in his ears. The green-lighted lines of the Head-Up Display moved before his eyes. The targets were F-111s, simulating Soviet sweptwing Fencers, the Su-19s, presumed delivering nuclear threats and coming like bats out of hell at 1.2 Mach, about a hundred feet off the ground—a job the F-111s were made for.

Sweat dripped down into his eyes. He knew what Topper was going to do.

From 30,000 feet to the bottom of the desert in one long pounce—miss it, and you're an omelette on the desert floor. Topper would do it, too. A six-G conversion in pure vertical. Upside down. Straight down. Supersonic.

He saw Topper roll inverted.

On your back now, to pull the Gs.

He thought, Topper, I don't want to die in some fake Air Force war.

There was no way out of it. He rolled inverted, the Eagle flipping over eagerly. His mind braced—*keep sharp*.

He turned the Eagle's nose down. He slammed the throttles forward. Down. The world turned upside down. The Mach numbers on the HUD rolled up before his eyes. Through Mach. The air screamed—1.1 Mach. Brown dirt coming up fast. He grunted up the blood into his belly, into his lungs, to keep from blacking out. World's best fighter jocks. Jesus. 1.4 Mach.

A hand grabbed deep in his intestines and started dragging down and out. Going to kill both of us. He heard himself— *aaagh, aaagh, aaagh,* straining and grunting. Eyes bulging, face dragging. God, that hurts.

But suddenly, surprised, he was happy. He thought, euphoric: Hell, why not? The black *Star Wars* tube was narrowing deep inside his head, vision tunneling with the terrible Gs.

At the bottom—shoot the sons of bitches and pull out. If you can.

The airframe began to shudder. It continued to shudder.

The committee room was almost empty of spectators and reporters, drawn away by the morning's exciting event of the Space

Shuttle launch. Only the television camera crew remained. The slender blond young man with the deeply suntanned face took his seat at the witness table before the microphones and laid his brief-case before him. The subcommittee counsel, Garland Blitzstein, leaned over from the upper table where the Senators sat to instruct the stenographer to begin at the point where the testimony had stopped the day before. He consulted the typewritten sheet in his hand. The stenographer nodded.

Sitting back down in his seat, Counsel Blitzstein said, "Mr. McGillicuddy, we'll begin from the discussion of the 'fixes' in the F100X engines—"

Senator Mastracchio touched Counsel Blitzstein on the sleeve, and the young lawyer bent his head to listen. This went on for some minutes. The engineer from Trueham Engine Company opened his briefcase and took out his papers. Counsel Blitzstein looked up.

"Mr. McGillicuddy," he said, "in consideration of time involved and the length of some of the testimony we've had before us, we note that the subcommittee has a transcript of your complete testimony on the 'fixes' in the F100X engines which you began to list for us yesterday and which subcommittee members have been able to give a reading. So this material stands as noted, unless you have anything further to add." He swung around in his seat. "And Senator DeLean has a question."

Senator DeLean hitched himself nearer the microphone. "Mr. McGillicuddy, about these modifications, these 'fixes' which have been installed in the F100X engines now, and which you say are taking care of a good many of the problems like stall stagnation, like the proximate splitter in the compressor, uh, inlet lip"—Senator DeLean was reading from notes prepared by his staff—"and this PLAP in the fuel control which are, I take it, designed to upgrade the F100X engines—what I want to know, for the general information of this committee, is, these were pretty serious problems, weren't they?"

John McGillicuddy, his face reddening under his tan with the look of a shy man about to be prodded into a bolder move than he had intended, said, "Yes, Senator, the problems with the F100X engines in the F-15s have been serious; I don't think I want to give the impression that they weren't. But if you don't mind—if the subcommittee has already accepted the rest of my testimony as submitted in the report for its records—

before we close this out, I'd like to bring a few things to the subcommittee's attention. For one thing"—he paused slightly here and then said rapidly—"in all the volume of testimony the committee has heard this week, I don't think anybody's made the point that Trueham Engine Company *built and delivered the engines they were told to build and deliver.*"

Senator Mastracchio, who had been writing on a pad before him, looked up.

"For instance," the engineer said a trifle loudly, "we didn't exactly agree with some of the testing the Air Force insisted on after the original specifications had been followed, and that is, testing at thirty-one and a half hours at full afterburners which—as an engineer—I can tell you is more use and stress without maintenance than any turbofan engine in any military fighter is going to see in its lifetime. And at two point five Mach. And at a thirty-thousand-feet simulated altitude. Remember," he said, his face quite flushed, "these were not Trueham Engine Company's test specifications. They were the Air Force's."

Both Senator Foutts and Senator DeLean started to speak. John McGillicuddy kept his eyes on the microphone stand before him.

"However, at no time during these tests were we told by the Air Force to evaluate and test for more than—and I want you to make note of this, Senators—more than *twelve* throttle excursions per hour-and-a-half combat mission. Throttle excursions are when the fighter pilot slams his throttles forward for a sudden burst of speed, using his afterburners, and then back down again. And when he needs another burst of speed in a tight maneuver, the same thing again. These are your throttle excursions. However, it was a hell of a surprise for me to find—because I worked on these tests myself at our site in Florida—that when the Eagles went operational, the Air Force pilots were hotdogging these engines in excess of *sixty* throttle excursions per hour-and-a-half combat mission. Which meant that every time the fighter pilot shoved the throttles up to full military power and then back down again, and up and down and kept repeating this, the F100X—which is a high-powered, hot-running, lightweight engine to begin with and exactly what the Air Force told us to *build*—was heating up and cooling down and doing this over and over again under heavy demand, with mounting temperatures in the turbine section. Actually, over twenty-three hundred degrees Fahrenheit. And hell, yes—the turbine blades could be expected to burn up, some of them, in that kind of heat and that kind of use. No Trueham engineer ever told the Air Force they *wouldn't*."

All the Senators were silent now, giving him their undivided attention. The subcommittee counsel rested his elbows on the table, his chin in one hand, staring fixedly.

Senator Foutts cleared his throat and said, "Well, what I wanted to ask you was, if I understood your testimony yesterday, why you said the F100X engines did not pass the, ah, original acceptance tests."

The Trueham engineer took a deep breath. "Senator, no one has mentioned the role of General Banks of the Air Force in the acceptance tests so far, but it's my understanding that General Banks was appointed by the Air Force command in a special extraordinary capacity four years ago to get the engine program for the F-16s moving, when it looked as though engine production was lagging well behind airframe readiness. It's true that when the F100X engines were subjected to the rigorous tests I mentioned, they didn't perform well, but these tests were, in part, designed by. General Banks himself. They were far more demanding than anything any of us had anticipated or that we had been warned about when the engine was designed. And I personally failed to see the reason for their severity." John McGillicuddy looked up. "But the time period then was critical—the growth of the Soviets' air power and their new MIGs indicated we needed to free up the F-15 program and get it operational on an accelerated basis. So General Banks *did* accept the engines for the Air Force, even though, as I have pointed out, their initial performance was disappointing. But as Undersecretary of Defense Parsons said, a lot of the maturing process in the F100X engines had to take place *after* they were installed in the F-15 airframes and in service. When some troubles developed, this led to the Component Improvement Program—"

"I'd like," Senator Foutts interjected, "to go back to this business of engine acceptance, when the engines failed to pass the test. Now, you said—"

"Senator," John McGillicuddy persisted, "I want to say this, if you please—if General Banks had made his decision to pass the F100X engines in spite of their disappointing performance, and if after that they had turned out to be relatively trouble-free, as he had every right to anticipate, then General Banks would have been a hero—the man of the hour. That's not such an exaggeration. Air

Force Development and Acquisition is a hot seat and becoming more so. The military is closer to the edge of new technologies; the military makes first use of any revolutionary aviation concept— and it's out in front in risk-taking. I guess it wouldn't hurt to say here that in spite of that, in spite of some of the problems connected with superadvanced equipment we've been examining, we've still come a long way. The engines in World War II fighters, such as the Spitfire, the ME-109, the P-40—it's a long list, I won't go into all of it—went less than *twenty-five* combat hours before replacement. And it wasn't unusual for those engines just to burn up while in use."

Senator Foutts said, "I'd like to go back to this engine acceptance when they didn't pass the tests."

His face set and flaming, John McGillicuddy said, "Sir, I'm just trying to give you an indication of some of the things that have happened that haven't been brought out in testimony before this subcommittee. Senator, I've been in this committee room every day, and I've listened to all the references to the viability of defense contracts in areas of the country where there's a concentration of skilled but highly unionized labor, as we have, for instance, in the northeast where Trueham Engines are located, and the speculation of witnesses about low production as a result—or even faulty production or whatever you want to call it—and the wisdom of giving contracts like the one for the F100X engines based on need, or the company having enough power to influence the giving of them—" The engineer appeared to choke or stumble on his words. He coughed. "And I guess I've already deviated from my original testimony about the engine fixes enough—and you must be aware I'm speaking on my own now—"

Subcommittee counsel Blitzstein said, "Mr. McGillicuddy—"

"I wish you'd just let me finish." The engineer's voice was quite hoarse. "A year or so ago, the F100X engines were averaging three to four stall stagnations per thousand engine flight hours. The rate is now down to one point three, and with the modifications Trueham Engine Company has developed with the Air Force—and believe me, we've busted—we've exerted every effort possible—we will cut this down to point fifteen shortly. Senators," he said, leaning into the microphone to be heard above the voices, "believe me, I understand it's part of the American process of self-government to mount these investigations, to explore, as you have done here—and I don't want to give the impression that I don't think subcommittee investigations aren't worthwhile, because I'm sure they are—to go into every little detail that might have gone wrong or caused excessive trouble where the taxpayers' money is concerned. I certainly think some of that has been aired to good effect. Certainly, a lot of the work connected with the F100X engines might have been done better to begin with, especially in cooperation with the military—I've worked with the military, and I think I have a reasonable view of that. But what we're examining here, the F100X engines and the whole F-15 advanced tactical fighter program, is still a product of American minds and skill, and I firmly believe—I *know*—they're the best in the world. I think we lose sight of that. But if I didn't believe that, being connected with this project and knowing it about as well as anybody, I wouldn't say it! Senators, the F100X is the finest fighter engine ever developed—there hasn't been a witness before these microphones who's denied that. They've testified to its problems, and I've tried to outline to you what's being done to solve them. But—" Here John McGillicuddy's arm raised spasmodically. The corners of his mouth jerked. He blurted, "If you don't believe me—ask the Russians!"

Simon McAllister recovered, felt the Eagle shudder as he hauled up. It was bonecrushing stress to put on any equipment; the Eagle pulled out of the dive smooth as grease. But he was not in such good shape. He put the Eagle into a banking turn and almost slid out of it; for a moment, it was a sensation like a three-dimensional slide on ice. For several seconds, he saw only blackness, and he was in pain. He was hyperventilated from grunting against the Gs coming down and generally surprised he was still in one piece. His lower colon felt as though it had been pulled loose inside him. Topper, he saw, was somewhere on his left and below.

Still groggy, he swiveled in his seat, trying to keep sharp for attackers. From the radio transmissions, it seemed that Beeper and Nizzard were still around. In his earphones, he heard Beeper calling that he had one F-5 at six o'clock, breaking hard.

His nose was bleeding. Blood was trickling down inside his mask and into his mouth. But he told himself that he had made a vertical snap down from 30,000 and lived, caught a trailing F-111 and eliminated it. And he told himself that he was as crazy as Topper.

At two o'clock, he saw Beeper's Eagle cut into full afterburners and roar into a twisting, spiral climb. The F-5 was right behind Beeper, hustling to maintain positional advantage. He had to watch. Both fighters rose, the F-5 painted like a MIG 21 in Soviet-style red and brown camouflage, the F-15 Eagle a sleek, elusive ghost-gray. Their tailpipes glowed against the sky, both nose-up, moving in flashing, ascending corkscrews. But the Eagle's spiral was sharper, tighter; like a needle-nosed spinning rocket, it pulled ahead. The F-5's airspeed was rapidly bleeding off. The F-5 began to lose power. Shuddering, shaking, the F-5 came to the top of its climb and stalled. Beeper's Eagle still climbed above the attacker.

In a beautiful floating moment, the F-15 hung there, truly Eagle-like, predatory, waiting for the simulated MIG to stall and fall away. When it did, the Eagle's nose dropped, turning on a dime. The angle was too high for a missile—he figured Beeper got off a cannon shot.

Beeper's voice blared in the radio: "Gun kill on F-5!"

By the computer clock, the whole thing had taken from fifteen to twenty seconds.

Almost immediately, Beeper's voice said, "I'm Bingo fuel, friends; checking out, westbound."

The air was suddenly empty. He looked around. Dolphin flight had probably run out of fuel after the first strike and was on its way back to Nellis. He saw Topper closing on the left, hand-signaling. *Now what?* he thought.

From what he could see, they had done all right. The actual scores would be waiting for them in the mass debriefing, but the first strike of six F-4s and six F-5s had been designed to knock them off station and sweep the area, making way for the F-111s to come swarming in and drop their nuclear stuff on the airfield. It hadn't worked. Some of the F-111s had gotten through, but they had definitely been hassled off target. Twelve Aggressors and six simulated Su-19 Fencer fighter-bombers up against the combined Topper flight's eight Eagles—actually eighteen against *six* Eagles in the beginning because they had gotten caught on tanker at first strike. The Eagles were coming up against heavy odds at this Red Flag. Tactical Planning was working hard for some positive data—and getting it.

He was wing-on with Topper, heading west, and Topper was still hand-signaling.

"Topper, check."

He couldn't believe Topper was out of gas. But Forty Thirty-three ran on Murphy's law; whatever could go wrong, did. Just for that moment, he allowed himself some sneaking satisfaction that even Topper had trouble with the thing.

He followed Topper's lead, slowly throttling down.

"Where to?" he said into the mask.

"Home. Direct."

He couldn't believe his ears. He felt his skin creep. Then he told himself he must have misunderstood. Home, direct, would lead them across all restricted areas, even corner-clipping the AEC Dreamland. For Christ's sake, he thought, exasperated; he was getting so he expected anything.

There was no way in the world to argue.

He said cautiously, "Okay, let's stay low, under it." At least their radar would break line-of-sight with ground stations. "I hope you've got the gas."

He didn't want to be down there on the desert floor again with SAR looking for them.

"Positive."

In spite of himself, he felt a surge of resentment. All you ever got from Topper was military monosyllables.

They dropped down. Low meant plenty low, under radar tracking, down with the lizards and the snakes. And all he could think of was that he wanted to get the hell out of Nellis without being caught in anything crazy, even with Topper, without blowing his chances to test pilot school.

The AEC area rose up, looking like any other piece of desert. If it was Dreamland, if it glowed in the dark, you couldn't tell the difference—except that they weren't supposed to be there. He still didn't know why Topper hadn't declared an emergency.

Topper said, "Moonbird, my inertial NAV system has dumped."

The sunshine beat brightly through the canopy. The sky was streaked with high-altitude cirrus clouds. A beautiful day, calm and clear. It didn't seem the time for anything as bizarre as this to be happening. Like sneaking home through restricted areas. He saw the computer wasn't showing the right heading. The desert floor slid by. Minutes going by. Same heading. He stared at it. Somewhere, Red Control eyes were on the lookout for those who committed gross transgressions, like slipping over Class One restricted areas, waiting to bust them forever. He told himself that he was sick and tired of the feeling that he had had in the pit of his stomach for two whole weeks at Red Flag.

"Topper—two."

"What?"

Cautiously he said, "Top, I've got us twenty north of a direct course." He hesitated. "Listen, what's your gas?"

He waited. Finally Topper said, "Still fifteen hundred internal, two thousand in the wings."

He tried to keep his voice calm. "Topper, dammit—your *wings* aren't feeding." Then the worst part. "Top, listen, are you lost?"

There was no response for a long moment. The brown desert rushed by. They were minutes from Nellis if disaster didn't catch them first. He looked over and saw the black oblong of Topper's visor, Topper looking at him. They were at 150-feet altitude, roaring over the desert ridges, going nowhere. And Topper should have been on emergency a long time ago.

Topper said, low and distant, "Moonbird, you've got the lead."

He looked out through the canopy. He could get a visual on Mount Charleston overlooking Las Vegas if they swung right. Topper had given him the lead to take them back.

He thought, God, I don't believe this.

19

As if magically self-generated—the previous day had been, by any standard, ordinary enough—it appeared that the euphoria of the late sixties and early seventies had returned. The news of the successful Space Shuttle launch had swept Capitol Hill. When Senator Glass returned from the President's press conference at the White House, he saw that the doors along the hallway of the second story of the Russell Senate Office Building stood open, and in almost every Senatorial reception room, portable television sets blared forth in concert with the familiar, nostalgic clicks of shortwave radio transmissions and the laconic voices of Houston Control talking to the orbiting astronauts. Senator Glass noted an unusual number of telephones ringing.

Coming into his own office, Senator Glass found the television set there turned to live coverage of the crowds gathered in downtown Helsinki to watch the Space Shuttle on a giant outdoor television screen. An announcer's voice-over narration reported the number of NASA tracking stations in the Indian Ocean and Australia and their observations: all systems go, the astronauts feeling fine, equipment functioning well.

The Senator's administrative assistant followed him into the inner office and shut the door. Yoder carried a handful of pink message slips which he read off as the Senator quickly shuffled through his mail.

The office of the Secretary of Defense had called to inquire about a working lunch with the President's National Security Advisor, Professor Wojniak, and a representative from the Joint

Chiefs of Staff (suggested—USAF Commanding General Joseph Morehouse) to discuss the Industrialization of Space bill now slated to emerge from committee and be scheduled for debate in the Senate.

The Chairman of the House Defense Appropriations Committee wished Senator Glass to return his call.

The Majority Whip in the Senate, Robert Murphy, wished the Senator to return his call.

"I'm having lunch with my daughter at twelve-thirty," Senator Glass said. "I have to get moving. Some restaurant called The Monocle here on the Hill. Must be in the telephone book."

The Oval Office had called again (second time).

The Senator's presence was desired at a press conference at the House of Representatives, Room 212, 3 P.M., with members of the Overseas Press wire services.

"No," he said, and shook his head.

Newsweek and *Time* had both called for possible interviews on the proposed bill for space development by private industry. Mr. Fred Lightfoot of *Finance* magazine would like to talk to the Senator about the Senator's proposed strategy for the funding of a solar energy platform by the nation's utility companies.

Senator Glass peered around his desk, looking for his other pair of bifocals. "Are you kidding? That guy never quits, does he?" But his voice held no rancor. The copy of the issue of *Finance* that had caused them so much difficulty still lay prominently displayed by the framed photograph of his daughter. The Senator reached over and dropped it in the wastebasket.

Mr. Bernard Gould of AAASI had called and wished Senator Glass to return his call, ASAP.

Senator Vincent Mastracchio wanted the Senator to call. He was waiting in his office. It was urgent.

Senator Glass snorted. "Call Vinnie Mastracchio, and tell him I said we're going to break camp on the subcommittee hearing. General Monkfield's just scheduled himself as the last witness on Monday."

At the White House that morning, the President's National Security Advisor had cornered Senator Glass prior to the press conference on the Space Shuttle launch, and in a few words Professor Wojniak had conveyed surprise and acute disappointment over the public airing—even if, as the Professor understood it, all inadvertent—of any criticism of the Show the Flag mission to Saudi Arabia. Which, Professor Wojniak had been careful to point out to Senator Glass, was a mission not only calculated to promote good Saudi relations, but a joint endeavor, at least in its initial planning, of both the National Security Advisor *and* the President.

Senator Glass said with some irony, "I've just been informed the Air Force wants equal time Monday to say it doesn't have any engine problems at all, it's all been fixed up, and there wasn't anything there in the first place."

Gus Yoder looked startled. "But *Finance* and the Washington *Post*—"

"Well, that was yesterday. Now the Space Shuttle's up and doesn't look like it's going to fall down, and there are other things to write about."

The administrative assistant was silent for a moment; then he consulted the paper in his hand again. "I don't know if you want to look at these invitations. The Astronomical Society of the Smithsonian in New York—if you can make a date in February."

The Senator grunted. He looked around. "What did I do with my umbrella, Gus? It's raining out there."

"Senator Mastracchio—"

"Yes, I know. Schedule him for lunch next week. I'll tell him what a good job he did."

Senator Glass went to his coat rack and took down his raincoat and an Irish tweed walking hat. He winced as his assistant helped him into the coat. His shoulder was cramped from shaking hands at the White House.

Yoder said, awkward in his sincerity, "Senator, I want to be the first to say it's a real triumph. After all these months— It's been a long haul and not much thanks for it. But credit is certainly due to you and the very few others who've carried the burden of work on these space programs."

For a moment Senator Glass said nothing. He cocked an ear to his outer office where the telephones were ringing, the television set adding to the racket. A voice, ostensibly on TV, was saying:

"—a spacecraft which can be used over and over again, unlike the rockets of the past which fell into the ocean at the end of one voyage. But the Space Shuttle is a machine of incredible complexity, a workhorse and a real spaceship. Shown here in animation, the Shuttle is about the size of a DC-9 and will act as a way-station link to outer space. With its

successful launch and orbiting this morning, the President of
the United States said, 'The human race has made another
giant leap of conquest and future exploration and development
of space.' In the next decade, the Space Shuttle will facilitate
the construction of permanent space stations—"

Senator Glass buttoned up his raincoat, wincing again from the
pain in his sore hand and arm. With unaccustomed abruptness, he
said, "Gus, I want you to get out the Congressional lists this afternoon and start telephoning. You've got our fence sitters color-
coded; see what you can do about getting them on the hook while
they're still watching their television screens." He added over the
sound of shrilling telephones in the next room, "It's not like it was
a week ago, is it? I couldn't even get anybody to come over to the
house for a free meal and drinks."

It was an exaggeration, but Yoder knew what he meant.

Senator Glass's sour mood did not dissipate. As he came
down in the elevator, Senator Murchison of Oklahoma singled
him out from the back of the car to comment, "Well, Mort—
it looks as if you space people can write your own ticket now."
Senator Glass's rejoinder was short. He reminded Senator
Murchison that he was going to count on his help. Something
he had not been able to do in the past.

A chill rain was falling as he came out of the Senate office
building and crossed Independence Avenue, and the air was
somewhat colder than it had been when he had come from the
White House. He had not been able to find his umbrella; for
a moment, he considered the fairly futile prospect of a cab and
saw two go by already occupied, as was usual on the Hill when
it rained. He squared his shoulders dutifully to walk, rain or
no rain, for the benefit of exercise and started off in the direction
of Fifth Street toward Stanton Square. Too late he remembered
he had left the slip of paper with the address of the restaurant
at his office when he switched coats. His irritation grew. It was
too much to ask, naturally, that his daughter would, sensibly
and considering the weather, elect to take lunch in the perfectly
comfortable surroundings of the Senate dining room. He knew
the answer. Nancy's standing complaint was that she had grown
up in the Senate dining room and considered it painfully boring,
representative of those values and institutions which she now

rejected. If he wanted to take lunch with his daughter, he had to go where she wanted to eat and nowhere else.

Senator Glass found that he had turned down a side street unknown to him somewhere back of the Capitol. The area had grown unfamiliar, and he could find, after looking about, no indication of a restaurant. The neat whitestone houses, so recently slums, had, in the past five or six years—Senator Glass could not remember exactly since he seldom walked or even rode across this part of Capitol Hill—been renovated and had increased in value, some of them a hundredfold. A new Georgetown, as it were. He looked at the fronts of several houses of the late Edwardian period and judged them too small, certainly not in a class with the elegantly restored brick and walled gardens of the Georgetown section.

The rain poured, a dreary autumn torrent. Senator Glass looked about him with increasing impatience. He disliked walking. His daughter's petulant summons to lunch in some out-of-the-way place, which, if it followed the patterns of the past, probably served up a menu of some inedible ethnic stuff or vegetarian bean sprout and soybean messes, was an indication of the longstanding sorry state of their affairs. And growing worse, as far as he could see.

There seemed no resolution to Nancy's current lifestyle, the moping about the house now with the ending of college, the apparent fading of all desire to focus her life, to do something with it—Senator Glass cast about in his mind for comparisons with other girls, the daughters of his contemporaries of his daughter's age and social class. In years past, someone like Nancy would have been settled by now, married and accepting of life's considerable rewards and busy with her children, his grandchildren. He didn't see why that was such a damned unpalatable prospect, but, he had been told, that was not the style anymore. The style, as much of it as he had seen in his daughter's friends, exhibited the same discontent, the same lack of purpose as he had observed in Nancy. His daughter's friends were living in communes in southern California. Or working—if it could be called that—in something defined as community organizing or antinuclear lobbying. Or installed as adepts in offbeat religions featuring saffron robes and begging bowls. Unmarried, most of them, they often joined together in curious liaisons, not all of them heterosexual, and often with small untidy children appended quite casually, the

children seemingly fending for themselves. If there was any
bright spot, he supposed, it was Nancy's obvious unhappiness.
None of the friends, the classmates, were too damned happy,
either, but Nancy at least had not yet made her choice. No choice
at all might be, he was realizing, the better part, considering these
alternatives. But he was baffled and cross, a familiar feeling. He
supposed lunch, if not carefully managed, would be one of their
unsatisfactory and recriminatory encounters. Nancy still held
him responsible, in ways she had never bothered to state, for her
mother's death. And felt that this had inflicted upon her the disruption, the destruction even, of a safe and happy girlhood. Not
the *loss* so much, as he understood it, of a parent, but the dep-
rivation of her rightful happiness—and she had been damned
unforgiving and punitive since.

And yet he loved her. Their relationship had become in the
past few years eminently unrewarding, but she was still his
child. More than once he had contemplated, sorely confused,
the sweet and sunny little girl who had been so inexplicably
replaced by a vengeful young adult and had wondered—does
it ever heal? He had thought, held out hope, that there would
come a time when one faced one's offspring across the battle-
field of insoluble adolescent conflicts (inescapable, he had
come to believe, since so many of his acquaintances had suffered through the same) and called a weary grown-up truce.
But he had come to the conclusion lately that he was ready to
pass this seemingly irreconcilable turmoil onto someone else.
A husband.

What gave him hope was that Nancy appeared genuinely
interested in the Air Force captain and had hinted more than
once that if she were unhappy, then this might be the answer.
The more she thought about it, he found this solution eminently
acceptable. The reasons for this attraction he had not—did not
dare—examine, but he ascribed them to the mysteries of love.
He would be vastly relieved to see her married, would even
promote it enthusiastically. At lunch he intended to bring it up,
to commit himself to the most elaborate and celebratory of
weddings, to propose St. Timothy's Episcopal Church (being
military, he counted on the Captain's having some official
religious affiliation), to plan on hundreds of guests, to foot the
bill for the honeymoon—

Fretfully, Senator Glass turned and started back down the street again. He was lost. He was somewhere off Fourth Street—or was it Fifth? He could find no street signs. It was an attractive residential block with carefully tended, newly planted trees, guy wires and burlap sacking wound around their trunks. The rain dripped off the brim of his hat annoyingly, and he was aware that the lower parts of his trouser legs were wet. He felt undignified. He told himself he would have to look for a corner grocery or service station on Massachusetts Avenue and call the restaurant for directions. Sliding on a patch of wet pavement, he lost his balance and knocked against an iron railing. He hit his shoulder and rubbed it. The continuing pain made him consider bursitis, and this made him cross. He detested signs of ailments. It never did him any good, he warned himself, to fume about Nancy.

The arm continued to ache. Obviously there was something more there than just soreness from shaking hands at the press conference. He considered the foolishness of being lost on Capitol Hill only a few blocks from his office, when he could easily have called for his car and been driven in dry comfort. And if he hadn't been so set on walking for the sake of exercise. Awkwardly, encumbered by the folds of the raincoat and suit jacket under it and the bulk of his body flesh, he reached up to rub his shoulder. And just as suddenly he was alarmed by a quick and mortifying feeling that his stomach was about to do something unexpected. That he was, perhaps, going to throw up right there on the street. Salty saliva filled his mouth. He grabbed the wet bark of a small tree and clung to it. The branches scratched his face. His mouth opened of its own accord, his stomach erupted brown bile in a projectile that spewed into the rain and down the front of his coat. Fighting fear, he sank to one knee. Pain shot from his arm down into the fingers of his left hand.

Some people were coming up the sidewalk, a woman with an umbrella. Helplessly preoccupied, he saw them as only blurs, heard voices. His mouth opened again and he strained, vomit spraying. He felt dizzy with pain. He leaned his face against the tree trunk, pressed against the soggy burlap. God-awful thing to have happen. A tremendous pressure weighed on his chest, like someone sitting on it. The voices passed him by.

Think I'm drunk, he thought, outraged. The light was beginning to fade, filled with gray rain. He fell. The concrete came up and hit him in the nose and chin, mashing his face with a stunning blow.

20

Simon McAllister put his mouth up against Beeper's ear and shouted, "I'll tear your head off if you go off and leave me with this, you understand that?"

He had to shout to make himself heard over the racket of the live band in the Nellis OC bar. It was Friday night, the end of Red Flag. The disco dancer gyrated in her strings of beads up behind the liquor bottles and out of reach. In the snack shop where a crowd had taken their drinks to watch the Space Shuttle, two televisions were going full volume.

Simon held his place in the jostling around the bar, watching Topper going down the tables, picking up the little plastic net-covered patio lights, lifting them to his mouth, and drinking the hot melted wax. Topper was fairly steady on his feet, considering that he was roaring drunk. A crowd of young fighter jocks from an A-10 squadron lurched along in Topper's wake. Every once in a while they surrounded Topper, held him still, made him show his beet-red eyes to anyone who would pay attention, yelling about the vertical conversion of the morning from 30,000 feet during the attack on the F-111s out at Quartzite Mountain. Son of a bitch, they marveled. They pushed Topper around playfully, straightened his flight suit, patted him. It takes a *hard* man. A patch of dried blood still rimmed one of Topper's nostrils.

Staring at him, Simon thought: he looks like holy hell.

He shook his head, turned back to the bar. In the bar mirror, his own eyes looked as bad as Topper's; it hurt just to see them. If his eyes didn't clear up by morning when they were due to go out, he decided, he was going to have to go over to the Nellis infirmary. But he didn't want any delay; all he wanted was to get back to Langley the shortest way possible. He made a face, opened his eyes wide. A lot of the capillaries had hemorrhaged. Lurid, he thought—the real stuff. You're as bad as the rest of them, he told his image.

They had planned, this last night at Nellis, to go down to the Vegas Strip and had, the four of them, counted on joining Dolph Bauernhauser's crowd. They had even rented a car, and Nizzard had called the Desert Inn and made reservations for the dinner show—Wayne Newton, one of the best acts in town and just right for their big celebration. Red Flag was over. When they came in for touchdown after the area defense out at Quartzite, the ground crews had told them the news of the Space Shuttle launch. The *Columbia* up there now and orbiting. Nellis was full of the news, and they knew Las Vegas would be jumping. It was the whole moonshot era back again. The entire country, they heard, was watching it on television. The United States was out in front again.

They had been ready for it. All they needed was to clean up, change into civilian clothes, and head for town. And Simon had decided that sometime during the evening, he was going to break the news that he was pretty sure his application to test flight would be approved—without divulging any details, naturally—so they could celebrate it all in one big basket.

They had come into the OC bar from debriefing, high on the success of the Area Defense at Quartzite, still in their flight suits, for just one drink. Everything had stalled right there. The rented car was still sitting in the parking lot.

Nizzard came up with a girl by the hand and put his arm around Simon's shoulders, pulling him to one side.

"Listen," Nizzard shouted, "I'll see you all in town. I got a ride with some friends."

He was having enough trouble with Beeper, who was drunk and, as usual, damned uncooperative. He grabbed Nizzard by the front of his flight suit and held him. He could see a sudden flurry in the crowd around Topper. One of the little bar tables had gone over. The crowd milled. People mopped up drinks.

"Don't you go anywhere, either," he told Nizzard. He was tired of shouting. "I've got to get him out of here."

Nizzard broke his grip on the flight suit. "Hey, listen, man, be *cool*." Nizzard was drunk, swaying on his feet. Owlishly he said, "Moonbird, you don't know it, but this is the *Air Force*."

He let him go, disgusted. Over their heads, the Marines were climbing into the rafters. Damned lunatics. Beside him, Beeper rested his chin on the surface of the bar, licking up his spilled beer. The bartender strong-armed two RAF pilots who wanted to climb up and pull down the disco dancer. She watched, alarmed.

On the other side of him, a Lieutenant Colonel in a class B uniform leaned to put his mouth against his ear and shouted, "Look what your buddy's doing."

Topper was standing on something—he supposed a chair, since Topper's head and upper body rose above the young fighter jocks pressed around him. Topper held a beer can at arm's length. Deliberately Topper drew his lips back over large white teeth and bit into the side of it. Beer spurted out of the beer can as he pulled it away. Topper held a chunk of aluminum between his teeth. He stood there above the crowd, grinning, and the metal gleamed.

Simon grabbed Beeper by the back of the neck and pulled his face up from the bar. "Are you too damned drunk to help me?" he wanted to know.

Beeper shook his head.

He pulled Beeper off the bar stool, pushed him through the crowd ahead of him. They fought a wall of bodies. Somebody poured a drink into his hair. He kept going. In the snack shop, they were screaming over something. A fight.

"C'mon, Top," he said, putting his arms around Topper's knees.

They pulled him down. Topper came down suddenly relaxed, all his body weight falling on them. They staggered. When they got him on his feet, they turned the wrong way, had to struggle back through the crowds again. One of the A-10 jocks wanted to claim Topper. Simon told him he'd kill him if he didn't let go.

They dragged Topper through the lobby.

"Where the hell's Nizzard?" he wanted to know.

He never got the right kind of help from any of them. Uncooperative bastards.

Going down the steps outside, Topper slipped from their grasp and fell, sprawling on the gravel. When they hauled him up, his eyes were almost closed. But he was grinning.

"You dumb sons of bitches," Topper said. He belched.

They got him to his feet. Upright, he was nearly more than they could handle. Topper looked around. "Jesus, I'm drunk," he announced.

"Listen, Top," Simon struggled to hold him up. His arms only reached around Topper's chest. It was dark outside the OC, the air cool and crisp. Cars came and went in the parking lot noisily. Some pilots from the F-106 interceptor squadron at Langley passed them going into the club. They didn't stop.

"Take the car," he told Beeper. "Go into town, dammit. Nizzard's got the keys."

"No, hell, I'll help you." But Beeper lurched off in a circle, drunk.

Topper said, "Moonbird." He put both hands over his face and rubbed it hard.

"Yeah, Top," he said.

It was a long walk to the barracks on the outer end of the airstrip. And it was dark. He could see Topper falling down somewhere. He could see Topper sitting in the street somewhere, drunk as a pig and stubborn. God, he told himself. Slowly he steered Topper toward the road that ran in front of VIP quarters. It was going to be hard as hell.

At the intersection, Topper stopped, and he couldn't budge him.

Topper said, drawing himself up, "Moonbird—listen. I need my wife."

"Yeah, Top," he told him.

Topper wouldn't move. "I need my little girl. I have a little girl two years old. Name's Emma."

He gave Topper a shove.

"I need Candy," Topper said. "I need them both."

The next morning, they had an early-go at 6 A.M. out of Nellis. Once out of bed, Topper was, as always, a little puffy but steady on his feet, totally operational. The rest of them were a little shaky. Beeper and Nizzard had come in from Las Vegas late and looked like corpses.

As they came out onto the flight line, Spearman, the acting

chief, said, "You all look like a maxed-out bunch of turkeys."
But not loudly.

All he wanted, Simon told himself, was to get home. Just
before leaving, he dropped the final bunch of letters to Nancy
in the mailbox in front of the base post office.

They had trouble right away.

Dolph Bauernhauser had scheduled a coordinated air refueling sortie for both flights down on the Casa Grande tanker
track in Arizona without consulting Topper. Dolph had asked
for it on the grounds that Dolphin flight was deficient in tanker
sorties, which were hard enough to get back east, and he needed
the opportunity to do some square-filling for his flight. The
arrangements had been made Thursday night in the OC bar
with a friend of Dolph's from Davis-Monthan who knew about
tanker availabilities. They could do their air refueling exercise
on the tanker track at Casa Grande, shooting a rendezvous
without actually taking on fuel, and stop at Bergstrom, Texas,
before heading home.

Topper, for once, was mad as hell. He stamped up and
down the flight line, talking to himself. They heard Dolph
Bauernhauser say, "Well, when the hell was I supposed to tell
you—last night?"

They all knew where Topper had been last night and in what
condition. But no one had ever done that before to Topper.

They were going down to Casa Grande, home by way of
Arizona and Texas. They were late on takeoff. On the taxiway,
Topper's engines flamed out.

On the radio, Topper's voice said: "Ground control, Topper
flight has a problem; stand by."

The next second, Forty Thirty-three's engines caught with
a roar.

"Jesus Christ," Topper's voice said.

It was a beautiful day. A northwest wind scoured the sky
clear of clouds. The weather reports noted a high pressure
system all the way to Saint Louis. North of Tucson, they picked
up Albuquerque Center and the tanker refueling track, the oval
pattern running north and south through the sky over southern
Arizona.

Albuquerque Center came on frequency 351.8 and said, "Your tanker is a KC-135, Rubber Duck."

Up ahead, the tanker responded, "Confirm working Rubber Duck on frequency two-eight-nine point seven."

Simon reached down and selected the tanker refueling frequency. He was tired, the muscles in his hand were tired, and his reactions were a little stale. He wondered how Beeper and Nizzard were doing. They had a good hour or so ahead while they made runs on the tanker, racking up Dolphin flight's refueling hours. And it was bumpy, a little clear-air turbulence feeding off the mountains. It didn't help. The coffee in his stomach sloshed uneasily.

Topper, as flight leader, was first up. Albuquerque, looking on their radar scopes, said: "Roger, contact your tanker. Confirm headings; make sure reciprocal."

Topper could do this in his sleep. The trick was to slide up on the racetrack pattern with the tanker, matching airspeed, and fit neatly under it. He could see that Topper was about thirty degrees cold. At that moment, Topper got a visual on the KC-135 and said so.

He was on Topper's wing. In a minute, he heard Topper say, "Moonbird, give me a fuel check."

He read off his numbers: "Roger, Top, eight-five-zero-zero square." He thought, *Now* what the hell is wrong?

Topper's voice said in his ears: "Something's off. Now I've got a fuel gauge problem."

Above them, the tanker informed them, "Rubber Duck halfway through turn."

They were really into clear-air turbulence here, some nasty little updrafts. He held the Eagle steady. The voice of the tanker reported the CAT, warning them. Topper had the tanker on position at twenty-six degrees left, at about twenty-one miles separation. Beyond them and behind, Nizzard's Eagle bumped and swayed like a bobbing cork.

Topper said, "Well, this tail number's doing it again. I'm reading eleven hundred pounds. Moonbird, have I been venting any fuel?"

He hadn't seen any and told him so.

He hoped it wasn't a replay of the day before, when Topper had selected "Stop Transfer" on his centerline tank while refueling, thinking he had trapped 4,000 pounds of gas and then found he hadn't. Once again, it was clear that you couldn't trust Forty Thirty-three's crazy systems, its gauges, sensors, or engines.

Topper made up his mind. "This is Topper One. I'm going for real and take five thousand pounds of fuel now and divert to Davis-Monthan to check fuel gauge before we go cross-country."

It was the only thing to do. But by now, they might as well be going home by way of South America. Slower and slower.

The tanker came easing down on them. The voice of the boomer up in its belly, flying backwards over the desert with his chin on a bar to keep his vision steady, said, "This is Rubber Duck boomer, radio check. How do you copy?"

He dipped into a pocket of unsteady air. If they had been on an airliner, the stewardess would have them strapped in, shutting off their drinks and bathroom privileges.

Topper had shut down his radar for the tanker contact.

"Note your altimeters," the voice of the boomer droned. "And check your noses cold."

Topper turned off his armaments. "Topper One, nose is cold."

He moved his Eagle up to position off the tanker's right wing to wait. The air was really rough: he could see the wings of the KC-135 moving up and down, flapping like a real rubber duck. He was having difficulty holding his own position.

"Rubber Duck, ready, cleared to contact position."

He could see Topper bouncing around down below, riding the bursts of CAT. The boomer saw it, too, and said, "Topper One, stabilize."

He thought about Linda Criscio—he hoped she wanted her turkey back. He knew the squadron was back from Saudi; Dolph Bauernhauser's wife had called them before they left Nellis.

Under him, Topper reduced his power and brought the Eagle's airspeed down to match the tanker's. The tanker turned, making 420 mph on the nose. The mountains below rolled by. At 20,000 feet, the highway north to Phoenix was a straight line against the brown desert floor. He took a bounce, put his hand up on the canopy to steady himself. The KC-135 was moving up and down on his left. He was close enough to see the rivets in its skin. The tanker was dipping five to six feet with every jolt.

The boomer missed. Or Topper missed. He looked down and couldn't believe it. In Vietnam, Topper said, you owed a case of beer if you couldn't hit the end of the fuel probe right on the mark called the apple and bring the intake up to halve it. The boom passed within two feet of the clear canopy and Topper's helmet. He saw the shadow of the boom against the plastic, only an arm's reach away from Topper.

The voice of the boomer, wide-awake, said: "Two feet right, Topper One."

Topper said, "Roger."

It was all routine; it was a two-inch tube of steel right before your face, feeling for the Eagle's left wing root and the intake. One of the basics, done all the time. He felt his stomach contract around an unknown feeling.

The voice of the boomer said, "Topper One, *stabilize*."

The CAT was severe now. They were turning into it, right over the mountains.

He saw the boom swing into position over Topper's canopy. He saw every second of it in infinite detail. The boom hit the intake. For a moment he thought it had connected, but it veered off, bounced off. A gust of invisible air took the Eagle and the tanker and mashed them together. The boom hit the transparent bubble over Topper on the left side. It sank down through the canopy into the cockpit.

The voice of the boomer yelped: "Rubber Duck—break away! Break away—break away!"

And another voice inside the tanker, almost simultaneously, "Roger, break away. Break away, Rubber Duck."

The tanker hit all four throttles, a big volatile tub of kerosene scrambling away from danger, calling emergency procedures. Below them, Forty Thirty-three staggered away, its canopy shattered, a 400-mile-an-hour wind tearing through the hole. The Eagle teetered uncertainly, then sideslipped.

There was silence only for the space of a second. They were forty miles down-track and forty miles out of Davis-Monthan Air Force Base right outside of Tucson. Help was near, but nearness didn't count. Simon slammed the throttles forward and turned into a dive. The air rattled with radio transmissions from the tanker, from Topper and Dolphin flights.

The tanker, urgently: "Topper One, Topper One, what's your status? Repeat, what's your status?"

No answer.

He yelled into his mask: "Topper, this is Moonbird! For God's sake, are you okay?"

He was closing. Topper couldn't be dead because the Eagle was still flying. He thought about the boom chewing into Topper's body, into his shoulder or his face. Topper without a face. He knew the cockpit had decompressed because the moisture in the air had condensed—Topper was sitting in a mist of cloud. Something black was spurting on the acrylic canopy where it was still intact. Dark red. Blood spurting on the canopy.

Albuquerque Center called the tanker. "Rubber Duck, this is Albuquerque, do you need assistance?"

Worried about the damned tanker. He inched his Eagle closer to Forty Thirty-three, which was falling now.

Beeper's voice in his earphones: "Moonbird—canopy is broken on the left side. I'm going down for a closer look."

Beeper was above him, and Nizzard.

"Negative," he yelled. "Negative—stay out of my way!"

Nizzard said something, then Dolph Bauernhauser's voice. The tanker was trying to talk to Albuquerque.

He yelled into his mask: "Top—this is Moonbird! Top, say something! Top, this is Moonbird, acknowledge, acknowledge!"

The Eagle was dropping, but not out of control.

Just then, a strange voice said, "Moonbird—T-two."

It was Topper. T-two was marginal.

The voice of Albuquerque said to the tanker: "Roger, state emergency, number of souls on board, armaments—"

Someone else's voice blared: "Go to guard, go to guard—channel two-four-three-zero." Beeper, with his head on right, giving the international emergency frequency.

Topper was still dropping. Coming off the tanker track, he was headed for Tucson and Davis-Monthan, but losing altitude. From above, the Eagle with the hole in it looked battered, crazy, unreal. If Topper would just say something—They heard Beeper setting up for enroute descent for Davis-Monthan, trying to get Topper home, and the radio responding quickly, clearing out ahead.

Topper's voice, suddenly. Blurred and thick: "Moonbird, I read *no* gas."

No damned gas. And without its power, no way at all to keep the Eagle in the air.

On the emergency channel, a cool female voice was telling Topper to descend and maintain one-five-zero, that these were radar vectors to precision approach landing, Davis-Monthan, runway one-two.

His mind kept telling him that Topper was as good as dead. He promised himself, raging, that he would see that damned Forty Thirty-three never flew again if he had to dismantle it with his own hands. There was no telling how badly Topper was hurt. Maybe Topper couldn't get out.

The Eagles buzzed around the falling shape of Forty Thirty-three, radios squawking. They were running parallel to Highway I-10 below, and Topper was still coming down, not going to make it.

They had a handoff to Tucson Approach. Tucson was saying, "Topper One, we understand emergency, you are twenty miles north of Davis-Monthan, fly heading—"

They would never make it. The Eagle was dying, out of gas and systems failing. It kept losing altitude. He was right on Topper's wing; he could see the gray bulb of Topper's helmet, Topper's head bent. The canopy was spattered with blood. Topper still held his course for Tucson straight ahead.

The ground was coming up. There were little blocks of houses under them, the Tucson suburbs marching up the side of Mount Lemon on the left. Crowds of houses; it looked as if the earth was paved with them.

He started yelling, "Topper, eject! Topper, you're not going to make it! Eject, if you hear me!"

The rubber handle between Topper's legs took fifty pounds of pressure to pull up, if the mechanism wasn't damaged. If Topper was hurt badly, he'd have to fight it. If he could pull it, if it was still working, the canopy opened and the rocket motor responded to the eject handle, blasted the whole seat and the man in it out of the cockpit; then another charge snapped him out of the seat when he was clear.

There was always the chance that even if he got that far, clear of the Eagle, the seat wouldn't free up. That might be busted, too.

Beeper knew what was happening. "Topper," Beeper was warning, "get out *now! Now!*"

There wasn't any time left. Incredibly, they saw Topper turning east, into the mountains. There was a crazy chorus in his earphones. The whole flight yelling. *Topper—eject!* Both engines had just flamed out.

Gas all gone now. He was watching a man die.

Forty Thirty-three began slowly rolling on its longitudinal axis, corkscrewing lazily on a long glide through the air. It turned toward the slopes of the mountainside, rolling heavily.

He knew Topper wouldn't eject now, even if he could. He was right over the streets. Topper would hang in there, not drop it on the houses below.

He was tracking Topper so closely he was no more than five feet off Topper's wing. Still no radio transmission. If not dead, then dying. His throat muscles closed painfully. Not Topper. The airspeed fell to 200 miles an hour. The earth slid up in their faces.

He heard the yelling suddenly. Beeper and Nizzard. "Moonbird, *pull up! You're going to hit the mountain!*"

He had forgotten about himself. All reflex action, he yanked the Eagle's nose straight up, hit the afterburners in a bursting, roaring vertical climb. He saw the mountain hanging overhead. Trees and rocks. Close enough to touch.

A second before, a toy man had popped out into the air. The earth screamed by, the mountain circled and whirled away, too late. Below him, Forty Thirty-three zigzagged at 500 feet, dropped, augered its way into the stones of a cliff. The air shook, filled with metal pieces. He felt the air trembling all around him.

He yelled into the mask: "I have a chute! I have a good chute!"

His voice bubbled out of him crazily. But he had a dayglow orange, white, and olive-drab ball visible in the air below and dropping. The airframe around him shook. Beeper circled close above him. He saw a red and yellow flaming flower where Forty Thirty-three was still exploding, burning itself to death halfway up Mount Lemon in the trees and rocks.

"Roger, I see it!" Beeper answered.

He twisted the Eagle into a right turn to come down for a

visual pass. He kept shouting into the radio: "I have a good chute under me. It's good!"

For those few seconds, he saw only that Topper had bailed out. Then the chute was down on the mountainside in the trees, and nothing moved.

It hadn't taken long enough to drop. The parachute lay there, its wedge-shaped colors spread out. Five hundred feet—less— was too low to eject and live. Nothing moved.

X marks the spot.

Stunned, he thought: It's all over.

Sergeant Amos Schuld looked up; Sergeant Linda Criscio stood in the office doorway. There had been no noise; it was Saturday and the hangar was empty, and there had been only the uncanny sense of someone standing there and watching. He felt his skin prickle.

"Jesus, why didn't you say something?" he growled.

The girl was in coveralls; she'd been working, but she had pulled off her cap. She reached up and tugged at her hair. Something's wrong, he thought.

She stared at him, delicate face pale and set, the lips curved, indented at the corners of her mouth. Not smiling. He waved his hand for her to come in.

She stayed where she was.

"Amos," she said softly, "when are you leaving?"

Surprised, he started forward in his chair. Then he said, craftily, "Leaving for what? We just got back."

She knew better. "You're leaving. Everybody knows. That you've put your papers in."

That was not exactly true, but he had made up his mind. That she knew, that the word was out, did surprise him. He put a good face on it.

"Aw, that's just flight line gossip," he said. "Honeybunch, everybody's got to retire from this man's Air Force sometime, just like they gotta die. I'll level with you. I'm thinking about it. I might do it. All right, I'll *probably* do it, but you keep that under your hat. I'll put it in channels when I get good and ready."

"If you go," she said, "I'm going to OTS."

He jumped up from the chair and came around his desk in

a hurry. He reached out and took her by the arm and drew her inside the office. He kicked the door shut.

"Now, say that again."

She simply looked at him.

"Now, you're not going to do that," he said. "You don't want to be no snot-nosed butterbar hanging around back here, shuffling papers. Sweetie, you're too good for that. What made you think of that? Woman, you're the best maintenance hand I've ever seen; you don't want to go and mess up." Falsely hearty, he said, "I'm not going to let you do anything like that."

She said, "I'm going to get a degree in engineering."

He stared at her. "The hell you say."

The pale lips moved. "Aeronautical. I can go to UCLA. Then to officers' training school."

"Well," Sergeant Schuld said. He moved around in a circle, not sure he wanted to stand or sit. "Well, *hell*." Irritably he said, "Well, sit down, why don't you?"

Before he left, he had planned to put her up for production superintendent. It was a little early, and she was damned young for Master Sergeant's stripes, but nothing was impossible. He had surveyed the current structure and figured wing command was ready for it, what with affirmative action and all. Among other things, it was a good showcase move. Now she had come up with this. Even had the school picked out—UCLA—using the bootstrap program to get into OTS. He walked back and forth across his office while she watched him, trying to think.

Finally he said, "Now, sweetheart, all you want is your old hog. Forty Thirty-three's coming in today or tomorrow; then you can play with it all you want. You're just lonesome."

She looked at him as though she would never understand him.

He waited through the silence.

"Hell," he said finally, "you just go ahead and do what you want to do, then. I guess you will, anyway. But I'm damned if I understand it. What's wrong with you? You act like I've gone and done something." He peered at her. "I don't know what in hell goes on in your head, Linda, I swear I don't. Just what in hell," he wanted to know, "is the matter?"

She made a small, futile gesture.

"Nothing lasts," she said.

Part 5

O:
EAGLES

21

Major Fuchs bent ungracefully—she was a tall, stout woman with an awkward body that did not show up to particular advantage in uniform—and put a copy of the Tucson *Times-Observer* on the table in front of Captain McAllister. Since he was still talking on the telephone, Major Fuchs gave him a sympathetic look but made no move to go away. She patted the newspaper with her hand, *there,* to draw his attention to it and continued to gaze upon him warmly.

Major Fuchs had—and she would admit it—done a complete about-face in her original attitude toward young Captain McAllister. At first, doubtlessly reacting to the confusion and disorder attendant upon his presence in her duty area, she had firmly objected to his settling in at the table and virtually monopolizing the telephone line which, as she had pointed out, was not only for his, Captain McAllister's, use, but also for others on the floor. Major Fuchs had also viewed with great disapproval the sheets of paper and forms scattered about, the unemptied ashtrays, and the accumulation of paper bags, cups, and cardboard containers Captain McAllister brought in from the cafeteria with his meals. In the nearly four days he had been there, Captain McAllister had persisted in making quite a mess.

Major Fuchs was not, however, totally inexperienced with this sort of thing, nor with fighter pilots, whom she had found to be generally disruptive, independent, and sometimes even questioning of her authority. But in Captain McAllister's case,

she had been forced to make an exception. Particularly since
the Captain appeared to be attracting attention not only from
a stream of field grade officers from base operations office, but
also the public relations staff of TAC. All of which had to do
with, Major Fuchs surmised, the number of calls Captain
McAllister was receiving from Washington, D.C.

It was always a woman's voice, Major Fuchs knew, listening
avidly, a young woman's voice, and, from the pitch amplified
in the telephone receiver, conveying tones of great distress. In
fact, from what Major Fuchs could hear, it was decidedly weepy.
Having let down her guard this far and having developed a certain
proprietary attitude toward Captain McAllister as a consequence,
Major Fuchs was dying to find out what was going on.

When Captain McAllister terminated his conversation and
hung up the telephone, Major Fuchs smiled at him with a
certain encouraging eagerness. He probably needed to tell his
troubles to somebody, she assured herself. Four days—and as
far as anyone could tell, not a break in all that time! The
accident, she knew, had been a terrible experience, and he had
hardly had a moment's rest since then, what with all the safety
board members coming and going to interview him and take
his testimony. He was so young, Major Fuchs thought, watching him, and so engagingly handsome—it was impossible not
to want to help. Captain McAllister's thin, well-bred features,
the dark, expressive eyes with thick lashes, his tanned, almost
satiny complexion were ingratiatingly boyish. She thought: no
wonder some girl's calling him all the time.

Major Fuchs said, "What's the matter, Captain—girl trouble?"

Captain McAllister looked up. He began to gather in one
untidy pile the sheets of names and telephone numbers and
scribbled notes.

"Funeral arrangements," he said shortly.

"Oh." Major Fuchs was a little startled and immediately
saddened. So *that* was what was going on! To cover her confusion and the several questions which rose to her mind, she
reached across Captain McAllister's knees and briskly began
to gather up the litter of paper coffee cups and wrappings.

"My goodness, it never rains but it pours," she said. "You've
really had your share lately, haven't you? I guess you think
the skies have opened up and dumped on you this week. But

you know," she said firmly, "no matter what's going on, you have to give some thought to yourself; see you eat regular meals, for one thing—which I can say right now I don't think you've been doing—and get yourself some rest. Sleeping out here in the visitors' lounge on the couch isn't going to help that, is it? But you've got to remember you're not made of iron, even at your age. Nobody is. Haven't they billeted you in VOQ? I'll bet they have. And I'll bet you haven't spent fifteen minutes over there since Saturday. I'll bet you haven't even changed your clothes."

Captain McAllister said indifferently, "I'm okay. Really."

Major Fuchs reached over him and opened up the newspaper she had put on the table before him. In a special center section, the *Times-Observer* featured photographs of the Russian spacecraft in orbit that had, as the *Times-Observer* commented in a long editorial, confounded and mystified the whole world. Major Fuchs had thought the photographs of the Soviet thing would take Captain McAllister's mind off his troubles for a while. At least the photographs, just released by NASA and the Defense Department, were a lot clearer than the blurry object being shown on live television.

Major Fuchs had watched it all on television at home and then had studied the *Times-Observer*'s pictures over breakfast, and in her opinion, the Russian object looked like a giant erector set. It was shaped like an oil drum—or the ill-fated Skylab of a few years ago—and it had been photographed with its middle section opened and giant manipulator arms reaching out into space. There were supposed to be three Russians aboard. Tracking stations around the world monitoring the Russians' radio frequency said there appeared to be that many voices replying to earth.

But she could see that it was no time to discuss this with Captain McAllister. Not if he had a funeral to think about.

"Well, there it is," Major Fuchs said. She gathered up the cups she had neatly flattened and stacked them in a box with the remains of a half-eaten hamburger. "That's really something, isn't it? And we thought we were going to be the first to get a space shuttle up! I mean, we *were*, but who ever expected the Russians would be a day or two behind us with something of their own? Those Russkies," she said and shook her head. "You just know whatever it is they're doing is not going to be for the benefit of mankind, like ours is. And, boy, they certainly don't let anybody know what's going on, do they? Not a word out of them. I saw the special news on ABC last night, and they had a panel of experts guessing what it was the Russians had up there and what it was doing, and some man, somebody from the Defense Department, said you couldn't minimize any potential military threat. How about that?" Major Fuchs bent over Captain McAllister to look more closely at the pictures. "Doesn't look like the Space Shuttle, does it? On television, they said those arms would probably be used to construct some sort of space station. Can you imagine that? Of course, they don't know for sure—somebody else said they might be putting up another satellite. They might even be building something to send to the moon."

Captain McAllister said nothing. He was busy sorting out his papers. He balled up a sheet and tossed it into the couch cushions behind him.

Major Fuchs put her hand on one hip and pursed her mouth critically. "Now, you know, I've been thinking—what if the Russians got to the moon first this time? And put a building on it, a moon base. It just goes to show you, this country should have gotten started on these space programs a lot sooner and not let things slide, the way we did when the astronauts stopped going up. They said last night we even had programs ready to send men to Mars, only nothing came of it."

Captain McAllister did not appear to be listening.

"Well," Major Fuchs said, "I thought you might want to look at the paper later, since you don't have a television out here."

He looked up. "Oh, yeah, thanks—I saw all that. Thanks for the paper. I'll look at it in a little while."

"Well," Major Fuchs said, "the whole world certainly has been in an uproar. I think it's going to be another big setback for the United States. We thought we were so far ahead, and now look. That didn't last for more than a few days, what—last Friday? Time really flies." She sighed.

Captain McAllister gave her an abstracted look. There were, she saw, big dark circles under his eyes. *Whose funeral?* she thought. She wanted to come right out and ask him.

"You ought to get some sleep," she said again. "Nobody goes on and on forever, you know."

Captain McAllister said, "Oh, I sleep."

Major Fuchs clucked at him. "Yes, I know, but *real* sleep, in a real bed. That's a different thing entirely. You give it some thought. You look like you could use it."

"Sure," he said. He reached up and ran his hand through his hair. "Right—I'll think about it. I just want to get some of this stuff out of the way first. I've got to go over to the safety board again for another deposition. There's all this"— he gestured vaguely. "I think I've called just about everybody now. My girl's father just died."

Ah! Major Fuchs thought. She said quickly, "Oh, that's terrible—I'm so sorry to hear that. Well, you really have had bad news, haven't you? I declare, I don't see how you've managed."

He stared at her. "Dropped dead on the street," he muttered, "just like that." He rubbed his hair again. "It's in the paper, was in Sunday's paper. Senator Mortimer Glass. Now they're putting him—now he's lying in state in the rotunda. Of the Capitol," he added, knitting his brows. "The whole thing. Like Hubert Humphrey."

Captain McAllister's voice trailed off to an absent mumble. She thought he said something about a hell of a week.

"Well, the poor girl," Major Fuchs said. But she was thinking: My goodness, Captain McAllister knowing the daughter of some U.S. Senator. She had heard of Senator Glass. "Why, Senator Glass was an important man; he's been in the Senate for years and years. He was in the Senate when I was a girl. I hope," she added, "somebody is helping your—"

"Fiancée," he said.

"Yes, with you all the way out here."

"She has an aunt," he told her, "and there's a committee from the Senate to make the arrangements, I guess, about everything else. She's making out all right, but she's pretty upset, naturally. I told her I thought I could get two days' leave for the funeral, even with all this here." Looking around, he said, "I think I've made pretty much of a mess out here."

Major Fuchs said quickly, "Now, you're not making any trouble, Captain; just don't worry about a thing." She was glad, at last, to demonstrate a generous and understanding nature. "You just keep right on with what you're doing, and you be sure to let me know if you need anything, you hear? If anybody says anything to you, you just tell them Major Fuchs said you could stay right here and get your things done." She looked around. "It's a pity we don't have a little office for you where you could be by yourself. That would be a lot better, wouldn't it? Now, downstairs in radiation there's a little space—"

Captain McAllister gave her one of his sudden, disarming smiles. "That's really nice of you, Major, but I'm all right here. That is, if you don't mind it, I don't."

The telephone on the coffee table in front of Captain McAllister began to ring again. He lunged for it and grabbed the receiver. She had warned him about letting the sun porch telephone ring too long before he answered it; that was the only thing she had to be really strict about.

Taking her small accumulation of garbage in her hands, Major Fuchs started down the hallway from the visitors' area. She was glad he had remembered about the telephone—not that there wasn't plenty of noise already on the floor. In all the rooms she passed, the televisions were going, most of them turned up too loud for the comfort of the other patients. It was hard to keep that sort of thing under control. She noted that she had better send Nurse DiFalco around to check them out and see that the volume was turned down a little. But she could understand the excitement, what with the television coverage of the American Space Shuttle and now the Russian spacecraft in orbit.

She had told the staff on duty at the nurses' station, however, that there would be positively no television out there. Monday night, someone had sneaked a portable TV to the desk for the night duty nurses, and she had gone right to her office the next day and typed up a memo on it, reminding them that television sets on the nurses' station were absolutely unauthorized; she had seen to it that the memo was posted on the board right where they couldn't miss it.

When she came out into the main area of the surgery floor, Lieutenant DiFalco was standing up behind the low glass partition in front of the desk, waiting for her.

"She's *here*," Lieutenant DiFalco declared. The white nurse's cap with its bars of rank was perched like a sitting bird on top of her puffed and bundled hair, making her look both pert and severe. Lieutenant DiFalco pointed in the direction of the elevators. "That little redheaded Sergeant who sneaked in here twice yesterday afternoon. I wish I knew where she *goes*.

I saw her come in, and she saw me, too, but she took off down B side before I could say anything to her. But I'd just like to catch her. I know she hasn't got a visitor's pass, because she's supposed to check in here at the desk."

"All right," Major Fuchs said grimly. "I'll get her."

"She knows it's unauthorized to go roaming around up here without a pass," Lieutenant DiFalco continued. "Especially in Post Op. Unless she's trying to bother somebody."

Major Fuchs started off toward B section, her rubber-soled shoes making a faint squashing sound.

"I'll get her," she said over her shoulder. "You just keep an eye out. Watch down this side if she makes a circle to come around."

Lieutenant DiFalco leaned over the glass partition to watch Major Fuchs disappear around the corner that led to the elevators.

"No telling what she's doing," Lieutenant DiFalco muttered.

For Major Topper James, it was a frustrating experience. He kept rising to the light like a swimmer, going under, then floating upward toward the light again. There were even the same roaring noises, the same bubbling voices one heard when one was underwater. Then he realized that he was losing and regaining consciousness over and over again. Be still, don't struggle, he told himself. It's the damned tree again.

This time, the tree held him fast. This time, no room to sway, hanging there. He couldn't move either his head or his body, but he knew if he thrashed around, he'd get tangled in the parachute shrouds, maybe get them around his head and neck and strangle himself. He thought: don't do that. He remembered that from before.

He heard Moonbird's voice. That was luck. He tried to tell him, "Moonbird, get me the hell out of here," but no one answered.

Every time a voice floated past him, he tried to tell them that his left arm and shoulder were caught fast and that was what was holding him there. His face was wedged in the branches. Something was sticking up his nose.

It took a damned long time.

Three days hanging in a tree in the jungles of Nam was something he could do without. Even the first time. After a

while he had managed very cautiously to haul himself rightside
up—the only good thing he had managed to do the whole time.
But after that, nothing. Just fading in and out of consciousness,
half dead. He had visions of dying in that damned tree if the
choppers didn't find him. Just hanging there, his corpse drying
out eventually like some giant seed pod in the leaves.

The curious thing was, it didn't smell at all like the jungle.
Tied to memory, smells were vivid—mud and heat. This time,
the stinks were sharp and acidic and sometimes as gassy as
ozone, bothering him considerably.

Then came the hallucinations. Right on schedule.

A doorway appeared out of nothingness, like a hole in a
cloud. And a pale little girl with orange hair staring at him,
white as a ghost.

Her mouth moved, and she said softly, "I just had to come
up and see you. I'm not supposed to be here; they won't let
you have any visitors, but this is the third time I've been up
here. The other times you were asleep."

She whispered, "I have to keep my voice down."

She came closer. He saw her hands flutter as if she wanted
to touch him. "Oh, my God," she whispered. "Oh, my *God*."
Her eyes, round as teacups, filled with anguish and tears. "They
said you nearly lost your arm. It's a wonder you're alive."

He kept staring at her. He didn't have to speak.

The ghost girl said, "I can only stay a second, really. But
I just had to see you. I just hope you're going to be all right."
The big eyes moved over him distractedly. "I know you think
this is crazy of me, coming in here like this. I know you
probably don't even know who I am. But I was stationed at
Langley—air traffic control. I've talked to you from the tower
just lots and lots of times. I had duty for your demo flight
every Friday. But I guess you wouldn't know that, would you?"

The voice rippled on, like silk in the wind.

"I've really got to go. The nurses are beasts up here—if
they find me, I'm in trouble." The eyes moved closer, filling
up his field of vision. "I guess you're really doped up. You
probably don't remember anything at all. If you just want to
nod your head—but I don't want you to move any of those
tubes or anything—"

He closed his eyes, and when he opened them again she had
just faded away. But it had all been very curious and pleasant.

Not all of them were like that.

A voice came in cheerfully. It put something cold in his groin and said, "Major, do you hear me, Major? Let's let down a little peepee now; we don't want to swell up."

Not an hallucination.

They came back and threaded a catheter into him. Godawful. He could hear them talking about it.

A male voice said, "Well, he could have crushed his urethra on impact. Or it's an abdominal trauma of some sort."

Miserable pain. It felt like a baseball bat inside him.

Then Candy came.

Candy.

It *was* Candy, warm and smelling of perfume, as real as the real thing. He wept. Blistering tears welled up in his eyes and dripped down his cheeks like a stone face crying, impossible to help it. They held him down.

They said: "Okay, Major, just take it easy. We don't want you to move around too much. She's here. You just be nice and lie still now and just hold her hand. That's right, you just hold her hand, and we'll put you back to sleep."

All the things in his nose and mouth kept him from telling her. He tried to pull them out. They held his good hand.

Candy's soft lips were against his face. "Honey," Candy's voice said, "just lie still and hold my hand. I'm going to stay right here."

He cried. Inside him, all kinds of things struggled painfully. He felt as though he was tearing himself apart. *Just let me talk to you,* he tried to tell her. *I'm going to die without ever having said a word to you of what I want to say.*

For some reason, he went back to sleep.

He woke up again and it was lighter, some small light, and the good hallucination was still there. It held his hand and spoke to him in Candy's low, murmuring voice.

He thought: *When am I going to get something to eat?*

Candy said, "Honey, do you want some water?" and stuck a tube in his mouth.

He drank the water. But he really wanted to get the tube out of his dick.

Time passed.

It was always dark, and things came and went in it. He told them: *For Christ's sake—hurry up and find me!*

And a male voice said, "What's the prescription for Tegratol for?"

These hallucinations now were not too great.

"Hi there, big fella—I want you to look up at me. Just let me get both your eyelids pulled back here a minute."

A blinding light came out of the dark, boring into his head, all the way back into his shrinking brain.

"Look, I've got a spasm in these fingers, a really live reaction! See them move? And feeling, too. Well, how about that? Just take it easy, boy, we're not going to hurt you. When he came in here, it looked as if we were going to have to do a reattachment; I thought the arm was all the way off. He got a glance-off on the canopy; then the boom broke through into the cockpit, but those few inches saved him. As it is, we have a lot of tendon damage and a large mass of muscle tissue just ripped right out—"

They moved around, banging things. He could see shapes.

"Now, Mrs. James, we're going to change his medication just a little. Dr. Turner and I have something we want to tell you. You sit down over there out of the way, and I'll explain it to you."

The deeper voice said, "Yeah, but I don't want those neck muscles to atrophy; that cast comes up too high. Get somebody in here to cut some of it off."

He groaned.

"He's all right, Mrs. James; they're just changing the neck dressings. If I could have your attention for a minute. That's right. Now, when we took Major James down to neurology before we operated to check out those nerves in his arm and shoulder, we gave your husband a little test. It's called an EEG—that stands for electroencephalogram. No, it's absolutely painless; it just measures brain waves. It's like an EKG—have you ever had an EKG? Well, we just put some electrodes up here and hook him up to a little monitoring box; he doesn't feel a thing. This was a precautionary measure not only to check out the damage to his arm and shoulder, but also to look for any other possible neurological involvement, such as whether he had sustained some injury to his head that we couldn't see from the outside. And we found a very interesting thing, Mrs. James, while we had the Major on the table, he had a little seizure. Now, it wasn't anything much—in fact, we wouldn't have known anything was there if he hadn't been hooked up to the EEG and we weren't getting a reading right at that very minute. But our printout showed your husband probably has had an old trouble for a long time—my guess would be some old injury—and he probably didn't know it himself. And nobody else would, either, since apparently he doesn't show anything visible except a little eyelid flutter. But he could have had some symptoms from time to time, like a momentary distraction, some little visual things like flashbacks, daydreams—or some sort of slightly exceptional behavior. What kind of behavior? Oh, any kind of behavior, actually, as long as it was a little more exaggerated than it used to be—but very benign, nothing to bother him. This is a damned hard thing to describe, actually. The only thing we saw physically, outside of the EEG reading, was a little fluttering of the eyelids lasting not more than one or two seconds. Actually, he's a very healthy man—the fact that he's still alive proves that. This type of epilepsy—no, not born with it; that's a common misconception. Most cases we see of epilepsy are caused by automobile accidents. Sometimes from a prolonged high fever. Or sometimes nothing at all; it just shows up. Now, Mrs. James, what Major James shows is what we call complex partial seizures. It's so slight that it probably hasn't bothered him before, and it's probably not going to bother him at all in the future, because we've put him on an antispasmodic called Tegratol. It's one of the epilepsy drugs, and it's probably going to take care—"

"That doesn't look bad at all," a voice said, close to his ear. "Boy, that's lucky. See how close that is to the carotid artery?"

But he wanted to hear the other voice.

"—the nurse will bring you some booklets on epilepsy to read. It's a very fascinating field, Mrs. James, because we know so little about its causes. When I complete my tour of duty here at Davis-Monthan and get out of the Air Force next month, I'm going to specialize in trauma-related epilepsy. I'm really very lucky I had a chance to run that EEG on your husband and catch him right in the middle of a seizure. A CPS of this sort is so tricky—you could take a flight physical, as I'm sure your husband has, all the time, and not show a thing, unless you had an EEG hooked up to you *and* you happened to have a seizure right on the spot. Here we have a textbook case of past trauma that's been so well modulated and concealed—"

If only he could get out of that damned TREE.

He was surrounded by dark and clouds, the tantalizing light always just breaking through.

"I'm going to cut out that sedation. Hell, he's only fighting it, and we'll have to lower it, anyway, with the Tegratol doses. Look at him—he's all over that bed; the whole arm is moved around in the slings."

"Okay, buddy," a voice said. A very military voice. "Okay, buddy, now let's just *hold it down*."

He was coming up into the light, like coming up from drowning. It was getting lighter.

"Damn, Major, now I know why that refueling boom didn't kill you. Just hold it down, will you? I don't want you jumping right out of this bed."

Yeah, well, never mind. He was getting loose. FOUND. He was coming down now, in safe hands.

There was Candy's face right in front of him, so sweet and so beautiful. He could never believe that lovely face. Behind Candy's head were slatted blinds, striped with sunshine. Bright daylight. Candy's voice.

"Honey," Candy said, "you're just raising hell. Can you hear me? If you can just lie still, you'll come awake so easy. Oh, honey, I'm right here with you. Just don't move around."

He clutched at her with his good hand. She was real. Everything was real. A big plaster cast on his left side held him from neck to belly and covered his shoulder and arm. He saw his fat purple fingers sticking out of the end of the plaster mass hanging over his head.

He said thickly, the tubes flapping against his mouth and cheek, "Candy, don't leave me." He had to get that out first.

And Moonbird, standing there. He couldn't get his eyes focused to see.

"Moonbird," he croaked. He tried to make his voice a little louder. He wanted Moonbird to bend down so he could whisper to him.

He said hoarsely, suspiciously, "It's a room? No trees?"

Moonbird said, "Top, you're flat on your ass in the hospital."

"Good boy," he said, relieved.

He let himself relax. Candy took his hand in hers and held it.

"Okay," Major Topper James said. He tried to smile. "Okay, I'll buy that."

22

Lieutenant Roger Gazenove brought his Eagle into Davis-Mon-than Air Force Base late in the afternoon on Tuesday. He had wanted to schedule a cross-country for himself on Sunday and get right out to Tucson, but he had been delayed by a Monday morning conference at Langley on the Saudi mission. Simon McAllister met him on the flight line, and they walked over to the base hospital together.

"How's he doing?" Roger Gazenove wanted to know.

Simon said: "Well, he's off the critical list; they took him off this morning and upped him to 'satisfactory.' Everybody says you can't kill Topper, and you can't keep him in bed, either. That sounds like Top, doesn't it?" He tried for a smile. "They're still shooting him up with painkillers and he's a little slow, but he can talk. When you see him—I think I told you on the telephone he has a tube down his throat because of the swelling, and another one up his nose, and a couple of IVs in his arm—he looks like some kind of crazy hydraulic system. And then there's the big cast because of all the fractures. But now they say definitely they think he won't lose his arm, and he might get some of his shoulder movement back. I think I told you they took out a hunk of his collarbone that was splintered when they operated."

The squadron commander never walked: briskly, short-legged, he trotted down the streets at Davis-Monthan toward the hospital, mostly in the middle of the road, ignoring the sidewalks. A jeep passed, and a Major turned around and looked at them.

"Topper's kind of swelled up. He looks like he's gained twenty pounds. He had some internal injuries—for a while, they thought he might have ruptured his spleen when he ejected or when he hit the ground. All you hear around the hospital is that it's a damned miracle that he's alive. Of course," Simon said somberly, "you have to consider that if that refueling boom had been a few more inches to the right, Top would have taken it dead on, in the middle of his chest."

Or in his face.

He was glad no one knew about the nightmares that had dogged him since the accident. Topper without a face. Topper without a head. Cropping up in his sleep. Worse than any horror movie. He had gotten so that he deliberately tried not to sleep.

Even now, he didn't want to think about it, had to make a large effort to talk about it normally, though he had had to talk about it for hours to the Air Force board investigating the accident, to the hospital people, to the doctors—to everybody he'd called on the telephone originally. He was beginning to feel trapped in it—the semiofficial explanation of how Topper James had nearly killed himself trying to keep from dropping that damned Forty Thirty-three on the population of Tucson. And he was sure he had been over most of this several times with Roger Gazenove on the telephone.

He tried to remember if he'd left anything out.

"Something else I guess I should tell you, in case Candy doesn't bring it up." This was the worst part. "When they did an electroencephalogram before the operation, they found Topper had some kind of seizures. They think maybe it was due to something that happened to him in Vietnam."

He didn't want to use the word "epilepsy" right away, especially to the squadron commander. It conjured up all sorts of pictures of people writhing on the ground, spitting foam—stuff like that—and he would never bring himself to think of Topper in that way. Out of the corner of his eye, he looked at Lieutenant Colonel Gazenove to see if there was a reaction. *Maybe he knows about it already,* he thought.

"Otherwise, he's the same old Top. They had a hard time holding him down in bed when he was doped up. Now he keeps yelling that he's hungry. But I don't think they're going to let him eat anything with all that swelling in his throat. And he keeps talking about his little girl." Suddenly curious, because he hadn't had time to ask Candy about it, he said. "Where is she, anyway?"

Lieutenant Colonel Gazenove gave a short, barking laugh. "Tearing up my house."

He had to say one other thing because he wanted Roger Gazenove to take special note of it. "You knew Topper drove that damned crate into Mount Lemon to keep from killing a bunch of people. We were right over the suburbs out there."

"You told me."

"That's why he nearly killed himself. I know he could have ejected at two-zero. There wasn't anything wrong with that seat; it wasn't jammed."

The eyes shot him a sharp look. "Do you *know* that?"

"Sure, I know it. Topper knows it, too—he'll tell you so when he gets around to it. You know how hard it is to get anything out of Top."

Lieutenant Colonel Gazenove only said, "Well, we'll see. We'll see what the safety board comes up with, what they say in the reports when they finish looking over the crash site." He shook his head. "Moonbird, you haven't changed much. They've been telling me you have, but I don't see it."

He ignored that. He said, "Look, Rog, they're not going to find much of anything out there. When Forty Thirty-three burned, it really burned. Topper had plenty of gas in his wing tanks—that was the whole damned trouble—and it had happened before. And that's why it burned so good. There's nothing left of that monster but a powder."

"I heard there was more than that."

"They sure as hell aren't going to be able to rebuild it; there're only scraps left. I hope," he said fervently, "they dig a hole out there on the mountain and scrape it in and bury it forever." He saw that Roger Gazenove was watching him, and he said, "I'm just tired."

When the other man said nothing, merely kept looking at him, he said, "Well, I am tired. But I'll get rested up—now that Candy's here, I'm going to go over to my room and sack out for a couple of days. A day, anyway."

"You play golf?" They turned into the hospital driveway. "They've got a good course here in Tucson, and you'll have plenty of time to learn if you don't know how. These boards of inquiry never take less than thirty days; you might as well settle in. And you'll be around to keep Topper company."

He said, "Topper's got Candy; he doesn't need me."

The look again.

"Well, he doesn't. They just sit and stare at each other all day and hold hands. Which is all right with me," he said quickly, "don't get me wrong. I'm glad to see they've got things sorted out, for a change."

He held open the front door to the hospital lobby, and as Roger Gazenove started to pass through, he caught his arm. "I told everybody here what Topper did. I wanted it to go on the record."

The squadron commander said, "Moonbird, I'm sure the investigation board will take your opinion under consideration."

"That's why all the PR people came around, wanting to know if it could go in the newspapers."

"What happened?"

"The Russian orbiter went up, and everybody forgot about it, I guess."

They went toward the elevators. Roger Gazenove said, "Don't worry about it. They'll get around to it later."

"Nothing ever gets in the newspapers later; you know that."

"Oh—" Roger Gazenove said, remembering. "My wife cut a clipping out of the Hampton paper of your girl's father, the Senator, lying in state in the Capitol. I've got it somewhere. There wasn't much of a story, only pictures." He paused. "Have you been hearing from her?"

He nodded. He said, "I guess all the news came in just this one week."

But it struck him suddenly as funny. He knew the Senator wouldn't have liked that, to be lost in the back pages of the newspaper because of some Russian spaceship. But it was appropriate.

After a few minutes, he left Roger Gazenove to sit with Candy and Topper in Intensive Care and went out on the sun porch to gather up his papers and his DOP kit and the other things he'd left about. Right away he noticed that someone had been around, really cleaning up: everything had been put in one big pile on the coffee table with the shaving kit on top; the cushions of the couch had been straightened and fluffed up; the

magazine rack had been returned to its former place by the
wicker chairs and the magazines put back in it. And the telephone was gone. Someone had unplugged it and taken it away.

Signs of the times, he told himself. Topper was out of
danger, so he had just been moved out. Notice served. It was
probably that old bitch, Major Fuchs.

He had lived in that corner of the sun porch on the post-
surgery floor at Davis-Monthan Hospital for almost four days.
Four of the strangest days of his life. He felt curiously bereft.
Not that he ever wanted to go through that again, he assured
himself, but it was as though the corner there, *his* corner, had
grown around him like a nest, and he wasn't sure he wanted
to be booted out of it yet. A crazy idea.

He stood at the windows in the sunshine, looking out at the
parking lot and the neat and tidy streets of the base, the moving
traffic, the blocks of yellow brick administration buildings, and
the distant circling of aircraft over the field. The military. In
peacetime, a safe community isolated from the world, assured
of common interests, connections, the regulations of—in some
ways—a very satisfactory life. Knitted together, too, in a network of people who knew each other, everybody having been
stationed with somebody, somewhere, at one time or other;
they partied together, raised their children together, watched
each other jostling for position on the promotion ladder together, and wove themselves into interdependent, mostly
workable systems. If you wanted to know where somebody's
estranged and separated wife was, you called your squadron
commander, who called his wife, and *she* knew.

If he wanted to, he supposed he could stay in. The alternatives were not so great: he didn't want to be an airline pilot,
nor did he want a job with some aircraft company as low-to-
middle-range engineer. He could stay in the Air Force and
probably be a squadron commander some day like Roger Gazenove, especially if that was the only way to keep flying
advanced equipment—and he didn't know that he was interested in much else besides that. He wasn't going to go into
some aircraft engineering office and spend his weekends with
the local flying club.

Listlessly, he went back to the couch and sat down and
started sorting his papers on the coffee table. There was a lot

of stuff he could throw away; he didn't have to carry all of it back to the VOQ.

But in going through the papers, it was like reviewing the whole past four days again, and painfully. Scribbles on a piece of paper, Saturday afternoon: Roger Gazenove's duty number and home telephone, to tell him that Forty Thirty-three had crashed and Topper was in the hospital and why. At that time, with Roger on the line, so racked-up he couldn't finish; Nizzard had to come in for him, then Dolph Bauernhauser, acting detachment commander, wanting to check things out with Gazenove. Then trying to get in touch with Candy. The number of her mother in Omaha, then her brother's number in Lincoln, to find she'd gone to stay with her other brother in Sioux Falls. Only the brother in Sioux Falls didn't know where she was. Then back to Roger Gazenove again to find out, via Amy, that Candy had gone to her cousin's in Denver. Then the terrible conversation with Candy in Denver to tell her he didn't know whether Topper was going to live or not, but that he would call her back and give her the TWA schedule from Denver to Tucson. The TWA telephone numbers. The telephone number of the Great Western Motel in Tucson to make Candy's reservations.

He balled up the sheet of paper and looked around. There was no place to put it. He threw it on the floor.

Then all the numbers of the preliminary investigation team: Colonel Jacobs; the pilot member—he had more numbers than he needed for Captain Galliardi—he was the one he had talked to the most. Then a whole page of names and Nellis base numbers to call to make appointments for his depositions; the safety captain's number, and on and on.

He folded that sheet up and stuck it back inside his flight suit. He would be devoting plenty of time to these people from now on as they raked over every burned piece of Forty Thirty-three's wreckage and his own recollections. When Topper was well enough, the board would begin with him. What would come out of it, finally—and he had himself seen enough accident reports—would be something the size of a book with, hopefully, some recommendations based on the findings that would see that it never happened again. Linda Criscio was in it, too; somebody back at Langley on the safety board there would interview her, if they hadn't done so already.

In his own testimony so far, he had been drawn into things

they all knew would have repercussions, especially Topper's not declaring an emergency the last day at Red Flag over the trouble with the fuel feed in the wing tanks. He felt filled with frustration. It was almost impossible to explain about Topper, about their once-in-a-million near-perfect performance at Red Flag that Topper had driven them to with maximum jeopardy, about Forty Thirty-three and its demon-ridden systems. About anything.

The bottom sheet said across the top: Nancy. In Washington. Call the base operator.

He hadn't known the Senator was dead. In the midst of everything, while Topper was still on the operating table and all of them were sitting out in the visitors' lounge, grimly waiting—Dolph Bauernhauser and Dolphin flight, Beeper and Nizzard—there had been Nancy. Who had thought, naturally, that he would be able to drop whatever it was that he was doing and fly right into Washington.

He couldn't remember how he had explained to Nancy that it was impossible under the circumstances, that the accident board at Davis-Monthan would rule out any request for leave for at least the first two or three days, and that it was useless to put in for it. Neither he nor Nancy had been in any shape to understand each other, and he was amazed that they had, that they had managed to comprehend that though something terrible had happened to both of them, they could still talk to each other, depend on each other. He had felt really sorry for Nancy. She had sobbed uncontrollably when she told him that she could say now that her father was a good man, a really good man, in spite of the things people said about him. After all, she wept, he was her father. He hadn't known what to tell her to console her.

He suddenly remembered that he hadn't asked Roger Gazenove about getting two days' leave now to go to Washington for the funeral Thursday.

He rolled the remaining papers into a cylinder and held them in his hand. After a while, after standing there for long minutes brooding about other things, he thought: I need a rubber band. He knew he wouldn't find one anyplace in the hospital.

He had managed to get through it all somehow. He had even managed to do a lot of things right. But he hadn't remembered until late Sunday afternoon to think about it. What it meant to him now that Senator Glass was dead.

There wasn't one damned soul he could talk to about it.

23

As Captain Thomas Turner approached that point in the cafeteria line where he had to choose between aged slabs of Boston cream pie and glass dishes of a dessert known among the medical residents of Davis-Monthan Hospital as "mystery lumps" (although the latter was identified reassuringly on the daily menu board as fruit custard), he noticed a peculiar phenomenon taking place at the cash register. Just beyond the checkout stand, Drs. Feeney and Rentner and two or three members of the hospital administration staff seemed to be suddenly afflicted with some strange motor disability: their eyes became fixed, apparently, on some sight to the left of the main cafeteria room, and their attention thus captured, they wavered, staring, then scuttled sidewise, generally forgetful of their trays and their direction. Dr. Feeney and Dr. Rentner came together with a clash of trays and spilled coffee, and one of the administration staffers recovered himself only just in time to avoid running into them.

Sliding his own tray along the rail toward the checker, Captain Turner could finally see what it was that was creating the traffic hazard at the end of the cafeteria line. The delectable Mrs. James, whose husband was a patient down in Post Op, sat at a table by the back windows, sipping a Coca-Cola and reading from some pamphlets spread before her. Frowning slightly, Mrs. James was absorbed in what she was doing and did not look up at the noise. Her sleek head, its mass of light brown curls swept up to a loose knot and cascading charmingly from there down upon her shoulders, her clear-cut profile with adorable short nose, downcast eyes with long lashes, sweet full mouth accentuated by some artful pink gloss—not to mention, Captain Turner noted hastily, that totally distracting body in yellow sweater and designer jeans clinging tightly to each and every curve—certainly wrought an immediate visual havoc. He almost left the cash register without his change.

But Captain Turner was quick to seize this lucky opportunity; he had met Mrs. James just a few hours ago, and he was sure she remembered him. He approached her table confidently with a winning smile, conscious of the eyes of the room upon him.

"Hi, there," he greeted her. "I see you're catching up on some reading. Stuff Dr. Rohrback gave you? How's it going? Mind if I sit down?" Smoothly and without waiting for an answer to any of these questions, he put his tray on the table and slid into the seat opposite her.

Mrs. James looked up, those wide blue eyes innocently dazzling. He said, introducing himself, "I'm Tom Turner, resident in surgery. I came in today to chip a little off that cast on the left side where it was binding up under your husband's ear. The guy with the little electric saw, remember?"

He was rewarded with a slow, ripe smile, the gleaming lips parting over perfect white teeth. For a moment, fascinated, he forgot what he was going to say. He murmured, looking at the booklets on the table, "Complex partial seizures—that's what Dave Rohrback found on the EEG, wasn't it? Well, that's going to be tough."

Now she gave him her full attention.

"Yes," she said, "I think I've read just about every one. Dr. Rohrback told me they'd be easy, written for people to understand, and I guess they are. But I never knew there were so many kinds of epilepsies—there's not just one, you know. It's sort of an electrical storm in the brain." She held up a copy of a paperbound book for him to see: *The Epilepsy Fact Book.* "It's not really what people think it is. I mean, so many people think of fits, at least that's the impression I had, although I'd never really thought about it much. You know, I've never even *seen* a person with the sort of epilepsy most people think of, the kind with convulsions. But the book explains it's a sort of short circuit of the electrical currents in the brain, just an interruption in the body's regular functions, and not so frightening if you know what it is." She looked somewhat bemused. "I never knew there could be these small, momentary seizures that you could hardly detect," she murmured.

She was, he could see, really picking up the jargon. As he watched those softly curving pink lips, Captain Turner told himself she could sell him on an epilepsy lecture anytime. But neurology was not his field; he was a resident in surgery. He tried to change the subject to his advantage. But he was still thinking. After all, you can't expect her to sit around a hospital room all the time. He wondered if, later on and as a purely friendly gesture, Mrs. James might like to take in a movie.

He said knowingly, "The medication your husband's taking is not going to make his CPS much of a problem, you know. What he's really going to have to work on is that banged-up arm and shoulder that he nearly lost when the refueling boom hit him. No matter what Dave Rohrback may have told you, there's just bound to be some nerve damage there, and he's lost a hunk of muscle and bone out of the sternum area. He's got to regain the use of all that, and we're not going to know what we're dealing with until he gets that cast off and goes into physical therapy."

"Will you be there?" she wanted to know. She seemed to hesitate. "I mean, I know Dr. Rohrback told me his Air Force time is up, and he's going out of the service and into—"

"Oh, I'm going to be around for a while," Captain Turner assured her enthusiastically. "If the Air Force doesn't decide to switch me around, that is. I expect I'll be here when the cast comes off, unless they want to transfer Major James out of here. Lackland's got a bigger medical installation and a bigger physical therapy setup; they might want to put him over there, after a while."

Mrs. James assumed a deeply thoughtful expression, not really listening, and he stopped.

"It's going to take a long time, isn't it?" she said softly.

"Oh, it's going to take a *long* time—at least a couple of months for that cast, maybe some sort of interim immobilization of the arm after that, depending on what the bone people say. Then maybe a small cast for the upper arm. Maybe even bone grafts," he offered, full of hope.

The blue eyes continued to regard him.

"A year?" she said.

"Maybe more than that. Say eighteen months. Depends on how much nerve and bone regeneration you've got, and—"

But she had drifted away from him again.

"Oh, Topper. No active duty," she murmured.

"I'm afraid not," he said, frowning. "Has Major James said anything to you about wanting to get back on active duty? Because if he has, I guess you know what the score is there."

He hesitated, not knowing how far to pursue the subject, but sensing that, for some reason, she was thinking of other things. He said stiffly, and not quite sure why, "I guess you can count on one long second honeymoon ahead of you. After the cast comes off, that is." He tried to laugh.

She kept staring at him. Then she gathered up the literature that the neurologist had given her and opened her pocketbook.

"You know," Mrs. James said suddenly, "you can want something for a long, long time and think it's about the only thing in the world you really want." She caught her lower lip between those pearl-like teeth and, for the briefest of moments, looked heartbreakingly mournful. "I mean," she said, her voice slightly husky, "it really doesn't pay to think just of yourself and what you feel you have to have to make you happy. Because when you get it—sometimes it's the worst thing to have, after all. I think what you really have to look for is what other people need to make them happy. If you love them, that is. That's right, isn't it?" she asked him.

"Right," he said, thoroughly confused. "If you say so."

She stood up. "I want to thank you, Doctor," she said. "You've been really sweet. I guess I'll be seeing you around."

"Yeah, sure." He stood up hurriedly, watching her walk away across the cafeteria with that superb, undulating loco-motion, oblivious to heads turning and the chaos attendant on her passing. He heard the sound of breaking glass and scattering silverware from the hot food line.

Captain Turner sat down again. She had not, he realized, been much aware of him. They had had a conversation, but for all the personal impact he'd made, he might just as well have been the paint on the wall opposite. Total zero. She probably wouldn't even recognize him the next time they met.

Well, some lucky people had it, he thought. Obviously the big blond object down in Post Op was what Mrs. James was focused on to the exclusion of all else right now. Another faithful and devoted wife. He didn't see how some of these bastards did it. He took his spoon and plunged it gloomily into the dish before him.

He'd selected Mystery Lumps this time, just for the hell of it. Looked like, he thought, examining a green crystalized bit on the end of his teaspoon, the remains of the fruitcake they'd been serving in the cafeteria last Thursday.

While Candy was downstairs, the evening news came on. Simon McAllister was holding a cardboard container of orange juice with a glass straw in it for Topper when in the hallway outside he heard the recorded sound of teletypes with which CBS opened the evening news. He said, "Dammit, Top, I want to see Dan Rather. I want to see what the Russians are doing now."

There was no television set in Intensive Care; he usually went down into the Post Surgery section to watch the TV news from the doorway of one of the other patients' rooms. He didn't want to leave Topper alone, but Roger Gazenove had jumped up from his chair and was already in the hall.

He put the orange juice on the stand beside the bed and said, "I'll tell you about it when I get back," and followed the squadron commander outside.

The first room around the corner in Post Op was the one he most often used: the Lieutenant Colonel there was ambulatory, recuperating from a hernia operation, and liked to have company. They found the Lieutenant Colonel sitting on the edge of his bed in bathrobe and bedroom slippers. He waved them inside. Dan Rather's voice filled the room.

"Without a doubt," the newscaster was saying, "the unveiling by the United States Defense Department of this new tactical fighter weapon is in direct response to the events of the past four days and serves notice to the Soviets that their latest entry into space, for whatever purpose, will not go unchallenged."

Lieutenant Colonel Steed was a large, bald-headed man attached to the Adjutant General's office. He turned around and said, "You can come on in and sit down, if you want to. Plenty of chairs, and you can see better on this side."

Roger Gazenove said, "That's all right; we can see fine from here. We just wanted to take a look at the first few minutes, see what the Russians are doing up there."

But the Soviet mystery ship, as the news media was now

referring to it, was not being shown on television, nor was the American Space Shuttle, *Columbia*. Instead, some grainy film was running of a strip of desert somewhere and a shape moving on it.

"—just released," Rather said, "at Edwards Air Force Base in California."

At almost the same time, Roger Gazenove and Simon stepped into the room. They watched in silence as the thing rumbled down the runway at Edwards.

"Son of a bitch," Roger Gazenove said softly.

The film had been shot from a considerable distance, no doubt for security reasons, but it was clear enough to show the shape barging down the concrete, slowly gaining speed. A trail of what appeared to be thick gray smoke followed it. At last, when it seemed it had eaten up most of the runway length and its takeoff was marginal, it nosed up precipitously and bounded from the surface with a muffled roar. The shock waves of its ascent made wavering lines of the desert background, and the camera focus blurred. As fast as it took the eye to record and follow it, the shape was airborne, pointed almost vertical; it shot up and above range and disappeared.

"Goddamn," the Lieutenant Colonel cried. He clapped both hands down on his robed knees. "Did you see that? Son of a *gun!*"

Roger Gazenove said, "What the hell are they using in that thing? That's not a jet fuel."

Dan Rather's face returned to the television set against a rear screen projection of the blue-green globe of the world as seen from space.

"And that, ladies and gentlemen, was the first glimpse, and not much more than that, of the United States' incredible new tactical fighter weapon in a film just released today. The Hybrid Tactical Vehicle, or HTV, as it's called, is equipped with dual propulsion systems that will take it to the limits of the earth's atmosphere at approximately one hundred thousand feet and then launch it into suborbital space, where, according to the information just released by the Defense Department, another system of rocket-powered engines will maneuver it for tactical purposes in and out of low orbit. It's assumed also that some of the assists now installed, or soon to be installed, in the Space Shuttle, as well as other devices now in our satellites, will guide and direct the new manned HTV to any potential security threats up there."

The newsman paused and said, "We will be back with this and other stories in just a minute."

A woman appeared on the television screen with a mop to demonstrate the properties of liquid floor wax, and Simon McAllister slipped out of the room.

He stood in the hallway next to a high metal cart full of plastic dinner trays and watched a stream of traffic coming and going on the post-surgery floor, mostly relatives of and visitors for the patients there and an occasional nurse in her rubber-soled shoes and uniform pants suit. No one took any particular note of him; it wasn't unusual to see visitors standing in the hospital halls, waiting for some treatment or service to be rendered inside the room, usually bedpans. And he wanted to be by himself for a minute. Most especially, he didn't want to be drawn into any discussion with Roger Gazenove and the Lieutenant Colonel about the Hot Victor. Since he had seen the drawings that night in the Senator's house, he was well aware that he knew more about it, probably, than anyone except the people who were actually working on it.

It was not a dream now; it was real. The HTV program was far enough along for the prototype to be making test flights at Edwards and for the early results to be good enough for the United States to announce it to the world to counter the launch of the Soviet spaceship. But to be out of everything that mattered and with no apparent hope of getting any closer to it now that he was there at Davis-Monthan, with nothing to look forward to but a month of sorting out the details of Forty Thirty-three's crash on Mount Lemon, filled him with the deepest misery. It surprised him how badly he had wanted that appointment to test flight; an excruciating sense of disappointment and defeat reached down to his very innards. Every damned expectation he'd had was down the drain, he could see that; there was virtually no possibility whatsoever that Senator Glass had managed to do anything on his application to test flight before he died.

For the first couple of days after Nancy had told him of the Senator's sudden heart attack, he had held out some small hope, but the more he thought it over, the more unlikely it seemed. If the Senator *had* made a note of it, if he had asked someone in his office to get right on it after that day at the Middleburg horse show, it was probably still in channels somewhere—and whoever's desk it had landed on would know by now that Senator Glass was dead and there was no longer any immediacy operating. He couldn't think of anybody in the military structure who would want to do a favor for a dead politician.

He was pretty sure now that the Senator had waited on the matter. If he had himself been in the Senator's place—and if he understood the Senator's wishes the way they had been presented—then *he* would have wanted to wait and see how things turned out before doing anything. No need to pass a recommendation down through the Pentagon that somebody's application for test flight be pulled out of the files and given consideration when you didn't know for sure whether or not the person involved was going to be your son-in-law.

The more he thought about it, the more he figured he was probably right; certainly it was the way he himself would judge these things. But on the other hand it wasn't as though he didn't deserve, couldn't qualify for test flight in his own right. It still bothered him; he couldn't get over the curious, inexplicable injustice of it all.

He bent his head wearily, put his hands over his eyes and rubbed them hard. That left Nancy. He was so damned tired of thinking about it. He really wanted to get to Washington as fast as he could, to be with her and help her out and, yes, do a little lovemaking in the upstairs bedroom of the Senator's house without being hassled for once. When all was said and done, he supposed he really missed Nancy; she was the one he always turned to, for some reason; she was the only one he could depend on to talk to.

But get *married?* he asked himself.

Jesus God, he thought. Life is so goddamned complicated.

Roger Gazenove said: "I found the Saudis pretty nice people. They entertained the hell out of us, took us on sightseeing tours, gave the squadron a big dinner in a tent they put up right on the runway at the airfield, and I was invited to the home of one of the Royal Saudi Air Force colonels, met his wife and kids and a couple of his brothers in the Air Force. Whatever was going on behind the scenes, and whether or not we sold the Saudis on the idea of this trip, is another story. They might have been too polite to say otherwise, but I got the feeling they were impressed. The Saudi military people were impressed, but then they've been impressed all along—all they want is to get their hands on some Eagles, and they don't mind saying so. I enjoyed it," he said. "We got the equipment there and back without any trouble, and it's something to remember. At least I got to do that much."

"Oh, right," Simon McAllister said, remembering the squadron commander had only a few weeks more before his transfer to a desk job in Washington. It was strange to consider that even Roger Gazenove had problems of a sort.

Before he could say anything about it, Lieutenant Colonel Gazenove went on: "Well, with what's going on in space and announcing we've got the Hot Victors up our sleeve—in case the Russians didn't already know it—I don't think any of it's going to matter a whole hell of a lot now. The Saudis'll get their F-15s; we'll probably hustle some over right now to reinforce the whole Middle Eastern area while the world's attention is on this stuff in orbit. That's what I'd do."

They had eaten late, after leaving the hospital, at a Mexican place in Tucson where the squadron commander always went when he was at Davis-Monthan. Roger Gazenove had remembered to buy a carton of enchiladas to take home to his wife. They left the taxi at the Davis-Monthan gate and walked through the quiet streets of the base toward the flight line. The night was cool and soft, crystal clear in the pure air of the desert, and the sky was filled with stars. They heard the constant crack and thunder of night fighters taking off from the distant runway. A figure in fatigues passed under the lights ahead of them, riding a bicycle, and turned down the street toward enlisted personnel barracks. Somewhere across the highway a dog barked.

They cut through the empty parking lot in back of the Air-Ground Support building, and in that open space, the wind off the airstrip caught them. Roger Gazenove folded the box of enchiladas protectively against his chest. Simon put his arm up before his face and sidled into the gusts.

"God, I hate the wind!" he exclaimed. "If it hadn't been for the damned—"

He cut it short. He had almost brought it up again, and he certainly didn't want to talk about that anymore. The largest part of the conversation at dinner, even with their talk about the unveiling of the HTVs, had been about Topper's accident on the tanker at the Casa Grande track and the outcome of the investigation by the accident board. And he was sick of it. It was only making him more aware of how tired he was and how depressed.

Roger Gazenove peered at him. "Moonbird, what's eating you, son? You aren't beating on yourself, are you? I thought we settled that. You did everything you could; I think you ought to let it rest."

He said, "It's okay, Rog."

"Well, it's not okay—your face is still hanging down in your shoes. Listen, son, there are always crates around like Forty Thirty-three. Everybody's flown them at one time or other; everybody hates them. The hell of it is, your jinx equipment usually keeps flying; you can't seem to get rid of them; they just go on and on. This time we were lucky. It died, and Topper didn't."

"Yeah," he said.

Lieutenant Colonel Gazenove said, "Moonbird, you need to do something besides hang around the hospital and keep going over this thing with the accident board. I'm going to call Mack Pierson when I get back to Langley and have him put you on regular flight while you're here. You need the work time."

"I'm okay, Roger," he told him. "You don't have to worry about it."

The other man laughed. "Well, be nice to your girl friend when you go to Washington. She's had a pretty bad time, losing her father like that, and funerals are hard on everybody. Take it from me; I wish I never had to go to a funeral again myself. but you forget your troubles and take care of her, y'hear? Mack cut your orders for Thursday and Friday, and I told him to throw in Saturday and Sunday. You might as well have the weekend; nobody's going to need you around here before that. Candy's here to look after Topper." With the friendly intimacy that had grown up between them in the past few days, the squadron commander said, "What do you think about that situation? It looks like they're going to work it out all right, doesn't it?"

He said indifferently, "Oh, yeah, I suppose so. Candy's got something to keep her busy now; Topper needs her, and God knows Topper could use some looking after." He was glad to get out from under that himself. He said quickly, "Rog, I think Topper *knows*."

They had reached the flight line. Now they walked down the apron under the white lighted glare from the hangars. The night was busy. The air traffic taking off on night sorties kept up a loud, intermittent roar.

"You know Topper," he continued. "Topper wouldn't say a damned thing. It isn't the arm, either—Topper would make that arm work right if it took him two years to do it and if that was the only thing that kept him from flying. But don't you notice? He just sits there and looks as if he knows something you don't know." It was a subject they had avoided up to now; he supposed they might as well talk about it. "I mean, I *know* Topper."

He found, suddenly, that he could not express how well he knew Topper after two years of living and flying with him; it was too awkward, too much the sort of thing he always resisted. He was not going to fall into the trap of making some great Air Force speech about flight leaders and what their faithful wingmen came to feel for them. Choked, he said: "I guess you always look at the other guy and think: what if it was *me?* When I don't have night—when I'm not thinking about that damned boom coming down on Topper, I think about Topper not flying anymore. I just can't believe it. Not *Topper*."

Roger Gazenove stopped, turned, and looked at him. "Is that what's bothering you?"

"Sure, it's bothering me. Hell, doesn't it bother you?"

When the squadron commander didn't answer, he said, "I mean it. Suppose somebody had to tell me that. I don't know what I'd do, Rog. Flying—well, certain kinds of it, anyway—is all I want to do. I haven't prepared myself for anything else in this life, I'm beginning to realize, and neither has Topper. God, Topper won't even be able to fly Piper Cubs on weekends! I know he won't; he won't even be able to pass a Class Three FAA flight physical if he's got a record of seizures, no matter how mild they are." He said anxiously, "The Air Force will give him a desk job or something, won't they? I mean, Topper's not going to have to pull all the way out, is he?"

Roger Gazenove said, "Moonbird, I guess they can, if he wants it. Somebody's going to look out for him—we're not going to let anybody step on Topper." He cocked his head to one side and regarded him. "You've got a strange idea, boy, of what this life is all about. Don't like it much, do you?"

"Oh, hell, let's not discuss the military. It doesn't have

anything to do with anything right now, how I feel about it. But why Topper, of all the people it could have happened to? Why did it have to be the best?"

Roger Gazenove said, "Moonbird, you've made a big mistake. I don't think you know what's been going on. What Topper's been doing for the past ten, twelve years has been maximum risk—I don't have to tell you that, do I? I thought you knew that. Do Topper a favor. Don't sweat it."

He stared at him. "I don't know what in hell you mean, Roger."

Lieutenant Colonel Gazenove said, "Now listen, son— Topper James chose to go into a service academy, chose the professional military; that's what he wanted. Topper is a career fighting man; he's a combat soldier who flies supersonic equipment. In peacetime I suppose you could say that we tend to lose sight of that, or at least most people do, but that's what he is. And don't you kid yourself—he knows what happens when the breaks don't fall right. When the breaks start coming in ass-end up, everything goes to the wall in a hurry. There's no in-between. Now, you're not old enough to have been in Nam, but that's how it was—one second's reaction error, some piece of equipment somebody forgot to fix right, and you'd had it. Before you start," Roger Gazenove said, "before you even consider this business, you've got to think about that—that all it takes is just one little thing, anytime, anyplace. If you don't know that, then you've got no damned reason being here. And listen, it isn't just the equipment that's pushed to the limit of the performance envelope; it's us, too. And God knows we're subject to the same kind of variables. All of which reminds me," he said, unzipping the front of his flight suit and reaching into the inside pocket, "I've got to give you your orders before I forget it."

He handed Simon a small manila envelope. "Go ahead and open it," he told him. "I started to give it to you in the hospital, but there was just too much going on."

It was a thick wad of paper, more than just orders for temporary duty at Davis-Monthan. Beyond them, some A-10s were lining up on the taxiway, advancing their engines, and he couldn't hear what Roger Gazenove said.

The squadron commander lifted his voice over the noise. "I think you're making a mistake; I think there are plenty of opportunities where you are right now, only you haven't looked them over. And God knows, I hate to lose a good fighter jock. I want you to promise me one thing—that when you get back to Langley, you'll come in to see me, and we'll talk about it. I want you to be sure you know what you're doing. Test flight is a damned dull—"

"No." He almost shouted it.

He had the papers unfolded, and he held them up before his eyes. There wasn't enough light from the hangars to read them. "What the hell does it say?" he demanded.

"It says in sixty days you report to test flight at Edwards."

He let out a whoop. He waved his arms, flapping the handful of papers. Almost as abruptly, he stopped, remembering where he was, who he was with. He let his arms fall.

"Roger," he began, "I want to thank—"

The squadron commander waved it away. "Thank Randy Slyke. He's the one who worked on it. Take him out to dinner when you get back."

He said, "What?"

Lieutenant Colonel Gazenove shifted the white cardboard box he was carrying to his other hand. Very deliberately, he looked down at his fingers, rubbed them together, frowning slightly. "Randy kept on that for you all the way. When we went to Saudi, he had somebody he knows stay on it up in Washington. When we got back, he called right away, got the final list, and you were on it. The papers came right in."

"Oh, my God," he said.

Lieutenant Colonel Gazenove looked up and smiled. "Moonbird—hell, you act like you thought you weren't going to make it. Listen," he said, "I'm keeping somebody waiting around here. I've got to find my tub."

"Wait." He wanted to walk out to the flight line with him and get a minute to think, maybe talk it over. He knew what had been said, and he supposed he understood it; it was just something he could hardly make himself believe. Randy Slyke, he told himself.

Then, just at that moment, when he was trying to absorb this, he was struck with the strange and sudden realization that he was the one whose future, as they saw it, had been granted him, and not Topper. Not able to speak, he stood there and looked at Roger Gazenove and saw the other man knew what had happened and what he was thinking and that there was not, now, any need to bring it up.

Lieutenant Colonel Gazenove said, "Moonbird, while you're at it, you might as well wait a few days." He paused. "You can tell Topper about test flight when you get back."

The squadron commander turned and walked away. After a few feet, he stopped and said over his shoulder, "Get some sleep."

A few steps beyond the light from the open doors of the hangar he passed into the dark and between the silent rows of F-15 Eagles.

Sergeant Regina Murphy dragged open the heavy metal door of the traffic control tower on the ground level and rushed toward the stairs. If she ran up each and every flight, all the way to the top, she would make it right on time for the midnight shift.

There were rumors that somewhere in the world there were Air Force traffic control towers equipped with elevators, but Sergeant Murphy had never heard them identified either by name or place, nor had she ever met anyone who had actually been in one. All the towers she had ever known had scrupulously observed the rule that elevators were installed only when they exceeded the height of one hundred feet or more. As a consequence, somebody had seen to it that they were unfailingly constructed to reach ninety-nine feet, sometimes less, but never more. And traffic controllers were known for their great legs.

She heard the earlier shift coming down inside the tower, their voices floating in the stairwell. They leaned over the railing to greet her.

"Ha—you're late!"

"Murph's never late; she's bucking for more stripes, aren't you, angel?"

"You better get your ass up here, kid—it's two-four-zero hours."

Wordlessly, she waved at them. The outgoing shift was a friendly crowd. They knew she was stuck with the graveyard shift since she was newly transferred in from Langley and had low priority. It would be her lot in life for a while. They passed her, grinning sympathetically. Tech Sergeant Morris gave her a pat on the rear to speed her upwards. They continued down the stairs, and she heard the door slam below.

On the level just below the tower room, she stopped to get a drink at the water fountain. She gulped the cold water, making an effort to stop puffing, and threw her uniform cap on top of the locker. Then she grabbed the rungs of the ladder and swung herself upward. She could already hear the noise of air traffic and the voices of the controllers. It was midnight, but it sounded as if things were hopping.

The ground controller going off duty was waiting for her.

"Hi, Murph—here's the picture." He was in a hurry. "You have Demon One-One, a flight of two A-10s; they've started engines and their taxi is on request. Saber Two-One is taxiing now, that flight of A-7s." He pointed through the glass wall of the tower to the concrete paths below where dark shapes were moving. "We haven't heard from Eagle Zero-One's departure. He hasn't started his engines. But he's a single F-15 bound for Langley, and his ETA is—"

Sergeant Murphy took the headset and clamped it on. She moved the mike button nearer her mouth and nodded as he continued talking.

"Everything else is quiet, except for aircraft traveling on the ground. And you've got a tug—Rocket Two, that's holding short of the active runway to cross to west. Tug R-Two is pulling a munitions convoy—I think those are bombs for the A-10s when they arm up. All communications are green." As a last thought, he said, "And baby, it's busy."

"You can say that again," Regina Murphy told him. She flashed her dimples at him. She didn't remember his name; she didn't know everyone's name just yet, but she had seen this controller over at the NCO club and he had an adorable wife and the most beautiful baby you would ever want to see.

She turned back to the console.

"Rocket-Two," she told the tug pulling the flatbed loaded with munitions, "you are cleared across the runway."

Off to her right in the tower she could hear the local controller talking to a flight of the new fighters, the F-16s, coming in on base leg.

"R-Two, call when clear," she reminded the tug. She checked the A-7s still taxiing out. Lifting her voice, she told the local controller, "Rocket-Two has cleared the active."

Now they were over on the other side of the field. "Davis-

Monthan ground. Demon One-One taxi, two A-10s, standing by to copy clearance."

She checked the lighted ramp below her and saw the bomb convoy moving on the far west side. "Roger, Demon One-One," she told the Warthogs, as the ugly new attack fighters with their bulbous engine pods under their tails were called, "you're cleared to taxi. Wind is zero-six-zero at eight knots; altimeter is three-zero-one-niner."

A voice in the tower, watching the F-16s as they appeared from the left and swept toward the field for touchdown, said, "Hey, don't those birds look good! They say they roll those couches back to ninety degrees—that's practically on your back, man—to pull more Gs."

A new voice in her headset, slightly older, leisured but friendly, said, "Ground, Eagle Zero-One. Taxi one F-15, clearance on request."

That was the Eagle going back to Langley. Regina Murphy looked down to the taxiway and saw it was an F-15B, a two seater. Some squadron commander, she told herself. But she didn't recognize the voice.

She was busy with the sound of the young, crackling voices of the F-16s coming in to land that, for a second, drowned out all else. Impatiently, she stood on one foot and rubbed the toe of her shoe against the back of her leg, conscious that she had scuffed it up when she had stumbled, running back from the hospital. Her big toe still ached. *Rush, rush,* she told herself, *that's what you get.* But she had just wanted to look in at the hospital reception desk and find out how Major James was doing. It was, she had promised herself, her last trip over there; Major James's wife had arrived now, and she supposed he would be doing just fine. In fact, he had just been taken off "guarded" and put on "satisfactory."

So you see, she told herself, it's turning out all right.

What with one thing and another, she hardly had time to catch her breath. Concentrating and frowning a little, she cleared the runway of the F-16s that had just landed and got them onto the taxiway. While they were moving, Sergeant Murphy leaned closer to the glass window walls of the tower and looked up at the sky. The night was calm and clear over the desert, covered in a canopy of infinite stars like diamonds thrown down across a bolt of black velvet. Quickly, because she didn't have time to allow herself more than one look, Sergeant Murphy bent forward and turned her head to peer up and out. They said you could see the orbiters—the Space Shuttle *Columbia,* on an inclined orbit which swung over the western hemisphere and intersected the equator each time around, and the other one, the Soviet spaceship, which was somewhere up there. But not at midnight, she told herself. She really hadn't had time yet to read the newspapers and figure out the positions and know what was what.

It was exciting, though. She felt a little prickle across her shoulders and the back of her neck just thinking about it. From now on, they'd be up there. And in time, she supposed, people would get used to it.

The A-7s at the end of the runway, cleared for takeoff, cut to full military power. The cracking scream of their jets filled the night, heard only as a dim noise in the tower. Then the dark bodies of the attack fighters rose, tailpipes glowing like meteors, and met the black sky. After a second, they banked sharply, two shooting stars now, and they were followed by two more A-7s taking off.

"DM ground, Eagle Zero-One," the firm, mature voice said in Sergeant Murphy's ears.

The squadron commander in his Eagle.

"Roger, cleared for taxi, Zero-One," Sergeant Murphy responded.

And she added silently, *There you are, Commander.* When he reached the end of the taxiway, she would put him on a few minutes' hold to let the A-7s vacate the pattern, then clear him for takeoff. Feeling suddenly sentimental, she thought: *Say hello to everybody back there at Langley for me.*

Sergeant Murphy leaned forward again to get a better view of the sky overhead. Traffic was clearing out now. The dwindling stars of the A-7s had disappeared among the myriad lights of space. And far off, she saw, the small pale moon was coming up.

The author wishes to express thanks to the following for their help in making Air Force background and technical details available:

Langley Air Force Base: Headquarters, Tactical Air Command, Hampton, Virginia

General W. L. Creech, commander, TAC, United States Air Force

Colonel Donald Miller, 1st Tactical Fighter Wing (F-15 Eagles)

Colonel John Price, Public Affairs Office, TAC

Lt. Colonel George Devorshak, commander, 27th Tactical Fighter Squadron

Lt. Colonel James Cash, commander, 94th Tactical Fighter Squadron

Lt. Colonel Ron Lindeke, Public Affairs Office, TAC

Major Mike Penacchio, flight operations officer, 94th Tactical Fighter Squadron

Major James Wray, assistant flight operations officer, 94th Tactical Fighter Squadron

Major Robert Nicholson, 1st Tactical Fighter Wing Public Affairs Office

Captain John Baker, flight leader, 94th Tactical Fighter Squadron

Captain Thomas Young, wingman, 94th Tactical Fighter Squadron

Captain John David Mullins, flight surgeon, 94th Tactical Fighter Squadron

Captain William Kurey, simulator officer, 1st Tactical Fighter
   Wing
Lieutenant Dee Jaffee, 1st Tactical Fighter Wing Public Affairs
   Office
Lieutenant Larry New, wingman, 27th Tactical Fighter Squad-
   ron
Senior Master Sergeant Michael Mayor, 1913th Communica-
   tions Squadron (GCA)
Master Sergeant W. W. Lynshesky, Life Support Systems,
   27th Tactical Fighter Squadron
Staff Sergeant Beverly Davis, Asst. NCOIC, 94th Tactical
   Fighter Squadron
Senior Airman John Dowling, F-15 crew chief, 94th Tactical
   Fighter Squadron
Airman First Class Debbie Worth, F-15 crew chief, 94th Tac-
   tical Fighter Squadron

Westover Air Force Base, Chicopee, Massachusetts

Major Mike Choffel, 1917th Communications Squadron
Master Sergeant Tom Bullock, Air Traffic Control (West-
   over tower)
Staff Sergeant Daniel Samis, information officer

Bradley Field, Windsor Locks, Connecticut

General Ray Lilley, commander, Connecticut Air National
   Guard
Lt. Colonel Anthony Cichoki, commander, 103rd Tactical
   Fighter Group (A-10s)
Lt. Colonel Charles Parker, USAF advisor, 1118th Tactical
   Fighter Squadron
Master Sergeant Tom Wilson, administration

Nellis Air Force Base (Red Flag), Las Vegas, Nevada

Major General Robert Kelley, commander, Tactical Fighter
   Weapons Center
Lt. Colonel Richard Graham, commander, 64th Fighter Weap-
   ons Squadron (Aggressor F-5s)

Lt. Colonel J. P. Roberts, chief, presentations division, Tactical Fighter Weapons Center

Lt. Colonel David Michael Wallace, director, Public Affairs Office

Lt. Colonel T. C. Skanchy, commander, 433rd Fighter Weapons Squadron

Major Russ Everts, operations officer, 433rd Fighter Weapons Squadron

Major Roger C. Curtis, executive officer, 440th Tactical Training Organization (Red Flag)

Captain Bill Hamilton, instructor pilot, 433rd Fighter Weapons Squadron

Captain Dale Cooke, Thunderbirds Air Demonstration Squadron

Captain William Peterson, Range Control Center

Captain Robert Barca, Public Affairs Office

Captain Michael Schoenfeld, F-15 demonstration pilot

Lieutenant Donna Mitzschke, assistant maintenance supervisor, 57th Aircraft Generation Squadron

Chief Master Sergeant William Smith, maintenance senior manager, 57th DCM

Chief Master Sergeant John Schloss, maintenance superintendent, 57th Aircraft Generation Squadron

Senior Master Sergeant James Miller, production supervisor, 414th Fighter Weapons Squadron

Indian Springs Auxiliary Airfield, Nevada

Colonel Weston Smith, commander, 57th CSS
Captain Robert Haber, Jr.
Master Sergeant Rollins Stallworth

And special thanks also to:

John Allen, Rockwell International Corporation
Richard Gary Davis